Libby snuck out of the house,

leaving the front door ajar. She ran down

the stone steps to the back of the house where

she stopped short. There, at the edge of the

rainforest, was a stone archway, shaped as a perfect

circle. At its base, a knee-high stone was partially

covered with leaves and Libby got to her knees

to clear the debris, and read:

Always loved. Never forgotten.

Born in Australia, **Amanda Geard** has lived all over the world, from a houseboat in London to a Norwegian Island, before settling in County Kerry in Ireland. Her writing has appeared in *The Irish Times*, *The Journal*, *writing.ie*, *Nordic Reach* and *Vertical Magazine*. Her short story *Not Yet Recycled* won the New Irish Writing Award in October 2019. Her debut novel *The Midnight House* was a Richard and Judy Book Club pick.

Also by Amanda Geard

The Moon Gate
The Midnight House

THE
MOON
GATE

AMANDA GEARD

REVIEW

First published in 2023 by Headline Review
An imprint of HEADLINE PUBLISHING GROUP

I

Cataloguing in Publication Data is available from the British Library

Hardback ISBN 978 1 4722 8375 7
Trade Paperback ISBN 978 1 4722 8376 4

Typeset in Bembo by CC Book Production

Printed and bound in Great Britain by Clays Ltd, Elcograf S.p.A.

HEADLINE PUBLISHING GROUP
An Hachette UK Company
Carmelite House
50 Victoria Embankment
London EC4Y 0DZ

www.headline.co.uk
www.hachette.co.uk

For Dad, who knew Tasmania's west coast,
and its treasures, best of all.
I wish you could take me exploring one more time.

Bass Strait

★Northport

● Launceston

Southern
Ocean

Towerhurst

Westford ★ ● Queenstown

TASMANIA

Macquarie Harbour

● Brighton

Hobart ●

AUSTRALIA

The location of real (●) and
fictional (★) places in
The Moon Gate's Tasmania

Prologue

The edge of the ocean, County Kerry
December 2004

The letter opens a hole in the earth, and through the darkness she tumbles. Falling. Falling. Slowing. Slowing. Until she reaches light and arrives at an island on the other side of the world. The place where she once was. The place where *they* once were.

Tasmania.

She only glances at the page, but suddenly she's back a lifetime ago, smelling the sweet sassafras, waking to the chatter of a thousand birds, turning her face to the sun; that burning antipodean glare.

She shuffles the letter beneath the pile of post. Something to face later. Outside the wind whistles, coaxing white caps from Kenmare Bay, and she busies herself with the remaining mail her eldest son delivered with an accusatory look that morning. The post box is up the boreen and she walks to it, and beyond, every day. But occasionally she leaves it full, stuffed with unread words; she just walks on past as though she hasn't a care in the world.

୧

Later, the storm has moved inland and there's a freshness in its wake, as though it stole away the electricity that pulsed through her when she sat at the table, opening the envelope.

She takes a sip of sherry, her gaze lingering on the fire where peat smoulders and glows, its liquorice smoke curling up the chimney and away. Beside her, on the coffee table, the letter is half hidden in shadow as though it's just an idea, but in her heart she knows whoever wrote it thought very hard indeed. All the signs are there. The careful text, the quality of the envelope: heavy, textured, olde-worlde.

Like her.

It's addressed to Mrs McGillycuddy, and the sender's details are written on the back in tiny, whispered text, as if this woman, this Libby Andrews, was writing an apology. And part of her address is familiar. *Grosvenor Square, London.*

It is a coincidence, that's all.

Still, she contemplates striking a line through her details and writing 'Return to Sender' so the letter can drift back to where it came from.

But you can't plough a field by turning it in your mind, as Daniel used to say.

Even before she reads the letter in its entirety, she knows something about Libby Andrews. She clearly takes care over the little things. And although she doesn't want to, she likes her already. She feels a cautious warmth emanating from the page, adding to the glow of the fire. The letter finishes with placations: *Only if it is suitable for you.* Formal for an Australian.

She walks to the window, gripped by a need to look into the darkness and see what's peering back. Outside, the clouds have lifted and moonbeams cut the bay, separating her peninsula from the next.

Libby Andrews wants to ask about Daniel. That is all.

She takes a pencil, and sharpens it slowly.

And in the dying light, she replies.

Chapter 1

London

November 2004

Three weeks before the letter . . .

The absence of greenery in Covent Garden wasn't so much a surprise to Libby Andrews as an inevitability. The city she thought she might recognise from Monopoly boards, Dickens and programmes on the telly was buried beneath a shiny present that concealed its history until she peeled away the layers and searched for what hid beneath. From the bomb-scarred facade of the V&A to the muddy course of the Thames, itself a repository for centuries of the city's flotsam, London's piled past was slowly coming alive for Libby as she walked its endless streets. But it wasn't the city's history that had brought her to the dingy waiting room a stone's throw from Waterloo Station. It was her own.

'Number thirteen!'

Libby stood quickly and stepped up to the counter, cursing her superstition as she slid the docket and her letters through the square hole in the glass with shaking hands. If only she'd left her aunts' apartment earlier and not boarded the wrong bus, indeed if she'd overcome her doubts sooner, and done this immediately when she'd arrived in London, she might well have been number one. But when had she *ever* been first? She never won, never pushed herself forward, and even now she stepped back from the counter to give the rotund man behind the glass plenty of space.

Immediately, she began to babble. 'I wrote to the coroner's archive six months ago to confirm the box hadn't been destroyed. You can see the dates on the two letters: the first one in 1975 and the other in 2004. Can't you?' She hesitated, but the man remained unmoved. 'I've come a really long way. From Tasmania, in fact . . .'

Usually, mention of the island piqued interest, prompting a story about a visit, or more often than not an *intention* to visit, but the man only turned her letters over with chubby fingers as though doubting their authenticity, oblivious to the charms of Australia's southernmost state and those who hailed from it. Behind Libby, three people waited, each clutching their little blue tickets, each perched on one of the uncomfortable plastic seats lined up along the wall. Feeble daylight washed down from a high window that showcased passing feet splashing through the downpour, the sound of rain-pummelled pavement drowned out by a grumbling vent whose warm air ruffled the diminutive foliage of a palm standing bravely next to the counter. That plant, Libby thought as she watched the man's concrete expression, was the only indication that a human being worked here at all. The room smelled of wet dog and yesterday's lunch, and although Christmas was less than a month away it was nowhere to be found amongst the signs that barked at those who waited.

TAKE A TICKET OR TAKE A HIKE.

ABUSE OF STAFF WON'T BE TOLERATED.

NO ID, NO ITEM.

'ID?' said the man, finally raising his eyes, his gaze hovering over her shoulder to the waiting numbers.

Libby slid across her Australian passport.

'You're not *Willow* Andrews, then?'

'Willow's my mother.' She took a copy of her birth certificate from her pocket and pressed it against the glass. 'And Ben Andrews was my father.'

'The deceased?'

The ceiling vent chose that moment to stop its grumble, and several of the waiting numbers looked in her direction. The *deceased*? A ribbon wound itself around Libby's heart, and from somewhere deep within, familiar pain burbled. She'd felt it thousands of times over the years: on Father's Day, the anniversary of his death, the times friends bemoaned frustrating moments with their dads as though having a dad wasn't by itself joyful enough.

'Yes,' she said quietly.

'What?'

'I said: yes.'

Only the day before, under the cavernous roof of the London Transport Museum, she'd felt it as she stood before a single, tiny display. It said nothing more than she already knew, but somehow reading the words here in London, instead of half a world away, had sucked the moisture from her mouth.

The Moorgate Tube crash, the plaque read, *was the worst peacetime disaster on the London Underground. At 8.46 a.m. on the 28th of February 1975, 43 people died after a train failed to stop at Moorgate Station, the terminus of what was then the Northern City Line.*

There her father's name had been, right at the top. He was the man who'd left her life before it had even begun, and yet she missed him, and what might have been. From the museum, she'd walked to Moorgate Station itself to watch people pour out of the Britannic House exit at rush hour, blissfully ignorant of the accident that had taken place there thirty years before. In a wholly visceral way, the sight had flipped her stomach and, with a wave of regret, she wished she was still back in Tasmania, still living in her small, shared terrace house with her unreliable flatmates, working dead-end jobs she hated. She felt a sudden, terrible sense of loneliness and realised her mum had probably been right all along: even though their small island state hung off the end of the world, it had everything anyone could want. There was no *need* to go to Europe, Willow had explained, peering over her red glasses as they'd sat at a pseudo-French café drinking Italian coffee, because 'Europe comes to us'.

The man slid her documents back. 'Your *mother* will have to collect the belongings.'

Libby paused. 'But it's been thirty years . . .'

'Regulations.'

'The letter says . . .'

'The *letters,* madam, are both addressed to Willow Andrews.'

'She's in Tasmania. She can't just jump on a plane and collect them.' Though that wasn't strictly true. 'What am I supposed to do?'

'Not my problem.'

Libby glanced at the ABUSE OF STAFF WON'T BE TOLERATED sign. Taking a shaking breath, she continued, 'Please, I—'

He tapped yet another regulation stuck haphazardly to the screen. ALL COLLECTIONS ON BEHALF OF OTHERS REQUIRE A DOCTOR'S LETTER OR DEATH CERTIFICATE.

She's sick, Libby wanted to plead, though that would be a lie. Her mum was as fit as a fiddle. Strong. A strength that Libby herself hadn't inherited, along with any of her other features.

'Next!'

Libby was bustled aside by an impatient number fourteen, and her vision blurred with tears as her obedient feet took her out of the waiting room, up the stairs and onto the rain-battered street. There, she leaned against the entrance and felt her heart break as she gazed at her fingers, picturing this opportunity slipping through them, lamenting how close she'd felt these last months as she planned her move to London to finally retrieve a piece of the father she'd never had.

Tears dropped onto her black coat and rolled down the wool to the already wet pavement. Libby bit her lip, trying to stop the flow, but it was all too much. She was pathetic, completely pathetic. Some soulless paper-pusher had got the better of her and, as usual, she'd simply let it happen.

She sniffed and turned to the wall, hiding her face from the passing commuters. She should go back in, she should demand to see the manager. She should make a fuss. And yet . . . she wouldn't. She would retreat meekly to her aunts' apartment and wonder what on earth she'd been thinking, and why she'd hung so much on getting her dad's belongings. After all, if her own handbags were anything to go by, the satchel probably only contained an old receipt, half a packet of chewing gum and some slightly sticky coins saved for a rainy day. Still, she would have *liked* to find those things. Was that so shameful to admit?

'Are you all right, dear?' asked a small woman who seemed to appear from nowhere, her blue rinse the brightest thing on a dull street. 'It's just you're sobbing on the steps of a public office. A great offence, you know?' The woman smiled kindly, to show that she was joking.

Libby wiped the mascara from her eyes. 'I'm fine. Fine. Thank you.' Sniffing, she stepped aside. 'Sorry.'

'No need to apologise, dear. Any delay in getting to the desk suits me just fine.'

Libby smiled, her eyes stinging, and dug into her deep pockets, looking for a tissue, but all she found were three receipts, a pocket map of London and the documents she'd submitted to the clerk not five minutes before.

The woman looked down, catching sight of the letters. She nodded to herself, unclipped her handbag, and withdrew a pristine white handkerchief. 'For the mascara,' she said.

'Oh, I couldn't.'

'I have more.'

Gratefully, Libby took it and dabbed her eyes. 'Thank you.'

They stood in silence, watching a sea of dark umbrellas bob through the downpour.

'Will this rain ever stop?' said the woman finally, and Libby gave a small smile. The English and their weather. 'It's very wearing, isn't it, love? And there's too much work to get through before the holidays. Not at all good for the mood, is it?'

'Really, I'm fine. Just a bit of a wobble.' Libby scrabbled for an excuse. 'New city and all.' In fact, too much work would be a good thing. Next week she'd start applying for jobs; her Australian dollar savings would *not* hold up well to the pound.

The woman glanced again at the letters. 'I might be wrong but ... I suspect you've had a run-in with the notorious Computer Says No?' She waved a hand, indicating somewhere beyond the closed glass doors. 'What was it? Your collection letter too creased? That man's nothing but a menace.'

The doors opened and number fourteen spilled out, empty handed, and with a face like thunder.

'Well?' The woman raised an eyebrow. She was an entire foot shorter than Libby, who herself was less than average height.

'I wanted to collect a box the coroner archived,' Libby admitted. 'I should have insisted, but I just ... couldn't find a way. It's under Mum's name, you see? She lives in Tasmania.'

'Ah, *Tasmania!*' said the woman. 'My husband and I wanted

to visit on our honeymoon in sixty-five. But it was a long way to go back then.'

Despite herself, Libby grinned. 'It still is.'

A nod. 'Now, let me guess: Computer Says No insisted on a doctor's certificate?' She sighed again, with the resignation of someone familiar with this carry-on. 'And you can prove you are your mother's daughter?'

Libby's heart leapt. 'Yes . . .'

'You're sure about that?'

'Absolutely.'

'Well, come on then, let's take another look at that paper-work and see what we can do.'

૨૦

Libby was bustled into a small office wholly in contrast to the waiting room outside. Tinsel hung from the cornicing, and a small coffee machine filled the room with a welcoming aroma.

The woman held out her hand, all bustling efficiency. 'Now, what've you got for me?'

As she passed across the letters, her passport and the birth certificate, Libby's voice was snatched away by hope, and she stood mute, a feeling of desperation deep in her stomach.

'*A satchel containing documents and personal effects.*'

A gulp. She was close, so close. Whatever lay inside that satchel might tell her who Ben Andrews had been. Who he'd really been. Not the pale shadow her mum had painted of him.

The woman opened the passport page, noting Libby's birth date, August 1975. 'Twenty-nine years old . . .' She compared it to the birth certificate, then examined the photo carefully. 'You must never have met your father?' she said, looking up. 'What a *terrible* thing.'

'He died six months before I was born.'

'Oh, love. A tragedy, that is. I was working on London

Wall at the time. Half the city came to donate blood as word spread. I joined the queue quick smart, I can tell you. They were operating on poor souls down in the station, you know? Did your father . . .'

Libby shook her head. 'From what I understand, he died instantly.'

The documents were placed gently in Libby's hand, which itself was patted by the woman's cool touch. 'Now, you sit yourself down there. Can I make you a coffee?'

'No, thank you.'

'OK. Box 9462, is that right?'

Libby frowned and looked at the reference number in the two letters – one of which had been sent to her mum's old address in 1975, the other to Libby's rented address only six months before. Both were labelled *Attention: Willow Andrews*.

'You don't . . . need my mum to collect it?'

The woman paused at the door. 'I thought you said your mum was ill?'

'No, I . . .'

'Really? But I *saw* the doctor's certificate myself, didn't I?' She raised her eyebrows and nodded almost imperceptibly.

Libby wasn't good at lying, so she merely dropped her gaze, smiling weakly, willing her lack of confidence not to mess up the second chance she'd been gifted.

૨૨

An hour later, the 139 bus crossed Waterloo Bridge with Libby on board, the grubby window throwing back her reflection as though it didn't much care for it, as though it was judging her for doing something of which her mum would certainly not approve. She felt incurably guilty for the deception, for stealing the letter, for lying to Willow about the reasons she wanted to go to London.

'A gap year? A bit late, isn't it?'

'It's never too late,' Libby had said in reply, a practised response, and at those words, her mum had looked away.

But other feelings already threatened to overwhelm her guilt. On her lap sat the weathered satchel that had belonged to her father and inside it she hoped to find traces of the man he'd been. She had resisted the urge to open it then and there in the kind woman's office. Instead, she'd asked if she could leave the box, then slung the satchel over her left shoulder and bitten her lip.

'I don't know how to thank you.'

'There, there. No more tears now.'

'But really, this means the world to me.'

The woman had held up a palm. 'You need say nothing, my dear. If we can't help one another now and again, then what's it all about? Now, you get yourself settled at home before you open that. Reaching into years gone by can be a traumatic affair. You never know what you'll find,' she'd said with the certainty of someone who had seen this sort of thing before.

But as the bus halted in traffic, Libby could contain herself no longer. Just a little look. A glance. A peek into the past. *Her* past, in a way. Carefully unbuckling the straps with tingling fingers, she lifted the flap, releasing the scent of time, neglect, and the feeling she was doing something she shouldn't. Before she could close her eyes, look away, or change her mind, she peered into the two large compartments, one containing several documents and a book, the other full of everyday items: pens, a soft packet of Fisherman's Friends, a ticket for the tube that made her hands shake. Postage stamps of the queen, a stack of pounds (British and Irish) and a passport. Libby's heart flipped as she removed the latter, opened it and came face to face with her father, his features familiar from the few grainy photos she'd seen. She felt he was looking right at her as she traced a finger over his image, pausing when a photo slipped from between the passport's pages. Taking a deep breath, she withdrew it.

Mum.

There she was, Willow Andrews, wearing those large red glasses and the seventies bob she'd stubbornly retained all these years. But on her face she sported something unfamiliar: a wide, happy smile. In one hand she held a set of keys, and her other was wrapped around Libby's father, embracing him like she'd never let go. The aura of excitement surrounding them was so strong that, despite herself, and the painful chasm opening up inside of her, Libby smiled.

Looming behind her parents was a magnificent weatherboard Federation home, the type that lined Tasmania's oldest city streets. But this house wasn't in the city of Launceston, where Libby knew her parents had lived. Rather, it was surrounded, suffocated, by trees. She squinted, looking closer, a strange sense of familiarity scratching at a hidden part of her mind. On the far right of the photo a tower stretched up and away.

She shook her head and a memory dislodged. A house in a rainforest. A turret reaching to the sky. She was hit with a realisation: she *knew* this place. Slowly, she turned the photo over and, sure enough, there it was.

Willow and Ben, Towerhurst. 1974.

Towerhurst! She had *been* there, just once, and Libby's mind was dragged back two decades, settling on a childhood memory from which the haze began to clear.

Chapter 2

Towerhurst, west coast Tasmania, Australia

September 1985

They'd only just got out of the car and already Libby's hair was plastered to her head. She huddled in a bright red coat that was far too big, though according to the label it should fit a girl who was already ten.

'What *is* this place?' she said, sidling up to her mum, who waited by a sign so creaky it threatened to tumble onto the mossy ground below.

Towerhurst, it read.

'Come on,' her mum muttered, and they started up the drive. She'd been in a mood the entire trip, and Libby knew exactly why.

Old Mrs Murphy had called at 7 a.m. to say she couldn't, as had been agreed, babysit for the day: her own grandchild had chickenpox, and it was safer Libby stay away. 'No worries,' Mum had said sweetly down the phone, replacing the receiver calmly before huffing and puffing. 'There's no time' – she'd glanced at her watch – 'you'll have to come with me.' Softening then, as though realising she'd been a terrible grump, she'd given a weak thumbs up. 'It'll be fun.'

They'd driven for hours across the state, one picturesque scene giving way to another. Gone was the dry scrubby forest that surrounded their home on Tasmania's north coast, gone were the waves lapping at its shore, gone was the smell of salt in the air. Everything turned green, an endless emerald carpet that rolled over the hills, the whiff of livestock heavy on the wind. Libby had fallen asleep, an open book in her lap, and when she'd woken, the Tasmania she knew had disappeared, replaced with a desolate landscape that might have been on the moon.

'West-coast mining country,' her mum said as she navigated the turns winding through bare landscape that had been, she'd said, cleared of trees a century ago when pioneers dug for copper.

Over the next mountain the forest had returned, a morphed version of the one Libby knew: taller, thicker, crowding the road. It was as lush as she imagined the Amazon to be, and it seemed quite as unfamiliar. The narrow road had cut through the vegetation like a knife, and soon enough they'd glimpsed grey ocean, before turning north, following the coast, bumping along the potholed road until they'd reached an impassable track that snaked up a hill, and the creaky sign to Towerhurst.

Their boots splashed in the mud as they trudged past the inquisitive ground ferns, past the trees with their glistening leaves. Running water gouged the mossy track. As Libby skipped to keep up, she repeated what her mother had told her moments before.

'So, you're showing this house to some people?'

'Yes.'

'Why?'

'Because they want to buy it.'

'From who?'

With a sharp intake of breath, her mum stopped abruptly, and Libby careered into her side.

'Mum?'

No answer.

'*Mum?*'

'I'm helping sell Towerhurst for . . . a friend. I've never been here before.'

'What friend?'

Overhead, a currawong broke low from the trees, flying so close that Libby saw rain splash from its glossy black wings. Only then did she register what lay beyond, what had halted her mother.

A house, just visible at the top of the track, peered down at them like a schoolmaster might regard his students. At its front, two large windows looked out from a sweeping verandah, a prominent monobrow over watching eyes, the deck warped in a way that only time could manage. But it wasn't this part of the house that was remarkable, nor the upper floor where four windows lined up like watchmen. The schoolmaster, it seemed, wore a hat; a tall hexagonal turret – a single round window in each face – rose above the forest canopy.

'What *is* this place?'

'A legacy,' her mum said quietly.

Before Libby could ask what that meant, a roar cut through the rain. Behind them, a vehicle climbed the steep track, its wheels barely gripping the mud. It rolled to a stop and the driver wound down his window, leaning out with a grin.

'You're Willow?'

'That's right.'

The man reached out a large paw. 'G'day,' he said, switching off the engine. The silence made the rain louder still as it hissed on the bonnet, turning immediately to steam. 'I'm Denny and this is Jess.' He leaned back, revealing a petite woman whose brown hair was piled into a topknot. She waved, giving a wink; she had remarkable eyes: one blue, one brown.

Mum managed a weak smile. 'Not a great day for viewing.'

'It's . . . authentic,' Denny said. 'Wouldn't be moving to the west coast of Tassie for the weather!'

'No,' said Mum as she fished in her pocket for the keys.

⁊ઢ

The lock was jammed, but a sharp shove pushed the door ajar. Mum stepped back as they filed through, Libby sandwiched between Denny and Jess, blinking in the gloom.

Towerhurst was a mess: debris covered the floor, paintings hung askew and a soft layer of mould coated the wide, beautiful staircase that led up into the beyond. 'Looks like you've had a visitor,' Denny said, pushing a pile of droppings with his boot. 'Or more than one . . .'

When there was no answer, Libby turned. She frowned: her mum stood rigid in the doorway, eyes wide, hands clasped together. Then her expression cleared, and she stepped inside.

⁊ઢ

Most of the rooms were in a similar state; possums had moved in, making the house their own. But the windows were intact and it was dry, or dry enough, so Libby overheard Denny whisper to Jess.

They poked around the first floor, then the second. The house was a warren of rooms, more than a dozen in total, connected by airy hallways themselves linked by that impressive golden staircase. 'Huon pine,' Denny murmured to Jess, barely containing his excitement, as he scratched beneath the banister.

A strange door led from the end of the second floor. It was a perfect circle, almost as wide as the hall itself, and Denny whistled when he saw it, a low drawing in of breath through his blond beard.

Mum paused, blocking the way. 'Can't say what state the tower's in.'

'If it's like the rest of the house' – Denny shrugged – 'it'll be all right.'

'Might be dangerous. We'll get a professional to have a look . . . when you're serious about buying, that is.'

Jess gave Denny a look. He nodded. 'We *are* serious.'

'But you've only just arrived.'

'All the same . . .' He ran a hand over the door. 'It's like something out of *The Hobbit*,' he laughed at Jess.

Mum wasn't amused. 'No one's been into the tower for more than a decade. I'll get an engineer in, then we can go up.'

'Funny you should say that,' Jess said, with that wink of hers. 'I happen to *be* an engineer. Didn't I mention that?'

'No, you didn't.'

The only sound was the pat of rain on the roof, a muffled echo in the hallway.

'Look, Willow,' Denny said, 'we aren't interested in playing games. My wife and I *love* the house. It's exactly what we're looking for.' He linked a hand through Jess's. 'Exactly what we need to fill our life.'

Libby watched a look pass between them: sad, quiet. Something only adults could understand.

Mum nodded, softening.

'And we know about what happened here. We read about it in the library archive. Don't worry, it doesn't bother us. Do you have any information on the body—'

'No,' Mum interrupted, turning quickly to Libby. 'You'd better wait in the front room, love.'

'But I want to come up to the tower.'

'You can have a look another time.' Mum knelt before her, still with that soft look on her face. 'And when I say wait in the front room, I mean it. Do not – I repeat – *do not* go outside. You'll only get soaked to the bone.' She reached over to touch the backpack slung on Libby's shoulders. 'You've got your book in there?'

Libby nodded, turning to go. Then she paused at the top of the stairs, listening to the creak of the tower door, and the gasps of amazement as Denny and Jess started their ascent.

さ

There was nowhere to sit in the front room. The couch, which may have once been deep red, was now pink under the mould. At Libby's feet peeled wallpaper lay like sloughed snakeskins, and before her dark paintings showed Australian scenes: garrison towns on wide open plains. So different to the landscape outside.

Beneath the mantelpiece were the remnants of an unlit fire and she pulled out a page of newspaper, smoothing its crinkled surface. *The Examiner.* Launceston's local paper. Dated January 1975.

The room was flanked by two large windows. One at the rear, where the rainforest stood close, almost touching the glass; one at the front overlooking the verandah. The rain had stopped and a thin mist rolled across the driveway, hugging Denny and Jess's ute in a soupy embrace. It was quiet inside now without that thundering on the roof, but outside the world had woken, the air full of calls from birds she didn't know.

And then: a sudden movement. Beside the ute, then disappearing. Again, there it was. Small, the size of a dog and reddish.

Then it was gone.

さ

She followed because she could. Sneaking out of the house, leaving the front door ajar. Running across the wooden verandah, down the stone steps, past the ute to the very back of the house where she stopped short. There, framing a trail that led into rainforest, was a stone archway, shaped into a perfect circle, just like the door that led to the tower.

Libby stepped closer. She was afraid to pass beneath it – what if it should tumble? Just as she reached out to touch it, to test its strength, her foot knocked against something hard hidden beneath a thick layer of moss. She got to her knees and pulled away the sopping-wet vegetation to reveal a low cut stone. A message was carved into its surface.

Always loved. Never forgotten.

She wasn't sure what it meant, but the stone was beautiful; swirls of purple and green like she'd never seen before. Brushing off her knees, she stood, eyeing the archway once more. Fingers of fog rolled through it, swirling on the other side as though beckoning her through. On the trail beneath her feet, animal footprints peppered the mud. Wallabies or pademelons probably, elongated tracks Libby had studied at school. With tentative steps, she followed them, taking a deep breath as she passed beneath the moon-shaped archway, and disappeared into the rainforest beyond.

❧

She heard the waterfall before she saw it: a heavy thrumming that filled the air, getting louder and louder as she continued until finally she was upon it. A wide wall of tumbling tannic water the height of four men, diving from above to slide effortlessly into a round pool below. Leaning down, she scooped the water into her hands, and let it trickle away.

A narrow path traced the water's edge, cutting into the dark stone, and with one hand held out for balance she followed it. Step by step she went, until the tiny track took her behind the falls.

Libby wasn't, as a rule, a child prone to disobeying her mum, but now, as she stood in this cave, the falling water forming a frosted glass at its front and the smooth stone at the back inviting her to sit, she felt her moment of rebellion had been entirely worth it. This was a kingdom. She sat down, leaning her head against the rock all the better to feel the rumble.

Above her, something was amiss; a straight line, ill at ease in the natural surrounds. Stretching on her tippy toes, Libby reached up onto a ledge just visible in the gloom to discover a small blue-and-red biscuit tin, its coating lifted in places by bubbles of rust. *Arnott's* was emblazoned on its lid. She knew the brand well. Every Australian did. Mum loved their Monte Carlos, cream-filled biscuits that she dunked in her tea as she painted. She shook the tin: it rattled dully.

Her heart leapt.

Something was inside.

෨෧

As she emerged from the rainforest, her mind still fizzing, Libby was pulled roughly from her feet and gathered into an embrace so tight she felt the thump of her mum's heart through her coat, but almost as soon as the moment of abandon arrived, it vanished as if it had never been.

Her mum set her on the ground, and knelt, utter fury on her face. 'Where *have* you been?' Her brows were drawn up and away as though trying to escape. Which was just, at that moment, what Libby wanted to do. 'I *told* you to wait in the front room.'

'I thought I saw something . . . a creature . . . it ran away. I just wanted to see . . .' Libby trailed off. 'I'm sorry—'

Jess emerged from behind the house – 'Thank goodness!' – and a moment later Denny called from a round window in the tower. It swung outwards, a disk hanging precariously.

'Can't see anything from—' He stopped short, clocking the three of them below. 'Right-o.' He disappeared from sight.

'You gave us quite a scare, love. You were gone for ages,' Jess said as she knelt next to Mum.

Libby could have sworn she had disappeared for only a moment. 'I found a waterfall.'

'A waterfall, eh? Sounds amazing,' said Jess, her smile quickly slipping at a glance from Mum. 'Still, you shouldn't have gone off like that. It's not safe in the rainforest.'

'Why not?'

Both the women paused awkwardly, before Jess left and met Denny at the door, where they talked in hushed whispers, pointing all the while to the house's hidden features.

ε

Afterwards, at the car, Libby asked, 'Did they like it?'

'What?' Her mum had been silent on the walk back down the drive.

'Jess and Denny. The house?'

Mum nodded, opening the back door. '*In,*' she said.

Libby did as she was told, her streak of rebellion fading as fast as the light around them. She opened the window, leaning out to breathe the last of the fresh forest air. So sweet, so damp. She liked it, actually; she wished they could stay. 'Where're you going?'

'Toilet break,' said Mum, stepping behind a tree. 'It's a long drive home.'

When she was out of sight, Libby reached back across the seat. Tucked at the bottom of her backpack, wrapped in her dry fleece, was the tin.

She lifted the lid, sifting through the now-familiar contents: a tattered copy of Banjo Paterson's poem 'The Man from Snowy River', a ballad written on airmail paper, a heavy pendant on a tarnished silver chain and a sprig of herb pressed between two small sheets of glass held together with tape.

Outside, there was a retching, then her mum appeared, her eyes red and swollen.

'Something I ate,' she said, getting into the car and fastening her seatbelt. With a sigh, she turned the key and the engine reluctantly spluttered to life.

Libby slipped the tin away. Out of sight. But not out of mind. And not complete. Because one item was missing. The pendant – a fox with a dark blue jewel as an eye – lay in her palm, and as they drove home across Tasmania she traced the cool contours with her thumb, imagining where it had come from, wondering to whom it had belonged.

Chapter 3

Grosvenor Square, London

July 1939

Sixty-five years before the letter . . .

The fox pendant, and its shining chain, spilled out of the box into Grace Grey's palm. The gift was so unexpected that she merely stared at it until her mother rolled her eyes, indicating it was clearly the reaction she'd predicted. *She's such a dull creature*, Grace had overhead her say only last week to her laughing friends.

She smiled, but her mother had already looked away. Anyway, it wasn't so much that Grace wasn't pleased to receive a present, it was that the giving of *two* identical necklaces somehow made hers only half as special.

'Thank you,' said the second, appropriately grateful, recipient, and Grace's chaperone for the long journey to Tasmania. Rose Munro held up her pendant so that its sapphire eye twinkled at her in the sunshine, which was hardly unexpected; Rose was exactly the kind of young woman who inspired winks and lingering glances. She was physical perfection in every way.

'The chains might be silver, girls, but the fox pendants are platinum.' Edeline Grey took the necklace from Rose to hang it gently around her neck. 'They'll never tarnish. They'll always be as beautiful as the day they were made.'

'It will remind me of you,' Rose said with love, in the way she always talked to Edeline, as if it was Edeline who was her mother and not the housekeeper, Molly Munro. Grace could see Molly's short round frame silhouetted just inside the front door as she observed the scene from a distance, as though she was an outsider and not party to the farewells at all. Grace gave her a small wave, and Molly rewarded her with a warm smile.

Surely it was Molly, and not Rose, who truly deserved this gift? The housekeeper had worked for the Foxton family long before Edeline had become a Grey, apparently showing loyalty though through thick and thin. Grace didn't know which part of her mother's life had been thick and which had been thin, though she had a sneaking suspicion that the marriage to Kingston Grey was one of these, her own birth being the other.

She hadn't dared to tell Edeline how worried she was about leaving England, but Molly seemed to understand, as though last-minute journeys to the far side of the globe were par for the course, and three days was plenty of time to accept a life turned upside down.

'A great adventure is what it is!' she'd said after Edeline had coolly delivered the news moments before disappearing to one of her beloved political meetings, leaving her housekeeper to manage the fallout.

'It's for your own safety, Grace,' Molly had soothed. 'And your uncle Marcus is a fine man. I knew him, you know? Before.'

Before what? Grace had wanted to ask, but Molly had ploughed on, her voice bright, as though perhaps she wished she was going on this 'great adventure' herself. 'And Australia! Tasmania, no less. Van Diemen's Land. Convicts. Kangaroos, Tasmanian tigers . . .'

Grace had wrung her hands with anxiety. The thought of sailing across the world to live with her uncle Marcus and his Australian wife Olive, neither of whom she had ever met, turned her stomach inside out. And she may as well have been going alone; Rose seemed no more likely to be kind to her in Tasmania than she was in London. But the world around them was mobilising and it was inevitable that Grace, who had never been able to hold her ground, would be swept along in the end.

'You'll be just fine, love,' Molly had added, her gaze falling on Grace's clasped fingers. 'We will all have to walk a new path with what is to come.'

But even as troop trains spread across Europe, much of the city seemed to be wilfully, or ignorantly, oblivious. Londoners were enjoying the summer, drinking and dancing, lovers lying on their backs in the parched city parks, looking to the sky as though it would always be safely empty, turning their faces away when barrage balloons blocked the sun.

'Don't they understand what is about to happen?' Rose (who considered herself an expert on all things political) had said to Edeline two days before. 'What's wrong with them?'

And although Grace wasn't inclined to agree with much that her chaperone said, she had to admit that the taxis rolling sedately past the American Embassy, and the quiet laughter spilling from a nearby pub, gave London a deceptive air of normalcy considering war was, by all accounts, inevitable. Even now, whistling soldiers assembled an anti-aircraft gun on the square behind them while three school girls giggled happily down the street. It was the sight of the girls, not the guns, that caused Grace's heart to tug. These students, with their private jokes and swinging hair, would never have welcomed her in. Perhaps it was a blessing that she'd been educated at home. She was scrawny and ugly after all, and not particularly bright. Nothing like her mother, so tall and elegant, whose blonde locks framed a perfect face. Or Rose, who lit up a room, while Grace's colourless complexion caused Edeline's friends to ask what afflicted her, and if there was even a smidgen of hope for her future.

Across the square, a window opened and a young face peered anxiously – and somewhat furtively, Grace thought – up and down the street. It was Elizabeth Winman, a name Grace only knew because Elizabeth's father was a government paper-pusher and Edeline had met her mother at some society do where the Winmans had apparently overstepped the mark. 'That flat's rented, you know. It's on the Westminster books,' her mother had said. 'They're reaching far above their station.' But Grace had always thought, from her brief glimpses, that the Winmans seemed contented enough. Was it better to be squeezed happily into a rented flat than to own a cavernous house that would never be filled with love?

When Elizabeth's gaze alighted on the small gathering outside the Grey household, she threw them a wave, and Grace's heart leapt, but before she could return the gesture Rose elbowed her out of the way and shouted goodbye. Had Grace behaved in such a way, Edeline would've scowled, but she only snapped her fingers at the chauffeur and said that time was ticking, and the boat at Liverpool wouldn't wait for their arrival.

So, the two girls, with two bags, and five years between them, stepped into the car and said farewell to their respective mothers: small, lovable Molly Munro who gave Grace a genuine smile, and tall, elegant Edeline who did not. Both Grace and Rose's fathers were absent, but only Rose's had an excuse, in that he was dead and gone, while Kingston Grey was not. Grace wondered briefly when she'd once again see Grosvenor Square and how changed it would be.

As the car pulled away, Elizabeth Winman appeared from

her front door and edged carefully onto the street, sliding –
to Grace's surprise – into a shadowed nook where a man in
uniform, a boy of eighteen perhaps, threw his arms around
her. Elizabeth, Grace knew, was only seventeen, two years
older than herself. Yet here she was entwined with a lover,
and it made Grace feel that her life was already marching by.
Although she would be sixteen in September, she wasn't even
close to becoming a woman, being as weedy as an urchin,
though better dressed, and so flat chested she might as well
have been a boy. In fact, *better* she'd been a boy, then perhaps
her parents might have loved her after all.

While Rose glanced back over her shoulder to where Edeline
and Molly waved goodbye, Grace was fixated on Elizabeth and
the boy who bent forward to kiss her, saying something to
make her laugh. She nodded, holding his hand as he walked
away so that their arms outstretched until their fingers finally
let go. And Elizabeth held her nerve, never faltering until he
disappeared out of sight, at which point she sat heavily on her
front step, her shoulders shaking as she cried. Grace gripped
the fox pendant that hung around her neck and in her heart,
that heart which her mother dismissed as unlovable, she understood she'd never experience a moment like the one she'd just
witnessed. As the car turned from Grosvenor Square and her
old life, she wondered what it might be like to fall in love, be
swept away, and pine for another human, knowing that it was
only when you were with them once again that your heart
could possibly be full.

Chapter 4

Grosvenor Square, London
November 2004

Libby stood in a trance at the foot of the steps that led to her apartment in Grosvenor Square. Well, not *her* apartment, precisely, but the one she was gratefully borrowing from her exceptionally generous aunts just until she 'found her feet'. The satchel hung heavily on her shoulder, weighed down by expectation and guilt. She would go up, pour a glass of wine, take a deep breath and . . . and . . . and yet the thought of opening those buckles again, of meeting a part of the man she'd never known, caused her stomach to flip. Already it had spilled a secret and, as she'd descended the steps of Bus 139, realisation hit her hard: Willow, her mother, had lied.

'I'm helping sell Towerhurst for . . . a friend,' she'd said that day back in 1985. 'I've never been here before.'

Never been here before. But in the satchel Libby had discovered irrefutable proof that that wasn't so. In 1974 – the year before her father's death – her parents had stood before that unmistakable house wearing grins as wide as their faces.

'Seen a ghost, my dear?' said the elderly woman who had appeared like an apparition at Libby's side, both of them static in the swirling Friday night bustle.

'Not a ghost,' Libby replied, 'so much as a memory.'

'You're far too young to be living in the past.'

It was true, of course, though sometimes she felt she resided nowhere else.

'Well, don't just stand there,' said Miss Winman, Libby's eighty-two-year-old neighbour, as she extended her arm. 'Won't you make yourself useful, and help me up these steps?'

❧

An hour later, stood at the window with a glass of wine in hand, it wasn't Grosvenor Square Libby saw before her but Towerhurst, that strange trip with her mum now a vivid swirl of sensation in her mind. The smell of the damp humus, the currawong's call overhead, the light behind the waterfall.

Putting aside her untouched glass, she went to her bedroom to retrieve a wooden box she'd packed in Tasmania ten days before. Ten days already? Where had the time gone? How long would it take to find a job, a place of her own, a life? 'Let go of the past,' her mum had said, spying the shoebox tucked inside her daughter's open suitcase the morning of the flight. 'Leave it here.' But Libby could never do that, literally or metaphorically, and now she sighed as she pulled it from beneath her bed, and opened the lid.

It was her memory box, the place that she kept the secret parts of her life she always wanted with her. There, on top – because they were the only items she regularly looked at – were Krish's letters, his handwriting chaotic as though he couldn't wait to get out all the things he'd wanted to say. Libby lifted them to her nose, even though all scent of him had vanished long ago, erased by that same *time* that people promised would ease the pain. Gently, she put them down, removing the other items from the box one by one: theatre stubs, photos that she dared not look at, a bracelet wrapped in velvet. At the bottom, she located what she was looking for: a small biscuit tin, blue, red and partially rusted, the word *Arnott's* emblazoned on top. She opened it, sifting through the four items inside: two poems, the fox necklace and the sprig of heather pressed in glass.

She picked up the first poem, carefully unfolding the typed pages.

> There was movement at the station, for the word had
>   passed around
> That the colt from old Regret had got away,
> And had joined the wild bush horses – he was worth a
>   thousand pound,
> So all the cracks had gathered to the fray . . .

It was 'The Man from Snowy River', Australia's darling poem, written by Banjo Paterson in 1890 and as quintessential to her nation's identity as the kangaroo, the eucalyptus and the wide and open plains. Every Australian child learned it at school, but it wasn't until the day when Libby had stepped beneath what she now knew to be a moon gate – that circular stone archway leading into the rainforest – and ventured behind the waterfall that she'd *really* read it, tasted its cadence. Felt the goosebumps prick her skin. Sitting here now, at the foot of her bed, legs stretched before her, she still heard the sound of that rushing river, felt the thrill of stumbling across a secret kingdom.

She put the page aside and picked up the sprig of heather, holding the glass to the light to see that the white bell-shaped flowers remained beautifully preserved. As a child, she hadn't known what the plant was – it was an invasive species in Tasmania – but she later discovered its identity (as she had with so many things) through the pages of her novels. All those heroines wandering moodily over heaths, their hands trailing through heather.

Next, she unfolded the second poem, carefully smoothing

the thin paper. Its title – comically – was 'The Ma'am from Joey River' and its cadence matched, more or less, 'The Man from Snowy River', though it told an entirely different tale, that of a group of boys trying to score a kiss from a girl to win a bet. Conspicuous in its absence was the name of the author, and it seemed a great shame to Libby because the poet had taken *such* care: the words framed in a flawless, sloping hand, a tail on each G and flourishes on the Ys.

Putting the poem carefully aside, she picked up the final item, recalling the guilt of the theft (or was it *really* theft?). The moment they'd returned home from Towerhurst, she'd raced to her room and flung the tin, and all its contents, into her memory box – its privacy always respected by her mother – far beneath her bed.

She lifted the chain so that the pendant dangled free, its sapphire eye twinkling in the fuggy light of her bedside lamp, and for the first time in nearly twenty years Libby hung the fox around her neck. Its heaviness surprised her. It seemed to press against her breast bone, as if trying to find a way to her heart.

❧

Ten minutes later, she sat at her computer, her finger hovering over the *Enter* button. According to Skype, her mum was online, though it was early morning in Australia, and soon she would be lost to her work. A month before Libby's departure, Willow had started teaching, something she'd said she'd never do. Still, she'd gone ahead with her plan, and a girl called Ciara was her first student: mid-twenties, Irish, a barista at the local café. The last time she'd poked her head into the classroom – Willow's studio, hidden at the bottom of the garden – Ciara and her mum had been as thick as thieves, laughing at some unknown joke. Something had tugged at Libby then. Jealousy perhaps, though perhaps not, because when she'd seen Ciara leave, a happy flush to her features, she'd felt not the slightest bitterness. But she *was* envious. Envious that Willow *could* laugh that way with someone else. And sad. Sad that her mother never lost herself with Libby, never relaxed. Never let go.

She hit *Enter* and, to her surprise, her mum answered on the second ring. There she was in her red glasses, her short grey bob shining in the bright Tasmanian summer sun which illuminated the kitchen in a brilliant glow.

Within five minutes they'd covered the week since Libby had last called, her walks along the Thames and her visit to the V&A – but not her visit to another museum she wouldn't mention, nor to that dingy waiting room – and now silence descended. Willow hadn't asked this time about her daughter's social life, and Libby was forced to face reality: her octogenarian neighbour, Miss Winman, was her only true acquaintance in London and her mum clearly knew it. Was Libby *really* so predictable? She was somehow surprised that her mum should know her so well when their relationship had always seemed so . . . so *functional*. Functional discussions about functional things, rarely anything deeper. Certainly nothing as deep as the thing that Libby needed to say.

Mum, I collected Dad's satchel. I'm sorry.

It was on the tip of her tongue when Willow said, 'Oh!' and waved towards the front door, a wide grin spreading across her face. 'Ciara! Come in! I'm talking to my daughter.'

'Libby in London?' said a lovely Irish lilt.

Willow nodded, and Libby's heart flipped. She'd never considered that her mum bothered to mention her to others.

'She's definitely in London, wrapped up in wool. Probably wearing slippers!'

Laughter – kind laughter – came from Ciara. 'You know what they say? Cold feet, warm heart.' She made a murmur about using the toilet, and with the sound of a closing door she was gone.

Self-consciously, Libby removed her black woollen shawl. Across the world, there was a sharp intake of breath, and Willow paused, the screen appearing to freeze.

'*Where* did you get that?' her mother whispered as Libby leaned back, realisation dawning. *The necklace.* She'd forgotten it was still looped around her neck. Whatever had possessed her to wear it?

'This?' Libby had never been a good liar. 'I . . . found it. Ages ago.'

'When? Where?'

'It was . . . it was when we visited Towerhurst—'

At the name, Willow drew breath.

'Back when I was a kid. Do you remember?'

Her mum reached out as though trying to touch the fox pendant, to take it in two fingers and turn it this way and that, to peer into its sapphire eye.

'I'm sorry. I should've told you I found it. It just didn't seem important because you were so worried when I disappeared . . .' She trailed off, remembering how guilty she'd felt. 'Do you know who the necklace belonged—'

A creak of the door, and her mother's face smoothed. 'Ciara,' she said, 'let's get started.' She nodded goodbye, quickly ending the call so that this time her face really *was* frozen, captured on the screen, her searching gaze fixed somewhere in the middle distance. The necklace, it seemed, had conjured a memory and Willow Andrews had been whisked away into the past.

Chapter 5

Launceston, Tasmania

November 1974

The solitary envelope waiting on the doormat was nondescript, and Willow Andrews juggled an armful of shopping as she scooped it up to read the printed address.

> Mr & Mrs Ben Andrews
> 27 Acacia Drive
> Launceston
> Tasmania

She turned it over, examining it. This wasn't a redirect from her parents' home; whoever sent this knew where she lived, and that made her smile. They were finally official. She glanced at the ring on her finger – a find from an antiques store in Launceston – a non-fussy slip of a thing. Like their wedding had been: just them, Willow's parents and her sisters, back from Sydney. No one on Ben's side, of course, which was why they'd gone for a small registry office affair, followed by dinner in town. They'd been half living together for two years, much to the horror of Ben's neighbours, and now that they were married everything had changed.

She took a knife from the kitchen counter, and sliced the paper open.

えん

A day later, she and Ben sat in the plush office of the Launceston solicitor whose name had been printed in deep blue ink at the top of the letter, *Doyle & Son,* while Mr Doyle himself – the senior by the look of him – peered intently over his glasses.

'It's not as abnormal as you'd think,' he said, leaning back comfortably in his captain's chair, his pen lined precisely parallel with a pile of documents intended for signing. 'Houses are often left in trusts like this.'

Willow wrinkled her brow. *Trusts.* The domain of the rich, or those who had something to hide.

'But who's it *from*? Who left it?' She spread her hands, then folded them away when she noticed the blue streaks on her fingers, bits of paint she'd missed. *So much colour, so much life,* Ben always marvelled when he admired her work, *just like you.*

'I'm afraid I'm not at liberty to divulge that,' Mr Doyle said. 'The trust goes to you, and your husband, as the new beneficiaries. You may use the property as you see fit.'

There was a long silence. Ben leaned forward. 'You mean the house is effectively . . . ours?'

'Yes. In a roundabout way.'

Willow wanted to laugh at the ridiculous nature of this unexpected situation. 'Why us?'

'As I said, Mrs Andrews, as executor of the will in question, I've been tasked with carrying out very specific instructions. The only thing I may say on the matter is that the benefactor was a particular fan of . . .' He paused, glancing at the folder. 'A particular fan of the arts.'

She reddened. After years of struggling to find her way, years of temp jobs, scraping and scrimping, working in her parents' spare room, everything had changed with one sale. One *big* sale – her painting *The Reckoning* – and the series of commissions that quickly followed. Now her work was in vogue. She squeezed Ben's hand. Yes, in the three years since they'd met, things had been going very well indeed. He was her lucky charm, sat there in his brown suit, the trousers so flared at the ankles she had to laugh. His hair was slicked back in a way she'd never seen before, quite comical really. It was unusual attire for Tasmania's greatest – so she felt – literary talent.

'Well,' Ben said in a formal tone Willow planned to tease him about later, 'shall we go over the paperwork?'

'Of course.' Mr Doyle handed him an envelope and Ben slid out two large documents, each held together with a bulldog clip. *Terms of Engagement: Doyle & Son* was typed in bold print across one. The other simply said: *Foxton Trust*.

Ben passed them to Willow.

Mr Doyle cleared his throat. A clock chimed a merry whistle from the waiting room, where an immaculately dressed secretary had coolly welcomed their arrival with a swift sweep of her eyes half an hour before. 'It was the benefactor's specific instructions the trust only be transferred when the primary beneficiary had married.'

Some old-fashioned notion, Willow thought. Her mind went to Ben's neighbours; their raised eyebrows, the twitching curtains and pointed questions. They too held on to the sentiment that marriage was the turning point for couples to do what they wanted. Woe betide those who tried to live their lives prior to the big event. Hopefully, their new neighbourhood would be less . . . conservative.

She touched Ben's hand, then turned back to the lawyer. 'Where is this house, anyway?' In all the flurry neither of them had asked; they'd only speculated the night before as they watched the sun set over Launceston. 'I'm hoping for somewhere near the river,' Willow had said. 'A brick Federation house that needs a bit of sprucing.'

From a desk drawer, Mr Doyle took a lumpy envelope. He tipped it upside down, spilling a set of keys and a map of Tasmania, which he stretched like a piano accordion, pointing to the island's west coast.

'The house,' she said, 'it's not in *Launceston*?'

A bemused look. 'Did I say it was?'

Willow glanced at Ben, who appeared to be on the verge of laughter. This was about as far from her urban waterside fantasy as it was possible to get. Tasmania's west coast was not somewhere anyone *planned* on living. It was remote, wet and wild. *Very* wild. A place where people went to escape the world.

Mr Doyle continued. 'It's close to the sea. You may even catch a glimpse of the ocean from the . . . upper levels.'

Ben leaned over the map. She could almost see his mind at work: a ready-made writing bolthole away from everything and everyone. His reluctance seemed to dissipate in an instant. 'What's it like, this house?'

'*I've* never been there,' Mr Doyle said as though Ben had asked if he'd once visited the moon. 'I'm more of an east-coast man myself.'

Ben put a hand over Willow's, squeezing gently. *Let's see where this goes*, was his intimation. 'What about the tax implications?' It was the most officiously adult thing she'd ever heard him say.

'The trust has sufficient funds to cover expenses,' Mr Doyle said. 'If this were an inheritance, then you'd be up for death duties. An outdated notion.' It was the kind of opinion given by men with enough money to give it.

Mr Doyle looked pointedly at his watch, and Willow wondered whether they'd stayed long enough for him to bill a full hour to her trust. *Their* trust, she corrected herself. 'I'll leave you to go through the documentation. You can sign when you're ready.'

When he left, Ben turned to her. 'Who could have done this?'

She shook her head and leaned over the documents, flipping through the pages. *The Foxton Trust*. It didn't ring a bell. She gave Ben a sideways grin, and he leaned in to kiss her.

'What was that for?'

'I couldn't resist your smile.'

She laughed. 'Perhaps it's because I'm a householder now?' She shoved him. 'Gold digger.'

He raised an eyebrow. '*We*. We're householders.'

She kissed him back. Her heart could burst. Life wasn't going to plan; it was going much better. They signed on the dotted line.

෧

In the end, with all the excitement, they simply couldn't wait. By the time the sun was up the following morning, they were already winding their way past the outer suburbs of Launceston into open farmland. Willow lowered the window, letting the breeze pick goosebumps on her bare arms. A concertinaed map lay in her lap, a dog-eared guidebook tucked underneath. Their yellow Renault 16 burst at the seams and, aside from the kitchen sink, Ben had packed almost everything they might possibly need for a trip to the west coast: woollens, waterproofs, walking boots. Pasta, rice, beans. Sleeping bags. Tent. And – Willow had raised an eyebrow as she peered into a holdall – books. Quite a few, actually.

'We're only going for three days.' She'd flicked through a battered Ian Fleming.

He'd tucked an orange woollen hat into the top of his pack. 'Be prepared,' he'd grinned, making the Scouts sign, though he'd never been one because he'd never had the opportunity to try. It was something, he'd said, they would make sure their boys did. Campfires, bushcraft, knots.

'Knots?' She'd made a face when he'd told her.

'Yes.'

The only knot they'd tied before that conversation was the marrying kind, and she'd liked that one very much indeed. But there was another knot. One that sat in her stomach. Worried at her. Tightening a little more each month. Willow *would* get pregnant, the doctors said, there was nothing obviously wrong. But though he never expressed it, she knew in her heart that Ben was worried that he'd never have a family of his own.

'You have sisters now,' she'd told him on their honeymoon. 'Ash and Ivy love you almost as much as me.'

'I hope not,' he'd laughed, but she could see that he was pleased.

'And Mum and Dad can't get enough of you. They treat you as though you were their own.'

He'd pulled a face. 'That's all a bit Tasmanian,' he'd said, referring to mainlanders' jokes about an inbred state. With four hundred thousand people the island was hardly a village, but locals took the jesting in their stride. And Tasmanians laughed at mainlanders too: the madness of Sydney's rat race, the snarled Melbourne commute, the long hot summers that burned them to a crisp.

Willow observed the landscape slide by: scattered sheep in russet paddocks, garrison towns like sandstone guards of honour, stands of eucalypt waving lazily in the breeze. And the endless blue sky watching – unblinking – their progress. The road wavered in heat haze but the air was fresh, though they were now thirty miles from the sea. Tasmania was like that. An island that couldn't be defined by a single climate, a single mood, a single landscape. Rolling hills and jagged gorges.

Rocky shores and sandy embraces. Cities and empty spaces. Dry forest, low forest, high forest. Wet forest. An island that hung on the edge of the world. An island with something for everyone.

ॐ

The sign was obvious, just as the solicitor had said: half a mile past the ford ('You won't be able to reach it at high tide,' he'd warned them), the house's name flashed up in the headlights, ghostly in the darkness.

Towerhurst.

They turned right, climbing the steep track, the little Renault's wheels spinning in the moss as they chatted nervously – Willow about dinner, Ben about visiting the nearest town tomorrow – until they came to an abrupt stop.

'Oh my God,' Willow gasped.

There, before them, was a magnificent Federation house, large but not ostentatious, in two shades of white: crisp alabaster on the lower half, peeling ivory above, as though someone had set down a paintbrush at the end of the work day, gone home for tea, and never returned. Eight windows peered from the elevation and a deep verandah promised sundowners and shelter from the west coast's famous rain.

But most remarkable, and most out of place, was the tower that reached from the house, rising above the red corrugated iron roof and soaring over the canopy. A sea view, indeed.

Ben turned to Willow, throwing her a nervous grin. Immediately she knew what he was thinking. He loved it. He was swept away. He was gone. Somewhere in the recesses of his imagination Towerhurst was already becoming a muse.

'Will we?' he said.

She put her hand in her pocket and touched the keys, as she had done so many times on the drive. Would one of these *really* fit? Surely, they'd made a mistake. Missed the turning for a tiny cottage, or a tumble-down shack? And yet Mr Doyle had said: *Towerhurst.* They'd followed the directions precisely.

She stepped up to the door, and on her first attempt — as though they were returning home after a stay away — it unlocked.

Ben picked her up, swinging her small frame into his arms with a mock groan, muttering something about the size of her lunch.

'What're you doing?'

'Carrying you into our new home.'

She laughed. 'Why?'

'What do they say it's for?' He paused, thinking. 'So that demons can't follow?'

Her arms looped loosely behind his neck. 'Isn't it a wedding thing?'

'Well, we're newly married!'

'Something about the wife not showing herself to be too keen for the bed?'

Quickly, he set her down. 'We don't want any talk like that.' He looked over his shoulder as if checking for neighbours whispering behind net curtains. But there was no one to see, only a thousand trees standing like sentinels.

'Thank you, Foxton Trust,' he said.

'Thank you, Foxton Trust,' she whispered, determined that they'd one day discover who'd done this.

Ben stepped aside. 'Your castle, madam' — he swept low — 'awaits.'

With a gentle push, the door yawned open, and Towerhurst awoke once more.

Chapter 6

Tasmania

September 1939

A driver was waiting at Hobart's docks to ferry Grace and Rose to Towerhurst. He was a young man – Rose's age at most – with ash-blond hair that curled on the crown of his head, and he folded their sign away as they approached. He had a way about him – leaning against a lamppost, a week-old newspaper tucked beneath his arm – that feigned a casualness Grace didn't quite believe.

'Miss Grey?' He gave Rose an appreciative look over a nose whose enormity, Grace could now see, wasn't merely a trick of the light. Your uncle sent me.' There was no mention of Olive, Uncle Marcus' wife. 'I'm the chauffeur,' he added in an accent so thick he pronounced it *show-fa*.

Rose was amused by the mix up. 'How delightful. But *this*' – her smile only widened as Richard's fell away – 'is Grace Grey.'

'Oh . . . well.'

He bustled them into the car, and Grace sighed as she was designated to the backseat, listening to Richard as he asked Rose all about herself and the journey on which they'd just been.

It had taken eight interminable weeks to sail from England: down Africa's western coast, across the Indian Ocean, and along Australia, the size of which Grace had vastly underestimated when she'd pulled out a dusty old atlas to research Tasmania on the day after Edeline had announced their trip. 'Lovely beaches, though the people are monstrously unrefined,' her mother had said, as though they'd merely be taking a weekend jaunt rather than a journey to the other side of the world.

Was it a bad omen, Grace had wondered, that Tasmania appeared on page thirteen of that creaky atlas? The island itself was a little triangle-shaped smudge, home to a few scattered villages, names stolen from their English counterparts: Launceston, Brighton, the Tamar River. She estimated that it was 180 miles south of Melbourne.

They rolled out of Hobart and into the city's outskirts in quick order. There, the houses changed from sandstone to brick, to weatherboard, mostly painted white, with ornate fretworks and overhanging verandahs. But the decoration decreased the further west they went so that Grace felt that they were being driven out of civilisation, and she turned to watch the city disappear from the car's rear window.

'How many people live here? In Tasmania?' she asked from the backseat as they rumbled along a corrugated dirt road.

Richard gave a low whistle. 'A couple of hundred thousand? Mostly in Hobart, though. Not many living where we're headed.' He glanced at her in the rear-view mirror; his eyes were the colour of coal.

'Is that an oak tree in the field?' she asked a little later.

The spare wheel attached to the black Buick's bonnet rattled in time to his laughter. 'No. Most things round here're eucalypts of some kind or another. By the way, it's *paddocks*, not *fields*. But where we're headed, things are a bit . . . different from here. Cut off from the rest of the state, see? By the West Coast Range. Over there, there're species no one's even identified and ten steps off the track you'd be lost, taken by the rainforest in one giant gulp.'

Rose tapped his shoulder playfully. 'Richard!'

'Children love that kind of thing,' he'd replied.

I'm not a child, Grace had wanted to say. *I'm fifteen.* Instead, she'd said: 'What type of animals?'

'Snakes, for one. And Tasmanian devils, too. They shriek in the night. You'll hear them. There's an Irish family lives near your uncle's place, and they say the devils' call is just like the banshee; that's an omen of death, you know?'

'Terrifying.' Rose batted her eyelashes. 'Have *you* heard them?'

'Plenty of times. I live in Westford, not far from Towerhurst,' he said pointedly, casting her a glance. 'I drive this route to Hobart a few times a week.'

Grace leaned forward. 'How far to go?'

'We're still hours away. Towerhurst's north of the ford. We need to make it before high tide, otherwise we'll have to bunk down for the night.' He winked at Rose, and Grace watched her turn away, a grin as wide as her face.

੨ཱ

They made the ford in time. It was a thin crossing paved with flat stones that lay across the mouth of a river slicing from the edge of the forest.

'Why is it so brown?' Grace asked. The water was the colour of weak tea.

'The button grass in the plains above; it releases tannin. Sometimes the river runs pretty clear, sometimes it's like this. Depends on the rain.'

'What's it called, this river?'

'The Joey River,' Richard said, answering to Rose, even

though she'd not asked the question. '*Joey*, like a baby kangaroo.'

Rose nodded and turned away, her interest in his Tasmanian facts clearly having waned substantially in the preceding hours.

Above the Joey River, vegetation closed into an archway that framed the dark heart of the rainforest. Trees crowded against each other, marching downstream and making for the ocean, like lemmings off a cliff, stopped only by the alabaster beach that stretched as far as Grace could see.

'That's Ocean Beach,' Richard said. 'When the water's in, you lose the sand . . . it's shallow, and at low tide you can walk far out to sea. You don't want to be there when it turns, though. Easy to get caught. It's happened before.'

Grace couldn't swim, so she planned on staying as far away from the beach as possible.

As they rolled across the ford, thick plucks of water splattered the windscreen. 'Better get used to this,' said Richard. 'On the west coast of Tasmania, it rains two hundred days a year.'

જે

Towerhurst was nothing like Grace expected, nor was her uncle Marcus Foxton, who barely resembled the few photos of him she'd discovered in an album at the back of the Grosvenor Square library. He was, it was true, tall and fair like Edeline, with those same blue eyes, but in the twenty-odd years since he'd left England – at the end of the Great War – he had grown in both girth and hairiness, the latter in a rather alarming manner.

'Welcome to Towerhurst,' he said, with a hybrid English-Australian accent. 'Remarkable, isn't it?'

The top of the house was a turret that stretched heavenward, up and away. It seemed to Grace like a child raised up on an adult's shoulders so that it might see over a crowd, just as she had witnessed other fathers do to their daughters, both parties laughing happily.

Rose stretched her arms as she stepped from the car. 'It's fantastic,' she said. She looked ready for a night out in Mayfair: her skin flushed, her blue eyes shining, her hair a bright light in the dim afternoon. 'We've had *quite* the journey, Mr Foxton.'

Uncle Marcus smiled, and Grace caught her breath. Momentarily, Mother appeared. Right there, hidden in that expression, and she felt a pang. Not of longing – she didn't miss Edeline – but a sadness of sorts: when she herself looked in the mirror that distinctive Foxton smile had ever been absent.

Her uncle nodded. 'Olive sends her apologies. Her mother's ill, so she's staying with her for a few days.' Grace felt briefly disappointed. Mother had visited her brother here just once, and always called Aunt Olive 'the Australian wife' with such a sneer of disapproval that she was curious. 'She saw that dinner was left for us, and even I can heat up a stew.'

Uncle Marcus laughed then fished in his pocket for an envelope, handing it to Richard, who'd already taken the trunks and put them by the front door. Now he hovered.

'Well, I'll be going,' said Richard, a little too loudly. Rose – the obvious object of his lament – stood on the porch, leaning over its picket fence, peering into the forest. She made a fine silhouette from where they stood. 'Goodbye,' he said vaguely across Grace's shoulder.

Uncle Marcus smiled again, deep lines etching the corners of his eyes. 'A long old trip, isn't it?'

Grace's weariness overcame her. She nodded.

'Well, my dear girl, I'm sure things will improve,' he said, patting her shoulder, then turning to lead her up the steps, 'now that you're out of London and perfectly, wonderfully safe.'

Chapter 7

Hyde Park, London

December 2004

If someone had asked Libby to choose her favourite place in this incredible city she wouldn't hesitate. Even in wintery grey, Hyde Park was beautiful, with its bare trees – oaks, beech, hazel, so different to the eucalyptus Libby grew up with – and the distant bustle that seeped from the encircling streets but never quite reached inside. She'd found havens of tranquillity in its nooks and crannies, and now she sat on a bench overlooking the Serpentine, watching two swimmers brave the cold. It was a slow Saturday morning, hindered by the several glasses of wine she'd had the night before and the fact that she woken with the feeling that the conversation with her mum must have been some strange dream. But there was no doubt about it: Willow had *recognised* the fox pendant, and *more* than that, she'd physically recoiled when she'd discovered where Libby had found it. Their discussion had ended as quickly as it had begun, with the unsaid hanging between them.

Still, Libby was one to talk. She too had her secrets, one of which sat on a marble bench in her aunts' apartment; a message from the past that she wasn't ready to read. And yet already the satchel had told her things she hadn't known before: her parents *had* been happy, at least in that moment captured on camera in 1974, and the knowledge comforted her no end.

And comfort was something Libby had always desired; she wasn't one for rushing around or rocking the boat. *Normally.* It was something Krish had always said he envied about her; her ability to just be. *Be what?* she wondered now. She thought of her wasted life and all the time that had passed since, and the sense of guilt she carried about his death that she'd never confessed to anyone. They'd only been together three years, though it had felt like a lifetime, and they'd rapidly reached the stage that they could laugh and love and fight, always knowing it would be okay. It had felt supremely mature, the fact that their relationship transcended all the others around them: twenty-year-olds in the will-we-won't-we game, newly released from the watchful eye of their parents, let loose into the world. But Krish and Libby; they were inseparable. Until they were separated for ever.

A gentle huff of wind puffed at the branches above her and two solitary leaves, the final gasp of autumn, gently fluttered to the ground to settle at her feet. She appraised them, still thinking of herself and Krish: he was gone, and she was gone in almost every sense of the word, and she ached for the life lost when he'd turned on his heels and gone to that party alone.

'I need to work harder,' she'd said, still seated at her desk as he'd hovered in the doorway.

'You hate med anyway, Libby. Study literature, like you always wanted. You have a choice, much more than me . . .'

She'd watched from the window as he'd driven off, knowing that he knew her better than she knew herself.

How she missed him. She took a little comfort from the knowledge that he'd surely be encouraging her now. He, too, would be fascinated by the photo she'd found in her father's satchel. She had confessed to him – and only him – about that day behind the waterfall, when she'd finally read 'The Man from Snowy River' as though for the first time, and felt something shift in her mind.

'And "The Ma'am from Joey River"!' he'd always added, laughing.

Now, Libby twisted the fox pendant between her fingers; it was cool to the touch in the crisp London morning, just as it had been the day she'd first held it. A thought struck her: had her father, had Ben, been there, behind that waterfall? Had her mother? Had one of *them* left the tin? She shivered.

Across the grass, a young couple walked arm in arm, her swollen belly already part of the family and, not for the first time, Libby wondered if her father had known of Willow's pregnancy before he'd died. She'd been born in August 1975, six months after Ben's death, so it was possible, wasn't it? Of course, she'd never asked. But she had often imagined both the tranquil scene before her, and the one that followed: the moment when Willow learned that she would raise her child alone.

Surely, if her mum had really *loved* Ben, then Libby's existence might have been some – however small – comfort amidst the grief? She had considered this a thousand times since losing Krish, when she had thought this shared, tragic experience would draw her mum closer, rather than leaving them both, separately, still drowning. For Willow, wouldn't a daughter have been a gift to cherish for ever, someone whose life would be inextricably entwined with her own?

❧

As she walked home, Libby passed the Australian War Memorial on the park's southernmost corner, its long wall of granite sweeping her in as though someone had placed a hand gently on the small of her back, ushering her forward. Before her, two tourists with Australian accents perused the names, which were places, not people, signifying the towns and cities from where Australia's fallen had come. She walked along the wall until she reached *Launceston*, the city in which she'd gone to school. How many soldiers from there had died? she wondered. It was a history she knew so little about, and she suddenly felt ashamed of her lack of understanding of Australia's home front, compared to all she knew about Britain.

It was one of the first things she'd done when she'd arrived: a war-time tour of London led by a guide wearing battledress. Forty thousand civilians had been killed in the Blitz, he'd said, as he'd directed them past shrapnel damage scarring the V&A, then indicated a shelter sign on a red brick wall faded almost beyond recognition. 'Traces of the past are still visible,' he'd said, 'if only you know where to look.'

As Big Ben signalled midday, Libby's mood became sombre, and in the silence that followed – as if the last post had sounded – Laurence Binyon's famous poem came to her unbidden:

They shall grow not old, as we that are left grow old:
Age shall not weary them, nor the years condemn.
At the going down of the sun and in the morning
We will remember them.

Libby thought of those who'd lost their lives in wars, but the words also tugged at her heart for another reason, for the men she'd lost who'd never been to war. Krish and Ben. Both so young when they'd died. With Krish she had something to hold on to – letters, mementos, memories – and that at least was some comfort, but when it came to her father, Ben, she realised with a sudden starkness that, *at the going down of the sun, and in the morning*, she didn't know how to remember him.

⁊

Half an hour later, as Libby opened the door to the apartment, a Skype ring tone filled the room. Removing her coat, she answered the call, and immediately two near-identical faces beamed at her from a hotel lobby across the pond: Ivy and Ash, her twin aunts.

'Libby,' her aunts crooned in unison, before Ivy added efficiently: 'Just between breakfast meetings. How are you getting on? All sorted?'

They'd talked twice in the last week, and Ivy had asked her the same question each time. Libby couldn't help but admire her apparent optimism. Perhaps she thought this time her niece would leap to her feet, exclaiming that life was great, and she'd got a job, and friends, and – why not? – a boyfriend too!

'Good, good, yes,' she said, satisfied that the answer wasn't entirely a deception. She *was* getting on okay, but she wasn't exactly *sorted*. 'I've started looking for a place . . .' she added for good measure, trailing off as the lie caught in her throat.

Ash flapped a hand at the screen. 'No rush, no rush.' And when her aunt said that, Libby knew she meant it. Neither Ash nor Ivy were prone to beating around the bush, nor were they patient with others who did. Although for their niece they'd always made an exception. She supposed this deliberate ignorance of all her failings came from a place of pity, because her life had been threaded through with a grief that Ash and Ivy's hadn't.

'We might,' Ash said, 'pop back to London for a few nights next week, on our way to . . . Lucerne?'

'Geneva,' said Ivy, glancing at her sister with affectionate exasperation.

'Yes, yes.' Ash beamed. 'Geneva. Lovely lake and all that.'

In the background, the clink of cutlery was muted by murmurs, deals being made on a Saturday morning in a city that didn't sleep, while in the foreground a waiter appeared, wearing full tails and an expression of deference. He bowed slightly, proffering a piece of paper, which Ivy took, waving him away with a five-dollar bill.

'You're busy,' Libby observed, 'we can talk later.'

Ash's hand disappeared off screen only to reappear holding a martini glass filled with dark liquid. 'We always have time for our favourite niece,' she said, before taking a giant gulp.

'Your *only* niece, and' – Libby gave her a look – 'an espresso martini? For breakfast?'

Ash lifted her drink in acknowledgement. 'Just a dash of Dutch courage.'

Libby knew better than to believe her. Her mother's younger twin sisters were the dream team for whom *courage* had never been a problem. Between them they had run half a dozen companies – no time for husbands – and in their early retirement they had taken to investing in small enterprises, flipping their fortunes: vineyards, publishers, a boutique guesthouse on the Cornwall coast. Anything that interested them. If a new acquisition failed, they simply moved on to the next. The past, it seemed, held no sway over Ash and Ivy.

As Ivy looked once more at her watch, Libby said quickly, 'Actually, before you go . . . I wanted to ask if you remembered something about Mum.'

Two sets of eyebrows went up.

'Did she and . . . Dad . . . ever live anywhere else other than Launceston?'

There was a pause, then Ivy shook her head just as Ash nodded.

'*Riiiight*,' said Libby, leaning forward. 'Does the name *Towerhurst* ring any bells?'

'No,' they chimed in belated unison.

'No, I don't think so,' Ivy repeated, glancing at her sister, something secret passing there. As an only child, Libby was fascinated by her aunts' ability to connect in ways she couldn't understand. *That* wasn't unusual, but *this* look was. They were known for colluding, but always in front of Libby, never – as she felt at this moment – behind her back.

'It's just,' she persisted, 'I found this photo.' She held up the image of her parents, turning it over so the caption was clear.

'Oh, *Towerhurst?*' they said, as though they hadn't understood the original question.

'Yes, Towerhurst,' said Libby dryly. 'I think Mum sold it when I was ten?'

'Oh yes, I recall that now.' Ash drained her drink, a small moustache of froth remaining on her top lip. She'd always been easier to read than Ivy, whose demeanour could best be described as *level*.

'Did Mum and Dad *live* there?' asked Libby. 'When did they buy it?'

'Buy it?' started Ash. 'Oh no, poppet, they didn't—'

'I think your father,' interrupted Ivy, 'wanted a quiet, out-of-the-way place to write.'

Out-of-the-way was right. Even on today's roads, Towerhurst must have been a five-hour drive from Launceston.

Libby held up the fox necklace. 'Do either of you recognise this? No? It's just that . . .' She told them about her visit to Towerhurst when she was ten, and the way her mother had acted. 'Did something happen there? With Dad?'

'Darling,' said Ivy with unusual softness, 'I know it must be difficult being in London where Ben . . .' She trailed off. 'There's no need to dig up the past.' Behind the screen someone must have beckoned her, because she quickly disappeared, leaving Ash alone.

'Mum looks so *happy* in this photo,' Libby said. 'I've never seen her smile like that.'

'They were happy.' Ash paused to recall a memory. 'Your

mum used to smile like that all the time. She was a ray of sunshine.' There was something in the way she said it – *was* a ray of sunshine – that made Libby's heart ache.

'She changed when Dad died?'

'Yes. Understandably.' Ash cleared her throat. 'So, you're looking forward to seeing us?'

'Of course, I can't wait.' A hesitation. 'It's lonely here.'

Ash gave her a sympathetic look.

Libby pushed her advantage. 'I just thought while I was here, between jobs – *settling in* – I could find out a bit more about Dad. Mum and I were having a great chat yesterday and I asked about Towerhurst when one of her students interrupted us.'

'How's the teaching going?' Ash said.

'Great. But . . .' Libby laughed a little desperately at the attempted deflection. 'How can you *sell* a house you don't even *own*?'

'I didn't say she didn't *own* it.' Ash pulled at her collar. 'I said she never *bought* it.'

'What? She didn't . . .' Now this was interesting. 'Mum didn't . . . *inherit* it, did she?'

Looking over her shoulder nervously, Ash pushed away her martini glass as if she suddenly regretted her Dutch courage.

'Who from?' persisted Libby.

Ash shook her head.

'Come on, tell me.' An old house in the rainforest, a secret legacy, some hidden history her mum wouldn't talk about. 'Tell me!'

'I don't know! She never said. It was anonymous.'

'Anonymous?'

'Yes.' An exasperated sigh. 'Willow called – we lived in Sydney then – to tell us the news. The very next morning she and Ben left for Towerhurst, but your mum never went back . . .' She trailed off nonchalantly as Ivy took her seat with an air of busyness that suggested their conversation was at an end.

Libby couldn't leave it there. 'Ash, what *happened* at Towerhurst?'

Ivy glared at her sister. 'We'd better be going, darling,' she said, smiling tightly. 'But we'll see you soon.' Ash waved guiltily, already hurling a barrage of excuses at her sister, as Ivy cut the connection.

Libby picked up the photo of her parents. They had been there, at Towerhurst, in 1974, and for some reason – until that day ten years later – Willow hadn't returned.

Chapter 8

Towerhurst, Tasmania
November 1974

Ben's buoyant voice cut into the morning. 'Something *incredible* has happened.'

Groaning, Willow rolled over to snuggle deeper into the pillow. It was so *comfortable*. She wanted to say, *What, Ben, what?* but nothing came; her mind was too thick with delicious sleep.

'It's not raining!'

Catching the smell of coffee, Willow opened one eye. Still dark. No, not quite dark. The room was layered in shades of grey. Dawn approached.

'What time is it?'

'Dunno.' Ben returned to their bed – two mattresses beside the fireplace, their sleeping bags in a tangle – and pressed a cup into her hand.

They'd explored Towerhurst a little the evening before, tiptoeing through the hallway in dusky light, Ben fumbling for a light switch, which he'd flicked with bated breath. Nothing. He'd left to fetch their torches from the car, leaving Willow alone to listen to the whispers of the house, its secrets muffled by the first urgent taps of rain. Underlying the smell of old carpet and dust was a sweet pine fragrance; resin that hung in the air. She'd run her hand along the wall, feeling the undulations of the paper that covered it.

'It's hideous,' she'd remarked when Ben returned, shadowed by a beam of torch light that swept the hallway, revealing wallpaper covered in faded tiny rainbows that looked like a thousand grimaces.

He whistled. 'Someone went to town on this place in the fifties.'

At the hall's centre lay a wide wooden staircase, the golden timber leading to the floor above. They turned right into the sitting room, then left to discover a kitchen with an astounding array of appliances, drawers stuffed full of utensils for every requirement: egg slicers, melon scoops, a contraption for shaving ice. Like the other rooms, it was a time capsule encompassing several bygone eras. Three bedrooms led off the hallway, and another three off the hallway of the floor above. Small bathrooms hung off rooms like question marks, and every window gazed over that dark, watchful forest.

Finally, at the end of their exploration: a tunnel.

'No,' Willow said as their torch beams picked out the round shape blocking their way, 'not a tunnel . . . a door.'

It was perfectly circular, almost as wide as the hall itself, forming a full stop at its end.

'A single slice from an enormous tree,' Ben said breathlessly, examining the undulations of the timber, his hand chasing the torch beam around the door's circumference. His expression suggested he'd discovered the back of the wardrobe, that he believed Narnia might be on the other side. And it certainly *looked* like an entrance to another world. A *locked* entrance, as it turned out – one for which they didn't have a key.

In the sitting room, Ben had glanced at the fireplace. *Will we?* his raised eyebrows had asked. It wasn't cold, but the house felt damp. She nodded. Wordlessly, she'd returned to the car, gathering their things while Ben inspected the log box. When he was satisfied with the chimney's draw, they'd settled, her in the crook of his arm, each lost in their own thoughts, staring into the flames as though the house's secrets hid there.

Now, finishing his coffee, Ben threw back the sleeping bag. 'Come on,' he said, 'time to explore.'

Willow closed her eyes. She wanted nothing more than to go back to sleep. If only Ben would get the fire going again and maybe some breakfast . . .

'Nope,' he said when she mentioned it. 'We need to take a photo first. For posterity.'

'You're kidding?'

'Why not?'

The dawn was cool, but not cold, and they stepped outside into stillness. The lingering scent of rain – a damp richness that clung to the forest – was so fresh it was almost minty.

'God,' Willow breathed. It was beautiful, but how on earth would they look after this place? Towerhurst needed work, serious work, and money. Painting, heating, airing. Love. Someone would have to stop the forest from marching across the weed-choked gravel to climb up the weatherboard walls. It was all so overwhelming. All so . . . *sudden.* But still . . . she felt a ripple of excitement: this place had *potential.*

They balanced Ben's camera on the car's bonnet, setting the shutter release and giggling all the while. Afterwards, Willow wasn't at all sure if they'd captured the shot – her holding the keys with one hand, and him with the other – before the camera had slumped forward as though tired of their childish delight.

Ben took her hand, weaving her fingers into his own. 'I reckon we should go to town, call someone to connect the power.'

'Already?'

'We can explore Westford. Get a few supplies. In case we want to stay longer. And maybe someone will know something about the legacy?'

She kissed him, and they lingered, both clearly thinking of the night before. Sleeping in front of an open fire, it turned out, was really rather romantic.

'Let's see,' she murmured, her whole body tingling. 'But now,' she said, 'carry me back over the threshold, will you? I'd like to re-enact our first night at Towerhurst.'

Ben grinned, and lifted her into his arms.

Chapter 9

Towerhurst, Tasmania

September 1939

At half past nine on Grace's first evening at Towerhurst, war was declared. Hitler had marched into Poland two days before and now there was no going back.

'Well,' Rose said, lounging in the sitting room, 'that's that, I suppose.' She turned to Uncle Marcus. 'What do you think of the situation, Mr Foxton?'

'Marcus, please.'

Grace watched quietly as Rose gave a small, acquiescent nod of her head. 'What do you think of the situation, *Marcus*? Not unexpected, I suppose?'

'I'm glad Menzies has come to his senses. Our prime minister is somewhat an admirer of Hitler. Toured Germany as attorney-general only last year, if you can believe it. Said – and don't quote me – that there was something rather magnificent about the abandonment of individual liberty, that sort of thing.'

'Didn't he admire the Germans' willingness *to devote themselves to the service and well-being of the state?*'

Uncle Marcus looked at her anew. 'Well, I never! I believe that's *exactly* what he said.'

Rose laughed lightly. In doing so, she gathered years she

hadn't yet earned. She had always been a chameleon who blended effortlessly into her changing surrounds, flirting at the servant's door as easily as she welcomed guests graciously at Grosvenor Square's grand entrance with all the haughty aplomb of a daughter of the house, rather than the housekeeper.

Now, as she sat before the crackling fire, Rose talked of Menzies' volte-face as though she was born to politics. To anyone else, her insight seemed remarkable, but to Grace, it wasn't a surprise. It was Edeline talking, really; Rose had always been a sponge for her words.

'I don't suppose Australia has any choice in the matter?'

'On the contrary,' Uncle Marcus said. 'I think the choice is clear.'

'Follow the mother country?'

'Perhaps, though I wouldn't put it like that round here.' He frowned. 'Australians are proud. We might be part of the Commonwealth, but we've been our own nation for forty years.'

'*We?* Do you feel Australian, Marcus?' The way she said his name made Grace glad that Aunt Olive wasn't here.

'Somewhat, yes.' He looked sharply at Rose, and she quickly shifted her gaze, a small piece of her facade crumbling away.

'I'm sorry, that was rather rude,' she said. It was a turn of phrase Mother would use. *Rather* this, and *rather* that. Rose had never spoken like that before, and Grace crossed her arms, staring in amazement at her chaperone.

The movement caught Uncle Marcus's attention. Probably he'd forgotten she was there at all, that was normally the way.

'What do you think about the news, Grace?'

'Me?' Why was he asking her opinion? No one had ever done that. She was immediately lost for words. 'I . . . don't know.'

'It can be frightening, knowing the world is about to change.

I remember when King George announced the Great War.'
He came to sit by her. 'At the time, I thought it was exciting.'

'Exciting?' Grace thought that preposterous. 'That's a little
silly.'

Rose inhaled quickly, half standing. 'I think perhaps we're
all tired . . .'

Grace glanced at Uncle Marcus. If he thought her rude, he
didn't show it. Instead, he said, 'It *was* silly. Ridiculous! I can
hardly imagine it now. But back then, I didn't know what war
was.' He drained his glass. 'Now I do.'

He'd fought in that war, the one before, the *Great* one, lied
about his age to join his uncle Cornelius's regiment. Grace
knew her mother had hated Cornelius. 'He stole a precious
thing from me,' she'd always said. 'Marcus was only sixteen
when he left for France, but he'd aged decades three years later.
War does that, steals the years, steals futures.'

At the end of 1918, Uncle Marcus departed for Australia,
and had never set foot in England again.

Earlier, at dinner, Rose had asked: 'What do you do here,
Mr Foxton?' They were eating beef stew, and the carafe of
wine was already half empty. Outside, the rain came down
in buckets, hammering on the iron roof, a rowdy guest in the
room.

'Ah, yes, good question. One I've been asking myself for
years.' He had smiled in that good-humoured way of his, laying
a slab of butter on his bread. 'Nowadays, not much. My uncle
Cornelius had a dozen mining leases, both here, and nearby in
Queenstown. He signed them over to me as a wedding gift.
He'd had his fill by then, seeking pastures new.'

Queenstown was fifteen miles inland from Towerhurst.
There, copper had been stripped from the hill like a skin while
the on-site smelter belched poison into the air, making the rain
so acid that nothing more would grow.

'They call it a moonscape,' Uncle Marcus had added. 'I'll take you there, if you like?'

'I'd love that.'

'Really? Well . . . I'll see if we might visit the smelter. It's no place for a lady, though I'm sure we can arrange a tour.' He'd turned to Grace. 'You're not keen on the stew?'

'It's lovely, but Mother says I shouldn't eat too much meat.'

'Colette will be disappointed; she loves to make a hearty Irish stew—'

Rose interrupted: 'Colette?'

'Colette McGillycuddy. She comes in three days a week. She and her husband, Ned, live on the only other property this side of the Joey River with their nephew, Daniel.' He hesitated. 'He might have been a good playmate, Grace, although I believe he's quite a few years older than you. Sixteen or seventeen.'

Grace bit her lip. 'I'm fifteen, Uncle Marcus.'

'Ah.'

Quickly, Rose had leaned forward, changing the conversation's direction. 'You don't look rough enough to be a miner.'

Uncle Marcus had laughed, shaking his head. 'True. I prefer to follow my passion.'

'Which is?'

'Literature.'

'You're a writer?'

'Occasionally.'

Grace had looked up in surprise. A writer? Strange that her mother had never said so, considering Edeline had many writer friends. They penned political pieces, opinions, treatises that Grace had to admit she didn't understand. When her father was away, they called at the house, talking long into the evening over wine and endless slender cigarettes. Over the years, Rose had taken to joining them, always seated next to Edeline, taking her cue. What Molly thought of the situation, of her daughter being politicised, Grace didn't know.

'How exciting,' Rose said, eyes sparkling. She was like glitter, the light hitting her in all the right places.

'Hardly. A slog, more like.' He'd written three books, he said, none to critical acclaim. His publisher had grown tired of his narrative – always too sombre – so he'd started writing poetry instead, to greater effect. Poems, he explained, were easier to keep light, the ending already in sight before the narrative found its darkness.

'That's fitting,' Rose said, 'because life is a thousand shades of grey.'

He'd appraised her appreciatively then, as they'd finished their meal, and he did so again now in the sitting room as Rose stood, empty glass in hand, stepping up to the wireless to turn it off. 'I imagine life will change with this war, even here, in the back of beyond,' she said, not without relish.

'You can be sure of that, Rose.' Marcus drained the final, blood-red drops from his glass. He paused for a moment, staring into the gently sighing flames. 'Nothing changes lives like war.'

Chapter 10

Grosvenor Square, London

November 2004

The contents of her father's satchel lay before Libby and she already knew one thing: Ben had not come to London only to 'do a reading', as her mum had told her. At least, the documents she'd placed in a pile for examination told a different tale.

Examination. She almost smiled at the way her mind was running away with her.

She picked up the first piece of paper, a clipping from *The Times* dated 20th February 1975, titled 'A Snippet of Yet Another British Fascist' and written by a man, or woman, called Milton Twiggs. Quickly, she scanned its contents. It was a short profile of an Edeline Grey (née Foxton) who had been imprisoned during World War Two for her political beliefs, which were, to be frank, extremely unsavoury. She had been a leading member of the British Union of Fascists, also known as the Blackshirts or the BUF, and a good friend of the party's founder, Oswald Mosley, not to mention thick as thieves with the notorious Diana Mitford. A little was written about Edeline's early life – born in Hampshire, grew up in a village called Rotherwick, three brothers, one of whom (Marcus) had moved to Australia and married – and her husband, Kingston, who had never joined the BUF. There were several paragraphs about her political activism, including references to articles penned for Mosley's *Blackshirt* and the *Fascist Week* newspapers. One had been about a trip to Berlin, just prior to the 1936 Olympic Games, where Edeline met key members of the Nazi Party. The author – this Milton Twiggs – noted that there had been rumours her daughter, Grace Grey, accompanied her. Unsubstantiated reports suggested they had met Hitler himself.

When Libby reached the final paragraph, she read it twice.

In 1940, Edeline was interned at Holloway Prison for five years. On release, her passport was confiscated, and she returned to 45 Grosvenor Square for a time, before vanishing entirely. As with so many of Britain's fascists, her current whereabouts remain unknown.

45 Grosvenor Square? Libby glanced out of the window to the opposite side of the green, where number forty-five was no longer a home, but a series of offices – charities, stockbrokers, advertising agencies. It fascinated her that her father, it seemed, had been interested in someone who had lived so close to where Libby did now. For the first time, it occurred to her it was possible he had stayed with her aunts, who had purchased the apartment sometime in the seventies. They'd never mentioned it, but then – as with so many things – she'd never asked.

Libby leaned forward. A familiar colourful figure stood on the pavement below, holding up a hand and, by some miracle, London's traffic stopped in its tracks. Despite the turmoil that churned her stomach, as Miss Winman disappeared from sight, Libby couldn't help but smile.

She picked up the next document; the short story she had recognised as the bus rolled over Waterloo Bridge the night before. There was no doubt about it, 'The Selkie of Ocean Beach' was achingly familiar. She had read it before, discovered it online when she'd been searching her father's name years ago. Published in the *Telegraph* fiction supplement in late December 1974, this was the story, she was certain, that had brought him to London, just as her mother had said. Someone, her father presumably, had underlined several paragraphs, as if in preparation to read them out loud to an audience.

Putting the story aside, she picked up several pieces of paper stapled together and written in an entirely illegible hand, the only decipherable words the heading: *Interview with Olive Foxton, Our Lady of Mercy, February 1975*. She flicked back to the article her father had clipped from *The Times* about the fascist, Edeline Grey, and frowned. Olive Foxton? There was her name, buried in the third column. Olive had married Edeline's brother, Marcus, soon after his post-World War One arrival in Australia. Her heart leapt at the link. *Our Lady of Mercy?* What would that be? A convent? She scanned the pages again and some hidden part of her mind recognised the form of the script; it was shorthand. How hard could that be to decipher? She wasn't sure.

Three items remained in the pile: a book, a map of Ireland and a ticket for a return flight to Dublin, purchased in her father's name. It was due to depart on the 1st of March, which Libby realised with horror was the day after his death.

With shaking hands, she studied Ireland's unfamiliar geography, running her finger to the country's south-west corner where two places had been marked in pen. The larger one, *Killarney*, was denoted with a star, while the smaller – a village on Kenmare Bay – had been circled. *Ballinn* it was called, and a note had been written beside it: *To get to Ballinn, take a train from Dublin to Killarney, then rent hackney.*

Finally it was time to inspect the last item in the pile, and she picked it up with anticipation, wondering what the book would reveal about her father's taste in reading. What text had so consumed him that he'd carried the novel around London, perhaps snatching moments to read in a quiet café or a peaceful corner of a park? As she turned the book over, she gasped with delight:

The Ballads of Daniel McGillycuddy.

Her father, it seemed, was also a fan of poetry. For the first time in her life Libby felt a spark of connection with him across the years, and she couldn't help but imagine him turning the pages as she did now, scanning the ballads, choosing which ones to read again, deciding which one he enjoyed most. She slid her finger down the index. 'Life on the Death Railway'; 'When the Bomb Dropped'; The Boys who Held Timor'. These were ballads of battle, World War Two clearly, and even before she read them, she knew the feelings they'd evoke. Two years after moving across to the English department at the university, she'd written a paper on British war poetry, though it had focused on World War One. She had titled it *Songs that Won the War*, and she'd been immensely proud of it, still was. She believed with all her heart that there were great lessons to be learned from poetry, if only people chose to read it.

She put the book aside – her nightly entertainment sorted for the foreseeable – and picked up, once again, the article about the fascist, Edeline Grey. *45 Grosvenor Square*. How about that. She turned the paper over, interested to see what other snippets of 1975 had been captured – Margaret Thatcher's Conservative win? Miners' strikes? – realising immediately that, in her hurry to sift through the satchel's contents, she hadn't seen the photo that accompanied Milton Twiggs' article. It was uncaptioned, but considering their attire – mid-length cream skirts, high-buttoned black shirts, and black ties pinned with the fascists' famous lightning bolt – Libby could only assume it was Edeline Grey, arm in arm with a beautiful, smiling girl who must have been her daughter.

Chapter 11

On the track to Westford, Tasmania
September 1939

'I'm afraid Grace has been rather spoiled,' Rose explained as they rolled along the track towards Westford. Marcus contemplated this. Grace seemed reserved and perhaps a little sullen, but if anything she looked as if she would flinch from attention rather than demand it.

'I've searched her face for Edeline,' he pondered, 'but for the life of me, I can't see anything I recognise.'

'Oh, she might well be in there if you could only garner a smile,' Rose said, unfastening the top button of her black shirt, waving her hand against what Marcus considered to be spring's mild heat.

'And . . . how does one do that?'

'Do what?'

'Raise a smile.'

'No one ever has.'

The Joey River was just a trickle when they arrived, the hard surface of the ford an inch beneath the water. Marcus leaned over the steering wheel of his battered red pickup, taking the route with care. 'There's a tide table pinned to a board in the hallway. Three hours either side of low is the window.'

'What if it closes?'

'We keep a picnic in the vehicle for emergencies. Spam, chocolate, blankets.'

Half a dozen miles separated the river from Westford. Marcus explained that the village was first built as a temporary settlement following the discovery of alluvial gold in the 1880s, but nowadays most of its residents worked at the Mount Lyell copper mine in Queenstown, not fifteen miles away.

'Why did Cornelius build across the river? Why be cut off from Westford?'

'I loved my uncle despite – or perhaps partly because of – his eccentricity,' Marcus said. 'But most people thought he was rather strange. I think he simply liked the privacy. He was a good man, Cornelius. I fought with him during the war, you know? In an Australian battalion.'

'Wasn't that unusual? An Englishman doing that?'

He shrugged. 'There were Paddies fighting with the Brits, Aussies fighting with French, Brits who fought with the Anzacs at Gallipoli. Stories you rarely hear, but were really dime-a-dozen. I lived then in Foxton Hall, not far from where Cornelius's battalion trained at Larkhill Garrison. He visited quite often and one time I just . . . went back to the base with him. Lied about my age, as so many did.' They paused at a fork in the road where a sign pointed inland – *Queenstown* – then continued straight, following a potholed road that tracked south. 'After the war I came out to explore Cornelius's claims, but I wasn't much of a miner, as you rightly pointed out, so I sold out to Mount Lyell. It's Australia's largest copper mine, you know?'

Rose nodded; Marcus had already been impressed at how much she knew. Edeline must have told her all about the place she was coming to.

They pulled over to let a truck pass, its trailer heavy with logs. 'Still, there have been some benefits to Westford's lack of mining. Without the smelter, we've kept our healthy forests. The town might be poor, but our surrounds are rich.'

'What do you mean?'

'Huon pine.'

'Timber?' She sounded disappointed.

Ahead, a long narrow jetty stretched out to sea.

'That pier's made of it,' Marcus said, 'which means it will outlast us all. It's a miracle material, full of a substance called eugenol. Stops the wood from rotting. They sent convicts to the west coast to fell it for shipbuilding, imprisoning them on Sarah Island, over there in Macquarie Harbour. Truth be told, the guards didn't need chains to stop them from escaping.'

'Why not?'

He indicated the vegetation jostling at the road's edge. 'The rainforest is a fortress, very difficult to navigate. The piners do it using the river systems, floating the wood downstream to the mills. That's how our neighbours make their living.'

'The Irish family?'

'The McGillycuddys, yes.'

Finally, they emerged from the rainforest into open space, and Marcus observed her reaction. 'Surprised?'

She nodded.

'They say — and you'll soon learn to take what *they* say with a pinch of salt — that the first settlers didn't trust each other, such was the value of the claims. They didn't cooperate as the men in Queenstown did. Suspicion ran so deep that they arranged their tents in a circle, each keeping an eye on his neighbours. The tents grew into houses, though the "town planning" remained.'

'And the sentiment?'

He raised an eyebrow at her tone, and Rose gave him an appreciative smile. Was she flirting with him?

'There remains, as in any small place,' he said, 'a certain undercurrent, yes.'

Westford's few shops stood in a ring around a central green with a single, brave eucalyptus in its centre. A grand old brick post office sat with its back to the sea, flanked by the hotel and a small shop, and several people filed from Australia Post, chatting at a million miles an hour, their heads leaning close. A fizzle of excitement held the town in its electric embrace.

'Wars need metals and timber. Commodity prices will rise.' Marcus switched off the engine. 'There will be more work.'

'That's rather callous.'

'It's a long way from here to Europe.'

She hesitated. 'What if war comes here?'

'I don't think that'll happen.'

'Still, perhaps I can do my bit? Get a job?' There was uncertainty in Rose's voice as she glanced around the village. 'Won't there be work at the mine if the men go to war?'

'Yes well, let's keep an ear to the ground, shall we?' Marcus said cautiously. The government had been quick in discouraging Australian women from their campaign to join up, or do a man's work. *What? What do you mean?* a government minister had said only yesterday in an interview on the wireless, *a woman take a job from a man who's trying to support his family? Preposterous!*

He parked outside the shop, where a large sign in brown lettering read *Holmes' Grocers*, and on the wall beside it, a poster had been pasted haphazardly. It depicted three women knitting a long scarf in the red, blue and white colours of the Australian flag.

Join your local branch membership and help the war! Australian Country Women's Association.

'You're eighteen, aren't you?'

She laughed. 'Twenty already!'

'Well, you can join the CWA for starters, they have a branch here.'

'Great,' she murmured.

Marcus opened the car door. 'Come on. I'll introduce you to Mira, but be careful what you say: she's the least discreet person in Westford – which is really quite a feat.'

&

Marcus found himself seeing the interior of the shop afresh as Rose looked around. It was sparse: tinned food on one side, packets on the other. A meat counter at the back sold beef and chicken. There was no fish – 'People get that themselves,' Marcus told her – but there was a smattering of British brands that would have been familiar to Rose: OXO, Marmite, Bournville Cocoa. The newspapers on display were three days old, and a handful of magazines – *Woman's Weekly*, *The Australian Woman's Mirror*, *The Bulletin* – spread across the counter. If rationing was introduced, it could hardly get more austere than this.

A woman appeared from behind a shelf. 'Was told you'd arrived.' She had an alarming hooked nose that protruded from beneath thick glasses.

Marcus waited to see how Rose would deal with this. She didn't skip a beat. 'Oh, hello . . . Mira, is it?' she said, with what must have been her sweetest smile.

'I see you're well informed, missy.' She looked over Rose's shoulder, nodding to Marcus, then continued her gaze around the shop. 'Where's your sister, then?'

'My sister?'

'Richard said he dropped *two* girls off at Towerhurst. My son tells me *everything*.' The woman's eyes were orbs of unlit coal. 'You were the one travelling in the front, I s'pose?'

Marcus had taken a box and packed it quickly. 'Grace's up at the house. Working in the garden with Olive,' he lied smoothly, then he turned to Rose. 'Have you much of a sweet tooth?'

'Surely, I'm sweet enough?'

Mira Holmes watched the interaction with interest.

'Throw in a small tin of Arnott's biscuits, will you, Mira?'

The shopkeeper muttered something.

Marcus raised an eyebrow, clearly amused. 'What was that?'

She brandished the biscuits threateningly. 'I'll be rationing these.'

'Always one step ahead of the government,' Marcus said. 'We're lucky to have you.'

❧

Outside, the sky had cleared. A gentle breeze licked off the ocean, fluttering a collection of notices pinned to a board in the shop's doorway. The village, it seemed to Rose, was a hive of activity. Dances, societies, political groups.

Marcus called from the car as he loaded the shopping. 'Is there anything you want to buy?'

In her pocket, Rose carried some Australian pounds, changed in Melbourne when they docked. Edeline had given her a tidy sum. 'No,' she replied, as she slid into the passenger seat, 'I think I have everything I need right here.'

He smiled awkwardly, turning from her to watch a group of boys cross the village green. They paused momentarily under the tree at its centre to share a cigarette and, as Marcus stepped up into the pickup's cab, he spoke softly, so that only Rose could hear.

'*There were some gilded youths that sat along the barber's wall / Their eyes were dull, their heads were flat, they had no brains at all.*'

She laughed at the jingle. 'Where did *that* come from?'

'Banjo Paterson's "The Man from Ironbark". You've heard of him?'

'The man from Ironbark?'

'No. Banjo Paterson. He's our darling poet.'

'Our?'

'Australia's.' Marcus was at it again. Truly Edeline had been right: he *had* gone native.

'Perhaps I *have* heard of him . . . "Waltzing Matilda", wasn't it?'

He nodded, enthused. 'And "The Man from Snowy River", "Clancy of the Overflow" and "The Man from Ironbark", of course. Still' – a gesture over his shoulder – 'those youths aren't so bad. When I see the McGillycuddy boy among them, I'm not concerned.'

'Daniel?'

He glanced at her, surprised. 'Yes. How did you know?'

'You mentioned him the night we arrived. Said he might have been a friend for Grace if he were a little younger.'

'He's a nice boy. Poor lad's had tragedy in his life, but he bears it as best he can. Olive tells me he's handsome, caught several girls' eyes in town, though none have captured him yet.'

Rose's gaze lingered on the group. There was only one handsome boy among them; he had dark hair and the broad-shouldered silhouette of someone who wasn't shy of hard work. He stood a little aside from the others, grinning cheekily as the car rolled past, his expression changing from interest to awe as he spotted her.

'He lives just beyond Towerhurst, you say?'

'Came over from Ireland a few years ago after a tragic accident.'

'What happened?'

'He—' Marcus slammed on the brake and the pickup's tyres skidded, narrowly avoiding a small animal as it bounded from the trees. 'Sorry. Sorry!' he said, his face colouring under his beard as a few 'whoops' sounded from the green. He put the pickup back into gear, and cleared his throat.

'Where were we?'

'Daniel . . .' she prompted, just as he said, 'Banjo Paterson? Yes, yes.'

She hesitated, but he hadn't heard her, and so he launched into a potted history of the bard. She smiled and nodded politely, all the while glancing into her wing mirror, where she could see Daniel, stood apart from the others, watching her retreat into the distance, until the track turned and he was gone.

Chapter 12

Westford, Tasmania

November 1974

Westford was the strangest town Willow had ever seen. Its buildings clustered around a central green, a single towering tree lonely in its hub, but if its circular shape was a symbol of community, its demeanour was not. The post office, a grand redbrick building closest to the sea – its old sign still bravely holding on for dear life – had become a dejected-looking pub and several shops were boarded up. A small notice on the milk bar whispered: *Open Weekends.* Westford was lifeless, not a car in the street, not a soul to be seen.

She followed Ben across the green and paused beneath the mighty eucalyptus where a war memorial, carved with a dozen names, sat at its base. Willow felt her stomach tip in the way it always did when she stood before a cenotaph, a swirl of emotions setting her off balance. Sadness, grief, regret. Her own father had fought in World War Two – eventually seeing its end in Nagasaki – and had lived, unlike these men whose names survived in stone. Sometimes she couldn't fathom that the time between two world-changing wars had been less than the time passed since the last of them. What must it have been like to have lived through both? To fight in one and then watch your sons leave to fight the next?

On the plaque, she noticed a familiar name: it matched a
sign that they'd seen on the last bumpy miles to Towerhurst.
McGillycuddy's Fine Timbers, it had read. And here on the cenotaph was the name once more – *McGillycuddy* – this time
followed with the letter *D,* and Willow wondered, with a tug
of her heart, who her neighbours had lost.

'C'mon,' Ben said, 'I'll tackle the electricity connection.
You do the shop.'

'Surely we don't need anything?'

'Answers,' he said, as he turned towards the phone box.
'We need answers.'

When Willow entered Holmes' Grocers, it was empty. Rows
of tins lined the wall, and a small refrigerated display containing meat and milk hummed next to a shelf of shrivelled
vegetables. She took a basket and wandered the four narrow
aisles. Westford, it seemed, was on its last legs. She had read
last night, in their tattered guidebook, that its population had
dwindled after its first magnificent copper-hued bloom. It had
long since gone to seed, its families and industry scattered to
the winds.

Behind her, someone cleared their throat.

'Good day for it, missy?'

Willow turned to see a wizened woman with an alarming
nose and Coke-bottle glasses – that served to magnify her black
eyes – standing rather close. 'Oh! A great day for it,' she said,
taking a step backwards.

'On holiday, are you?'

Wishing the proprietor would arrive to provide an opportunity to dodge the interrogation, Willow said, 'Yes. A holiday
of sorts.' She held up her basket. 'Just adding a few things to
the esky.'

'An esky, eh? You'll be needing some ice with that, then.'
She turned to the freezer to dig expertly in its frosty innards.

'Sure . . .'

The woman, who clearly *was* the proprietor, handed over
the ice – rather too much of it – and looked Willow up and
down. 'Milk?'

'No.'

'Cheese?'

'Really, we have enough—'

A slab of Tasmanian cheddar was dropped into the basket
anyway, and Willow gave a reluctant nod of thanks, backing
away as she silently cursed Ben for the outing. She glanced
through the window; her husband was where she'd left him,
tucked away in the red phone box, the receiver pressed to his
ear, one hand waving at an invisible and – by the look of it –
intransigent person on the other end of the line.

The woman persisted. 'Where're you staying then?'

'Just north of here,' Willow said, returning her cautious
gaze to the proprietor's hungry eyes.

'*North* of here? With Colette McGillycuddy?' Her head
bobbed up and down in encouragement as if the movement
might coax a story.

'No . . .' Willow hesitated. In small-town Tasmania, gossip
spread like bushfire. 'We've brought the tent,' she said. It wasn't
exactly a lie.

'Oh.'

Not wanting to risk a show of interest in anything else,
Willow stepped up to the counter, adding a tin of Arnott's
biscuits to her basket with exaggerated finality as each item
was packed into a tote bag and its price reluctantly punched
into the till.

Tap-tap-tap.

'Not great weather for camping.'

'No.'

Tap-tap-tap.

'Your car's not made for crossing the Joey River, little vehicle like that. If you're camped that far north . . .' *Tap-tap-tap.* 'Are you?'

'What?'

'Camped that far north?'

This was the reason Willow hated lies. Hated secrets. Before you knew it, they were unravelling before your very eyes. Anyway, what was the harm in coming clean? This woman was, after all, *exactly* the sort of person who might know something about the legacy. The thought filled her equally with hope and inexplicable dread, but it was more than that. If they were to spend time at Towerhurst, Westford would be their local town. *This* would be their local shop. They might pop into the pub for a pint or a counter tea on the odd occasion. The house would be their shack. The thought made her smile – with its seven bedrooms, Towerhurst was far from a shack.

'Actually' – she cleared her throat – 'we *thought* we might need the tent, but the place we're staying is in good nick.' She hesitated as the woman's mouth dropped open. Tentatively, she added, 'Which reminds me – do you have a tide table?'

'You're staying at *Towerhurst*?'

'Well . . . yes.'

Displeasure rippled over the woman's features as she gestured to the window where a few faded real estate notices clung to the glass. 'Didn't know it'd been sold.'

'It was a . . . private arrangement.'

'Would've been better for you to go through the official channels. My son could've done your due diligence. We took over the estate agent when we bought up the post office years ago.' Behind her, a faded sign for Australia Post hung over a pile of blank envelopes. 'The old place is wrecked with damp, you know.'

'It's not that bad—'

'For *years* I encouraged her to sell up. She had no children, no family to speak of, so . . . she'd be better off in the city. Somewhere civilised. Somewhere like Hobart. That would've suited her.'

Willow picked up a copy of *Australian Women's Weekly*, flicking nonchalantly through the pages. 'Suited who?'

'Olive Foxton, of course! Don't you know who you bought it from?'

'It was through an agency—'

'I thought you said it was private.'

'A private agency. In Launceston.'

'Hmm.'

Olive Foxton? Willow itched to ask a dozen questions, but the woman began a tirade on the changing face of Launceston, the 'types' that were moving there: too many *mainlanders*.

'You're not from there, are you?'

'The mainland?' Willow hoped to convey a sense of shock. 'No. I was born in the north of the state.'

'Ah well, that's a *shame*. My family's Hobart born and bred. Fifth generation.' A certain sense of superiority stepped behind her, pulling back her shoulders.

'Hobart? Really? When did you move to Westford?'

'1930.'

Willow smiled. Hobartians never let go of their roots, she had to give them that.

'My father,' the woman continued, 'bought this place when things picked up in the pine trade. He was always reactive like that. Smartest man I ever knew. Passed that on to Richard, my son.'

'The pine trade?'

The woman observed her as though she might be daft, a sharp contrast, presumably, to Richard. 'Huon pine.'

'Of course.' Huon pine, Tasmania's golden timber. 'Was Olive . . . in the pine trade?'

The woman laughed. 'No.' Her gaze lingered somewhere beyond, and Willow turned. Ben stood at the shop window, reading the three *For Sale* signs that hung askew. 'Came from mining money, as did her English husband, Marcus. He was a wrong 'un through and through. Imagine deserting your wife like that? Leaving her all alone in *that* place. Well, you've seen the state of it, haven't you?' She took a deep breath to signal she was just getting started. 'And *literature*, that's what he said he wrote. High and mighty stuff. Shopped around too, didn't he?'

'Did he?'

'Yeah. Fancied his niece's chaperone, Rose—'

'Oh?'

The woman's white knuckles gripped the handle of the heaving tote bag. 'Interested in all that, are you?' She leaned across the counter. 'Remind me once more . . . how you found out about Towerhurst, again?'

'Just an ad in the newspaper.' Willow's palms began to sweat. 'We were looking for a . . . shack.'

'A *shack*?' An eyebrow was raised and Willow felt herself being reassessed: from a person who holidayed in a tent to the type with a second home. She slipped her paint-stained hands into her pockets. It had worked though, because the conversation moved swiftly forward.

'What's your husband do with himself?'

The woman had clearly watched them arrive in Westford together, then. 'He's a writer,' Willow said, trying to keep the pride from her voice. She loved what he did, but mostly she loved that he loved what he did.

'A writer, ay? Like Marcus Foxton? Not much of a reader

myself. I s'pose I can see the need for it. And you . . . do you work?'

'I'm a painter.'

'Is that so?' the woman murmured, as though this confirmed all her suspicions. Finally, she pushed the bag forward. 'Mira Holmes.' The name was said as less of an introduction and more as a form of inducement.

Willow slid her and Ben's first names across the counter with her payment. She felt, in terms of exchange, she had given the lion's share already. She shouldered her bag and said casually, 'What made Olive sell Towerhurst in the end, d'you think?'

Mira raised an eyebrow. The question seemed to please her no end. 'Went a bit batty, didn't she? Marcus's fault, I reckon. Poor old Olive Foxton, she wasn't a bad sort, really. No matter what people said.'

Chapter 13

Towerhurst, Tasmania

September 1939

From the first moment they met, Grace could see that Olive Foxton was not a woman to whom nature had been kind. It wasn't just the angry set of her gaze, it was that her looks – captured years before in the wedding photo that hung beside the fireplace – appeared to have hardened over time. She had narrow eyes three shades lighter than her wiry brown hair and bore a semi-permanent expression of distaste, lines sweeping from the corners of her down-turned mouth to add a decade to her forty plus years.

Grace had been in Tasmania for three days when Olive first swept through the sitting-room door and cast a critical eye over her niece, who was sprawled on the floor, an encyclopaedia open before her.

'It's not as bad as all that,' Aunt Olive said by way of introduction, when she saw what Grace was reading. 'Very few tiger snakes round here.'

'Thank goodness . . .' *Encyclopaedia Britannica* insisted that the yellow-bellied snake's bite could kill a grown man in eight hours.

'Well . . . stand up, then.'

Grace scrambled to her feet.

'Not very like your mother, are you?'

'I—'

'Well, anyway, day to day you won't see many animals round here, apart from the odd wallaby or roo. The rainforest's too thick.' She gave a sweeping look of disappointment in Grace's general direction. 'Welcome to Towerhurst,' she added as she turned on her heel and walked out, leaving her niece with a familiar sense of inadequacy.

It had to be said, though, that Aunt Olive took immediately to Rose, that hard expression of hers swept away by a cautious smile. Alone in her room, unable to sleep, Grace heard them laughing together late into the night, joking about Richard Holmes – the driver and son of the notorious gossip Mira – who had already asked Rose, unsuccessfully, to step out with him. The twenty years that separated the two women appeared to have dissolved on their very first meeting, as they'd linked arms, strolling over the verandah and disappearing into the 'garden', which Towerhurst didn't really have, not in any way that Grace was able to recognise.

'*This* is our garden,' Uncle Marcus said by way of explanation a day later, patting the trunk of something he called a *man fern*, its foliage tumbling like a weeping willow. 'The rainforest.'

'But what about *that*?'

'The moon gate?' At the back of the house a circular stone archway framed a path leading into the wilderness. 'Your great-uncle built it. He travelled extensively on the Silk Road, you know? That's where he got the idea. It's an oriental kind of folly. He loved the notion that to step through a moon gate is a rebirth of sorts. What do you think of it?'

There he was again, asking her opinion. 'I don't know . . .'

'Well, nothing at all wrong with that, my dear girl, but remember' – he tapped his temple – 'knowing your own mind is said to be the solution to all your problems.'

❧

Grace sat alone in the sitting room, watching a low mist roll
through the moon gate, when from behind her she heard the
sound of an opening door. Aunt Olive appeared.

'You might have gone with your uncle Marcus and Rose
to Westford this time.' It was a statement – or a wish – not a
question. 'Perhaps you should take a walk? Head out through
the moon gate. The track leads to a waterfall.'

'A waterfall?' Grace blinked. She had never seen a waterfall
before, only fountains in parks and gardens.

'Yes, yes.' Aunt Olive was all cool encouragement. 'There're
mining digs beyond, so I wouldn't go too far,' she warned
half-heartedly. 'I haven't been there for years, but Marcus tells
me the path's clear. The wallabies use it.'

'What about the . . . snakes? Tiger snakes?'

A hesitation. 'No. It's pretty safe, I'd say. Snakes only appear
when it's sunny, anyway. Cold blooded, you know?'

Grace looked out into the rain. 'Perhaps if you could . . .
accompany me?' she said, but when there was no reply she
turned to see Aunt Olive disappearing through the door, whatever she was muttering lost to the thundering thrum of rain.

Instead of venturing to the waterfall alone, Grace explored
the house, going from room to room until she reached the
strange round door on the top floor which – though usually
locked – stood ajar, a crescent of light spilling from its edges
like a waxing moon. She put a hand on the centre, cautiously
easing it forward so that light rippled over its surface. Beyond,
a narrow wooden staircase spiralled up and away, leading –
she knew – to Uncle Marcus's study. She hesitated for only a
second before slipping through and quickly pulling the door
to. Outside, weak sunshine chased away the rain, and inside
the air swirled with dust motes that danced in hidden eddies,

draughts from above. If she climbed those winding stairs – which narrowed hypnotically the higher they went – she would be at its top. From there, what would she see?

❧

Exertion stole Grace's breath, and with each step the thump of the pendant at her chest matched her pounding heart. 'Weak lungs,' her doctor had once said. 'Give her plenty of rest and keep her out of the sunshine.'

At the top of the steps, she paused, bewildered.

Her father's study at Grosvenor Square was neat, all dark wood and leather, with a magnificent marble fireplace at one end, and at the other, a sideboard heaving with decanters below a painting of the king, who always watched Grace's transgressions with a haughty stare. The smell of beeswax infused the room and, with the thick oak door closed, it was as silent as a grave.

This study, however – with its scent of smoke and stale coffee – was chaos. Piles of books (hundreds? Thousands?) lined the walls, stacked in towers, snuggling together at odd angles, each one's balance dependent on its neighbours. A potbelly stove dominated the centre of the room, and two small desks, covered in paper, huddled at opposite walls as though stinging from a fight. Grace moved towards the closest, stepping past scrunched notes that littered the bare floorboards, and picked up a scrawled page of messy verse. So covered in corrections was it, she could barely make out the words; something about a *piner*, whatever that was, and she put the page quickly aside, feeling that a trespass might be excused, but snooping could not.

Beneath one of the six brass portholes was a chaise longue and Grace went to it, crawling over the grey herringbone fabric to admire the view; the forest's emerald canopy – thicker and even more impenetrable from above than it was below – rolled in verdant hummocks to the sea. Grace blinked rapidly, becoming dizzy from the view, from the height, from the realisation that this island teetered on the edge of the world. It was thrilling and terrifying all at once, and for the first time she tried to comprehend just how far from London she was, which made her wonder – really wonder – how she'd ever make it back.

*

Later, Grace stretched like a cat. It had been so comfortable, that chaise longue – tucked away in the tower, no one to disturb her – that she'd lain back for just a minute, closed her eyes, and promptly fallen asleep.

Across the room: a scratching. She looked up in alarm.

Uncle Marcus was there, sat at one of his desks. Though he faced her, his attention was on his work, his brow so furrowed in concentration she feared it might drop to the page. He wrote quickly, line after line, whispering to himself, rolling the words in his mouth.

Grace held her breath, sitting ever so slowly. Then, on stockinged feet, she crept like a robber in the night towards the top of the stairs. It wasn't yet dark outside.

'Thought you might sleep for ever.' Uncle Marcus continued to write with a slow and steady hand. 'Now I see that isn't so.'

She paused, one foot hovering above the ground. 'I was . . . tired,' she said sheepishly.

'When I arrived, I thought a Tasmanian devil had broken into my office, but it was' – the tilt of his head hid what might have been the suggestion of a smile – 'just your snoring.'

Grace flushed in shame. 'I . . . I don't *snore*.'

'I'm afraid you do.'

She narrowed her eyes, a little flicker of rebellion firing in her belly. 'That's quite . . . rude.'

'Yes, *you* were rather. Breaking in like that.' Between them, a curl of smoke rose from the potbelly stove, and Uncle Marcus went to poke at the flames. 'I've written half a ballad since I returned from Westford. And you slept all the while. Quite a feat.' He glanced at his watch, raising an eyebrow. 'Quite a feat indeed.'

Two things stopped Grace racing down the spiral staircase and away. Firstly, Uncle Marcus didn't seem cross with her, quite the reverse. And secondly, she was curious.

'What do you mean: *ballad*?'

He looked at her in surprise. 'A song, a poem. A rhyme that tells a story.'

There was nothing, in Grace's opinion, worse than a poem. And poets. Mother had several poet friends, always speaking in riddles, praising their fellow poets in company, then scoffing as soon as their backs were turned. 'Sounds a little silly,' she said.

'Silly?' Uncle Marcus returned to his desk. 'You use that word a lot.'

Did she? She hadn't noticed. Suddenly conscious of how childish she sounded, shame needled at her again.

'Oh don't worry, I've found a use for it,' he continued, picking up his page to read. '*The son said: "Don't be silly / I won't drink tea from the billy."*' He laughed heartily, though Grace found nothing funny about it.

'What does it mean?'

'It's about a boy who goes panning with his father, and the father forgets to bring their tin mugs.'

Grace frowned. '*Panning?*'

'Panning for gold. You know?'

She shook her head.

'You put gravel in a pan, then move it like this' – Uncle Marcus rotated the horizontal sheet of paper like a slow-spinning top that had just tipped off its axis – 'until all the lighter material is washed away. If you're lucky, you'll find a speck or two of gold. It's heavier, you see—'

'Yes, I know gold is heavy, I'm not sil—' Grace stopped herself. 'It's just that I don't understand where the goat comes in.'

Uncle Marcus stopped his pantomime. 'Goat?'

'The billy *goat*, and the tea.'

He stared at her, then laughed. 'Not a billy *goat*. A billy*can*. Now who's silly?'

Sighing, she started for the steps.

'Grace, wait!' Uncle Marcus got to his feet and picked up the metal bucket that sat on the top of the stove, its handle fashioned from a piece of wire. '*This* is a billycan. Settlers made billy tea, see? Got mine at a junk yard.' From his grin, it seemed he was still pleased with his purchase. 'It was once used for transporting stew, or . . . *bouilli*. But nowadays billycans are just a symbol, really. Of the outback.'

Grace scrutinised the view out of the western porthole, where the sun was slipping below a quiet sea. 'We're not in the outback?'

'No.'

'So it's . . . just a big tin without a lid?'

It was Uncle Marcus's turn to be sheepish. 'Yes, well. That's about the size of things.' He hesitated. '*Silly* really.'

'Silly,' she agreed. A hairline crack opened in her mind.

Defeatedly, he studied the billy in his hands.

Grace cleared her throat. 'Actually it doesn't sound *so* silly in the ballad.' It felt nice to say such a thing.

Uncle Marcus glanced up. 'Do you think so? Well, it's hardly its best usage in a poem. Banjo Paterson wears that crown.'

'What did he say?'

'*Once a jolly swagman camped by a billabong / Under the shade of a coolabah tree / And he sang as he watched and waited till his billy boiled / "You'll come a-waltzing Matilda with me."*'

Grace didn't ask who Matilda was, and why they were dancing around the fire. 'Who is this Benjo Paterson?'

'*Benjo*? Ha! He'd love that, I'm sure.' Uncle Marcus put the billycan on the cook plate. 'He's Australia's finest poet. Andrew Barton Paterson. Banjo is his nickname.'

Grace bit her bottom lip. 'What else does he write?'

Uncle Marcus plucked a book from a pile underneath the chaise longue and flicked it open to a well-worn page. '"The Man from Snowy River",' he said. 'You know it?'

She shook her head.

'Goodness! We must fix that.' Without invitation, he began to read with unbridled enthusiasm, the poem rolling off his tongue.

'There was movement at the station, for the word had
    passed around
That the colt from old Regret had got away,
And had joined the wild bush horses – he was worth a
    thousand pound,
So all the cracks had gathered to the fray . . .'

Grace listened, transfixed, to the hair-raising story of the horse-back pursuit of this valuable colt. When it was finally located, its new herd descended an impossibly treacherous slope even the bravest riders wouldn't risk. Only one man – the man from Snowy River – had courage enough.

'And he ran them single-handed till their sides were
    white with foam;
He followed like a bloodhound on their track,
Till they halted, cowed and beaten; then he turned
    their heads for home,
And alone and unassisted brought them back.'

As Uncle Marcus finished, dusk nibbled at the last of the day. 'What do you think it's about?' he said.

He was at it again, asking her opinion, and Grace wanted to say, *I simply don't know.* But in that hairline fracture in her mind, something had appeared: an ember, glowing weakly. She rubbed her arms awkwardly; goosebumps covered them. 'It's about . . . an underdog?'

'Yes!' Uncle Marcus slapped the table with delight. 'It is! The very man they didn't believe could handle the ride – *A stripling on a small and weedy beast* – was the only one with not just the skill, but more importantly, the *courage*, to recapture the horse.' He took the book – *The Collected Verse of A.B. Paterson* – and returned it precisely to the haphazard pile from where it had come.

'But what does it *mean*?' Grace's tutors had taught her that literature always had a message that the reader must discern.

Without looking up, Marcus said, 'It means exactly what it appears to: never underestimate yourself, Grace, no matter what other people say.'

She hesitated, but something was happening to that ember in her mind. Oxygen gave it energy, so that it flickered hopefully. For the first time in nearly sixteen years, someone had told her she could be more. She turned from Uncle Marcus and slowly, shakily, descended the corkscrew staircase, hot tears that came from nowhere cooling in an instant as she spread them across her cheek. The moon door yawned tiredly as she stepped through into darkness, with only the flickering flame inside her to light her way.

Chapter 14

Towerhurst, Tasmania

November 1974

Ben rifled through the contents of his pack again – a coat, a small tin of Arnott's biscuits, a notebook – then pulled up the collar of his fleece as Willow appeared behind him, her reflection almost ghostly in the hallway mirror as it threw back the morning's light.

'Pay attention to where you're going. This is no place for a storyboard saunter,' she said, referring to his tendency to wander deep in thought when planning a story. She planted a kiss on his cheek. 'It's got the feeling of rain out there . . .'

He glanced out of the window at the finest wisps of clouds dancing over the treetops, then grinned as he pulled on his orange woollen hat so that his ears stuck out. 'There's no bad weather, only bad clothing.'

'Where're you going?'

He had no plans; he'd follow where his feet led. 'Perhaps in search of baby kangaroos?' he joked, but when Willow only raised an eyebrow, not getting his reference to the Joey River, he cleared his throat and added: 'I promise to return by lunchtime.'

'Twelve-thirty,' she said, brandishing a small paintbrush dangerously.

'One.'

'Twelve-fifteen, then.'

'All right, all right.'

He grinned, shouldering his small pack. 'See you soon.'

&

There was nothing else like it, west coast Tasmania's medicinal air: some said it was the freshest in the world. Ben removed his hat, shoving it in his pack, then inhaled deeply as he stood on the verandah, hoping to take in some inspiration. From the corner of his eye, he glimpsed movement: something rust-coloured darting behind the car, then emerging to whip around the side of the house. He rubbed his eyes. A fox? That was impossible; there were no foxes in Tasmania.

He stepped off the verandah, chasing the shadow to the rear of the house just in time to see a tail disappear beneath the strange archway – built of stone and perfectly circular – they'd inspected the previous morning.

'What's that?' Willow had said, peering out of the sitting room, coffee in hand, squinting into the forest beyond. Curiosity getting the better of her, she'd pulled on her boots and by the time Ben caught up with her, she was already standing beside it.

'It's a moon gate,' she said, her fingers tracing the perfect joints in the smooth stone blocks.

'A what?'

'They say that when you step through one, you're reborn.' And she'd done just that, then raised her hands theatrically above her head. 'How do I look?'

'Extremely beautiful . . .'

He too had stepped through the archway, intending to wrap Willow in a hug, when he'd noticed a small, pointed stone protruding from the ground. He'd quickly bent down to peel away the moss that covered it and, as words appeared, he'd jumped back. 'Is this a . . . a *grave*?'

Willow – bravely – had finished exposing the lettering. *'Always loved. Never forgotten.* I don't think so. Look . . . there's no date.'

Now, Ben ran his hand over the engraving, thinking that the stone was a remarkable colour; silky green with flecks of violet, the two hues marbled together like ink in water. Though he was no geologist, he *knew* this rock type, he'd come across it before. Atlantisite: green silky serpentinite, and purple stichtite. The stone was famously unique to Tasmania and, some years ago, he'd written a story about a woman who had healed her grief by wearing a small piece of it around her neck. According to his gem-loving protagonist, Atlantisite promoted compassion. He didn't believe in all that stuff, but his character had, and that was all that mattered.

In the cold light of day, he realised Willow was probably right . . . as usual. But, if this *wasn't* a grave, then the inscription was at least a memorial to someone, though to whom, there wasn't a clue. He stood, and inspected the moon gate; it too was constructed of Atlantisite.

At the edge of his vision, movement flashed on an overgrown animal track ahead. Abandoning his plan for the Joey River, and with one last glance at the mysterious stone, he slipped beneath the moon gate and into the trees.

⁊

He heard the waterfall before he saw it: a heavy, muffled noise that filled the air, and he quickly rounded a bend in the track to come face to face with a wide wall of tumbling water, the height of four men, that fell in a glossy stream to the pool below. At its far side, a stream drained away, seeking the sea, and it seemed to draw him in so that before he knew it, he was kneeling down to scoop the tannic water into his hands and drinking deeply. It was ice cold, and his temple began to throb, but still he took another gulp, enjoying the earthy taste.

He unzipped his backpack and took out a biscuit from his Arnott's tin. His watch read 9 a.m. Plenty of time to continue his exploration. To his right: a flash. Reddy orange . . . or was it? He wasn't sure, but still . . . The track – smaller now – steepened into the wall of trees. Hefting his pack, he took a brief backward glance at the pool, then turned left; up the hill and away.

Chapter 15

Towerhurst, Tasmania

September 1939

On the morning of her sixteenth birthday, Grace woke with a determination to do something a little wicked.

She swung her legs out of bed, wiggling her toes on the cold wooden floor, then slipped into a cotton dressing gown that was too small – her wrists poking out of the sleeves as though making a break for freedom – but which she much preferred to the silk one Edeline had wanted her to pack. *That* one hadn't suited her at all. It also didn't fit, in that it was far too big, although it had been a birthday gift from several years before. She'd left it hanging in her wardrobe at Grosvenor Square.

Now, she stood before another wardrobe and stared into its mirror, trying to remember how that dark blue silk had threatened to drown her. Would it have fitted her today, of all days? A girl's sixteenth birthday – according to fairy tales – was a magical moment, a point of transformation, when womanhood beckoned from just around the corner, but as Grace stared at her reflection, all she saw was the same image as yesterday: a pale face, mousy hair, and stick-like legs that protruded from the childish cotton gown.

'You'll be a woman before you know it,' Mother had said

the day she'd gifted the dressing gown. It was Grace's thirteenth birthday, and she'd opened it with excitement only to find she'd been given the kind of thing that Rose would love.

'It's huge,' she'd breathed. Everything Mother had ever given her was oversized, as though she bought gifts only for the daughter she wished her to be.

Her mother had sighed then, and leaned back. She was sitting on the bed, an intensely intimate gesture that had confused Grace, woken as she was from her slumber by the soft sigh of the mattress. It transpired that Edeline had plans and wouldn't be back until late. 'You are very, very difficult to love,' she'd remarked matter-of-factly, bending down to plant a perfunctory kiss on Grace's forehead before she departed. Her pale Mary Jane shoes barely made a sound on the carpet, and were quickly joined by a matching pair as Rose followed in her wake.

Still, the dressing gown hadn't really bothered Grace. It wasn't as if she'd requested a specific present; she'd never *wanted* anything before. She'd certainly never *asked* for anything. She may have had her faults, as she was often told, but she wasn't demanding. This year, however, for the first time in her life, she *desired* something: that ballad, 'The Man from Snowy River', by the writer whose name she'd forgotten. His work wasn't like anything she'd read growing up.

She *had* considered asking Uncle Marcus for it, for the book with the poem, but she was unaccustomed to making requests – though twice she nearly had. The first time, at the dining table, Aunt Olive had spoken over her, and the second time she'd been alone with him in Westford and, just as she was building her courage, a group of jostling boys swept past them, joking and teasing as she stared back, frozen in place by their familiarity and sense of belonging. Richard was there, though he didn't acknowledge her, only asked her uncle after Rose.

More than a week had passed since she'd fallen asleep in the tower office, and each day since she'd paused at the moon door and given it a push, only to find it locked. She merely wanted to read 'The Man from Snowy River' one more time, to feel the goosebumps on her flesh, and recall how Uncle Marcus had regarded her as though she were more than Mother's invisible daughter. So, yesterday, she'd hidden in the hallway cupboard as, like clockwork, her uncle descended the stairs from the study for his lunch. As had become his habit, he'd locked the door and – she'd observed – hidden the key under a vase in the hallway.

From down the hall: a creak, a shuffle. A slam. Grace held her breath, then – realising she was afraid of being caught merely contemplating a wicked deed – released it. What she planned wasn't *so* wrong, was it? The study was chaos after all; Uncle Marcus wouldn't even notice the book's absence. It would be a birthday present to herself, and why not? No one in the house had mentioned her big day. It would pass without fanfare, just as the previous fifteen had done. At least this year she'd be spared the ill-fitting clothes.

She paused, waiting until the pipes shuddered beneath her, followed by the sound of sleepy steps, then she went to the bedroom door and eased it open, peering into the dark hallway, her heart in her mouth. The moon door was shut, just a dark circle in the gloom. She looked left, then right, before her gaze fell to the floor.

She blinked.

There, shrouded in dimness, lay a small package wrapped in brown paper and secured with string. When she bent to pick it up, she saw that a message was written on it:

For Grace, on your sixteenth birthday. From Uncle Marcus.

Once more, she inspected the hallway, searching for Rose. This must be a trick. When she was certain her chaperone was nowhere to be found, she held her breath and tugged on the end of the string so that the knot fell loose. Carefully, she unwrapped the familiar book, then, with hammering heart, stepped backwards into her bedroom and clicked the door shut.

꿍

This was going to be her first good birthday, Grace thought half an hour later as she descended the staircase, fully dressed and ready for the day. She'd almost forgotten what the sun looked like, what it felt like, and for a fleeting moment, the beams streaming into the hall confused her as they bathed dust motes in spot-lit glory, sparking a reflection of her fox pendant's blue eye across the bare wooden floor.

In her hand, she held *The Collected Verse of A.B. Paterson*. She'd read 'The Man from Snowy River' twice already, the second time whispering it out loud, tasting its cadence. Goosebumps arrived unbidden each time. The next poem she'd chosen – 'Clancy of the Overflow' – had been a short piece written from the perspective of a lawyer sat in a stuffy city office who dreams of changing places with a cattle drover, who Grace pictured as a cow shepherd driving his herd over endless miles. She tried to envisage him riding those sunlit Australian plains, but couldn't. The view outside her own window was so very different.

On the verandah, she hesitated, peering into the trees with trepidation. Uncle Marcus had told her that, at the very waterfall Aunt Olive had once mentioned lay beyond the moon gate, a natural seat was set into stone. 'It's a magical place to read,' he'd added, and now, perhaps for the first time in her life, she wished for precisely that. Was it madness, she wondered, to venture into the rainforest alone? And yet this morning she felt a little mad, a little *bold*, as though the bravery of the man from Snowy River was infectious, and she had managed to catch a dose of it. Before she could change her mind, she stepped off the verandah, walking quickly behind the house, then passed beneath the moon gate, not letting herself look back.

ଧ

She heard the waterfall before she saw it. It was, at first, just a muted background rumble on the edge of her hearing, but it soon eclipsed all sounds and she paused, stopping to look behind her. No footprints, other than her own, led to where she stood. What if she got lost? Or stepped on a snake? She hesitated, but ahead, sunlight kissed the track through gaps in the canopy, and she threw off her concern. Already she saw water vapour hovering, a low rainbow-shimmer colouring the air. It called to her. She clutched Banjo Paterson to her chest, rounding the next corner with tentative steps so that the rainbow, always ten steps ahead, lifted up, arching beneath the cloud-speckled sky. The track passed the waterfall where, according to Uncle Marcus, the right fork led downhill straight to the main track from Westford to Towerhurst. '*Don't* follow the left fork, the track uphill, it's littered with old diggings. Terribly dangerous terrain,' he'd warned.

Now, on impulse, she stepped forward, kneeling down to do something she'd never done before: she drank water from a wild place. It slid silkily down her throat, leaving a pleasant tang of rock and time. She wiped her wet hand on her skirt, then went to the promised seat and sat, tucking her knees to her chest in a way that her mother would have scolded. Mother, however, wasn't here to disapprove, and Grace reached happily forward, removing her shoes to toss them aside and wriggle her toes against the stone.

ଧ

When, several hours later, dark splodges marked her page, she glanced up and remembered where she was. The rainbow was long gone and the waterfall, so soothing on her arrival, rumbled its discontent as fat drops of rain painted the pool's surface with concentric rings. She closed the book, suddenly feeling that she shouldn't be out there at all, and the sense of liberation she'd felt on her arrival evaporated as she hurriedly pulled on her shoes. Somewhere in the distance, a currawong called, and ahead, along the very path she'd arrived on, the undergrowth rustled violently. She halted, her heart pounding with the realisation that she'd told no one where she'd gone. There, again! The rustle. And was that . . . a tail? Richard's warning flashed in her mind: . . . *there're species no one's even identified and ten steps off the track you'd be lost, taken by the rainforest in one giant gulp.* She certainly didn't fancy being lost in a giant gulp, but she desired meeting an unidentified species even less. Remembering Uncle Marcus's words – that the right track followed downhill to the road – she neglected to retrace her steps and, aiming a pleading look at the weeping sky, trotted down the path, chiding herself for staying so long. Chiding herself for venturing out at all.

❧

At the road, she turned right, back towards Towerhurst, congratulating herself for not getting lost. What had she been thinking, coming out here at all? The man from Snowy River had taken her hand and led her astray.

Suddenly, her steps faltered and she stopped, then took three quick paces backwards, pausing again. Her heart quickened in her chest.

Ahead, a black rope with a sulphur-yellow stripe staining its belly lay across the corrugated road.

To her right was a low branch, white petals blanketing the ground beneath. It appeared flimsy but scalable, though Grace had never climbed a tree before. Children did it, so how difficult could it be? Without taking her gaze from the tiger snake, she side-stepped ever so slowly, then reached up and clambered onto a thin, waist-high branch. The beast didn't move, but she was certain it watched her, a beady eye following her ascent. Snakes couldn't climb trees, could they? She paused, clinging to the thin trunk, Banjo Paterson at her side. There was no sense in crying out, she knew, the rainforest would only swallow her call. Silently, she waited, but for what – and for how long – she did not know.

Chapter 16

Grosvenor Square, London

November 2004

Libby sat in bed plagued by a lingering thought: this wasn't the way most twenty-nine year olds in central London spent their Saturday nights. She sighed, setting aside her peppermint tea, and her reservations, in favour of the book which nestled in her lap.

The Ballads of Daniel McGillycuddy.

As far as she was aware, although it appeared he enjoyed reading it, her father hadn't written poetry; his works were purely literary in the sense that they'd gained all the acclaim and none of the sales. According to the bio in his short story collection, which she'd found tucked away in the Launceston Library when she'd been nearly twelve years old, he had won several national awards, and from the moment she'd turned the first page of his book she'd loved his writing, though she hadn't understood it. As she'd grown older, she had tried searching between the lines to glean what her father had *really* been trying to say, but she knew she could read a thousand different things into his narrative depending on what she wanted to believe.

A cackle of laughter rose up from the street outside her window, and Libby let go of her thoughts, blinking herself back into the soft, elegant room. Outside, she knew, the young and old were just beginning their night's revelry; she imagined them skipping arm in arm from one pub to the next, discussing life and love, letting off steam, making memories that they'd reminisce over the next morning with foggy heads and giggles. Libby had rarely, if ever, done that, though there was, she supposed, that initial period at university. The trying to fit in as she never had, the drinking, and the laughter that never *quite* reached her belly, as though she was always outside of the joke. But then she'd met Krish and no longer needed to look for understanding because she'd already found it.

She sniffed and wiped her cheek with her finger, finding it wet with tears she didn't know she was crying. In that moment, she felt a sudden familiar helplessness overcome her and – as if for the first time – she realised she was completely alone in a foreign city. Even her terrible flatmates in Launceston had been a certain comfort in her darkest days. Even her mum, though they never talked extensively about things that really mattered. It was, Libby supposed, the way Willow had dealt with Ben's death; by keeping her grief buried deep.

Sighing, she reached for her tea, and as she did so *The Ballads of Daniel McGillycuddy* tumbled to the floor with a soft thud. There, from between its pages, a card had slipped out. An old bookmark her father must have used? She reached down and picked it up.

> Roger Masters
> 22 Battledean Road
> North London
> *For all your biography needs*

A biographer? Next to Roger's name was a handwritten number and on the back was another name and a second number written in an older form, the type before STD codes were standard:

Rotherwick 5-6711.

Rotherwick? Libby recognised the name immediately. According to Milton Twiggs' article, that was the Hampshire village in which Edeline Grey had grown up.

As she turned the card over again, her phone pinged, and she opened the message to read good news from her aunts.

We'll be back earlier than expected. Tuesday. Hope that suits? Gives you enough time to clean up after all your wild parties. Ash x

Libby smiled. Perfect! She might well draw something else out of her aunt on the subject of Towerhurst . . . but not only that, she could do with some company and Ash and Ivy were the best of that. For now, though, Daniel McGillycuddy would have to do. She placed Roger Masters' card between the pages of the ballad collection, then turned to the back to read the poet's bio.

> Daniel McGillycuddy was born in Ballinn, County Kerry, Ireland, and moved to Tasmania in 1937 at the age of 15. It was in that harsh, unforgiving landscape that he developed a love of ballads, drawing influence from the great Australian poet, Andrew Barton (Banjo) Paterson. Daniel fought for Australia during World War Two.

A Tasmanian connection! From the satchel, which lay on the end of her bed like a loyal hound, Libby took her father's map and looked again at Ireland's south-west corner. Yes, there it was – *Ballinn* – right next to information about how to get there. Her father, it seemed, had been *very* interested in this Daniel McGillycuddy, so much so that he'd been planning to visit his place of birth. She sifted through the satchel and inspected, once more, the London–Dublin return tickets, scanning for a purchase date this time.

Her heart skipped.

Her father had bought these tickets the day before his death. *27th February 1975*. Her hands shook as she put them aside. It was strange, wasn't it? A last-minute travel decision like that in the seventies?

She turned back to the book, letting the pages fall open where fate ordained, and began to read 'Life on the Death Railway', a ballad with a cadence so beautiful and somehow familiar that Libby caught her breath. It was almost as smooth as Banjo Paterson's poetry, with a pacing and vernacular that matched, though these works must have been written at least half a decade later.

The next poem – 'When Grandma's Curtains Faded' – was a short ditty about the introduction of daylight savings during the war years, and she smiled at the cheek of it. She knew that imported Irish folk songs had played a huge part in shaping Australia's ballad culture, and she wondered how much influence that had had on Daniel McGillycuddy, a boy who had spent his early years in Ballinn before being shipped across the globe to Tasmania. In fact, many of the poems referred to life on the Australian home front, something she'd certainly never learned about at school. Hobart had had blackout rules? Bunkers were sunk into Launceston's streets? Fascinated, she learned that Bass Strait was mined in 1940 ('Explosions in the Shallows') and how Japanese submarines had been sighted off the state's east coast too many times to mention ('Beneath the Tasman Sea'). These ballads brought the war, the sense of an imminent threat to life, so *close* to Tasmania that Libby found herself thinking about her home state in a way she rarely had before. It was easy, she mulled, to look back and *know* that the island – and the majority of Australia, for that matter – never saw battle, but it was entirely another thing to capture the feeling that history *might* have been different (invasion, occupation, surrender?) had the war taken another turn.

There was no doubt in Libby's mind: the collection was fantastic inspiration for fiction – after all, fact was often stranger than anything the mind could conjure – and it made *total* sense that her father had been reading these ballads. It was only when she turned to the next one – titled 'The Far-Flung Distant Shore' – that she discovered she was wrong.

Chapter 17

West coast Tasmania
September 1939

By the time the jolly whistling sounded from around the bend in the road, Grace's legs wobbled like jelly. She had been there for ages – on her birthday! – and now that her initial panic had subsided she had to admit she felt mainly bored. She barely kept an eye on the sleeping snake, distracted as she was by her growling stomach, the tree's sweet-scented flowers reminding her of the bread and honey she'd had for breakfast many hours ago. Above, rain patted the canopy and, in the near distance, the gentle roll of surf formed a rhythmic background to her observations, a slow, mocking metronome ticking the time away. Vaguely, she wondered what Banjo Paterson would make of the situation: would he jest, or would he write a ballad where the weak girl, whom nobody had ever loved, conquers her fears and chases the creature away?

Down on the road, two legs appeared, the feet clad in tatty leather boots, walking with pace and purpose. Alarmed, but also buoyed, Grace called out in her most commanding voice.

'Stop!'

The boots halted, and the musical whistling ceased.

'I'm up here,' Grace said, shaking the branch, letting loose a shower of petals. She'd had enough of the Tasmanian

wilderness for a lifetime and cursed the fancy that had taken
her that morning. What had she been thinking? She blamed
Uncle Marcus, but also Banjo Paterson, who nestled between
her body and elbow, unopened since she'd climbed the tree,
for fear that she might fall.

The manly boots turned towards her. 'Now, what would
you be doing up there?'

At the sound of the voice, something uncurled in Grace's
stomach. Her mother had always warned her about the Irish;
thieves and liars, she said they were. But what choice did she
have?

'Can't you see I . . . require assistance?'

'Do you now?' came the quick and happy reply. The boots
stepped closer and a face appeared: green eyes above two
vertical dimples framing a more than mischievous grin. The
boy – or was it a man? She could hardly tell – removed his
flat cap, which was sopping wet, to reveal a handsome flop of
dark hair.

'That *thing* is blocking the road!' Exasperated, she added:
'I've been here for . . . for . . . for ever!'

He bit his lip, tilting his head to the side. 'Well, when God
made time, he made plenty of it.'

She gaped at him, and he held up his hands in surrender so
that the cuffs of his red plaid shirt fell back to reveal muscular
forearms. Perhaps he was older than she thought? It mattered
very little. She considered Rose, who always managed to get
men to do things for her. She almost, but not quite, succeeded
in softening her voice. 'Help me?'

The boy-man leaned forward, resting a hand against the
trunk. 'A grand sassafras, this one. You rarely see them this
big. Or climbable. You did a fine job getting yourself up there
like that.'

She let go of the branch with one hand and gripped the

fabric of her skirt to her thigh. Drops of rain filtered through the canopy, and he turned his head away.

'Now, how can I be helping you without so much as a please?'

Silence passed between them, racing up and down the trunk. 'Please,' she said eventually.

He nodded. 'And in return?'

A languid air of unease settled in the leaves. 'I'm sorry?'

'What will you give me in return?'

The nerve of the boy. 'I have nothing to give.'

There was something devilish in his glance. He stepped away from the tree, his feet making barely a sound on the soft ground. 'How about a kiss?'

Grace felt a swift, hot flush rise on her cheeks.

'A kiss,' he repeated, 'in exchange for solving your snake situation. On the cheek, is all. Nothing fancy.'

'Nothing *fancy*?' Her grip on Banjo began to slip, and she hesitated momentarily before releasing her skirt and letting the book fall into her hand.

The boy averted his gaze. 'What've you got there?'

'*The Collected Verse of A.B. Paterson.*'

''Bout music, is it?'

She laughed, then stopped. It felt strange to do that – laugh spontaneously. Even at his expense. 'No. Please hurry.'

'Can't be rushing a job like this,' he said, then added, 'you've only eight hours to live if a tiger snake bites you, you know?'

'Clearly God didn't make *plenty of time* for people getting bitten by snakes then.' The boy hid a small smile, and a flush of pleasure plucked at her skin. Had she just made some kind of joke? She wasn't entirely sure. She shifted the book so that it hid the crossed fingers of her hand. 'I will give you one small . . . *minuscule* . . . kiss – on the cheek – if you remove the snake.'

He glanced up in surprise, and was that ... guilt? 'Er ... grand.'

After a moment's hesitation, he turned, striding confidently towards the snake. When he was terrifyingly close, he stretched his arms wide as though preparing for a wrestle. *Tick, tick, tick.* He clicked his tongue rhythmically.

'What're you doing?' she hissed in alarm.

The rain seemed to hold its breath. Then, with a sudden movement, he leapt forward recklessly – the handsome fool was sure to be bitten. With the speed of a whip, he gripped the tiger snake's head, lifting its wriggling body over his shoulder and hurled it, with a primal yell, into the forest beyond.

ቈ

Grace huffed, then resignedly tucked the book into her waistband. She hadn't believed the boy would go through with it. Now what? Her cheeks flushed with the thought of what she'd promised.

Slowly, she began to descend the tree, its petals snowing around her. Three feet from the bottom, Banjo Paterson fell, tumbling to a splayed stop on the sodden ground. That really made her mad. Clinging to the branches, she said, 'I think you'll find that bribing a kiss from a lady is *extremely* bad luck.'

The boy raised an eyebrow. 'Didn't you know? We Irish are immune to bad luck.'

'How sill—' She shook her hair, letting petals fall free and feeling the fox pendant tap against her chest. Lowering herself gingerly to the ground, she turned to him. 'You'll find yourself cursed.' Where that came from, she wasn't sure, but it had the desired effect. The boy's face dropped. Fat drops of rain fell on his head, flattening his dark hair. 'So, if I were you, I wouldn't attempt it.'

He looked sheepish, then gestured forward to the shelter

of the tree. 'Can I? It's bucketing down out here.' Before she could even ask what *bucketing down* meant, he'd stepped close beside her and she closed her eyes, reluctantly turning her cheek towards him, hoping that the kiss would be quick. But nothing happened. She cautiously opened one eye only to find that he had settled at her feet, his back against the tree trunk. He had her book in his hands, flicking through the pages. 'I'll take a ballad, then.'

'What?'

'You just read me a ballad, and we'll call it even.'

No kiss? She felt . . . relieved? Surely? She narrowed her eyes and snatched the book back. 'Fine.' Turning to the well-thumbed 'The Man from Snowy River', she passed it to him.

'*You* recite it,' he said. The grin was back, and this time she felt a flush crawl up her neck. With a certain sense of trepidation, she sat next to him, and began to read.

'Get away with you,' the boy said when she'd finished.

'I *beg* your pardon?'

'What I mean is: what a story!'

'You speak so strangely.'

He shrugged. 'I'm Irish. Most of the lads here call me Paddy. Highly original.'

Grace closed the book and crossed her arms, watching the heavy rain fall in a sheet. She looked down at her mud-smeared stockings, wondering what Mother would think of her now. She smiled a little, despite herself.

'What's the craic?' he said, watching her.

'Would you *stop* it?'

'Stop what?'

'Being so . . . so . . . *Oirish*. No wonder all the *lads* here call you Paddy.'

They sat in silence for a moment.

'You're Grace, aren't you?'

She tried to mask her surprise.

'You're up at the big house with Marcus? With . . . Rose, is it?' Men always did that: asked about Rose in an overly casual way. He held out his hand. 'I'm Daniel McGillycuddy.'

Tentatively, she took it. 'Why are you here?'

'We live half a mile past you. I was walking home from fishing.'

She noticed, for the first time, the metal bucket he'd left out on the road. A rod leaned against it.

'I meant: why are you here . . . in Tasmania?'

He looked away. 'Came here two years ago to live with my aunt and uncle, so I did.'

'Why?'

'Because . . . because I had to. I'll get back to Ballinn one day soon though. It's in County Kerry. You know it?'

She shook her head.

'I'm saving for it, see?' He pulled some copper coins from his pocket, and stared at them as though they were a piece of his home country. 'Enough of these will buy me a ticket back.'

'You don't like it here?'

'I like Ned and Colette, and the place well enough.'

Grace nodded. Colette was always busy when she came to Towerhurst, but she never failed to be kind. Ned she didn't really know, but he seemed a gentle sort; so different from her own father.

'But it's not home, is it?' Daniel added with a shrug.

Grace wasn't sure. What was *home*, anyway? On the journey over, and during her first weeks here, she'd felt a pull back towards the familiar, but that was about the extent of it.

'I thought you'd be older,' Daniel said.

'Why?'

'They told me you were fifteen.'

'They?'

He shrugged. 'People in town.'

'I'm sixteen.' She felt a strange sensation, like she'd forgotten something but couldn't recall what it was. 'Today actually.'

'Sixteen? Today?' He appraised her, his brows furrowed. 'Well. May your . . . health always be like the capital of Ireland.'

'Sorry?'

'Always Dublin.'

She glanced away.

'*Doubling*. Get it?'

Despite herself she smiled, then rubbed glumly at the mud on her skirt. 'I don't think anyone will believe me . . . that I spent my birthday up a tree.' She smiled a little. 'Probably my best birthday yet. So, that's saying something, isn't it?'

Daniel cleared his throat. 'About the snake, I should tell you—'

A low rumble rolled over his words, then a vehicle appeared on the track, inching slowly forward. It was Uncle Marcus's red Ford pickup. Grace jumped to her feet, and when he saw her, his eyes widened.

'My God . . .' He cut the engine. 'Grace! I've been searching for you for hours.' His hair was a mess, and she noticed his skew-whiff shirt buttons as he opened the door. 'I thought you'd fallen down a mine.'

'I'm fine,' she said, quite surprised to find that she actually *was*. 'This boy' – she cleared her throat – 'that is, Daniel, he saved me from a giant tiger snake. It was asleep, blocking the road. I couldn't get past.'

Uncle Marcus raised an eyebrow, leaning an elbow on the car. His beard was salt and pepper. 'He saved you, did he? The snake was *sleeping*, was it?' He began to pack his pipe with feigned nonchalance while Daniel scuffed the ground with his boot.

Grace indicated a vague direction. 'He threw it into the forest there.'

Uncle Marcus held out a hand and took Daniel's, pulling the boy close. 'Thank you for saving my niece from such a dangerous, *lively* creature.'

'Well . . .' Daniel extracted his hand, picking up his bucket. 'I think I'll just walk the last mile back. Stretch my legs.'

Rain dripped from Uncle Marcus's brow. 'A good day for a walk, I think.' He turned to Grace. 'We were worried sick about you.'

Her heart flickered. 'Really?'

Opening the passenger side door, he said, 'There's a birthday cake waiting for you – marble cake, you said it was your favourite.'

'It is.'

'Jolly good. Best thank Daniel, then we'll be on our way.'

Grace appraised her water-logged saviour. 'Goodbye.' The words stuck like glue to her throat. Before she could pull the door to, he stepped forward.

'I'd love to hear some more of those ballads from yer man, Benjo Paterson.'

Uncle Marcus sighed, shaking his head, but Grace felt a flush of pleasure. *Banjo* was a ridiculous name, after all.

'How about next week?' said Daniel. He rested his hand on the car's bonnet.

'Well, I . . .'

Uncle Marcus muttered, then reached across, pulling the door shut and before Grace could answer they were on their way to Towerhurst, Daniel just an image reflected in the wing mirror, trudging through the rain.

Chapter 18

Grosvenor Square, London

November 2004

In the early hours of the next morning, Libby gave up on sleep and – grabbing the copy *The Ballads of Daniel McGillycuddy* – opted for coffee and computer instead. Her mind reeled as she settled down on the window seat in the front room, cognisant that for the rest of London it was still the dregs of Saturday night. She glanced down at Grosvenor Square, where a group of women in tutus looked rather the worse for wear as they piled into a taxi. Surprising herself, she realised she didn't feel any of her normal inadequacy at her lack of social life, but rather a certain gratefulness that her day stretched before her unhindered by fatigue.

She opened Daniel McGillycuddy's book, this time reading out loud the ballad that had so surprised her last night.

The Far-Flung Distant Shore
by Daniel McGillycuddy

Along the Kenmare River came the long and distant shiver
Of the steamer as she motored from the bottom of the bay.

As I watched her pass before me,
I was taken by a story;
The memory of a life in a place far away.

'Twas 1937, when my parents went to heaven
And a ticket to Tasmania was sent from Uncle Ned.
'His whole life lies before him,
Consider this a warnin':
If he stays in bleedin' Kerry then he might as well be
    dead.'

So I left my home behind me and took nothing to
    remind me
Of purple heather mountains where the faerie folk
    reside,
And all that lay before me
Was a yet unwritten story,
Six thousand distant miles across the oceans wide.

Cruising on that steamer, I became a ceaseless
    dreamer,
Poring over memories of the life I'd left behind.
I was an only child,
Kerry-born and wild,
And upon those far-flung shores, I knew not what I'd
    find.

Something that I've learned is that luck is never
    earned,
And my uncle was the kindest man I'd ever met.
But it wasn't him that dragged me
From the misery that nagged me,
'Twas the girl I one day found on the makings of a bet.

I'd heard there was a wager, 'We bet ye can't engage
   'er,
That one who thinks she's so much better than the
   rest.'
The local lads had made it,
But never yet had paid it,
Five shilling were the prize for the one who fared the
   best.

I was walking home from town across the sodden
   grounds,
<u>Towerhurst</u> hidden in the bushes on the right,
When I saw her in the branches,
What were the ruddy chances?
She was clinging to the tree, her knuckles white with
   fright.

She hollered then to warn me, pointing out before me,
To the rope as dark as charcoal that lay across the
   track.
'Twas curled, its belly yellowed
And it moved not when I bellowed,
So I sidled up behind it, and doubled round and back.

The Lord I'm sure forgave me, but to her squawk of,
   'Save me!'
I leveraged my advantage with a quick and charming
   grin.
'I'd be happy to assist, miss
For a single, honest kiss, miss.'
To which she nodded glumly, tears dripping from her
   chin.

'Look away,' was all I said as I grabbed its deadly head
And hurled it long and hard, through the bracken
    there it went.
And safety now before her,
I held my hand towards her,
And with a quick and haughty huff, she began her
    slow descent.

As she climbed off that tree a thousand petals tumbled
    free
And then she slipped and gave a cry,
But she landed safe and sound
With a flower faerie crown
And a fox around her neck, with a blue and shining
    eye.

It would have been amiss to commandeer that kiss,
So I pointed to the book that lay abandoned at her
    feet.
It spread its words before me
As though making then to taunt me:
'This world – of text and verse – and yours will never
    meet.'

So I asked and she agreed, delighted to be freed
From the obligation that I'd thrown upon her lot.
And she read the verses to me,
And the cadence in them threw me;
They reminded me of ballads that I'd almost long
    forgot.

And the guilt it overcomes me and my conscience it
    still shuns me,

That the snake I threw away had been killed by Uncle
    Ned.
But I couldn't really tell her,
'Cause no one trusts a fella
Who saves a frightened girl from a snake already dead!

But it's not the lie that taunts me, it's her memory that
    haunts me,
Of a girl that time forgot decades long before.
And yet she's here beside me,
As the twilight finally finds me,
And the steamer motors on, to a far-flung distant
    shore.

Libby took a long sip of her coffee and considered what she
now knew. Daniel McGillycuddy was important to the mystery
surrounding Towerhurst (the house was, after all, mentioned by
name in the ballad – and what's more, it had been underlined)
and that her father had been carrying a copy of his collection
wasn't merely coincidence, or a bit of light reading, it was a
clue. As was the fox pendant. She lifted it from beneath her
pyjamas, turning it this way and that so that it reflected the
yellow light of street lamps beneath her. 'Who did you belong
to?' she said, recalling the shock on her mother's face when
she'd caught a glimpse of it two days before.

And a fox around her neck, with a blue and shining eye.

Another part of the ballad her father had underlined.

She opened a browser on her computer, then turned to the
front pages of *The Ballads of Daniel McGillycuddy* where she
wasn't entirely surprised to see that the address of the book's
publisher – Stern Publishing – had already been circled.

The book was published in 1965 and, according to her
Google search, Stern Publishing still existed. There it was,

in black-and-white . . . literally in black-and-white: the most unimpressive website Libby had ever laid eyes on. A single page, with a long gallery of ballad collections, each book's cover captured in grainy greyscale. There was Daniel McGillycuddy's work, with a link to buy that said *Out of Stock*, just like all the others. She scrolled to the bottom of the page, searching for contact details, and was surprised to find that there were none, save an address that matched that printed at the front of *The Ballads of Daniel McGillycuddy*.

❧

An hour later, she stood on the towpath of the eastern extent of Regent's Canal only to discover – as she might have expected from the antiquated state of the website – not only that Stern Publishing no longer existed, but its building had, unfortunately, vanished altogether. She walked up and down the street, then paused to triple check she had the right place.

Stern Publishers, The Albatross, Graham Street, Regent's Canal.

She blew on her hands – it was so cold her breath fogged – then she opened her city map and frowned. She *was* in the correct spot, she was sure of it. This was the street, but instead of office buildings, it was lined with trees. The only shop sold booze and bread rather than books and ballads. Shivering, she sat heavily on a park bench and put the map away, letting her gaze wander across the calm, still water of the canal, which threw back the perfect reflection of the low buildings on its other side.

Buck up, Libby, she said to herself. This was hardly a dead end, was it? There were plenty more trails to follow when it came to her father's satchel. How about this Roger Masters, the biographer who lived – in the seventies at least – in North London? Ben must have known him, or at least met him. Or the Molly Munro whose number had been written on the back of Roger's card? Anyway, she could find Daniel McGillycuddy herself – if he was still alive. Could the authorities in Ireland give her his contact details? The *authorities*? She shook her head at the ridiculous notion. Even if she could find him, what on earth would she ask? Evidently the satchel contained a number of answers to questions she simply didn't know.

Over the canal, a pair of coots broke the water's smooth surface with an elegant landing before foraging around the base of the nearest narrowboat, whose colourful form was almost hidden beneath a collection of tatty flower pots. White coal smoke puffed from its rickety chimney and, as she shivered once again, Libby imagined how warm it must be inside. She stood, smoothing her black coat and wishing she had a crust of bread for the coots who were chatting happily, clearly delighted with the narrowboat's weedy hull, the growth so healthy it reached up above the waterline, threatening to cover the vessel's name.

But not quite succeeding.

Libby stopped. The vessel's *name* . . . it couldn't be? Could it? She took a quick step forward. *The All Tross*?

She almost laughed. The boat's name was missing half its *b* and an *a*, but . . . *The Albatross* it was. The publisher's office was a narrowboat on Regent's Canal? She couldn't believe it and yet, recalling Stern Publishing's website, perhaps she could. This boat, too – at least on the outside – was in a state of semi-neglected chaos. It was rather more colourful than the website, though, appearing cheeky and cheery and, truth be told, wholly in contrast to the look on the face of the man who had just appeared from the newly opened hatch.

He fixed her with a cautious gaze. 'You're early,' he said in a deadpan voice, as he upended a battered tin of Brasso onto a rag. '*Very* early.'

'I'm so sorry,' Libby said automatically, hating herself for apologising for nothing at all. Hating herself even more for the small flare of attraction she felt when he turned his questioning gaze to look her up and down. She glanced quickly away. Early for *what*?

'I haven't even had a chance to clean the outside,' he added dryly.

'I'm sorry,' she repeated, unnecessarily.

'What's that?' the man said, pausing to wave his polishing rag in her direction.

He was her age, she thought, or perhaps a little older, and his dark hair was wild in a way that might have been deliberate but, given his five o'clock shadow, probably wasn't. She looked down, trying to gather her thoughts. In her hand she still held *The Ballads of Daniel McGillycuddy*, proffering it like a shield. 'I . . .' she started uncertainly, 'I . . .'

'You?' The man's tone riled her and the flicker of attraction she'd felt only moments before was snuffed out. She narrowed her eyes, but that was as far as her confidence went, and when she opened her mouth the same, timid tone that she had always despised came out.

'Well . . . according to this book,' she said meekly, 'a publisher lives here. Or *lived* here . . .'

'Oh?' The man raised a single dark eyebrow, still rubbing slowly and ineffectively – Libby might have pointed out had she been so inclined – at a brass catch on the boat's roof.

'You see, my dad was looking for him – or *her*, maybe, I don't know? – in 1975. Possibly?' Her face began to burn. 'Although I know it's early and you seem . . . busy? I thought it was an office, you see. I just wanted a look. So I'm surprised to find . . .' She waved her hand in the boat's general direction.

A ripple of something that might have been amusement crossed the man's features. 'What . . . was the question then?'

'The question?' Libby plunged her hands deep into her coat

pockets. The cold had crept into her bones as she'd sat pondering her next move. '*Does* a publisher live here?'

He paused. 'So . . . you're not here to view the boat?'

'No . . .'

He disappeared inside.

'Hello?' she ventured, stepping closer, hearing the sound of clattering of crockery.

The man reappeared, a new expression on his face. He looked, if not delighted, at least quite welcoming. 'Coffee?'

'Oh, no, I can't—'

He disappeared once more. 'Sugar? Milk?' he called out of the hatch.

Libby stood on the towpath, unsure of what to do. A window opened and a hand reached out.

'Sam,' said the voice behind the hand.

She shook it, glancing over her shoulder to see if anyone was watching. 'I'm Libby.'

'You'd better come in, it's a bit chilly for coffee on the roof.' His eyes appeared in the window. 'The publisher was Lawrence Littleton. My father.'

Chapter 19

Regent's Canal, London

November 2004

The man – Sam – ushered her inside the narrowboat to a small table beside a potbelly stove, leaving the hatch open to pleasant effect: she was warm, but the fresh morning air brushed her face. A coffee was thrust into her frozen hands as she examined the boat's sparse interior with an inquisitive eye. It was immaculate, with no sign that a man might have lived there for more than fifty years, though the polished surfaces and lingering scent of varnish suggested that his presence had only recently been stripped away. It filled Libby with sadness; she was too late. Lawrence Littleton was gone.

As if confirming her suspicions, Sam said, 'I've finally had a bit of a clean-up inside. Haven't quite managed the outside yet. Slightly different sense of style, my father and me.' He dipped into his back pocket, pulled out his wallet, and passed Libby a small photo. 'He liked a rather more . . . alternative living space.'

'I'll say,' said Libby, observing *The Albatross* as it must have been many years ago: full to the brim with books, papers and clutter. The photo appeared to have been taken in the seventies, if the man wearing the brown flares was anything to go by. He sat at this very table next to a small, serious boy. Even now, she recognised Sam, with that black hair, and those wide blue eyes.

'You grew up on the boat?'

'Some of the time,' he said evasively, brushing past her to stoke the fire.

'And you don't want to move in now that . . .' she trailed off as he stood again, his head nearly brushing the ceiling. He was far too tall for the tiny narrowboat. 'No,' she said, answering her own question and considering her surroundings. It must be magnificent to wake up on a canal every morning, to leave the boat knowing that when you returned a small slice of tranquillity awaited; a stew left on the dampened-down fire all day, a night by the fire with a book. The cosy interior of *The Albatross* was perfect for Libby's short stature, she thought as she stretched her legs, relaxing in the radiated heat, surprising herself how comfortable she felt.

'Now, what's this all about then?'

Warmed by the fire, and his apparently genuine interest, she told him.

'So, in a nutshell,' said Sam, when she'd more or less finished her story, 'because your dad was looking for Daniel McGillycuddy, *you're* now looking for him, but you have no idea why?'

Libby nodded, feeling a little shame at how candid she'd been. She turned her gaze through the hatch to watch an elderly couple wander along the towpath with all the lethargy of a Sunday morning, noticing that the bench she'd sat on only half an hour before had been claimed by a well-dressed man who was ignoring his open broadsheet and had turned his face to the sun. Libby felt her own face flush with warmth when she glanced back at Sam, so she talked instead to her mug as though it might listen to all she had to say.

'I suppose it's all connected. The necklace, the ballad.

Towerhurst. And the reason Mum never wanted to return. And Daniel McGillycuddy? Perhaps he was somehow involved?' She ran a finger over the photo of her parents she'd removed from the satchel as she'd told Sam her story.

'There's no doubt about it, this mystery of yours is a mine-field, Libby.'

She crumpled under his gaze, looking away the moment their eyes met. What was *wrong* with her? She was here to find Daniel McGillycuddy's publisher, that was all; somehow – and she blamed being so chilled to the bone she'd lost her senses – she'd managed to spill her story to this stranger.

'. . . say about it all?'

Libby blinked, once, twice.

'I said: what does your mother say about it all?' Sam repeated. *Her mother.* She felt a zing of guilt. Mum was the one other person in the world to whom her father's story really mattered.

'She's . . . intrigued,' Libby said evasively, and Sam regarded her an instant too long before turning over a paper that appeared to be a list of people who would be viewing the houseboat that morning. *The Albatross* was in need of a tenant.

'Well . . .' he said, looking discreetly at his watch.

Libby drained her already dry cup, then hesitated, glancing around the boat's immaculate interior, thinking of the photo captured here in the seventies when books jostled against the portholes as if trying to take a swim. 'Was your father much of a note taker?'

Sam tapped his temple. 'All up here. That was Dad's way.'

Mr Littleton sounded as though he'd been a sharp contrast to his son, whose printed schedule for the day's viewings was now aligned perfectly with the edge of the table, which in itself was – in a way – a contradiction of his unkempt appearance.

He stood and she noticed that at some point he'd removed his thick woollen top to reveal a blue polo shirt, and the muscles in his arms rippled as he took their cups, washing them in the tiny kitchen sink, stooping so that his head didn't bump on the boat's roof.

'Still, I'm sure we can find out a bit more.' He wiped his hands with a tea towel. 'What are you doing Thursday night?'

'Thur— Thursday night?' she stuttered, her empty calendar roller-decking through her mind. Suddenly appalled at herself, at the look she must have been giving and at the thrill that raced through her veins to be asked out on a date by – she had to admit it – the most handsome man she'd seen in years, she stood quickly. 'I'm sorry, I'm not . . .' She wanted to say *Looking for anything*, but of course she was *looking* for something, just not romance or, worse, anything less meaningful. Picking up the satchel, she swept Daniel McGillycuddy and his ballads quickly inside.

A whisper of amusement crossed Sam's features as he wiped at some invisible mark on the wooden countertop. 'Dad's retired, but I'm sure he'll be able to point you in the right direction one way or another,' he said lightly, *too* lightly, clearly clocking her having mistaken his meaning.

But all that was forgotten. Lawrence Littleton was *alive*? Libby sat in surprise. They'd talked for nearly twenty minutes and yet he'd neglected to mention this *tiny* detail. 'You never said . . .'

He shrugged in a way that could only be described as cheeky. 'You never asked.'

She gulped down a rush of embarrassment and he spread his hands in a gesture of peace. 'And really . . . you seemed in need of a sounding board, sat there on that bench' – he indicated where the man with his face to the sun had now fallen asleep, snoring happily – 'debating with yourself.'

'I was not *debating* with myself . . .'

'Your lips were definitely moving.' She felt that his

amusement was teetering on a precipice and a little shove might push him over. He continued. 'Anyway, Dad moved out of the boat last month. He's got a place in Putney, something less . . . riparian. I'm sure he'd love you to join him at the Iliad Club. It'll be right up your alley, actually. They talk about literature, mostly.' He pushed the spreadsheet towards her. 'If you give me your number, I'll check with him and get back to you.' She hesitated long enough for him to add, 'Don't worry, Libby, I'm not trying to chat you up.'

She laughed awkwardly. 'No, I didn't think that . . .'

'Of course.'

'It was just that . . .' She scrambled for an excuse, and settled on a lie. 'I only have a landline, I haven't picked up a UK mobile yet.' Quickly, she wrote her aunts' number on the paper.

'Central London?'

'Yes,' she said, 'I'm staying with . . . friends.' It was another thing she needed to do: start looking for accommodation.

'Well . . . I'll call you.' He held out a hand and this time their touches were as warm as each other's. 'Old Street Station's straight down that street for half a mile.'

She recoiled. 'I don't ride the tube.'

'Yes,' he said. 'Of course. I'm sorry.'

'Goodbye then.'

'Goodbye.'

She turned quickly and started down the towpath, in the opposite direction to Old Street Station, the last stop her father would ever have made.

Chapter 20

Ocean Beach, Tasmania
October 1939

Three days after the snake incident, Daniel appeared on the steps of Towerhurst asking for Grace.

'I wondered,' he said awkwardly, as Uncle Marcus lingered behind and Rose eyed them with interest from the verandah, 'if I could hear some poems from that lad . . .'

'You mean *Benjo* Paterson?' Grace exchanged a glance with her uncle, wondering what on earth had got into her. Being shy and reserved was what she was all about. So her mother had always said.

'That's the one. I thought we could go down to the beach.' Daniel hesitated. 'If that's all right with your aunt and uncle, o'course?'

Aunt Olive was still in bed, and even if she wasn't, Grace knew she would have no opinion either way.

'I didn't think you were the literary type, Daniel,' Uncle Marcus said, crossing his arms.

'Should I take that as a compliment?'

'No.'

But it was agreed that Grace could go – 'for an hour, no more' – and she now walked across Ocean Beach, a potholed mile from Towerhurst, wondering why Daniel simply didn't purchase the book for himself. It was likely, she concluded, that their meeting had provided the perfect excuse for him to come to the house to meet Rose, and Grace was sure she hadn't imagined the admiring glance he'd sent her way. What had surprised her though, was that Rose had returned it.

'Here,' Daniel said, shaking out a tartan blanket.

'Here?' Grace pulled the top of her yellow blouse tighter against the sun, squinting at the endless white sand stretching as far as the eye could see. The tide was out.

'On its way back in,' he said, following her gaze. They were alone, which she thought improper, but apparently such things were little worried about in this strange place. She straightened her hat, Edeline's voice echoing in her mind: 'Keep out of that Australian sun, girls. I don't want you returning looking like withered prunes.'

'It's very bright,' she said, feeling as though she'd stepped inside a light bulb. They sat. 'Could we find some shade?'

Daniel surveyed the treeline, then looked at his watch. 'So, tell me about "Clancy of the Overflow" . . .'

Clearing her throat, she began to read, and with each passing stanza, she was sure he moved a little closer. 'What *are* you doing?' A gentle breeze pushed a prickle of sand across her bare feet and she tucked them underneath her.

'Listening,' he said, placing a hand over her own. She felt a flush of warmth – more powerful than the sun itself.

'I . . .' Words escaped her. Here was a *boy*, a handsome boy, leaning towards her, so close she saw the flecks of gold in his green eyes. Inches separated them, and Grace hesitated, unsure of what to do, but when his lips brushed hers, ever so lightly, she sighed involuntarily, a fire igniting her belly.

It was her first kiss, and when Daniel pulled away his touch still lingered, so that he might have been a part of her, might have left a piece of himself on her skin.

A moment later, a dozen cheering voices rolled over the sand from the mouth of the Joey River, extinguishing the heat in Grace's body. In a single second, she froze.

Rouge crept up Daniel's neck. 'Just' – he stood – 'wait here.'

'Who . . .' Grace surveyed the line where forest met the sand. Who would be out here? Surely they were alone?

They were not.

A group of boys appeared, whooping, slapping their hands in triumph. Daniel stormed towards them.

A flush rising on her cheeks, Grace threw down her book, and followed.

ॐ

The kiss was a bet. That's what she overheard as Daniel shushed his friends with a flap of his hand. He had the decency, at least, to start guiltily as he turned to see her standing behind him.

'You kissed me to win a *bet*?'

He took off his hat, holding it to his chest. 'It's not what you think . . .' but his voice trailed off, drowned out by his sniggering friends. She recognised Richard, his blond hair almost white in the blazing sun, his greedy dark eyes taking in her shame, presumably already embellishing the story in his mind, preparing it for delivery to his mother. She knew the faces – but not the names – of the other four. One stood to the side, a dumpy boy with red hair and pale skin. He caught Grace's eye, then looked away, embarrassed.

'How . . . how *dare* you!'

Daniel bowed his head. 'I didn't mean it to be like this . . .'

In Grace's sixteen years, barely a day had passed when she hadn't felt inadequate in some way or another: when Rose teased her, when Mother raised an eyebrow, when weeks went by during which her father didn't acknowledge her existence. Very few times, though, had she experienced true fury, and when she had, she'd run off, out onto Grosvenor Street and away. Over the square, past the embassies, across the bustle of Park Lane. She'd weave through the sparse crowds of Speakers' Corner and onto the banks of the Serpentine to sit, exhausted with rage, and look along its length to catch a glimpse of The Long Water. The lake always calmed her: that soft ripple, the reflection of a cloudy sky, the willows that wept at its edges. Mostly though, it was the chill of the water on her feet, for she'd always sit on the sandy bank, a stone's throw from the Lido where swimmers glided, arm over arm, through the silky lake. They looked at peace. 'Never let her swim; her lungs couldn't take it,' Grace's doctor had warned.

That's where Molly would always find her, her small hands gripping Grace's as she whispered well-meaning lies about Edeline being worried, before leading her home.

Grace turned away from the mouth of the Joey River towards the sea, which seemed so far out it appeared to have no intention of returning and, before she knew it, she'd taken off across the undulating expanse of beach and crossed the distance between Daniel and his laughing friends and the cold, wild edge of the Southern Ocean. There the waves tasted her toes and, within minutes, were lapping greedily at her ankles, the salty water stinging her legs in a way that made her feel alive. She dared not look back, dared not face her shame, dared not see if the gaggle of boys had dispersed, taking their taunts with them, so she fixed her eyes on the horizon where white clouds billowed like smoke, and waded forward.

࿔

Daniel watched Grace's form grow smaller in the distance, her yellow blouse a sharp contrast against the sea. This wasn't how he'd planned it.

'Why'd you come?' he said to his closest friend, Puds, the

only one of the boys who'd remained, the others having left their money, and taken their bikes, and their laughter, to begin the rough ride back to Westford.

Puds ran his hand through his red hair. It was the colour of a fox's coat, though the lad beneath it was anything but cunning. 'Heard Richard say you had the bet under your belt.' He was six inches shorter than Daniel, and pudgy, but the boy's old man was tall and Puds, Daniel knew, had aspirations of a six-foot future.

'I only told Richard Holmes because he's holding the money, I said I wanted *a single* witness.' He spread his hands: *is that so unreasonable?*

'Fair dinkum, Dan: it was cruel, everyone watchin' like that.'

'*You* were watching.'

Puds scratched his nose, from where a sprinkling of freckles had escaped and scattered across his cheeks. 'Didn't think you'd go through with it. Seems kinda grubby.'

'You know I'm saving to get home.'

'Yeah, well, this might've cost you more than you won.'

This was why Puds didn't really fit in with the other boys: he had a conscience. Daniel couldn't say where he'd acquired it from; Puds's father was a brute, and his mother long gone.

'What if she drowns out there?' His words cut Daniel deep. He could see that his friend hadn't immediately made the connection to his parents, but when he did, he glanced suddenly to the side, sweeping his red hair from his eyes once more. 'Dan, I'm sorry, mate, I didn't think—'

'C'mon,' Daniel said. The tide was advancing at a rate of knots. At the spot where he had been sitting with Grace, he picked up the blanket and shook it, spilling sand into the breeze. The lads had been wrong to make the bet – 'five shillings to the first who gets himself a kiss' – and he burned with shame, cursing his involvement in the folly. She had looked not just angry, but *alive*, and when she'd confronted him, her eyes flashing so vividly blue, he'd caught his breath, realising that someone else lay deep beneath that shy exterior.

Her book lay upturned and he picked it up, fanning its pages, knowing that sand would be for ever stuck in the spine. He really *did* love the ballads. They were famous, of course, but he'd only ever heard them spoken in an Aussie accent, and to hear Grace fumble over the unfamiliar words had made him feel less of an outsider.

'Hope she can swim,' Puds said with the surety of a boy who'd grown up where children doggy-paddled before they could walk. Daniel, however, was almost an adult when he had his first lesson a month after arriving in Westford, every stroke weighing him down with the knowledge that if his parents had learned, he wouldn't be there at all.

He shook his head, throwing away painful memories, then squinted at the horizon. There she was, just a tiny yellow speck, the water expanding around her as it raced towards the shore. 'She only needs to wade back,' he said, the words sounding hollow. 'Even if she can't swim, she'll be grand. Right?'

Puds looked uncertain. 'She'll have to swim across the ditch. There's no way round.'

'The ditch' was a channel the Joey River incised to the sea. It curved north, deceptively small when the tide was out, but adding four feet to the water's depth as the water rolled back over the sand. And four feet could be the difference between walking and drowning. Daniel shielded his eyes. The water was sure to be over Grace's head by the time she reached it.

Oh God, he thought, this is all my fault. He watched the tiny form out there in the waves, willing her back to shore, but if anything she became smaller still.

Daniel wrapped the book in the blanket, and gave the

bundle to his friend. 'Keep an eye on this.' He removed his shirt, adding it to the pile.

'You're going out there? You're a terrible swimmer!'

Puds could talk; he was built for floating, not freestyle.

'You want to come, then?'

'Sure . . .' Puds dropped the blanket and started to remove his own shirt but Daniel placed a steady hand on his friend's shoulder. The boy was shaking. Now, he thought, *that* was bravery.

'No point all three of us being washed away. You wait here. Raise the alarm if we don't make it back. Find Aunt Colette. She's good in an emergency. Yes?' He nodded, once, twice, then turned on his heels to run across the alabaster sand, and into the advancing tide.

Chapter 21

Towerhurst, Tasmania

November 1974

Stood on the verandah was a slender woman, probably in her seventies, with a grey rope of hair slung over her shoulder and a ginger dog with doleful eyes at her heel. She held a loaf of bread and a box of Saxa salt, and she passed both toward Willow with a smile.

'I'm a stickler for a traditional welcome,' she said with a warm Irish lilt. 'I'm Colette McGillycuddy, and this here is Rua the red setter.' She patted the dog's head. 'We're your neighbours.'

Willow reached out to accept the gifts. She wore a shirt stained with paint, her bare feet cool on the floorboards. 'Thank you. Come in, both of you. Out of the weather,' she said, wondering whether Ben had conceded defeat. It was past midday after all, and his cheap waterproof was no match for a downpour, unlike Colette's long Driza-Bone jacket.

'We're only a quarter of a mile down the road,' she said as she shook out the coat and hung it on a peg outside the door.

We, Willow discovered as she brewed the coffee, was Colette and her husband, Ned. The rest of their family had scattered in the breeze. 'Not much to keep them in Westford, I'm afraid.'

'What keeps *you* here?' They moved to the sitting room. A small fire crackled in the grate.

'Huon pine. We came to Australia after the war. Took advantage of the resettlement programme.'

'Must've been quite a journey in the forties?'

'Bless you! It was after the First World War, if you can believe.'

'You must have been *so* young . . .'

'We'd not been married two months.'

'And are you from Dublin?' Willow knew nothing of Ireland.

Colette drew a breath with mock-horror. 'You should never ask a Kerrywoman that.' She smiled. 'Run as far away from Dublin as you can without getting your toes wet, there you'll find County Kerry. The village of Ballinn, that's where we're from . . . right in the southwest.'

'Do you miss it?'

'You know what they say. *A good retreat's better than a bad stand.*'

'I'm sorry, I didn't mean to pry.'

'Not at all. The truth of it is, we had some bother. Ned fought for Britain in the war, and people at home weren't so fond of men who did that.' A deck of memories fanned across her face, but she quickly shuffled them away. Her gaze went to the window where rain kissed the glass, framing a canvas bathed in muted light. 'Oh my,' she said with exaggerated surprise, 'you're a painter?'

Willow laughed. 'I take it you've been to Mira Holmes' shop today?'

Colette's emerald eyes twinkled. 'Westford's not unique. I'll warrant every village in the world is just the same. Our parish in Kerry was shocking for it. The gossip ran rampant, but it's also a lifeblood.'

Willow murmured a vague agreement.

'Mira said you looked familiar. Are you well known for your work?'

'I'm not . . . *un*known.'

A smile. 'And your husband, Ben, he's a writer?'

'Yes . . .'

As if reading her mind, Colette shrugged. 'The only thing worse than being talked about is not being talked about . . .'

'Speaking of talking about people . . . Olive Foxton, the woman who lived here before . . .'

'You're wondering what she was like?'

A nod.

'She's about my age, and I'm no spring chicken.' Standing, Colette went to the wall beside the fireplace where a dozen photos hung in frames. 'Here she is on her wedding day to Marcus in 1920. Everyone in town was invited, even us, and we'd only just arrived. But then, so had Marcus. A shotgun wedding, so it was rumoured at the time. Though it couldn't have been.'

'Why not?'

'They never had children.'

Colette reached out to straighten the image and, with that single movement, Olive set her hard, unsmiling expression on Willow, who couldn't help but look away, her mind inevitably turning to her and Ben's own situation.

Not wanting Colette to see her emotion, she quickly pointed to a square frame in which a young couple embraced. 'Who's this then?' The girl wore a necklace, a pendant in the shape of what looked a dog – though it was difficult to tell through the dirty glass – and the boy looked smart in his Australian Imperial Forces uniform, though, instead of a slouch hat, he wore a Santa hat.

'That's my nephew, Daniel. Christmas 1940, I guess it was. A year or so before he left for the Pacific. Wasn't he handsome?'

'And the girl?'

A hesitation. 'That's Rose. Rose Munro she was back then; chaperone of Grace Grey, Marcus's niece by his sister. The girls came across during the war, evacuated from London. Poor old Grace had a rough time of it – caught rheumatic fever, so she did.'

'Is there a photo of Grace?'

Without so much as a nod to the wall, Colette answered. 'I doubt you'll find one. Olive wasn't her biggest fan—' She was interrupted by a whine, and turned to see Rua standing at the door. 'Excuse me.'

Two minutes later, Colette returned, the dog at her side. 'Bladder the size of a pea. I know how he feels.' She gave Willow a wink. 'Now, where were we?'

'Olive.'

'Oh, yes.'

'Was she an art fan?' Willow had found none of her own work in the house.

Hesitating, Colette considered her words. 'No. I wouldn't have thought so. Now, *Marcus* . . . he was a different story. He was mad for the arts.'

'Was he?'

'Oh yes. But didn't he leave the old place years ago? We missed him, so we did. It's remote out here' – Colette smiled – 'though we like it well enough.'

'It *is* an incredible wilderness.'

She nodded. 'Tell me, now . . . how do you find Towerhurst?'

'It's certainly . . . unexpected.' Willow smiled. 'We'd never set eyes on the place until two days ago.'

'Well, I admire your spirit. Buying a house unseen. Brings to mind our boarding that ship in Ireland all those years ago. Not a notion of what awaited us.'

Willow blustered, feeling guilty about the deception. 'Your

trip was a *bit* more adventurous than ours.' Thinking of adventures, she glanced at her watch. It was one o'clock.

Colette set down her cup. 'Well, can't be taking up all your day . . .'

'I'm just wondering where my husband has got to. He'd love to meet you.'

'We'll cross paths soon enough. You'll meet Ned too. Mind like a sieve, but don't we love them?' She rolled her eyes affectionately: *men*! From her pocket, she withdrew a key.

Willow's heart leapt: the key to the tower? Ben had turned the house upside down searching for it. At dusk last night he'd stood in the spitting rain, looking up at the portholes, side-stepping to view them from all angles. 'You think Rapunzel's up there?' she'd laughed. 'Locked in the tower?'

'I thought I'd best return it,' Colette was saying. It was, Willow realised, a match for the key that fitted the front door. 'Marcus gave it to me, in case we needed to get into the house.'

Questions tumbled over each other in Willow's mind as she turned the small key over in her fingers. 'You don't have one of these for the tower by any chance?' she said.

'Can't help you there, I'm afraid. Don't think anyone's been inside that room for over thirty years. Now . . . come on, Rua.' Colette tapped him on the shoulder and he opened one lazy eye. 'Deaf as a post, he is, but he's got *some* nose on him.'

The old dog heaved himself up, nuzzling Willow's hand as he passed. She wanted to reach out to Colette and beg her to stay. She had so much to ask – about Towerhurst, about the legacy – but didn't know how to do so without giving herself away.

As if reading her mind, Colette said. 'Call down to us, won't ye?'

Willow nodded. 'I'm sorry you missed Ben.' She paused by the door, peering out into the rain. 'He's off bush-bashing.'

'Bush-bashing?' Colette's wrinkles worried deep between her brows. 'Best stick to the tracks round here. 'Tisn't safe otherwise.'

'Will *you* tell him that when you meet him?' She laughed, rolling her eyes in the way that Colette had done moments before. *Men!* 'Ben never listens to me.'

🠞

An hour later – Colette's warning playing on a loop in her mind – Willow stood on the porch, peering into the fortress of trees surrounding the house. It was only a few hours until dark. She wrung her hands as the forest canopy swayed in the growing breeze. Where was her husband? She stepped off the verandah, calling his name.

'Ben? Ben!'

Running a hand through her hair, she ruffled it in frustration, trying to think rationally. Ben could – it was true – be somewhat scatterbrained, his storyboard saunters taking him miles in search of his muse, but this was different. Tasmania's rainforest was not an environment one could wander aimlessly through.

She went to the window, her reflection thrown back by building darkness. Every hair on her arms tickled, lifting from her flesh, the goosebumps violently illuminated as a shard of lightning split the sky. It felt astonishingly close. She squeezed her eyes shut, and counted, but before she reached *three* a boom shook the house to its core.

She opened her eyes.

Where *was* Ben?

Chapter 22

Ocean Beach, west coast Tasmania
October 1939

Daniel glanced over his shoulder to where Puds stood a hundred yards behind him on the beach before turning back to push through the waves. Frantically, he searched for the yellow blouse, though its disappearance could only mean one thing: Grace was already up to her neck in water.

He paused, lifting his hands to shield his eyes from the sun's glare, sweeping his gaze north to south. There! There she was now, just her head visible, bobbing in the waves.

Gripped by a sudden surge of fear, he drove harder against the incoming tide and, although he tried to run, his feet barely gripped the sand. Finally, the ground gave way to nothingness, and he went under, the chilled water stealing his breath. It was The Ditch. It couldn't be more than sixty feet wide – about the same length as the Westford public pool – and he thought about this as he kicked himself forward until his feet touched the other side, an undertow pulling at his chest. Now Grace was only a hundred feet ahead.

When she saw him, she grappled urgently for the sky as if his sudden appearance had shaken her from a stupor, but her splashing only angered the already-irate ocean, riling it into a frenzy. Her cry was smothered with a wave that took her under, and he felt he was tussling with an invisible enemy as he uselessly pushed water aside, trying to dig her out.

A cold limb. A soft wave of hair. Suddenly, she was there; just a shimmer of yellow under the waves and when he pulled her up she stared at him with eyes the colour of the sky, all traces of fury gone. As they turned for shore, he was aware of how cold she felt in his still-warm grip.

'You can't swim . . . at all? Grace?' he gasped, heaving for breath.

Whether she could or not, she didn't say. She was mute, tears mingling with the seawater that dripped from her fringe. Silently, he turned her away from him, putting his arms beneath hers, then – kicking his legs – he propelled them across The Ditch. He'd never swum like this before, towing another person; he went under, and under again, coughing seawater each time he surfaced. But still he held Grace aloft.

Finally his toes brushed sand, his feet finding purchase, and he carried her in the way a husband might his new wife, to take her over the threshold. With eyes closed, she put her arms around his neck, gripping tightly, silently, and for all the world he couldn't fathom what she was thinking. Or if she thought anything at all.

Puds splashed out to meet them in the shallows and together they carried Grace to dry sand where she sat, shivering, her gaze fixed on the horizon and her head tilted to the side as if listening for whispers. Puds wrapped the blanket around her while Daniel looked on, gripped in the throes of guilt.

This was his fault. Grace had nearly died because of his single-minded obsession with five shillings. Slowly, he knelt before her, taking both her hands between his own. 'I'm so sorry, Grace,' he said. 'Will you ever forgive me?'

She was still as silent as a lost soul. Then she blinked, her gaze returning from somewhere beyond, and the frown she gave him made him feel like she'd only just noticed he was there.

'I survived,' she said and, for reasons beyond his understanding, she began to laugh.

Chapter 23

Central London

November 2004

Libby's plan had been simple – ply Ash with espresso martinis, thereby laying the groundwork for a subtle interrogation regarding her parents' time at Towerhurst – but before she knew it she found herself spilling a story of her own; the one about her father's satchel.

'You did *what?*' her aunts said in unison, Ash's eyes wide with interest, Ivy's narrowed in concern.

They were halfway through dinner at a restaurant buried in the stone-lined wine cellar of a seventeenth-century pub recommended by *Time Out*. It was Libby's shout, she'd insisted – a thank you, really, for the accommodation – but even she had to admit the locale had a whiff of the inquisition about it. Still, her aunts had taken their seats, perusing the menu in a lively manner as if their red-eye hadn't landed at Heathrow that very morning.

Ash sipped her espresso martini. 'So . . . what was in it then? The satchel?' she said with an unmistakable twinkle in her eye. Libby felt the smallest lessening of her guilt – Ash, it seemed, was amused, if not impressed, by the news.

'Ash—'

'What, Ivy? He *was* her father.'

Libby nodded. What Ash said was true. Ben *was* her father, and she had every right to learn about him. How was she to know the satchel would reveal a legacy that her mother clearly wanted forgotten?

'A short story of his, a map of Ireland, tickets to Dublin, a few articles and notes,' she said vaguely. 'And a book: *The Ballads of Daniel McGillycuddy.* Perhaps you've heard of him?' She searched her aunts' faces for sparks of recognition and was disappointed to find none, but something – nonetheless – stopped her from telling them about her meeting with Sam on *The Albatross.* At the thought of him, she flushed, wondering when he'd call.

'I think you're reading too much into this,' Ivy said, setting her fork aside and asking if anyone fancied dessert. She quickly steered the conversation away to other – safe – topics: business deals in New York, Christmas gift ideas, a tentative plan to ask Willow if she might like to visit London.

'Mum? Visit London? You'll never get her to come overseas!'

'You'd be surprised,' said Ash. 'She always wanted to travel . . .'

Before Ben died. That was the implication, and Libby felt a familiar ripple of frustration. There he was, always on her mind, but never on anyone's lips. *Ben.* Whenever anyone spoke of him, and they rarely did, his name came in a whisper, followed by a shift of the spotlight to any topic but him.

❧

Later, over a nightcap in the apartment after Ash had gone to bed, Libby began to well up; emotion at seeing her aunts, and at voicing what she'd done, overcoming her.

'I just want to know a little more about him, Ivy,' she said. 'Who he was. What he was like.' It was the truth, although the mystery about Towerhurst, about Edeline Grey, and why her father wanted to find Daniel McGillycuddy was hardly a deterrent.

Ivy nodded, twirling a large glass of Baileys. 'I understand,' she said uncertainly. Of course, she couldn't understand, really. Dina and Rob – Libby's grandparents – had always been there as her mum and aunts grew up. There was no need for Ivy to search for her own father's past, whereas Libby felt a hole, a gap where a piece of her was missing.

It had hit her one day when talking to Krish, who had just finished a lengthy diatribe on a family wedding where siblings mixed with third cousins, mixed with great-great aunts, and everyone knew each other's business.

'Is that a *bad* thing?' Libby had asked as they sat on campus, watching a boat sail along the Derwent River and disappear into the distance.

'Sometimes.' He'd run his thumb over the palm of her hand, making butterflies dance in her belly. 'You'll discover what they're like,' he'd added in that way which said they'd always be together.

'Don't they look out for you?'

'Plan for me, more like it,' he'd said quietly. All his life, he'd been expected to study medicine, that was his fate from the moment he was born. Like his brothers and his older sister. Had he taken any other path, he would have disappointed those third cousins, those great-great aunts and, most importantly, his parents. 'In my family, our generation's purpose is to follow in the footsteps of our fathers.'

Libby didn't say it, but she *wanted* footsteps to follow. She needed inspiration, she felt like she'd been searching for it her entire life.

'Ben was wonderful,' Ivy said, putting her hand over Libby's, bringing her back to the present. 'Just like you.'

'Like me?' Libby turned away, tried to hide the emotion

that threatened to bubble over. 'I hardly think so. I've wasted my life, I've let the years slip by . . .'

'You've suffered great grief. I think you've done very well.'

'I gave up. Mum never gave up.'

Ivy hesitated. 'She had you to keep her going.'

'I can't imagine what it was like, losing your husband then finding out you were pregnant.'

'Your dad would have been so happy.'

'Did he know . . .' She paused. 'Did he know about me?'

'I'm not sure, love.'

Libby dropped her gaze. She thought about her mum as they stood there at Towerhurst almost twenty years ago, in the rain, looking up at the house as it peered down at them.

'Why didn't Mum want to return to Towerhurst?'

Ivy sighed. 'It was nothing really, Libby. Just a silly fear your mum had. Your dad, you see . . .' She examined the palms of her hands, clearly considering her next words. 'Ben had an accident while he was there . . .'

'An accident? What do you mean?'

Ivy stood and went to the window. Outside a sliver of moon smiled in at them through moody clouds.

'He disappeared for a while, in the rainforest. Your mum . . . she was afraid of the house, or the area, I think.'

'Afraid?'

'I'll tell you what happened, but afterwards . . . you must leave it at that.'

Libby nodded, though it felt wrong to deceive her aunt.

'Willow never collected Ben's possessions here in London because he'd become *determined* to uncover Towerhurst's history . . .'

'And my mother was not?'

Ivy shook her head. 'She was not. It all started the day he disappeared . . .'

Chapter 24

Towerhurst, Tasmania

November 1974

At midnight, a convoy of cars had arrived from Westford, just beating the tide as it swarmed across the Joey River. They planned to depart on foot at first light, and any guilt that Willow had felt in raising the alarm had evaporated as the hours ticked on. Ben was in trouble, and by the looks on the faces of those just arrived, they thought it too.

The largest man in the party introduced himself as Sergeant Griffin. He was plain-clothed but Willow picked him as police from twenty paces; that self-assured nature, the deference showed by the others.

'Tell me,' he asked, 'where your husband was headed?'

'I really don't know. He said something about looking for wildlife but . . .' she trailed off. She didn't have an answer.

The party laid out maps, discussing unlabelled local features – *Bill's Drop, Kelly's Gossan, Incline to Hell* – which only made Willow shake like a leaf. Colette, who was handing out mugs of sweet tea, leaned in close, whispering.

'They're mostly old digging works,' she said, 'just shallow shafts and the like.'

'Mines?' Willow glanced at her in alarm. 'We're nowhere near Queenstown.'

'There are a few exploration pits on Razorback.' The local name for the hill that rose behind the house. 'Nothing too dangerous. Most of the seams ran dry in metres.'

Willow could tell Colette was lying. The surrounding ground, it seemed, was Swiss cheese.

A weakness overcame her. She bowed her head, listening to the rain tap on the window, the odd bolt of lightning a thousand times more luminous than the candles filling the room. When a heavy hand pressed onto her shoulder, she looked up.

'Best get some rest,' Sergeant Griffin said.

ॐ

She came downstairs a few hours later, and peered into the sitting room where men sprawled in chairs, half asleep, the fire dying at their feet. Ned – who she hadn't even introduced herself to as she'd raced into the McGillycuddys' yard that afternoon – had driven to Westford to raise the alarm and was now snoring on the window seat, his face pressed against the glass. He was white-haired and wiry, with bright green eyes and that kind of vitality that suggested he would live for ever.

All was silent. Or . . . not quite all. From across the hall came the murmur of conversation, and Willow stepped into the kitchen to see Sergeant Griffin talking to Colette.

'I should have gone with him,' Willow said.

The sergeant raised an eyebrow. 'What? Have you both lost in the wilderness? No. No. Absolutely not.'

The thought chilled Willow even more. If she'd been with Ben, she realised, no one would have known they were gone. Colette would have called up that morning, Rua at her side, and rapped on the door, waiting for an answer. Would she simply have left the bread and salt on the verandah, or taken them with her to return another day?

ॐ

When Willow stepped outside two hours later, dawn had broken and the vicious wind, which had blown all night, took her breath away. Even amongst the trees it was wild, whipping the canopy back and forth as though undecided where to go, unlike the search party, who had a 'thorough' plan. She knew what they were really thinking, though; it was written so clearly on their faces that an author, like Ben, might have scrawled it there himself. The Tasmanian wilderness was so thick, so vast, that you could wander for days, for weeks, without stumbling across a town, or even a track. People had been lost before, never to be found again.

Colette had left to get supplies. There was plenty of bread in her freezer, and honey on the shelf, she'd said. 'Best . . . be prepared.' A memory of Ben using that same Scout's phrase two days before hit Willow so hard that it took her breath away. He'd been packing his orange hat at the time, the same one he'd pulled on that morning before he'd said he was off in search of kangaroos . . . *baby* kangaroos? Oh Ben! Willow shook her head. How could she be so stupid?

She hurried, pulling on her hiking boots and fleece, not even throwing a glance over her shoulder at the empty house as she raced down the steps. She'd just take a quick check. Ben had merely gone to the Joey River, he was there somewhere, perhaps he'd tripped, slipped . . . fallen? She'd find him. He was everything to her.

ॐ

Ben's body had dropped away. Falling, falling. Through the earth, as if God had whisked away the ground like a magician might a sheet, revealing emptiness beneath. A magic trick was all it was, he thought, and this had comforted him as he fell.

Later, he floated. Up and away, through the layers of life that might have been. He saw Willow, and a child. *Their* child, he knew with a sudden certainty. It was everything he'd ever dreamed of. Everything he'd ever wanted. A family of his own. He reached out to touch them, felt the warmth of their skin, but when he leaned towards Willow, she disappeared, and the child began to cry. Her tears were icy cold, and he felt them rise around him like the tide swallowing the shore.

He shivered and stepped away, further than he intended. To his endless stretch of childhood, to loneliness, to a time when he had nothing. No, he recalled, not nothing. He looked down. In his hands, he held books, so many books. He'd loved them all. Picking up one, he turned the pages, sure that he must look for something, but didn't know what.

Surely all of this – the sounds, the memories – were just in his mind? But the cold felt real. It seeped into his body so deep that it came out the other side. He opened his eyes. A cirque of grey hung above him, framing marble clouds.

Later, when he glanced at his hands, the book was gone, replaced with a tarnished silver chain and a pendant of shining platinum. A fox with a sapphire eye.

☙

Willow focused on anything but the chilled grip of the wind. She thought of warmer times. Ben writing in the sunshine, that flop of hair across his eyes. Ben holding her hand as they walked on Northport's golden sands. Ben with his palm on her belly only two nights before, the glow of flames illuminating the stubble on his chin.

The potholes were full to overflowing, and the hungry mud sucked at her boots as she arrived at the Joey River, which was running an angry torrent. Even at low tide, Willow doubted it would be possible to cross; not without a four-wheel drive.

Their little Renault would never make it, she'd be washed into the Southern Ocean and away, next stop Antarctica.

Her hood whipped back as she stepped up to the foaming waters, barely feeling the icy flow as it seeped into the leather of her boots. Only her ragged breath told her she'd run the last distance without realising it.

Ahead, something bright caught her eye, entirely out of place at the base of the emerald vegetation. She stepped forward, pulling the item from where it clung. It was Ben's orange hat. Slowly, she picked it up, tannic liquid dripping from the wool.

She looked to the foaming surf, screaming Ben's name. And then she turned and began to run.

ꖘ

By the time Willow made it to the front steps of Towerhurst, her lungs burned. 'Help . . .' Her voice faltered in a rattling breath. Behind a window, someone moved in the shadows. 'Help!' she called a little louder, brandishing Ben's hat.

Towerhurst's door flung open, and a figure appeared, weakly silhouetted by candlelight. 'For the love of God! *Where*—?' Colette used all her slight body weight to pull the door shut against the storm, then she started down the steps, her words whipped away by the wind.

'Ben's—' Still, Willow's breath rasped. 'The ocean . . . down at the beach.' She didn't know where to begin. 'The search party, Sergeant Griffin . . . they need to go there.'

Colette put a firm arm round her, helping her up the steps. 'They found him. They've found Ben. He had wandered off and . . .'

Willow heard nothing more as she let her head sink to her knees. She tried to slow her breathing, tried to swallow her sobbing relief as Colette pulled her tight, her voice muffled by the raging wind.

'. . . And tomorrow Sergeant Griffin will take three men to retrieve the body.'

In an instant, Willow no longer gasped for breath. She no longer breathed at all. She twisted her gaze to search Colette's face, but it was only a shadow. Ben's hat fell from her grip. 'I don't understand—'

'It's okay, everything's okay,' Colette soothed, pulling her shoulders towards her to wrap them in an embrace.

This was a dream, Willow was sure of it. A nightmare. She shook her head hard, splintering her thoughts into a million pieces. 'No, no. No.'

'We think—'

The front door swung open, slamming against the hallway, and a ghost appeared, wrapped in a blanket that flapped in the wind like a cape.

She blinked once. Then twice. Thump! Her heart began to beat.

Ben. She only thought his name; she couldn't cry it out loud, like it was locked away. She gulped thickly as he took two shaky steps towards her, pulling her into a one-armed embrace. 'We thought you were lost!' He followed her gaze, which had settled on his bandaged wrist. 'I don't think it's broken,' he said.

'Oh Ben. Ben.' Relief flooded her. 'I thought you'd been washed out to sea . . .'

'I'm sorry, love,' he said quietly.

Her sudden disappearance had, it seemed, triggered a second search, and now Sergeant Griffin pushed through the door onto the verandah sporting a thunderous expression. 'She's here,' he called over his shoulder, receiving a murmured reply from the half dozen men inside.

Ben held her hand as they walked up the steps, through the hallway and into the sitting room, where a fire – coaxed by the wind whistling down the flue – roared with life. In flickering candlelight, she could now see that her husband's hairline was congealed with blood.

She passed him the wet woollen hat, noticing the violent tremor in her hands. 'What happened? I thought you'd fallen in the river . . .'

'I must have dropped this at the waterfall. A stream runs from there to join the river, I guess?'

He glanced at Sergeant Griffin, who nodded.

'I only opened my pack to get a biscuit . . .'

'You and your Arnott's biscuits,' she sobbed.

'Your husband had gone beyond the track to the water-fall, fallen down a shallow mine shaft. Rua sniffed him out.' Sergeant Griffin paced the room, and for the first time Willow noticed his pronounced limp. 'He was only half a mile away.'

Willow's forehead creased in confusion. 'That close?'

'The forest's so thick that even if Ben had called out you'd have had no chance of hearing him,' Sergeant Griffin said. He paused. 'There's more . . .'

'Is someone from the search party missing?' Willow was alarmed. If she had caused this, she'd never forgive herself.

'No, no,' said Sergeant Griffin. 'Everyone from the search party is back.'

Relief rushed over her. Then she looked to the place where the old dog – Rua – had sat watching her that very morning. Where was he?

'There was a body in the mine,' Ben said. 'A body . . . down there with me.'

Something wet touched her knuckle. Rua stood at her side, gazing up. She laid her hand gently on his head, and he nuzzled it appreciatively. 'A body?' Willow's stomach tipped. 'Have you any idea who it is?'

The candle flickering over the fire hissed and died, its flame lost to a wisp of smoke as the room held its breath, waiting for an answer.

Chapter 25

Ocean Beach, west coast Tasmania

October 1939

Daniel and Puds treated Grace as though she were on her last legs as they flanked her stumbling form onto the potholed track where it crossed the Joey River.

'Are you sure you can walk?'

'I'm fine.' She laughed again, just as she had on the beach. How alive she felt! As though the waves had pulled off her skin, and beneath it was someone better. She was chilled to the bone but, although her fingers were numb, her heart was on fire. She batted away Daniel's supporting hand, and the proffered blanket, then paused, listening to the sound of a pickup approaching from the direction of Towerhurst.

It stopped beside them and, without a second glance at Daniel, Colette jumped out of the driver's seat and eyed her up and down.

'Heaven almighty, Grace, what on earth has happened to you?'

'I had a swim.'

'Your lips are blue. And your *blouse* . . .'

Grace glanced down and noticed that her undergarments were showing through the soaked yellow material. Only a few days ago she'd wondered what her mother would have thought of her mud-smeared stockings. But this? *This* was a whole new level of impropriety. She resisted the urge to giggle.

'Daniel? Puds?' Colette snatched the blanket from her nephew's grip and wrapped it around Grace's shoulders. 'Would either of ye care to explain? The girl's delirious, so she is.'

'It was an accident, Aunt Colette. Sure, I didn't mean—'

'Delirious?' Grace interrupted, throwing off the blanket once more. '*Sure*, I'm more lucid than a leprechaun,' she mimicked. Then her teeth began to chatter.

With a tight smile, Colette bustled her into the pickup. 'Let's get you home, pet. And you boys' – she turned to look through the open rear window where Daniel and Puds had clambered into the empty tray back – 'have some explaining to do.'

When they both started to talk at once, she shut the window, then started up the pickup and turned it on the potholed track.

੨ঙ

On the verandah, Olive inspected her knitting, exhaling in frustration. She couldn't believe she'd dropped another stitch somewhere along the way. Or – she looked a little closer – perhaps more than one stitch. She began to count the loops on the needle, annoyed at how few remained.

Swearing, she threw down her work. It was no good. The Country Women's Association would have to do without her promised pair of socks at tomorrow's meeting. Any soldier unlucky enough to be given them would need skinny ankles and – she glanced at her discarded knitting – a second pair to cover the holes in the first. She cursed again. She was distracted, that was all, and no wonder. A world war, she considered as she picked up her cold tea, was bound to be disruptive, no matter where one lived.

But it was *more* than that. More than battles in far-off places about borders bounding countries she was never likely visit. No, what bothered her was far, far closer to home.

She gazed at the wall of forest and shifted her position, shivering a little. It was probably time to go inside, though she'd only been on the verandah for half an hour at most, a futile attempt to clear her head from last night's revelries. Between them, she and Rose had polished off half of a bottle of gin and, truth be told, Olive felt it should have done her the world of good. What a laugh they'd had! Joking about Mira Holmes, and her gang of gossips at the grocers. They'd shared too – in whispered conversation – their thoughts on Grace, and it had felt good to speak honestly for once, instead of tip-toeing around Marcus, hiding her reservations about Edeline's daughter coming to stay.

'Dreadful, plain girl,' Rose had murmured. 'And that lank hair!'

She'd appraised Olive then, and leaned forward to touch her frizzy hair, saying that women in London would kill for locks with that much body. And in the silence that followed, it had been on the tip of Olive's tongue to confide that in the single visit Edeline had made to Towerhurst, she'd overheard a conversation during which she'd suggested to Marcus that 'you should really get your wife to cut and dye her hair'.

'To move with the times,' she'd said. 'If you're going to marry beneath you, at least make her look the part.'

But Olive had paused just an instant too long, and the gin-soaked conversation had carried on even as her memories lingered. And she recalled how Marcus had, in the face of Edeline's contempt, murmured a vague agreement, and that inability of her husband to side with his wife became a memory that had lingered ever since.

The front door opened and Marcus appeared. 'Is Grace back?'

Grace. Olive was tired of the fuss he made of her.

'I wasn't aware she'd—'

But her reply was interrupted by the familiar growl of the McGillycuddys' pickup as it rolled slowly up the track.

૱

As Daniel explained with a surprising amount of candour precisely why they'd returned from their poetry reading with one of the party soaked head to toe in water, Grace observed the assembly. There was Rose, who had emerged from the house moments into the furore and now leaned against the verandah, biting her bottom lip presumably to stop herself from laughing. There was Puds, his gaze downcast, his body immobile apart from his legs which took a stuttering shuffle backwards with each part of Daniel's explanation, so that Grace feared that by the end of the story he'd disappear into the forest entirely. There were the respective aunts: Olive, her hands on her hips, a single eyebrow raised; and Colette who had slung a protective arm around Grace's shoulders. And then, there was Uncle Marcus . . .

'Let me get this straight, boy. My niece almost drowned because of five shillings?' he boomed, his beard seeming to Grace a hairy megaphone.

'Sure, it wasn't quite like tha—'

'What was it like then? Explain it to me, because as you can see, I'm really very confused.'

There was something about her uncle's anger that made Grace's heart swell. Aside from Molly Munro, no one had ever been on her side before but, unlike Molly, Uncle Marcus was in a position to declare it. And declare it he did, telling Daniel just what he thought of him, and the actions of his 'knucklehead' friends.

'All right, Marcus,' Aunt Olive interrupted. 'Colette's

perfectly capable of giving Daniel an earful later. If he even deserves it.'

'Work away,' Colette said, shooting a glance at her nephew, though Grace could see there was a trace of humour behind it.

'For Pete's sake, Colette, not you too?' Aunt Olive poured the dregs of her tea to the ground, as though to signal the end of the conversation. 'I don't see why you're all making such a fuss. It was just a bit of fun. Boys will be boys.'

Uncle Marcus shook his head. 'What rot, Olive! I won't side with you on this. Do you not care *at all* for your niece?'

In the pregnant pause that followed, the forest held its breath. And just as she seemed certain to reply, Aunt Olive turned on her heel and stalked into the house, slamming the door behind her and leaving Grace to shiver in her wake.

Chapter 26

Westford, Tasmania

November 1974

'Ouch!'

'Stay still.' It was like trying to clean a worm.

Ben lay on the red sofa, his arm neatly wrapped in a new bandage. His wrist – the visiting doctor had said – wasn't broken, merely sprained, but he had mild concussion and had been given strict orders to rest 'both mind and body' for a fortnight or more.

Willow patted her husband's head with a damp cloth, trying to remove the remaining dried blood from his hairline. A shower would have been nice, but running water and electricity tended to go together, and Towerhurst had neither. Just a tank outside, forever filling with water from the roof and overflowing into the forest beyond.

Behind her, the fire crackled.

She got to her feet. 'I'm going to leave you to sleep.' The doctor had said he might be a little confused in the days to come, but he only needed time to heal.

'I'm not tired.'

'Get some rest.'

'Don't leave me.' A hand reached out.

'You're a terrible patient,' she said, sighing affectionately.

The day had dawned bright, but a shroud lay over the house; yesterday a body had been found not half a mile from here.

'Have you any idea who it is?' Willow had asked Sergeant Griffin the night before.

He'd hesitated briefly before shaking his head. 'No,' was his simple answer and the room had shifted uncomfortably. 'No, I haven't a clue.'

Ned had scoffed. 'I can't remember a single person who's gone missing in this area since we moved here—'

'Was there anything with the body?' Colette had interrupted.

'According to Ben,' Sergeant Griffin had said, 'a suitcase. Though its catches are rusted shut. We'll collect it tomorrow.' *With the remains*, he'd stopped short of saying, though everyone understood what he meant. 'We'll need to send . . . everything . . . to Hobart for forensics. It could be months before we know more.'

'The suitcase,' Ben murmured now, propping himself up on his good elbow. 'So strange, isn't it? Almost as though the woman was packed and ready to run away.'

'A *woman*?' Willow raised an eyebrow. The body had been down there long enough that only a skeleton remained. 'How on *earth* would you know that?'

'I just got the impression . . .'

Her husband's imagination was nothing if not overactive. 'The *impression*?'

He frowned, then let out a groan of pain. 'Thinking hurts.'

'I should say it does. With a knock like that . . .' She looked away, conscious that Ben had been lucky. *She* had been lucky. It hadn't been – by all accounts – a deep mine shaft, but had he fallen the wrong way . . . She turned to him, squeezing his hand, feeling the love flow from her to him. Without Ben, she'd be lost.

'The question is,' he continued, oblivious to her musings, 'did she die *before* her fall down the mine, or *because* of it?'

Willow sighed. 'Shall I get you a book?' She rinsed the blood-soaked cloth in the bowl of pink water. 'You're supposed to be resting, after all.'

'That Sergeant Griffin ... he doesn't seem very *capable*, does he?'

'He found you.'

'Technically, it was the red setter, Rua. Sniffed me out, you know? And perhaps *capable* is the wrong word. *Engaged*. He didn't seem particularly engaged. You know what I mean?'

'No, I don't.'

'A body was found, on the west coast of Tasmania. It's hardly a common occurrence, is it?'

That was true. It wasn't, though it was by no means unheard of. The temperate rainforest could swallow a person whole, as Ben should have been able to attest.

'So ... a book then? I could bring in your stash from the car. Or' – Willow went to the sideboard, where a pile of cloth-bound novels leaned drunkenly against one another, and plucked one from its dusty slot – 'how about Victor Hugo?'

'In fact, he seemed downright disinterested.'

She picked up another. 'Thomas Hardy?'

'Perhaps he feels out of his depth?'

'James Joyce?'

'Typical small-town policeman. I bet he's on the tourism committee. Probably wants to hush it all up—'

'I'll have a look underneath, shall I?' Willow knelt down, opening the sideboard's cupboards to reveal a jumbled mess.

'I mean, don't you think you'd be more *shocked* at discovering a body on your beat?'

She shifted through tattered papers, empty boxes and a Philips Bakelite radio that had clearly seen better days. Unable to resist, she said, 'I'd hardly call thousands of acres of bush a *beat*, would you?'

'Perhaps I'll go and see him.'

This was what Willow had been afraid of; Ben's overactive imagination placed squarely between a mystery and its solution. 'Oh!' she said triumphantly – and hopefully with a measure of distraction – as she withdrew a book nestled deep at the back. 'I've struck gold!'

'No mining references, please.'

'Sorry. But look . . . *The Collected Verse of A.B. Paterson.*'

'Oh?'

Success. She flicked to the title page. 'The original 1921 edition, no less.'

Ben appeared to recover from his tirade. 'Perhaps you might . . . read me something?' he said, cradling his bandaged arm theatrically.

'Sure.' She sat on the floor, nestling back against the sofa. 'Any requests?'

He squinted as he deliberated, an expression of his she found inexplicably charming. '"Clancy of the Overflow"?'

What a surprise, she wanted to say, but didn't. She loved that she knew her husband so well, knew that he'd choose the famous poem about the nameless lawyer living in an over-crowded city who yearns for the freedom of a drover's life.

'Not allegorical, is it?' she murmured.

'I like city living too,' he said, 'but it's nice to dream. My ideal would be . . .'

'Yes?'

'Towerhurst . . . and London.'

'You've never been to London!'

'I feel like it's in my near future. Roger's been inviting us there for years.'

'Roger?'

'Roger Masters.' Ben tucked a strand of hair behind her ear so that her tummy – even after all these years – fluttered. 'Summers at Towerhurst. Winters in London.'

'How will we manage that, then?'

Ben hesitated. 'Oh. I see what you mean. Two hemispheres, opposite seasons. Very pesky.'

'Pesky,' she agreed. 'Now, Clancy . . .' She opened the book, then ran her finger down the index, noting that a few specks of sand fell out from the spine; this book had been read on a beach. She cleared her throat.

'I had written him a letter which I had, for want of
    better
Knowledge, sent to where I met him down the
    Lachlan years ago;
He was shearing when I knew him, so I sent the letter
    to him,
Just on spec, addressed as follows, "Clancy, of The
    Overflow" . . .'

When she finished the poem, she said, 'My choice now.' She turned again to the index. So *many* familiar ballads. She'd studied them at school – every Australian child did – but she also recalled her father, Rob, reading to her at bedtime, the dim light from her lamp casting a shadow across the room to where Ivy and Ash slept in their beds, four years younger than Willow and yet to discover the words of Banjo Paterson.

'"The Man from Snowy River"?' she said.

'Bit predictable.' Ben laughed. 'But why not?'

'Pot, kettle.' She ran her finger down the index once more, then turned the pages; 21, 22 . . . 26, 27. 'I can't believe it . . . someone's ripped out "The Man from Snowy River"!'

'What?'

'That's treasonous!'

'I'll say,' Ben agreed.

Willow flicked through the book, looking for further sac-rilege, and as she did so, something slipped from the back.

'What's that?' Ben said.

'A card . . .' She picked it up, turning it over. 'No. Not a card. A photo.' It seemed somehow familiar, but not immediately recognisable. She peered a little closer. It was a picture of four young people, all handsome in their own way. Two men – both dressed in the distinctive World War Two Australian Imperial Force uniform – and two women wearing form-fitting skirts at odds with the wild background of the rainforest. One of the men wore a Santa hat.

Willow frowned. 'I recognise this photo, kind of . . .'

'Let me see.'

She gave it to him, then crossed the room to the square photo of Rose Munro and Colette's nephew, Daniel. There they were, him in his Christmas hat, Rose smiling, pulling him close. But it was just the two of them. Quickly, she removed the back of the frame only to discover the photo had been folded in half.

'The two pictures match!' she said, glancing at Ben, who was peering closely at the image as if he needed glasses. A sudden fear gripped her that his fall, his concussion, had damaged his eyesight. She turned the photo over and read the caption. '*Left to right: Rose, Daniel, Grace, Puds. Christmas 1940.*'

'But . . .' Still Ben stared at the image. Was he trying to see right through it?

Willow told him what Colette had said about Rose, Grace and Daniel.

'I don't know who Puds is, but by the look of this photo he's madly in love with Grace. See his expression? That's a smitten man if I ever saw one. Though' – she frowned – 'Grace doesn't look particularly pleased with herself. Gosh, what a sad-looking girl.'

Still Ben didn't answer.

'Love?' she said, sitting beside him.

'But . . . this necklace . . .' Ben said. He was pointing at both women – Rose and Grace – back and forth, and now Willow noticed they both wore an identical pendant in the shape of a dog. 'I've seen it before.'

'Really?' She raised an eyebrow. 'Where?'

'This necklace . . .' he said slowly, a memory clearly dawning, 'is the reason I think the body is a woman.'

'Why?'

'I saw it. I remember it . . . the hand.' He frowned. 'The hand, Willow.' He tapped the picture, pointing from one woman to the other. 'One of these necklaces was clutched in the hand of the body down that mine.'

ॐ

Sergeant Griffin stared at the photo. 'Are you sure?'

'I'm certain.' Ben pointed, just as he had done at Towerhurst that morning, from Rose Munro to Grace Grey, and back again. 'It's the *very* same necklace I found on the body.'

A sigh.

'And look! They're *both* wearing one! Doesn't that tell you something?' He hesitated, glancing uncertainly at Willow.

The two of them sat, rather like naughty school children, opposite Sergeant Griffin, in his sitting room. 'This is my home, just so as you know,' he'd muttered as he'd opened the door to find them huddled on the step, sheltering from the afternoon's onshore breeze. 'The station opens Monday afternoon.'

'We know,' Willow had replied. 'But my husband's remembered something you really need to hear.'

They'd been ushered inside and, despite their intrusion, served tea as black as a burned stump.

Sergeant Griffin set the photos in his lap. 'And where is this necklace now?'

'I . . .' Ben hesitated, glancing uncertainly at Willow, who gave him a small smile of encouragement. 'Well, I assumed you'd have it?'

'Me?'

'Didn't you find it when you retrieved the . . .' Ben's voice petered out. In the background, the mantel clock ticked, and the gentle roll of the sea sounded through the cottage's old windows. It was a stone building, out on the point, not far from the lighthouse. 'One of the original keeper's houses,' Mira Holmes had told them moments after giving over directions, and only seconds before openly asking the reason for their intended visit. 'We just want to call to say thank you for his part in Ben's rescue,' Willow had said evasively.

'Ben.' Sergeant Griffin leaned forward. 'I don't know how to say this, but . . . we found *no* necklace on the body.'

'But I *saw* it! Clutched in the hand of the . . .' Ben shivered. 'Of the skeleton.'

The sergeant took a deep, calm breath. 'Well, if there *was* a necklace . . . is there any chance you picked it up, put it in your pocket?'

'No . . . I don't think so.' Ben frowned. 'The whole thing was a bit of a blur. I slipped in and out of dreams.'

'Dreams?' The sergeant raised an eyebrow.

'Well, not dreams, as such.'

'Hallucinations?'

'No, I . . .' Ben trailed off as Willow squeezed his hand. He looked exhausted. Aside from his sprained wrist, he'd sustained a hundred bruises, and a concussion that was clearly more severe than the doctor had suggested.

'Look,' Sergeant Griffin said, his face softening, 'you've had a terrible shock. It's only natural that you'd be feeling a bit . . . confused.'

'No, I really—'

'Darling . . .' said Willow. She shouldn't have brought him here.

'But I did. I picked it up. It lay in my palm. A fox pendant with a sapphire eye.'

The sergeant nodded. 'I suspect you saw this photo before your accident, hence you imagined the necklace. Is that possible?'

It was possible, Willow realised. Gently, she took Ben's hand. 'We did glance at the photos, didn't we? On our first morning, after coffee?' And they had, as they'd lingered in the front room after their photo, after they'd made love. She flushed at the thought of it.

'I suppose so . . .'

'That makes sense, doesn't it?'

'I was sure she was holding—'

'*She?*' Sergeant Griffin frowned. 'What gave you the impression the body was female?'

'Well, the necklace . . .'

The silence stretched. 'I can see you've had quite a shock, Mr Andrews.'

Ben gave a muffled protest.

'I also appreciate you trying to help. But from the state of the remains' – at this, Sergeant Griffin gave a sad shake of his head – 'they must have been down there for decades. Though we'll know more in time. At this stage, though, I can tell you nothing. No identity. No sex. Nothing.'

Ben nodded slowly. He got to his feet. 'Can I use your toilet?'

'Down the hall, on the left.'

When he was gone, Willow gave a small grimace. 'I'm so sorry about all of this. About everything.' She felt embarrassed. Not because of Ben, but because of herself, for encouraging his imagination, which was overactive at the best of times. She should have listened to the doctor; her husband needed rest.

'You've made quite the splash in our little community.'

They'd certainly arrived on the scene with a bang. Was it possible they'd never heard of Towerhurst only days before? It already felt like a lifetime ago. 'My husband spent nearly twenty-four hours down that mine . . . I think he simply wants to know more. For his own sake.'

'As do we all, Mrs Andrews,' Sergeant Griffin said, standing, briefly rubbing his leg. 'I have a cold case in a place without any cold cases.'

'Because . . . he really is like a dog with a bone when he gets the sniff of a story,' Willow insisted, thinking of the look on Ben's face when he thought he'd made a connection – real or imagined – between the body and necklaces.

'There's no story here.' Sergeant Griffin paused. 'Crikey, he's not a journalist, is he?'

'A novelist.'

'Well, that's okay then.'

Willow sensed she'd let an opportunity slide by. 'But he has been known to dabble' – she crossed her fingers – 'in true crime.'

A raised eyebrow. A look of concern? 'Is that so?'

'Yes.'

Sergeant Griffin appraised her. 'Well, I tell you what . . . I'll keep you posted with anything we discover. Straight from the horse's mouth, so to speak. Off the record for now. How does that sound?'

Willow looked at him in surprise. 'You will?'

'There's no need to take this on yourselves. You just leave it to the professionals.'

'You?'

'Me.'

She looked at him over her red glasses. 'Out of interest, though . . . did you know the girls?'

'I'm sorry?'

'Rose Munro and Grace Grey . . . did you know them?' At the mention of their names, Sergeant Griffin cleared his throat. Or was that – Willow looked closer – a flinch? Then he laughed, a little insincerely, she thought.

'What did I just say? Leave it to the professionals.'

'It's more about researching the history of Towerhurst. So, did you know them?' She smiled. 'Off the record.'

He sighed, and pursed his lips. 'I knew them in passing.'

'And what were they like—'

With a flurry, Ben returned. He looked a little fresher, the remains of water clinging to the tips of his hair. 'Nice paintings,' he said, referring to several watercolours adorning the hallway's wall. 'Locally done, are they?'

The sergeant nodded. 'Now, Ben . . . I suggest you follow the doctor's orders. Rest for you.' He ushered them to the door, and Willow noticed – as she had the night before – just how pronounced his limp was.

'Did you injure yourself during the search?'

'Old war wound,' he said dismissively. 'No need for you to worry. About that. Or the investigation.'

The investigation . . . Willow turned, remembering something. 'And what about the suitcase?'

'It's all gone to Hobart.' The sergeant smiled reassuringly. 'As I said. I'll keep you posted. Straight from the horse's mouth.' And with that, he shut the door.

It was only after they arrived home, and she'd tucked Ben into a bed upstairs, that Willow noticed the empty picture frame hanging on the wall. She frowned. She'd forgotten to pick up the photos – those identical ones taken at Christmas 1940 – though she couldn't remember seeing them when she'd stood to leave. After she'd searched her bag and the car to no avail, she was forced to conclude that she must have dropped them. And perhaps it was a lingering guilt at her carelessness, or the mystery of the body down the mine, but that night she dreamed of Grace Grey and Rose Munro; two sepia-toned faces, and those twin necklaces glinting around their necks.

Chapter 27

Towerhurst, Tasmania

October 1939

During the night, cocooned in her warm bed, the last of Grace's lightheaded euphoria had ebbed away. She'd almost drowned, hadn't she? Because of Daniel? Run across the sand and out to sea to get away from him, and his 'knucklehead' friends. That Irish boy had humiliated her, tricked her, all for the sake of a bet. Even the pale dawn creeping feebly through the window couldn't shine a brighter light on that. And Grace couldn't help but think that perhaps Mother had been right. *More* than right. Not only was she very, very difficult to love, she was, it seemed, impossible even to like.

She reached to her bedside table and picked up Banjo Paterson. Even as she opened the book, grains of sand scattered on the bed, a sprinkling to remind her of the day before. She wiped them angrily away and, in doing so, knocked over a cup on her nightstand, sending a trickle of cold tea dribbling to the floor. She sighed, turning to page 148. There was one of her favourite poems: 'Hard Luck'.

> . . . I haven't got a bite or bed,
> I'm absolutely stuck;
> So keep this lesson in your head:
> Don't over trust your luck!

Here was a friend she could trust: ballads would never trick her, or betray her. Their companionship came without price. But she'd read all Banjo's works and now she wanted more. Perhaps, she thought, she might attempt to write something of her own? How hard could it be? From her bedside table, she took a sheet of airmail paper so transparent that it ripped under the tip of her pencil. Then, she'd lightened her touch.

> He made me angry so,
> Disrespect is such a bore,
> It made me tip my tea right over
> And knock it to the floor

She frowned, comparing her verse with *Hard Luck*, in which every second line rhymed. Her effort wasn't so bad, was it? She scrawled it out, and tried again.

> That day he will soon rue
> Disrespect I do abhor
> It made me knock my tea askew
> And tip it to the floor

No, no, no. She scrunched the paper, throwing it away.

> He'll remember what he did to me:
> He made a sordid bet
> Which caused me to flee,
> Then he showed a deep regret.

She scrawled a line through the verse and started again.

An hour after sunrise, Grace abandoned her efforts. Why didn't her poems sound like Banjo Paterson's? It was thoroughly maddening. His words were hardly Shakespeare, after all. Her various tutors had taught her the greats: Tennyson, Burns, Wordsworth. *Real* poets, not silly Australian bushmen who could only write in rhyme.

There was a knock at the door and, a moment later, Uncle Marcus cautiously peered around it. 'How're you feeling, my dear girl?'

Grace gathered the scattered pages. 'I'm . . . fine. Just fine.' To her surprise, she realised it was true. On waking, she'd been certain she would have a fever, that her ordeal would be the death of her, just as her doctor in Grosvenor Square had predicted. At the very least, all that salt water should have chaffed her skin, left her red and raw, but the mirror told a different story. In the muted morning light, her complexion was unlike ever before; a slight flush coloured her cheeks. In fact, she had to concede that she looked, if not pretty, at least tolerably nice.

Uncle Marcus picked up a sheet of paper, scanning its contents with a single eyebrow raised. 'You have some talent, I think?'

She flushed.

'Do you know,' he continued, 'what I love *most* about Banjo Paterson's work?'

'No.'

Tentatively, he sat on the end of her bed. 'His poems are often laced with humour. They poke fun at everyday life. They have a certain lightness about them.' He held out his hand. 'What else have you got?'

Warily, she passed him another sheet of paper.

'*He'll remember what he did to me / He made a sordid bet / Which caus-ed me to flee / Then he showed a deep regret.*' He pronounced *caused* with two syllables so that the cadence of the poem improved. 'I can feel your anger at Daniel. About yesterday.'

'*You* were mad at him too.'

'True, true.' Uncle Marcus was back to his calm self. After Aunt Olive had stormed off, Daniel apologised once more, and Grace saw that even her uncle had begun to thaw. 'I could see the boy was genuinely sorry. We all make mistakes, which means,' he conceded, 'we should all have the capacity for forgiveness, me included. Because holding onto bitterness, jealousy, anger, it's like . . . buying poison intended for another, then drinking it yourself. And what sort of madman,' he added, 'would ever do that?'

'I should forgive Daniel?'

'You could try. Perhaps start through your writing?'

Her writing? Grace flushed with pleasure. 'Lace it with humour?' she suggested. 'Like Banjo often does?'

He smiled. 'That's my girl.'

'But I don't know where to begin.'

'Begin,' he said, 'at the very beginning.'

In the end, she turned back to her favourite ballad – 'The Man from Snowy River' – for inspiration. She scrawled on every inch of paper. Wrote on front and back. Then, with a clean sheet, she copied her final version, then went to the window and peered down at the moon gate as she recited it in her head. It wasn't perfect. It didn't *quite* have Banjo's cadence, but what of it? She turned on her heel, seeking Uncle Marcus, the poem in her hand.

Chapter 28

Central London

December 2004

Libby left Paperchase and started back towards Grosvenor Square, a bag of stationery swinging from her arm. The day had clouded over and she relished the Dickensian gloom as she took a shortcut through an alley, wishing that gaslights lit the way.

She'd promised Ivy that she wouldn't look further into her father's investigations, but the story her aunt had told her had only piqued her interest. An unidentified body? In addition to an anonymous legacy? Libby couldn't help but wonder, as she emerged from the alley, if these two things were connected.

❧

On her return to the empty apartment, she spread her purchases on the kitchen bench – a notebook, a packet of sticky plastic tabs, and a Moleskine diary – opening the latter, and writing her address in pencil beside the text which read, *In case of loss, please return to.* Beneath that, on the empty line titled, *As a reward:* $, she crossed out the dollar sign, replacing it with a poorly rendered cup of coffee, grinning a little as she did so.

Ivy's revelation about her dad's experience down the mine certainly threw up far more questions than it answered. 'But,' Libby had asked, '*who* was the body down the mine? Why did it affect Mum so much? And what of Daniel McGillycuddy? Because Dad had definitely been keen to find him, or his past.'

Ivy had only shaken her head. 'I don't know anything about a ballad writer. We lived in Sydney at the time, love. It was only because of a phone call from Willow that day they drove back from visiting the sergeant that we knew the details. We didn't really discuss it again.'

Didn't *really*? Those final words played through Libby's mind as she clicked on the kettle, then leaned back on the bench, surveying her purchases, wondering what Krish would say to her now. He'd always laughed at her study ritual, and the amount of stationery it required, occasionally photocopying her extensive plans and trying, mostly in vain, to follow their military precision to a T. But that had been *before*, and her flair for organisation was something that had died along with him, at the same time as she'd locked away her feelings, speaking of them to no one, even when people asked. Then, after a time, they stopped asking altogether.

The click of the kettle brought her back to the present, and she glanced down to see that in her hands, she clutched two mugs, instead of the single one required.

❧

Twenty minutes later, tired of the solitude and her own racing imagination, Libby stood on Miss Winman's doorstep, armed with a packet of tea, the satchel, and a fairly flimsy excuse for company. 'It's a long shot,' she said, when the door opened, 'but did you know the Grey family? They lived across the square before the war.'

Miss Winman simply sipped the drink she was holding, which was suspiciously amber in the dim hallway light. 'The Greys?' she said, one eyebrow raised. 'I should say so. I wouldn't say our families were close, but . . .' She shrugged, swinging the door wide. For the first time during her weeks in London, and after several unaccepted invitations, Libby stepped inside.

❧

Moments later, despite an ineffective protest, Miss Winman poured a second stiff drink for her guest. 'It's just a little medicinal, my dear.'

'Thank you,' Libby murmured, beaten. What did it matter? It was over the yardarm somewhere. She observed the living room, which was charmingly trapped in a bygone era; green wallpaper, a portrait of the queen, a golden mantel clock that wasn't yet showing noon.

'You said once,' she fumbled, unsure of how to proceed, 'that you'd been here in this apartment since 1934?'

Miss Winman sat by the window, and Libby perched beside her. 'I see I shall have to be careful what I say to you,' she grinned. 'Though you're quite right. My parents moved here when I was just a girl. But that was many years after the Greys arrived. What part of their history are you interested in? The war?'

'Yes . . . how did you know?'

A laugh. 'My dear! There weren't many fascists on Grosvenor Square, I can tell you.'

Libby stared down at Franklin D. Roosevelt, whose bronze form had watched over the space for forty years.

'The Americans requisitioned the Greys' house during the war, did you know that?' Miss Winman continued. 'I believe that Edeline Grey *agreed* to it – though I don't suppose she had much choice – on the proviso she'd be given more comfortable accommodation at Holloway prison.'

'Did she return after?'

'For a time.' A hesitation. 'So, what's all this about, my dear?'

Libby produced Milton Twiggs' article as she explained

that her father had come to London thirty years ago, and had been researching Edeline Grey. She considered going into the details, but she didn't know what they were herself.

'It wouldn't be unusual for a writer to be looking into the Grey family.' Miss Winman scanned the article. 'Was your father a biographer?'

'No.' She thought of the business card – *Roger Masters. For all your biography needs* – that had slipped from between the pages of *The Ballads of Daniel McGillycuddy*.

'You're sure? There was a slew of profiles written about Britain's fascists during the seventies, it was quite *de rigueur*. Enough time had passed, I suppose, that people had stopped asking *what* had happened in the country's politics during the lead up to the war, and tried to understand *why*. But as far as I can see, some things are beyond explanation.'

'Did you know the family well?'

'Not really, but my father's job was to keep an eye on the comings and goings of the Blackshirts, of which Edeline was of course one.'

Libby raised her eyebrows.

'Oh yes, he was part of a department that followed hundreds of them. That's how we came to be here, actually; the apartment came with the job. My parents had the opportunity to buy it after the war. Not a bad investment.'

'Not bad at all.'

'Anyway, the fascism . . . although my father didn't tell me much about it at the time, I overheard things.'

'What things?'

'Well, for one, I recall my parents talking about this.' She tapped her finger on a paragraph halfway down the article.

'The trip Edeline Grey made to Berlin? With her daughter?'

Miss Winman frowned, clearly trying to recall. 'Like mother, like daughter, I suppose? Now what was her name, the girl?'

'Grace. Her name was' – Libby referred to the article again – 'Grace.'

'That's right. Not a very appropriate name, really. A terribly *ungraceful* girl, not much to look at. Slightly odd, apparently, too.'

'You never met her?'

'I never *talked* to her that I recall. I only saw her in passing.'

Libby unfolded the article to reveal the photo: a blonde, elegant woman, presumably Edeline Grey, smiling at the camera; a young, pretty, light-haired girl by her side.

Libby indicated the latter. 'This is her?'

Miss Winman leaned in and, from the top of her head, took a pair of glasses, and squinted at the image. 'Goodness no! But she *does* look familiar . . .' She tapped the uncaptioned photo with a gnarled finger. 'Yes, yes, this is . . . oh gosh, what was her name?'

'Grace,' Libby insisted.

'No, no,' said Miss Winman. 'A flower . . . Lily? Heather?'

'Erm . . . Dahlia?'

'No, no, no . . . Rose!'

'Rose?'

'That's the one. I went dancing with her on a few occasions. In fact' – her brow wrinkled – 'I was there when the two girls were evacuated from London. A last-minute decision, apparently. Oh yes, I remember that day.'

'You *remember* that day?'

A nod. 'It wasn't long before war was declared. I *remember* that because I used their departure as cover for my own kind of departure. *A departure from decorum,* as my father would have said.'

'What kind of decorum?' Libby prompted.

'Sorry?'

'What kind of decorum did you depart from?'

'The notion that I was too young for a sweetheart.' The memory brought a small sad smile with it. 'His name was Jonathan. The love of my life.'

'What happened to him?'

'He was killed,' Miss Winman said matter-of-factly, 'in October 1939. The phoney war, they called it. I can tell you, my dear, it wasn't so phoney for some of us. He was the only man I've ever loved.'

'I'm so sorry.'

'My father arranged a job for me at the ministry a year later as a secretary, but it was miserable watching the reports of death roll in. So I defied him.' A small smile. 'I became a nurse, and went to the front.'

Libby couldn't help but consider how differently she'd responded to her own loss. She had, in fact, been older than Miss Winman by several years when Krish died, yet the woman sat before her had upped and gone to war. What had Libby done? Nothing, that was what.

'That was brave. Rushing to help others.'

'It was a reaction really. I believed that if I could help just one man return to his sweetheart, I would have done my job.'

Libby smiled, but before she could ask more, Miss Winman glanced at her watch. 'By the time I returned from the front, Edeline Grey had gone from Grosvenor Square and Kingston was dead. I believe that Grace and Rose returned in forty-five, though I never saw them myself.'

'As late as 1945?' said Libby, thinking of her World War Two tour of London and the description the guide gave of chaotic evacuations of children to England's countryside. The older ones often returned to the city or joined up well before the war was over. 'Where on *earth* were they evacuated to?'

'Oh.' Miss Winman hesitated, realisation dawning on her face. 'I see this is *perhaps* something I should have remembered before. They went to Tasmania – to Edeline's brother. He lived in a remote part; I remember Rose lamenting it the last time I saw her.'

Libby's heart thumped. 'Not the west coast?'

'Possibly. It was an awfully long time ago. But from what you've told me about your father's fiction writing, it makes sense that he might have been interested in the Greys' Tasmanian connection?'

The *Towerhurst* connection more like it. Quickly – as Miss Winman glanced at her watch once more – Libby told her about her mother's legacy.

'And what does she say about it? Your mother?' Sam had asked the very same question on *The Albatross*, and with a small zing of something she didn't want to acknowledge she wondered momentarily whether she'd hear from him – as promised – before Thursday.

'I haven't . . . told her about Dad's satchel.'

'I see.' She sensed no judgement in her neighbour's tone of voice. 'I won't ask why, but let's play a game here. Say Marcus Foxton did own the house, perhaps Edeline inherited it from her brother and . . . left it to your mother? Hence your father's research?'

Both women looked a little disturbed by the theory. A fascist in the family?

'I do wonder,' continued Miss Winman, 'where they got to in the end, Grace Grey and that lovely Rose Munro. There were rumours that Edeline and Grace left – illegally – for Paris after the war, but—'

'What did you say?'

'Many of the Blackshirts had their passports confiscated, you see? So if Edeline and Grace left the country . . .'

'No, sorry . . . I meant . . . did you say Rose *Munro*?'

'Did I?' said Miss Winman, surprised.

'Yes.'

'Well, there you are then. Funny what the old mind retains.'

Libby had already tried to call both numbers written on Roger Masters' card – translating them into post-STD numbers with a little help from the internet – that morning without any luck. Now it seemed the tide had rolled the other way. 'My father had a contact number for a Molly *Munro* – do you have any idea who that might have been?'

Miss Winman set her face in a mask of concentration and after a time, it cleared, understanding dawning. '*Molly* Munro? Well, that must have been Rose's mother. The Grey housekeeper. There you have it then: your father was simply writing a biography on Edeline Grey.' She hesitated. 'Have you asked your aunts? What do they say on the matter of the legacy?'

'Very little,' Libby admitted.

'Tricky.'

'Yes.'

'Still, they're lovely girls, aren't they?'

'Who?'

'Your aunts. Bought the place in seventy-six, I think. It's true I rarely see them, but whenever they pop by we always have a wonderful time.'

In that moment, one of Libby's questions was answered. Her father *couldn't* have stayed with Ash and Ivy in 1975.

Miss Winman stood. 'Now, my dear, I must go. Tai chi. Want to join me?' She drained her drink, the wisdom of which Libby stopped herself from questioning.

She slipped the article back into the satchel. 'Another time, thank you. Perhaps I can come by again and . . .' But the older woman had already disappeared, only to return minutes later clad in an alarming outfit that might have come straight off a seventies ski slope.

Libby hesitated, but couldn't resist. '*That's* your tai chi outfit?'

A shrug. 'It's December. If I don't wear this I'm utterly frozen by the end. Now' — she looked at her watch — 'you're sure you won't join me?'

'No, but thank you.'

Bustling, Miss Winman looped a yellow headband around her brow, completing the colourful outfit. 'Why don't you find out who owns this Towerhurst now? Ask them a few questions? Perhaps they have the deeds.'

'Do you think that's possible?' asked Libby.

'In my limited experience, people living in old houses relish discovering their history. Have you found anything online?'

'I . . . I haven't looked.'

'You haven't *looked*? Honestly. And they say Generation X is resourceful.' Miss Winman stepped out into the hallway. 'Why not simply *oogle* it, my dear?'

And for the second time in as many minutes, Libby planned to do something she couldn't believe she hadn't done before.

Chapter 29

Grosvenor Square, London

December 2004

Back in the empty apartment, Libby watched from the window as Miss Winman's fluoro-clad form strode confidently down Carlos Place. She wished she had even a dash of the old woman's flair: her confidence was almost infectious and yet Libby realised, as she looked down at her black cardigan and tights, she was somehow immune. But she looked fine, didn't she? Smart. Neat. And anyway, black was useful. Black was practical. Black set off her blonde hair nicely, Ash had always said. Or had she *always* said that? Once or twice, Libby thought. Perhaps several years ago.

She went to find her new diary and, for the first time in as long as she could remember, wrote *To Do* at the top of a fresh page. Item number one, *Speak to Miss Winman* was technically cheating but allowed her to start as she meant to go on, ticking off each task as quickly as she could. Beneath that she wrote: *Go shopping for clothes*. Then beneath that: *Google Towerhurst*, before crossing out the *G,* and smiling.

She opened her laptop and, within moments, the house appeared on her screen, the star of a slick, sleek website. Towerhurst was almost, but not quite, as she recalled it. The corrugated roof, the cast iron detailing, the wide verandah spilling from the threshold to the beyond. And the tower, of course, reaching ever upward, the portholes like golden eyes in the sky. But things had changed: the paint no longer peeled, a neat lawn trimmed its edge, and a bright white gravel path led around the house, presumably to the moon gate and beyond.

It was a B&B now, and Libby scrolled with interest through the small but impressive photo gallery. Gone was the tattered wallpaper, musty carpets, and mould. The house had been tastefully restored to its former glory and sun streamed through the sash windows, painting the floor in squares of gold. The faded sign had been replaced: *Towerhurst Retreat.*

There was a photo, too, of the owners. Ah yes! That was them. Denny and Jess Joyce. Libby recalled with fondness the way that Jess had winked at her over her mother's shoulder, and there was no mistaking her eyes – one brown, one blue – nor had Denny's cheeky grin changed: it was exactly the same as the one he'd thrown her way as they'd paused at the top of the water-scoured driveway. Libby marvelled that, in the shade of the verandah, Jess might not have aged a day, albeit her topknot was now grey instead of brown.

The website was as tidy as the house's interior, with minimal information, a booking link to an external provider, and a single page – not several, as Libby had hoped – labelled *History.*

Towerhurst, a beautiful (if we do say so ourselves!) Federation house buried in the rainforest on Tasmania's west coast, was built in 1895 by Cornelius Foxton. After years travelling the Orient, his growing interest in geology drove him to Tasmania, where he pursued tin, copper and gold leases before finally settling in Westford. An eccentric who liked 'intermittent' privacy (according to his diaries) he set about building Towerhurst north of the tidal Joey River. He was a captain in Tasmania's 40th Battalion, and had a distinguished war record. In 1920,

Towerhurst passed into the hands of his nephew, Marcus
Foxton (1899–1974), a writer and publisher, who married local
woman, Olive Agnew.

There! Marcus Foxton *had* owned Towerhurst. And Olive
Foxton – the woman her father had interviewed in 1975 – was
his wife.

According to the records, Marcus sold his uncle's claims to
focus on his writing. He moved to Launceston in the forties,
though Olive (1899–1976) remained until 1973, after which
time the house was broadly uninhabited.

We purchased Towerhurst in 1985 and spent a decade
restoring her to her former glory. The house has a small historical archive, so we do hope you'll ask us more when you
come to stay.

Libby opened the *Contact* page, feeling somewhat foolish
for thinking that Jess and Denny might remember her, but
reminding them of that day in 1985, nonetheless. There was
an option for attachments on the form, and she uploaded a
photo of Martin Twiggs' article, then typed the last sentences
of her message.

Have you come across anything about Edeline Grey, who I under-
stand was Marcus Foxton's sister? I've attached an article here, but
this is all I have to go on. Also . . . did you ever discover the identity
of the body found down the mine behind Towerhurst in 1974?

Her fingers hovered as she deliberated – should she give a
reason for her questions? – then, making an uncharacteristi-
cally quick decision, she pressed *Send*, experiencing a zing of
satisfaction as she closed her laptop and crossed another item
from her new *To Do* list.

Chapter 30

Towerhurst, Tasmania

October 1939

Grace was anxious to get outside before the rain started again. As she entered the kitchen in a flurry, her bag slung over her thin shoulder, she stopped short. Rose was sitting at the table, sipping tea.

'I didn't expect you up so early.'

She could see Rose bristle at her words. Grace hadn't really thought of how she might be adjusting to their new life, but in London she had always been busy. Here, she seemed, maybe, a little lost. How odd that Grace was finding things so interesting, while Rose seemed simply bored.

'I'm off to see the mine,' she said, putting down her cup.

'The mine?'

'You know . . . where men dig in the ground for all that shiny metal.' Rose held up her fox pendant, flashing it in the morning sun.

'I thought you hated the wilderness?' Grace opened a cupboard, and put a tin in her bag.

'A mine is hardly wilderness. And you? Where are you going with Marcus's secret stash of biscuits?'

'To the waterfall.'

Rose frowned. 'Alone?'

'Yes.'

'Why?'

Grace paused by the door. 'Why not?'

Rose stirred a spoonful of sugar into her tea. 'Plenty of *water* there, do be careful, won't you?'

'I'll try my best,' Grace said, surprising herself a little with a show of nonchalance as she threw her bag back over her shoulder.

It had been less than a week since her adventure on the beach and Rose clearly felt obliged to say something more. 'Be . . . careful, won't you? Don't make a fool of yourself again. We're already the talk of the town.'

Grace hesitated, then smiled. She could see that, somehow, she had unnerved her chaperone, and it felt good.

&

Half an hour later Marcus finally came down for breakfast. His hair was dishevelled, and he was doing a fine impression of a scatterbrained professor; his tie skew-whiff, the bristles on his face forming a grey-blond mask of benign neglect. Rose held out a coffee; black and strong, just the way he liked it.

'I'm looking forward to today, Marcus.'

He looked up, as if he hadn't noticed she was there. 'Today?'

'Mount Lyell.'

Marcus took the cup, his hand brushing against hers. 'Ah, yes. Yes. Is that today?'

'It *is* Monday, isn't it?'

'You tell me.'

She laughed. It was a game they had begun to play; his vagueness cured by her clarity. 'We're due there at ten.'

He looked at his watch. 'Bags of time.' The large pat of butter he began to spread on a slice of Colette McGillycuddy's fresh-baked bread was soon covered in honey and piled on a plate. 'You can drive if you like.'

'I don't have a licence.' Though she *had* taken several lessons from Edeline's chauffeur over the years.

'I wouldn't bother too much about that down here, my girl, not really anyone to check. Apart from Sergeant Griffin, and I'm quite sure he'd let you off. Don't find yourself alone with him, though, will you? Wandering hands, and all.'

'I'll try my best.'

'Good, good. Borrow Olive's car whenever you like.' He glanced around the room as though he'd misplaced something of great value. 'Is Grace coming? Where on earth's she got to?'

Rose suppressed a sigh. 'She's gone to the waterfall.'

'Alone?'

'Of course.'

'Is that wise?'

'She's unlikely to go into the pool. She was hiding a book in her bag. You're encouraging her, you know?' They'd begun to talk like this. Candidly. Openly. Always when Olive was elsewhere. Which was often. She'd spent the last four days in Westford with her mother, whose health was fading daily.

Marcus chewed his bread thoughtfully. 'I think she's lacked encouragement in the past.'

'Who?'

'Grace.'

'What do you mean?'

'Does she get along with Edeline?'

Rose hesitated. 'As far as I'm aware. I'm only the house-keeper's daughter.'

Marcus appraised her, then nodded. 'Of course.'

His acceptance of her self-deprecation was demeaning. She waited for him to give her some encouragement – *You seem rather more than just a housekeeper's daughter* – as he might have done for Grace, but he only turned to the notepad in his hand, flipping to a blank page, pen poised. In the set of his brow,

Rose searched for signs of Edeline, but there was nothing there. He seemed to float through life unaware of the nuance of his surroundings, a complete contrast to his sister, who had a way of seeing the world with a certain clarity that meant little escaped her notice. From what Rose understood, it was both blessing and curse. True, Edeline had seen the war coming years before, but she'd also been unable to turn a blind eye to the mistress Kingston thought he hid so well. No . . . it was their marriage that was the greatest curse of all; a match made in hell, and instead of an heir they'd been left with Grace, who'd been sickly from the day she was born.

She emptied her cup in the sink. It was 9 a.m.

'Queenstown's a forty-five-minute drive, isn't it, Marcus?' She was looking forward to the time alone with him.

'Hmm?'

'Don't you think—'

Ratta-tat-tat.

Rose sighed. A visitor at this hour? She touched Marcus's shoulder gently as she passed.

ॐ

Daniel stood on the verandah, cap in hand, a bucket at his feet. He'd hoped that Grace would open the door, but instead it was Rose.

'Daniel.'

He saw her surreptitiously smoothing her hair as she smiled coyly. It made him wonder about Richard Holmes' claims that he was surely winning her over.

'Brought something for me?' Rose put her hands on her hips as she peered into the bucket at the spiky fish lying at the bottom.

'Well, no . . .'

'Gosh, that looks frightening.'

He hesitated. 'I wanted to see how Grace is.'

'She's fine.'

'I've been feeling guilty—'

'About the situation on the beach? It's about time someone gave her a little fright. It will have done her a power of good.'

If anything, this made Daniel feel worse. He looked over Rose's shoulder. 'I'd like to apologise.'

'You already did.'

'Properly.'

'With a fish?'

He blushed, and Rose laughed. It sounded cruel.

'So . . . is Grace in?'

Rose raised an eyebrow and leaned in close, whispering in his ear: 'She's gone to her secret place.' She put a finger to her lips.

From inside the house, a voice echoed down that hall. 'Where the bloody hell are my biscuits?'

Daniel picked up his bucket. 'Where?'

'To the waterfall.'

Before she could say anything else, Daniel stepped off the verandah, following the track around the back of the house that led under the moon gate, and into the rainforest.

࿐

From the edge of the clearing, Daniel watched Grace contemplate her next move. Her face was set in a grimace, one toe touching the water at the very point where – from his vantage point – the sun had set the glossy surface alight. In her white dress, with her hair loose, her fragility was almost pretty. It reminded Daniel of the moment she landed down from the sassafras, petals tumbling like confetti around her. In profile, she'd looked like a faerie queen. Then she'd given him a cool look, and the illusion had vanished.

Now she took a step into the water, determination and fear chasing each other across her pale face. Even from where he stood, Daniel saw the whites of her knuckles as she gripped the stony edge, kicking until she lay horizontal, spluttering, splashing. After a minute, she gave up, letting her feet sink. The water was only thigh deep, and her wet dress clung to her straight body. She slapped the stone in anger.

Daniel recalled his first days at Westford pool. The frustration, the way it felt to see tiny children leaping in the water without a care in the world, his embarrassment as he clung to the tiled edge. He felt a surge of compassion for her, admiration even, that she would attempt such a thing. Particularly after what had happened.

She pulled herself from the pool, and her chest heaved as she leaned her head against the rock, closing her eyes. It was a private moment, and he knew he should leave her be, but he felt her frustration, knew what it was like, and what was worse, he was surely the root of its cause.

There was nothing for it. Stepping quickly from the edge of the rainforest, he said, ''Tis a fine day for swimming.'

Grace gasped and wrapped her arms around her body, a familiar scowl returning. 'How *dare* you!'

He cleared his throat. 'I'm sorry. I didn't know you'd be . . .' He waved a hand in her general direction, half turning away.

'I . . . I . . .' She dug into her bag, then pulled a towel around her shoulders.

He laughed. 'It's not like you're in your birthday suit.'

'What *are* you doing here?'

'Free country.'

'This's Uncle Marcus's land . . .'

'Is it, so?' He wasn't sure that it was, but he could tell she didn't know either.

'Leave. Now.'

'I only came to see how you were.'

'I'm as you see.'

'Yes, I do see.'

She pulled her towel, and face, a little tighter, then knelt down, and began to gather her things – scattered papers, a book he recognised, a tin of chocolate biscuits that must have been melting in the sun.

He indicated the pool, though she wasn't watching. 'I can help, if you like.' Where the words came from, he didn't know. He was a boy who had only just learned to swim, offering to teach a girl who had nearly drowned because of him.

'You? Help me? I don't think so.'

'I'll teach you to swim.'

'What must I do in return? It's always an exchange with you.'

'That's hardly fair.'

She raised an eyebrow.

'Call it repayment for your near-death experience.' He grinned.

'Forget the debt,' she said dismissively.

'My father always said: *forgetting a debt doesn't mean it's paid.*'

She glanced sidelong at him. 'In exchange for nearly drowning, you'll teach me to . . . to *swim*?' Was that the trace of a smile?

He put down the bucket and stripped off his top before taking two steps to the natural pool, and leaping in with a whoop. The water was silky smooth, and he swam arm over arm to the base of the falls, the roar drowning out whatever Grace was saying. When he turned back, he saw that she'd stepped to the water's edge, watching him worriedly, then he disappeared beneath the waterfall to whatever lay beyond.

Chapter 31

The Iliad Club, Kensington, London
December 2004

True to his word, several days after they'd met, Sam Littleton had called the Grosvenor Square apartment and left a voicemail with arrangements to meet his father on Thursday night. He'd signed off with his name, but no number on which to call him back if Libby was disinclined to accept the invitation, which – she had to admit – she was hardly likely to do. The chance to talk to someone who had known Daniel McGillycuddy, and possibly met her father, was far too tempting to pass up.

❧

It was already dark when she arrived outside the Iliad Club, and she hurried off the street, where it had begun to rain so that the Christmas lights cast colourful reflections on the wetting pavement. Around her, Kensington High Street had been in flux, the working day bleeding into the evening, people going home, people going out. How she had envied those people – things to do, places to be – during her first week in London but now, as she smoothed her skirt and removed her black coat to reveal a brand new sapphire blouse (another item on her *To Do* list ticked off), she felt, almost, like one of them.

'Madam?'

A Maître d' peered at her with a single raised eyebrow. His expression was skilfully poised between welcoming and austere. 'Are you meeting someone?'

She shook her head, then nodded. 'Yes. I'm meeting a Mr . . .' Her mind went blank, distracted as she was by the noise emanating from within the club. She glanced through the French doors to catch a glimpse of a dozen grey heads, several of which had turned in her direction, and one of which – attached to a very small, bald man wearing a very large pair of black spectacles – gave her a grin that she couldn't help but return. The Maître d' followed her gaze, then waved her in, and Libby entered a whole new world.

≈

'How did you know it was me?' she said, lowering herself into a Chesterfield that was perfectly soft and worn in the way that only sufficient decades of use could produce. A martini she hadn't ordered was promptly placed before her by a waiter who bowed, then disappeared as quickly as he'd arrived with all the pomp and ceremony of a royal butler.

'My dear, look around you.'

She was, it seemed, the only woman there. But still, heads hadn't turned as she'd crossed the room; the men – whose average age must have been at least eighty – had returned to their conversations. 'Besides,' added Lawrence Littleton, who'd greeted her with a warm handshake, 'you look like him, you know?'

Libby caught her breath. It was the first time anyone had said such a thing to her. Over the years, she'd scrutinised the scant photos of her father that she could find, hunting for a resemblance that she wasn't sure was there. She smiled gratefully at Lawrence over her drink, from which she took two fortifying gulps. He was certainly as matter-of-fact as Sam, but he was infinitely scruffier, his high-quality tweed jacket fraying at the edges, his glasses held together with tape. Even his matching brown trousers looked suspiciously like the pair Libby had seen in the photo of him on *The Albatross*, when he'd had a head full of hair, and a slightly sad smile that matched that of his son.

When she didn't reply, he continued. 'I'll answer your question before you even ask it: yes, I met Ben, briefly, in February 1975. I was so very sorry to hear about his death. What a terrible accident, a terrible, terrible shock. How old were you when he died?'

'I wasn't yet born.'

'Oh my,' Lawrence said, drawing breath. 'I'm sorry. I should have known that. I'm sure Ben would have mentioned a daughter had he already had one.'

A plate of bread and olive oil appeared in front of them, its baked scent lingering with the sweet smell of beeswax and fresh lilies, the latter arranged in huge vases scattered around the room. Despite the turmoil that Lawrence's words created inside her, Libby felt at home here, and she smiled at him, wanting to put him at ease, grateful for the opportunity to dip into her father's past.

'Now . . . Sam tells me you want to know what we discussed when we met.'

At the mention of Sam, Libby took a quick sip of her drink. 'Yes, please. Whatever you can remember.'

'Well, the old mind's not quite what it used to be, but I'll do my best. Your dad came to us here at the Iliad Club to read his brilliant short story, "The Selkie of Ocean Beach".' Lawrence leaned forward. 'Back in those days, we could get good tax breaks by supporting the arts. Times have changed, of course.' He took a deep breath as though about to embark on a tirade which Libby wasn't at all sure she would be able to keep up with. She'd purchased few papers since her arrival, only glancing at headlines about the woes of the Blair government, and the war in Afghanistan. 'Anyway, at the end of the night, one of our members, Roger, stood up to read a poem by one of my authors—'

'Daniel McGillycuddy?'

'The very one. By the time he'd finished your poor dad was agape. He recognised the story, you see! And the girl it was about.'

She nodded, understanding. She had a sneaking suspicion that the ballad was 'The Far-Flung Distant Shore'; after all, he'd underlined several of its sections in the book.

'He seemed inordinately interested in Daniel's works about his time in Tasmania. Myself, I was rather more fascinated by his wartime ballads, but that's the beauty of poetry, isn't it? Everyone gets something different from it.'

It was true. Libby considered the ballads hidden away in the tin behind the waterfall and how 'The Ma'am from Joey River' had so captured her imagination even when held up against Banjo Paterson's most famous work. It was the cheekiness of the ballad, really, that struck her. A story about a girl who nearly drowns. It could be laced with anger, but it was filled with something else . . . an awakening of some kind, Libby felt.

'. . . must have made an impression on him.'

'I'm sorry?' Lawrence's voice brought her back to the present. He was peering at her over his glasses.

'You must have made an impression on my son. For him to arrange this meeting. He's not been on good form of late, so I'm glad of this . . . proactivity on his part.'

'I'm not sure I made an impression,' Libby laughed, bolstered a little by her martini, which she'd reached the bottom of in quick order. A second one appeared unbidden before her, three olives skewered on a toothpick lying at a drunken angle in the glass.

Lawrence raised an eyebrow, his knowing glance causing her to quickly look away.

She smoothed her skirt. 'And did he find a tenant for the boat?'

At the mention of *The Albatross* Lawrence huffed. 'No, he didn't. He's a picky man, my son. His mother lived there . . . once. He was only four years old when she died, you know. He went away to boarding school a few years after. I thought it was better than living in that cramped boat with me . . .'

A tingle rose up Libby's neck. 'I . . . I'm so very sorry.'

'I don't think he wants anyone else to move in,' Lawrence continued after a deep, steadying breath. 'Or perhaps it's more that he can't find the right person? Always been a perfectionist, Sam. Even worse since he returned from the war.'

'The war?'

'Afghanistan. Didn't he say? Been back a couple of months. Struggling to find his feet, poor boy.'

The hum of happy chatter in the room seemed to die around them, but it was, Libby realised, just her sense that things had got quiet. 'No, he didn't mention it.'

'Not surprised, my dear. He finds it difficult to talk about. Now,' he said, clearly keen to move on, though in her mind Libby was still in the boat watching Sam turn the pages of *The Ballads of Daniel McGillycuddy*, pausing over those war poems, frowning as he read. 'What is it you want to ask me, Libby?'

'I don't know,' she said truthfully, suddenly feeling hopeless, that the trail she was following was already as cold as ice. 'What was it my *father* asked you?'

'Well . . . I recall he particularly wanted to know if I had met Daniel.'

'Had you?'

'No, never. Daniel contacted Stern Publishing via letter. He'd seen our details in the back of *The Irish Times*.'

'He was back in Ireland, then?'

'Oh yes, he moved back to Ballinn after the war. Never wanted that in his bio though; said it was immaterial to the present. I guess he was right — all the ballads were stories of the past.'

'I see . . .'

'Daniel wasn't actually interested in publication. In his letter he said that he'd merely like to have his poetry bound in a book for his family. He'd read a review of one of our collections. Thought we might do a good job. We agreed . . .'

'We?'

'My wife — Sam's mother — Alice, and I.'

Before she could ask more about Alice, Lawrence continued. 'We sent off an invoice, but when he forwarded the manuscript . . . well.' He paused, smiling at the memory. 'We had to convince him that publication was the best way to go, and that *we* would pay *him*, rather than him paying us. Alice in particular felt the work was important.'

'Why?'

'The ballads . . . they captured life on the Australian home front for one thing, which is something we rarely heard about.'

Libby nodded. Even during her thesis, most of the works she'd studied were British. She realised now just how much she'd already learned from Daniel's ballads.

'But the way he wrote about the Pacific, Libby! About Timor, about Nagasaki, about the Death Railway, and the bombs that dropped on Darwin . . . I thought it was well done. We were in the swinging sixties by then, and everyone wanted to forget about the horrors of the past, no one more so than the soldiers who had made it home.' Lawrence paused. 'How on earth can we learn from history if we don't know anything about it? I persuaded Daniel the poems were historically important, though he explained he'd initially written them to process all the things that he'd seen. That they'd been an outlet that had let him . . .'

'Heal?'

'Yes.' He looked at her anew. 'Exactly. Eventually, we compromised. There was a single ballad he wanted removed if we were to publish it publicly. A request to which we reluctantly agreed.'

'A missing ballad?' Libby leaned forward. Had she had a mirror, she was certain she would have been able to see the gleam in her eye.

Lawrence laughed. 'That was the *very* way your father looked when I mentioned it. I can see where you get your inquisitive nature.'

She had never thought of herself as inquisitive. Not until recently. And perhaps that day behind the waterfall when she'd defied her mother by following a shadow into the rainforest.

'I did find the copy of the ballad for Ben, but I was going away, so I left it in the stern of *The Albatross* for him.' He hesitated. 'I'm sorry to say he never had the opportunity to collect it.'

Despite the tightness in her chest, Libby felt the overwhelming urge to comfort him. She leaned forward and touched his hand. Sometimes giving solace was the only way she felt it herself. 'I'm sure Dad would have been very grateful, had things been otherwise,' she said, kindly. 'Do you . . . do you still have the ballad?'

Lawrence reached into his bag.

'Is that . . .'

'It? Yes.' From an otherwise empty folder, he took two sheets of typeset paper, handing them to her. But Libby only needed to read the first line to know what it was. She gasped, then ran a trembling finger down each familiar verse, knowing full well that its handwritten twin sat, even now, hidden away in the Arnott's biscuit tin.

Quietly, she began to read – as she had a hundred times before – 'The Ma'am from Joey River'.

Chapter 32

Behind Towerhurst, Tasmania

October 1939

Grace traced the edge of the pool, slipping and sliding until she reached the bubbling water where Daniel had disappeared. The undertow had almost certainly taken him, surely he would be trapped – she thought, fearfully – in the endless submerged current?

Hearing the echo of her name, she turned, frowning, as a head appeared around the edge of the falls, followed by a beckoning which indicated a small ledge tracing the side of the pool. She hesitated, contemplating how to navigate it (and whether she even should) when Daniel stepped out to tiptoe along the rock edge and take her hand.

'Trust me.'

She almost laughed, but she followed nonetheless, with slow, careful steps.

෧

A whole new world lay behind the falls; it was a cave the size of her bedroom, cut off from the world by the shimmering, glossy stream.

'Oh!' she whispered, surprised that the sound of falling water was so muted, amazed that something so powerful could be that gentle. A mischievous light played on the walls, its effect intoxicating.

'Beautiful, isn't it?' Daniel touched a finger to the water, making a reflected rainbow dance.

She sat on a natural ledge, and he perched beside her, leaving space between them, unlike that day on the beach.

'Now, how about these lessons?' he said. 'You should learn how to swim if you're to become Tasmanian.'

'I'm not. I'm going back as soon as I can.'

He frowned at the ceiling. 'Me too.'

Just as on her birthday, when they'd sat under the sassafras, the admission surprised her. He seemed so settled here. So *at home*. He appeared to have friends and family that cared about him, and from what Grace had heard, Ireland could be savage.

'Kerry is the most beautiful place in the world,' he said, as though reading her thoughts. He stood, rising on his tiptoes, then reaching up, his hand disappeared into a ledge hidden above them. 'Ha! From over there, you can't even see this.' He felt around, clearly finding nothing. 'My village, Ballinn, is a bit like that ledge.' He sat back beside her, a little closer this time so that she quickly shuffled away.

'How so?'

'It's hidden from the world. We keep it secret, because we love it the way it is, but if you know where to look, you'll find it.'

'And you want to go back?'

'Ballinn's why I took the bet . . . five shillings for the first lad to kiss you. I'm sorry.'

She nodded. Just as Uncle Marcus had suggested, she had let go of the anger, and truly forgiven him. 'Can't your uncle,' she said, moving on, 'pay for your ticket home?'

'I couldn't ask him. Truth be told, he'd rather I stayed here. He needs me at the mill.'

Grace glanced at her hands. Colette had told her Daniel's parents were dead. 'You don't like Tasmania?'

'It's grand, all right. But it isn't home.'

They were back on the same topic again. *Home?* What did that really mean? She thought of her bedroom at Grosvenor Square, of the bustling streets that swirled beneath her window, of eating dinner alone before her parents dined. Which bit she wanted to return to, she wasn't sure. Home was something that Grace could never quite grasp, could never quite untangle: it was the smell of furniture polish, it was loneliness, and on some level, it was a lack of expectation that had held with it a certain comfort, though she no longer saw it that way.

≥≈

After her first swimming lesson, they sat on the warm rock while Daniel made a fire, flicking a flame from his lighter into shredded eucalyptus bark. It licked at the damp wood, throwing up steamy smoke that rolled low across the water. From the bucket, he took the fish, cutting out the spiny needles, then butterflied it using two sharpened sticks to hold it over the gentle flame.

Grace preemptively opened Uncle Marcus's Arnott's biscuit tin, eyeing the fish with suspicion.

'Can I?' said Daniel, indicating *The Collected Verse of A.B. Paterson.*

She nodded, and when he picked it up, a sheaf of paper fell from its pages.

'What's this?'

'Oh, I . . .' Grace scrambled forward, but Daniel was already on his feet, moving lightly around the edge of the pool, reading as he went.

'"The Ma'am from Joey River"?' he howled.

Before she could reach him, he was laughing so that his

words spilled over themselves, tumbling towards Grace as a blush rose on her cheeks.

   'There was movement at the Joey, for the word had
      passed around
   The girl from out-of-town would get away,
   She lived in wild Towerhurst and would glare you to
      the ground,
   So all the boys had gathered to the fray.
   All the young and older lads from the houses near and far
   Had mustered at the river at first light,
   For the boys they love a challenge and the Pom-girls
      really are
   And so they placed their bets with sure delight.

   There was Pudding, who weighed a pile and mostly
      loved to sup,
   And Richard with his hair as white as snow
   Was striding there beside him, though he'd surely not
      pay up
   He was known for being tightest with his dough.'

Daniel took a deep breath, dancing just out of reach. 'This is just like "The Man from Snowy River"!' he laughed.

   'And Paddy from the Emerald Isle who thought he'd
      win the bet,
   Handsome that he knew himself to be,
   A girl who might refuse him he'd never, ever met,
   And he sauntered down the beach with certain glee.

   The object of their ruse was a small and weedy beast;
   Something like a woman undersized,

With hair as dull as dishwater and forehead always
  creased,
She wasn't really easy on the eyes.
And if the lad could get his kiss, he'd earn himself a
  win;
There was hunger in his quick and urgent haste,
Because every penny put aside would go into his tin,
And closer to his home he ever raced.

So the boys hid themselves in the forest near the shore,
And waited for the show to fairly start,
Soon they were delighted with the spectacle before,
As Paddy stole the pieces of her heart.
He sat himself beside her and delivered her first kiss,
And his lips soon found the object of his mark,
Then her face it softened lightly, a ripple there of bliss,
And from behind them came the sounds of jeers and
  lark.

So she went; racing where the waves were white and
  grey
A wet and wild thunder on the sand,
And Puds, he gave the orders: "Don't let her get away,
This prank is getting mighty outta hand;
Paddy, you must save her; you must go and make this
  right,
Swim bravely and never fear the cold,
She'll be mad as hell, and she'll likely wield a fight,
But you did this, and now you must be bold."

He sent the sand grains flying, as he ran across the
  shore,
Clearing seaweed piles in his stride.

And the boy from Ireland's strokes never missed a
   beat,
As he swam beyond the ocean's wild tide.
Though the waves were rolling, he reached her
   without fear;
But saw it there reflected in her face.
He ne'er paused to breathe until they were fairly clear
And then, down on bended knee, he asked for grace.'

When she caught him, she snatched the pages back. 'That's grace with a lower-case G,' she muttered.

'Did you write that?' One hand was on Daniel's belly, the other over his mouth, laughter spilling from between his fingers. 'It's better than "The Man from Snowy River"!'

'Stop it! Stop it!' She grabbed her bag, throwing the ballad, the book and the biscuits inside.

'No, no. Wait.' Daniel put his hand gently on her arm. 'Wait! Sure, I'm not laughing *at* you. I liked it, Grace. It was grand! I mean it. It wasn't *quite* Banjo Paterson, but . . .'

She'd started to walk away.

'I *loved* it.'

When she turned back, she searched his face for signs of mirth. 'Don't tease me, Daniel.'

'Please don't go. I did. I loved it.'

She only half believed him, but the surprisingly delicious aroma of cooking fish, and his smile, and the soothing sound of the water, drew her back so that, before she knew it, she'd taken a place opposite him.

After a time, he said: 'So in the ballad you said . . . you'd never been kissed?'

She flushed. 'No. Who would kiss me?'

From his shirt pocket, he withdrew a shiny coin. 'I want you to have this.'

She frowned. It was his winnings from the bet. Aside from a few emergency pounds she had packed in her case, she'd never had money of her own; everything she'd ever needed had been provided. Fine clothes, fine food, a fine house. She looked at Daniel's ripped shorts, at the jagged state of his home-cut hair, and shook her head. 'I don't want it.'

'Nor do I.'

She pushed the offered coin away, proffering the tin of biscuits in its place. Daniel, who seemed to be a bottomless pit, having eaten three quarters of the fish and both the apples she'd brought with her, reluctantly pocketed the coin, but could barely conceal his delight at the chocolate-coated treats. After his first two, he took the empty tin, filling it with water, and handing it to Grace. She closed her eyes, wondering at the wisdom of drinking from a wild place, then, throwing off her caution, she drained the tin in three gulps, before – in complete mortification – letting out the whisper of a burp.

'Not such a lady after all, eh?'

She covered her face with her hands, but she couldn't help herself. Laughter flowed out of her like someone had popped a cork. She had never done such a thing in public before, and it hadn't been the end of the world as her mother had implied it would be. She peeked through her fingers to see Daniel smiling at her.

'You're surprising, Grace.'

'I'm not.'

He frowned as he went to the edge of the pool, filling the tin again. 'No, you are. You seem like one person, but actually you're another. You just don't know it yet.'

He poured the water onto the fire so that steam rose as a wall between them, and Grace was glad of it. Because at that moment, confusion rippled across her face, chased by an unfamiliar thing. A realisation. It was the second time in as many months that someone had said she underestimated herself. That she could be more.

Maybe there was something in it, after all.

Chapter 33

The Iliad Club, Kensington, London
December 2004

Her heart beating hard, Libby put the poem aside. No wonder Daniel McGillycuddy's words had seemed so *very* familiar. *He* had written 'The Ma'am from Joey River'. The poem that had sown a seed that day for her behind the waterfall when she was only ten years old.

She turned to Lawrence. 'Why didn't he want it included?'

Around them, the crowd at the Iliad Club was growing even more rowdy. By the open fireplace, several men were arguing over some disputed passage of *The Odyssey*.

'It was about the love of his young life, he said, a girl he'd met in Tasmania. And I guess his wife wouldn't have liked it. Or I got that impression anyway.'

'Who was the love of his life?'

'I'm not sure.'

'And did Daniel say what happened to her, this girl he met in Tasmania?'

'No. But this was all such a long time ago.'

Libby persisted. 'I think Dad planned to visit Daniel in Kerry. Do you know why?'

'Possibly he wanted to discuss something to do with his own writing? After his reading of "The Selkie of Ocean Beach" he revealed that his inspiration for the story's setting was the McGillycuddy place in Tasmania. He said it was built from that incredible timber . . . Huon pine? He told me a fantastic story about a misunderstanding over a heather plant that Daniel was supposed to bring on the boat with him from County Kerry for his uncle, and the poor boy brought the wrong one.'

Heather? Libby wondered whether she should mention the pressed pieces she'd found in the Arnott's tin, but Lawrence continued. 'I enjoyed Ben's story immensely. We often talk about it, Roger and I.'

'Roger?' It was the second time he'd mentioned a Roger. 'Not . . . Roger *Masters*?'

'That's the one! Roger was your father's good friend. If I recall rightly, Ben stayed with him while he was here.'

Libby reached into her bag to retrieve her copy of *The Ballads of Daniel McGillycuddy*. There, marking 'The Far-Flung Distant Shore' was Roger's card.

'*For all your biography needs.*' Lawrence laughed. 'Oh, but these are no longer his details. Let me get his number.' He took his phone from his pocket, then scrolled, before sighing and handing it over to her. 'Can you work this infernal thing? It's new.'

Libby rolled the Blackberry's button, searching for *Roger*. 'It's not here, I'm afraid.'

'What? The boy at the shop said he'd transferred the whole lot over. Used the words *in a jiffy*. Mocking me, I gather.'

Libby hid a grin.

'I'll be having words with Carphone Warehouse, I can tell you . . .' He muttered as he put the phone away. 'I'll get Sam to send it on. It's in my old Nokia. So reliable. Don't know why I changed . . .'

'That's okay, thank you. I was also wondering . . . you still have Daniel's details?'

'Daniel's details? What good would they do?'

'I'd like to contact him. See if Dad had been in touch.'

'I can give the Ballinn address' – at the name, Libby's heart leapt – 'but that's not likely to help you. Though perhaps you can ask his family some questions?'

'Why not Daniel himself?'

'Oh, my dear. Perhaps I should have mentioned before . . . but I'm sorry to tell you that several years ago I received word that your ballad writer, Daniel McGillycuddy, had sadly passed away.'

Chapter 34

The McGillycuddy place, west coast Tasmania

November 1974

The McGillycuddy property was surely a setting Ben would use for a future story, and he marvelled that although Towerhurst was grander, this place was just as unique in its very own way.

'Built it myself,' Ned said when he came across Ben loitering in the front yard. The old man wore an Akubra hat, seeming every inch an Australian, until he opened his mouth. 'Sure, it's grand. Started laying the foundations when we arrived in 1919, then worked up from there. Our little piece of paradise.'

It was a higgledy-piggledy collection of buildings. Huts of rough-edged horizontal planks overlapping like wooden waves, a sea of white surrounding them: spindly knee-high plants, dripping with tiny bell-shaped flowers.

'Heather,' Ned said, 'for the bees.' He pointed through the clearing, where half a dozen hives sat in neat rows as though waiting for instruction and, indeed, a faint buzz was audible over the sound of the ocean. 'Got my nephew Daniel to bring a few plants from Ireland back in thirty-seven.'

Daniel? Ben wanted to ask about Ned's nephew, but he was

steadied by the memory of seeing that name – *D. McGillycuddy* – on the village cenotaph.

'I thought Irish heather was normally purple?'

Ned nodded. '*Normally*, son, you'd be right. Apparently, during the thirties *white* heather was all the rage in Cork.'

Ben frowned.

'I *had* asked him to bring some Kerry heather with him. That beautiful Kerry heather. It's like God has thrown a purple veil over the land. Spectacular. But the boy forgot, only remembering when he was nearly at the boat, so he hopped out of the hackney, pulled up a few flowerless plants from someone's garden, then went on his way. *This* was what we ended up with. White flowers.'

Ben laughed. 'Whoops.'

Ned shrugged as he ran a gnarled hand through his grey beard. 'Nearly four decades later, I've finally grown used to it. And Colette says the honey's more fragrant for it. She always had a soft spot for Daniel though ... truth be told, the bees don't mind.' He wiped his dusty hands on his trousers, then appraised Ben. 'How are you holding up?'

'Fit as a fiddle.'

'Getting lost in this kind of forest for a night would drive some people mad.'

'You sound like my wife,' Ben joked, although he feared that it was somewhat true. Willow had suggested he stopped asking questions about the body's identity, just until he'd recovered. 'To be fair, I did have some wild hallucinations down there.'

Ned nodded at the bruise on Ben's forehead. 'Too right. I'm not surprised.'

They stepped into a long, low building with two sets of opposing double doors flung wide, forest visible on the other side. The ground was thick with wood shavings, the smell of resin pleasantly overwhelming. Huge planks of Huon pine were stacked neatly at the edges of the shed, and a mill stood at one end, with a neat rack of tools at the other.

'This is a brilliant setup.'

'We upgraded after the war, so I could carry on alone. This'll be here long after I've gone.'

Ben couldn't deny that he loved the idea of passing something on. He wondered what he would leave behind for his own family, his own children, if he and Willow could have them. He wished for that more than anything in this world.

'It's a legacy, all right,' he said to Ned, smiling. Yes, he thought, this is *definitely* a setting for a novel. Or a short story, at least.

'What is it I can do for you, Ben?'

'Well, I wanted to say thank you. For your part in the rescue.'

'Think nothing of it. Mind if I finish up?'

As Ned began to sweep the workshop's floor, Ben took a second broom and, with his uninjured arm, helped as best he could. As they worked in silence, he let his mind drift, imagining a story of a piner who'd built a honey-soaked paradise on the west coast. The house smelled so sweet that a selkie walked across Ocean Beach, drawn by the scent. She and the piner fell in love, but she missed the sea, so one day . . .

'So, we can pass the time of day, o' course,' said Ned, interrupting Ben's reverie, 'but I warrant there's something else you want to discuss.'

Not wanting to launch straight into the reasons he was here – did Ned have any ideas about the body down the mine? Why had Sergeant Griffin seemed so cagey, was he (as Willow had insisted) just doing his job? – Ben asked what had happened to Marcus Foxton.

'The poor man passed away a year or so ago. Cancer.'

'I'm sorry.'

Ned nodded. 'He hadn't been back to Towerhurst in nearly three decades, though I saw him occasionally in Launceston.' He searched the treeline as though waiting for a forgotten history to spill from between the trunks. 'Moved away from here soon after the war ended, so he did.'

'He and Olive divorced?'

'I don't rightly know. But there was no love lost there. When the girls – Grace and Rose – left, Marcus changed. Some people said . . . Ah, 'tis only rumours.' He hesitated.

'What *did* people say?'

Ned shook his head, tapping the broom against the wall. 'That Marcus was *very* keen on Rose.'

Just as Mira Holmes had told Willow. Ben folded the knowledge away.

'Spiteful gossip is all,' Ned said. 'People round here were jealous of Towerhurst. Marcus had everything without having to work for it, you see? You know how Australians are, tall poppy syndrome and all that begrudgery. He was a writer too, you know.'

Ben nodded.

'Not much success, far as I know. Got into publishing eventually – printing words, instead of writing them. Folk say he became depressed when Rose left. There was some kind of feud going on up there. The house was always unsettled. But then it had been full of sickness too, and that takes its toll.'

'Sickness?'

'Grace got rheumatic fever a couple of years after she arrived. I'd say it caused her to leave her childhood behind. She'd been skinny before but gaunt she was, in the year or so after.'

'What was she like?' Ben recalled her photograph from Christmas 1940, that sad look in her eyes.

Ned paused. 'Grace . . . Grace,' he said, thinking. 'I'd say she was a girl who didn't fit initially. The poor creature had a second skin, and it covered up what was inside of her. She was in love with Daniel—'

'Really?'

'But it was a one-way thing. There was a bet between the Westford lads; five shillings to the one who could secure a kiss from her. A difficult task, I believe. It certainly caused some trouble.' He told Ben a story about Daniel saving Grace from a dead tiger snake. 'Marcus wasn't too pleased about it, if I recall. He was quite protective over his niece.'

'He and Olive didn't have children of their own?'

A far-off flash of lighting lit the dim interior of the shed. 'Well, *Olive* never had any, at least.'

'What do you mean?'

Ned hesitated, his attention stolen by a yellow car arriving outside the shed. 'Your wife's here.'

Ben flushed. He'd lied to Willow; said he was off to the McGillycuddys to buy a jar of honey. 'I'm not going to ask any questions,' he'd insisted. 'I'll only be ten minutes.'

She wound down the window. 'It's about to rain and I was worried . . .' She looked pointedly at Ben's empty hands.

'Yes, the honey . . . we got distracted chatting about . . . the merits of Huon pine.'

'Careful, Ned. You'll find yourself appearing in his latest story.'

The old man nodded, then disappeared inside a small hut, returning with two jars of golden honey. She gave a thumbs up, then shut the window, blocking out the first fat drops of rain.

Ben paid. 'So, did she shed it?

'What?'

'I was wondering what happened to Grace's second skin . . .'

'Oh, she peeled it off, all right.' Ned inclined his head, smiling at a memory. 'And when she was done, you'd hardly recognise her. Sure, wasn't she the finest swan you ever saw?'

Chapter 35

Towerhurst, Tasmania

1940

As that summer progressed, pieces of Grace's old self began to fall away as though all her doubt, despair and despondency had once belonged to someone else. Buoyed by her new-found confidence, she began to sneak out of Towerhurst of a morning, learning to avoid the squeaky third stair from the top of the landing, though why she tried to leave undetected, she wasn't quite sure. Was it to hide from Aunt Olive's sharp tongue? Or to avoid her clandestine exits featuring in Rose's letters home to Mother? Perhaps she no longer wanted to see the look in Uncle Marcus's eye when she said she was meeting Daniel? The way he squinted, taking a breath as if wanting to protest, but clearly unsure how to go about it.

Her first swimming lessons had been less than successful; whenever she let go of the pool's side she sank like a stone, only to come up spluttering as Daniel lifted her out of the water just as he had from the sea all those weeks ago. 'I can't do this,' she'd said on her third lesson, huffing and puffing as she lay on a wet rock, and Daniel had said, laughingly, in reply: 'I've seen stones more natural at swimming.' And after her angry response, he hadn't come by for four days, and Grace found herself doing something she'd never done before.

She'd turned up at the McGillycuddys' house – her heart in her mouth – and paused, taking in the timber buildings scattered like seeds; they were somehow beautiful, and she sensed, rather than saw, that there was a strange order amongst the chaos. Large flowerbeds, containing dozens of young white heather plants, stood like little soldiers and, over the roll of the nearby ocean, a faint buzz of bees filled the air. Daniel had appeared, covered in sawdust, setting his hands on his hips. He wasn't wearing his trademark grin, wasn't sporting a cheeky expression, he only gazed at her with calm expectation.

Without preamble, Grace had apologised. It was done without making eye contact and into Daniel's hand she had thrust three pieces of paper, torn down their long edge from *The Collected Verse of A.B. Paterson*.

'Here's "The Man from Snowy River".' It had hurt her enormously to give it away.

'It's probably treasonous,' he'd said, 'to tear this from the book.' Then he'd grinned, and she'd smiled shyly back.

'I'm sorry for behaving so poorly,' she'd said before turning to walk away.

After that, the lessons had improved, and within a month she was swimming laps of the natural pool, gliding through the water, remembering those swimmers in the Serpentine and how she'd always envied them, and thinking that – when she returned – she would surely join them at that place of tranquillity in the beating heart of the city.

❧

Time seemed to pass differently each time Grace stepped through the moon gate, the days getting shorter and shorter until she finally realised it wasn't an illusion at all, but that autumn had finally come.

'It has at that,' Daniel said when she mentioned it. It was far too cold to swim but still they'd arranged to meet. 'You should see Kerry in autumn, Grace. It's like a piece of heaven fallen to earth.' As he talked, he lit a fire, and she took a seat nearby.

'Why is it heaven?'

'It's hard to explain.'

She leaned back on her favourite stone; it was curved just so, and her spine nestled into it perfectly. Lately, she'd noticed that it was even more comfortable, and that morning, when she'd pulled on her skirt her top button no longer fastened. She'd put on weight, and with it, height, two inches at least. What would her mother say? She felt she needn't worry about reports back to Edeline – Rose was too preoccupied with her new job in Queenstown to spend time concerning herself with Grace.

She glanced at Daniel. 'Try and explain.'

'I'm not good with words like you.'

'Nonsense.' She was only playing at her ballads and, anyway, writing rhyming ditties was a far cry from the easy manner of Daniel's everyday conversation. He blended in, moulding himself to each situation. Just like Rose, but without the calculated intent, quite the opposite in fact; she thought he did it to make whoever he was talking to more comfortable, rather than to show himself in a better light. With Ned he became a man, with Colette he became a son, and when he talked to her uncle he asked endless questions about topics that Marcus loved the most.

'How old's Banjo Paterson?' he'd said one day.

'Let's see' – Uncle Marcus always scratched his chin – 'mid-seventies, I'd say.'

'Is there anyone else writes these ballads?'

'Oh yes. Henry Lawson, for one. Great rivalry there.' Chin scratch. 'Thomas Kendall, of course.' Chin scratch. 'Mary Foott . . . she's a good Scottish influence.'

When Grace watched Daniel talk to Rose, she couldn't

help noticing the warm smile that played on his lips; and, in turn, she saw the way Rose admired him, the way she blushed when he made her laugh. The few years between them seemed to shrink at those moments. Daniel McGillycuddy could shed his skin with ease.

She said it to him now.

'Like you've done?' he replied. 'You don't think you've changed?'

She leaned back on the rock. Some months ago, an intimate question like that would have made her blush. She would have thought that whoever posed it was making fun of her, but even without glancing at Daniel's face, she knew that wasn't the case.

'A little, I suppose.' In her heart, she knew she had. 'Have *you* changed . . . since you got here?'

'Can't say as I have.'

Grace couldn't imagine that; a place like this *not* rubbing off on someone. It had, in less than a year, left an indelible mark on her.

'Do you have siblings?' It was the first time she'd asked him, and she felt a jolt of shame that she hadn't before.

'No. You?' They'd barely talked about themselves in any personal way; only swimming, Banjo Paterson, and how life was different in Tasmania. One time he'd asked her about her mother, and she'd shared some snippets that weren't really the truth. She'd left Daniel with the impression that Edeline was merely a cold fish, when in reality she was a shark.

'No. No siblings.' The closest thing she had was Rose, and that hadn't turned out so well.

'Most families in Kerry are big, but not mine.'

'Why not?'

He shrugged. 'Don't know. Sometimes Mam seemed sad about it.' She wondered what had happened to them, his parents, but before she could ask, he said, 'Kerry's different to here, o' course. In good and bad ways.'

'How so?'

She thought, because they had been discussing families, he would tell her about the people, but instead he said, 'Here there's a feeling of . . . opportunity. More than in Ireland. Like any man can make his own way.'

'And any woman?'

He scratched his nose. 'Colette tells me women got the vote here at the turn of the century. Didn't happen until 1918 in Ireland.'

She frowned. 'Opportunity is more than just getting the vote.'

'Do you think so? I'd say some people in Ireland would disagree with you.'

'From where I'm sat, I'd say Irish people are generally disagreeable.'

He laughed. 'No, but it's true, isn't it? The depression may have hit here, but it didn't seem so bad compared to other parts of the world.'

'I never really think about other parts of the world.' She wasn't embarrassed to admit it, though she felt it was something she should change. But then her lack of interest had been natural, hadn't it? She had no choice where she went, and what she did. After the war was over she would return to London, where her parents would marry her off.

Daniel threw a pebble into the calm pool. 'I think about the rest of the world all the time. It's why,' he added, 'I'm enlisting.'

She sat up. 'Enlisting? You can't be serious. The war won't come to Australia.'

'It's those people round the world I'm worried about.'

Last month, the Belgians and Dutch had surrendered, and, a week later, three hundred thousand Allied troops were plucked from the shores of Dunkirk right under the German guns. The Australian government, so Uncle Marcus had said, was having trouble deploying the men who had already signed up, and the nation was stumbling – rather than marching – into someone else's fight once again. War would never come to the Pacific; Australia's sons would die on soil ten thousand miles from home. So Uncle Marcus said last week. Aunt Olive, who had been knitting, scoffed and told him he didn't understand the Anzac spirit. That he was just another Pom. Grace had felt indignant on her uncle's behalf, then grateful that somehow she and Aunt Olive managed barely to cross paths these days.

Grace relayed her aunt's harsh words to Daniel.

'I'd say he understands war well enough. Just like Uncle Ned. They both fought in the last one. And the Anzac spirit is probably just like the British spirit, or the Irish, whether they're fighting for their own homeland, or another's.'

'Whose homeland will you be fighting for?'

'Not sure. Mine? Yours? Does it matter either way?'

Grace contemplated for the first time what life here would be like without Daniel. With him, so many things she'd once found dull came to life. 'It's not all spirit and mateship,' she said, repeating the words Uncle Marcus had said to Aunt Olive as he'd folded his newspaper before leaving the room.

Though it was cold, and they were both wrapped up, Daniel stood, stripping off his trousers to reveal a pair of shorts beneath. 'I'll make my money and return to Ireland after the war.'

He leapt into the pool, coming up gasping for breath.

'You will come back here first, won't you?' she said, but Daniel had, once again, disappeared beneath the surface, so she spoke to the ripples that shimmered across the pool.

'I don't believe you'll go. The war will be over soon.'

Chapter 36

Grosvenor Square, London

December 2004

Early on Friday morning, after a sleepless night and while considering her moves for the day, Libby's scattered thoughts were interrupted by the buzzer. She sighed, glancing at her watch. It was an ungodly hour, but any day, Libby had come to learn, with an A in it was suitable for rudely early deliveries. Before the bell could ring again – waking her sleeping aunts – she clicked the button without bothering to ask who it was, assuming that the package was for them.

That was something she quickly came to regret, because when she opened the apartment door she discovered a familiar – and rather attractive – man standing on the other side.

'Morning!'

'Oh!' was all Libby managed to say, pulling her dressing gown – a fluffy pink number of Ash's that she'd normally *never* wear – a little tighter. 'This is . . . a surprise.'

'I'll say,' said Sam, taking in her appearance with a look of subtle amusement. In his hand, he held her black Moleskine diary. 'This, I believe, is yours? You left it at the Iliad last night. Dad gave it to me this morning.'

'This morning?' It was only 7 a.m.

'I'm staying with him,' said Sam, 'for a while.'

'I see . . . and how did you find me?'

He opened the diary to the front where she'd written the Grosvenor Square address in pencil only days before.

'I thought an early visit would be payback for our unexpected meeting on Sunday.' Grinning, he leaned against the door frame, wholly at ease, such a contrast to the serious man she'd met on the boat and, what was worse, he was clearly enjoying her discomfort. His fleece hid a running top, suggesting that he'd already finished some kind of early-morning exercise; he glowed in a way that made Libby feel even more frumpy than she must have looked. And when he tapped his finger on the item she'd drawn next to *As a Reward* – the poorly rendered coffee cup – she swallowed down her misgivings, and said with a confidence she certainly didn't feel:

'Would you like to come in?'

❧

Back in the kitchen, Ash was digging in a cupboard, humming inharmoniously and modelling an identical pink dressing gown to the one Libby was mortified she wore.

'Well,' she said theatrically, as she spun around, her eyes dancing between her niece and the unexpected guest. '*Hellllo* there.'

Libby sighed. 'Sam, this is my aunt Ash. Ash, Sam. Sam's a . . . friend,' she said evasively.

'Is he now?' Ash leaned back on the counter, crossing her arms, an expectant look on her face.

'I would have come by later if I'd known you had . . . company,' Sam said to the room in general, his confidence slipping a little. 'Perhaps I can come back anoth—'

'Who's this then?' Ivy appeared behind them, in a matching hideous dressing gown and Libby swallowed down a strange urge to giggle as she watched Sam's composure crumble. The poor man. Entering the apartment with such bravado, only to find himself face to face with the inquisition.

❧

Later, as they strolled along a festive Regent Street, Libby couldn't stop herself. 'The look on your face!'

She laughed.

'You just left me . . .' he said, bewildered.

And she had. As soon as Ivy appeared, Libby had retreated towards her bedroom, indicating to her dressing gown, which was getting more embarrassing by the minute. 'I'd better change,' she'd muttered, leaving Sam at the mercy of her aunts.

'So, how did you two meet?' she heard Ash ask as she left, while Ivy leapt straight in with: 'And what is it you do for a living?'

Sam had seemed to gather himself, telling Ivy that he worked in government (a little white lie) and Ash that he'd met Libby while showing her a houseboat she wanted to rent (a very large white lie). Libby had grinned, feeling a swell of gratitude for Sam who, it seemed, could add discretion to his list of virtues.

Not, she'd thought quickly, as she'd closed the door to her room, that she was making any such list.

Ten minutes later, when she'd emerged, the aunts had evidently convinced Sam that it would be his pleasure to hang the artwork they'd brought back from New York, despite Libby's previous insistence that she would do it herself. She'd got in the way, trying to help, as he'd removed the painting from its travel packaging.

But Libby had gasped when the box fell away. '*More* of Mum's work?' This new painting – in Willow's distinctive style, with only a splash of colour – would join the other five hanging on the wall.

'We're proud of our big sister,' said Ivy, a little defensively.

'And it suits the living room,' Ash added, admiring the painting or perhaps – Libby looked closer – the man who was unwrapping it. Throughout her mum's career, the aunts had bought Willow's work from galleries. They wanted, it seemed, to support their sister in an anonymous way. And anyway, Ash was right: her mum's style *did* suit the apartment.

'It's beautiful,' Libby had said quietly as she traced a finger over the framing. It was a grey seascape with a single boat bobbling on the tide, its sail lemon yellow. It matched the new cashmere cardigan Libby wore; a gift from her aunts on her arrival from Australia. She had merely hung the beautiful garment in her wardrobe, admiring the bold colour, knowing it was something she would never have the courage to wear. But as she'd listened from her bedroom as Ivy asked Sam about Putney, where he was apparently living with Lawrence (*Ah, so you live with your dad? And how old are you?*), she'd snipped the tag from its collar and slipped the luxurious fabric over her head.

'They're just so . . . *so* . . .' Sam was lost for words as they turned into the bustle of Oxford Street, 'so *intense*.'

'You should see Ash after an espresso martini. At breakfast.'

He laughed. 'Invite me round for that, won't you?'

Libby looked away, a piece of her facade crumbling. She felt suddenly self-conscious in her yellow cardigan, striding down the street with a perfect stranger. As they'd left, Ash had given her a mortifying thumbs up, her only consolation being that Sam had been too fixated on getting out of the door to notice.

'So, coffee?' They paused at a café already stuffed full of suits on their way to work.

'That *was* the promised price,' said Sam, his arm lightly brushing hers as he ushered her inside.

❧

'So it was the late Daniel McGillycuddy who wrote "The Ma'am from Joey River", the ballad that you found when you were ten?' They were halfway through their coffees, and Libby had filled Sam in on the night before. He'd laughed at her description of the Iliad Club – 'an *old* boys' club' – and said he'd seen the two men by the fire argue over *The Odyssey* many times before. 'Dad tells me they've been at it since 1970, always in the same spot, always the same argument.'

'What? Wait, don't tell me: one of them thinks it's a comedy, the other a tragedy?'

'That it's been going on for thirty years is the *real* tragedy!' he laughed, looking at her theatrically with those bright blue eyes. 'You're a fan of the classics, then?'

'A wasted degree.'

'Ah.'

'Yes,' she said now, in reply to his original question, 'Daniel McGillycuddy is the poet I've been carrying with me all these years.' She touched the pendant, then – feeling self-conscious – dropped her hand to join the other wrapped around her mug. 'He was the reason I always wanted to study literature. One of the reasons' – she hesitated – 'I decided to quit medicine. Such recklessness hasn't served me very well, I'm afraid.' She thought of the string of dead-end jobs she'd had since. 'People, I'm sure, think me a failure, passing up the chance to be a doctor. I'm still not sure following my passion was the best life choice.'

'Well,' said Sam, 'I think you're incredibly brave.'

'Brave?'

'I walked into my job because it was the path that was laid for me.'

'You regret joining the army?'

'I see Dad filled you in.'

'He only mentioned it in passing because . . .' Libby grappled for an excuse. 'Because I was talking about Daniel's poems – the ones set on the front. I said I thought they must have been healing to write.'

'Healing . . .'

Libby swallowed, the lingering taste of coffee turning bitter in her mouth. 'Sorry. That's completely insensitive. I only mean . . . healing for *him*. But times have changed, haven't they? Wars have changed.' She hesitated. 'I think?'

'War hasn't changed, Libby. It's always been the same.'

'I'm sorry,' she said again. Her go-to words. Her way out.

'What I mean is: war has always been senseless. Conflict over what? Resources? Power? It all fades in the end.'

Libby thought about Daniel's ballad 'Death on the Railway'. In it, he described a line that cut through the Burmese Jungle, and how every six feet of 'progress' represented a life taken, and she'd wondered how many friends he'd lost.

'The thing is, Libby, I don't know much about the healing power of *writing* ballads, but I do know that reading poetry has taken me through some dark days. Kipling, Brooke, Owen . . . even . . . well, my friend, Simon – he was with me in the army – *he* was a fine poet. Captured life out there so brutally. With so much humanity, and layers of hidden meaning.' Sam looked away as though he might be embarrassed about what he was about to say. 'I feel,' he said, 'all that matters is what *you* take from any of these texts. For me, Simon's work expressed my own feelings of . . . grief, fear, guilt.'

Libby felt a strange sensation in her chest, a tightening, and she realised it must have shown on her face too, because Sam cleared his throat.

'Well, now that we're being so studious . . . what do you think about *The Odyssey*, anyway? Tragedy or comedy?'

The half laugh she gave him was laced with gratitude. She'd been gone then, thinking of Krish, thinking of her own grief, her own fears, her own guilt.

'It's a tragic comedy,' she said, sitting on the metaphorical fence.

'It's neither tragedy nor comedy. It's a romance. Odysseus struggles to return to his wife. Yet he loved her that whole time.'

Libby wrinkled her nose. 'He had a funny way of showing it.'

'Okay,' he conceded, 'he wasn't the most faithful . . . nor was she. But love won out in the end. He tried to get back to her for an entire decade. Loving an absent person for ten years! That's staying power.'

She looked away.

Oblivious to the change in her mood, Sam continued lightly, 'I wonder what Ash and Ivy would take from *The Odyssey*?'

'They're not great readers.' What had she been thinking, spending the morning like this, with her quick laughter and slow glances?

'Is your mother anything like them?'

Libby glanced up. 'Sorry?'

'Your mother, is she anything like your aunts?'

Chalk and cheese. 'They're quite similar,' Libby lied, suddenly wanting to be anywhere but sat here with Sam.

'Are you okay?'

'I'm fine. Actually, I need to go. I have to . . .' She scrambled for words then reached into her bag, grabbing a document she'd been carrying around for a week. 'I have to drop this off.'

'Shall I come—'

'No . . . no, I'm good.'

'Right.'

'Goodbye.'

'Oh, goodbye . . .'

She stood quickly, turning to go, knowing she was being insufferably rude, but telling herself it didn't matter as she'd

never see Sam again. When the café door stuck, she tussled
with it awkwardly until a courier came through from the other
side, casting her a withering look. Outside, she breathed cold
December air.

'Libby!'

She brushed past a jolly Christmas garland that had detached
from a hotel wall.

'Libby!'

Her steps faltered.

'Libby.'

Sam was there. 'I'm sorry.' His face was stricken, and he
was puffing, and for a split second Libby wondered whether
he too had tussled with the troublesome door.

They stood face to face. He hadn't said *I'm sorry that you feel
you have to go* or *I'm sorry if you took offence*. Sam was just sorry,
even though he didn't have an inkling of what was going on.

'I'm normally the one who says sorry for things I didn't
do,' she said softly.

His small grin brought dimples to his tanned face. 'I've
noticed.'

'It's just . . .'

'You don't have to explain.'

Libby considered her next words, though she couldn't think
what to say. That she too would have journeyed for ten years
to be with the love of her life? But that unlike Odysseus her
own soulmate was gone?

'It's just . . . I lost someone. Not just my dad.'

Sam nodded and, for a moment, she thought he had taken
her hand, but when she looked down she saw he'd merely
slipped a card between her fingers.

'This is Roger Masters' mobile number. Dad tells me he'll
be back tomorrow, and he's expecting your call.' He paused.
'He would love to see you.'

'He would?'

A nod. 'And the number below Roger's, it's mine.' He hesitated. 'You know, if you're seriously considering the boat . . .'

Despite herself, she smiled, and as he disappeared into the Christmas throng of Oxford Street she had to resist the urge to call him back.

Chapter 37

Towerhurst, Tasmania

Winter 1940

Two weeks later, when they met behind the waterfall, Daniel gave Grace a parcel. It was the size of an encyclopaedia, but with none of the weight, and it had been carefully wrapped in brown paper secured neatly with string.

'What's this? Christmas in July?'

'It's a piece of home. To remember me when I'm gone.'

When he was gone. He would leave soon, she knew; he'd lied about his age, and already had his papers. She wondered how she would be able to 'do her bit' if this war raged on as people said it would. Could she lie about her own age? There were whispers that women would play a larger role in this war than the last, and Grace scanned the weekly newspapers for evidence that such a sentiment had any basis, because although there had been little action, there'd been plenty of *talk*. Talk of a women's auxiliary to the army, air force and navy, talk of female deployment, talk of equal pay for equal work. Rose had taken matters into her own hands and, by her own account, was excelling in her administration role at Mount Lyell's smelter. 'All the shift managers have joined up, so I'm responsible for scheduling as well. It's exhausting!' she'd proclaimed, as though she was toiling down a dusty incline herself, pickaxe in hand.

Grace unwrapped the parcel and slipped out a canvas. On it was a painting of a beautiful valley of patchwork emerald fields that ran to the sea, tiny, colourful houses speckling the green. They looked to be marching towards the water, and the artist had painted them from the purple-topped peaks that wrapped the valley in a rocky embrace. The entire work was bathed in a golden glow.

She turned to Daniel. 'You did this?'

'No.' He pointed to a small squiggle in the bottom right corner.

She almost laughed. '*Puds?*' The painting was as delicate as its creator was not.

'Uncle Ned had an old photograph, but the view needed colour. I gave it to Puds, added a description, and he worked his magic.'

'It's really this vivid in Kerry?'

'Not every day. I described a perfect afternoon, in autumn. It's my favourite.'

He'd mentioned that before and she reflected that she didn't have a favourite season. The only discussion of *seasons* in the Grey household had been about the deteriorating quality of the societal kind.

He took the canvas from her, turning it towards the muted light. 'Autumn feels like you're looking at the world through a stained-glass window . . .' He coloured.

'Go on.'

'Well . . .' He leaned back against the rock, their heads nearly touching. The burble of the falls was soporific. 'Our village had this nice little church.'

'Catholic?'

'What do you think?'

She smiled. Finally she was getting used to this: the idea that people could answer questions with more questions that didn't need answering. That things left unsaid often meant more than those that were spoken, if only one took the time to listen.

'The stained windows threw this golden glow over everything, and the priest acted like God had done it. *Look how his benevolent gaze shines down upon us.* All that craic.'

'You don't believe in God?'

'Maybe. I sure did once, but' – he put the painting aside, inspecting his hands; they were bigger than Grace had noticed before – 'when that same priest said my parents were taken because of *God's plan*, you start to think there isn't one.'

She'd never asked him before, but now, in this cave that felt cut off from the world, with the cocoon of sound, with the way he'd let his shoulders drop and how he'd just pushed away that lick of hair as though casting aside a shield, she said, 'What happened to them?'

'They drowned. It was in autumn.'

Grace frowned.

'Odd, isn't it?' he said. 'To love that season? But it was beautiful altogether, that afternoon they left. It was just like this' – he touched the painting – 'just like the golden glow in the church. Only, I realised God didn't create it at all. It was just . . . there.'

She didn't really understand; she had no way of empathising, but she could see from the way he talked that his parents had been everything to him.

'I remember Mam bending down to brush a heather plant. She was laughing, saying how it was too early for such a beautiful sprinkle of purple flowers, and *weren't we just the luckiest people alive to be given this gift?* She always said things like that, Mam did.'

She smiled. 'She sounds wonderful.'

'For months,' he continued, 'the sight of purple heather was terrible altogether, and didn't Uncle Ned go asking me to bring some to Tasmania? He said Kerry's heather made God's own honey.'

'What did you do?'

'I brought white heather from a garden in Cork instead. Told him it was a mistake.'

Grace recalled the flowers that speckled the McGillycuddys' yard like flakes of newly fallen snow. 'I'm sorry.'

'Well, 'tis in the past now.'

They sat in silence, until Grace turned to him once more. 'Is . . . is autumn really golden?' She'd never noticed in London. One minute the trees were green, then they were bare, their leaves blowing down the streets, whipped by winter air.

'Sure, it's the turn.'

'What's the *turn*?'

He laughed at her. Six months ago, that would have hurt, but she began to laugh too. He said, 'The birch and the beech: they change colour, the last blackberries hang in the hedge-rows, then the hawthorn loses its leaves so that you finally see the spikes underneath, and remember that they were there all along . . .' He paused, embarrassed.

'Why, Daniel McGillycuddy,' Grace said, 'I do believe you're a poet and you didn't know it.'

He flushed. 'You've never noticed autumn?'

Now she thought about it, the trees in Grosvenor Square *did* turn to rust just after her birthday. When she returned to England, she would notice the changing seasons, she promised herself. Because she'd begun to enjoy *newness*, begun to appreciate that things don't stay the same for ever. Change, she thought, as she inspected her ink-stained hands, was something she had learned to enjoy, and could quickly grow to love.

One evening in September, over dinner, Grace discovered that Daniel had gone, left for the barracks at Brighton without so much as a goodbye.

'The McGillycuddy boy came by today,' Rose said as she sipped her wine.

'Daniel?' Grace asked guardedly, as though she might be referring to someone else. They were having a vegetable-rich stew, their meat stretching further and further each week.

'Yes, Daniel. I must say, a man in uniform is always something to behold.'

'Off to Brighton, was he?' Uncle Marcus said, apparently oblivious to Grace's discomfort. Brighton was Tasmania's main training camp, a base in the south of the state.

'I thought he was leaving . . . tomorrow.' Grace could barely get the words out. She had written him a letter; it sat on her bed.

'Richard Holmes and his Buick had been double booked, apparently, so they had to leave today. He went with that chubby boy . . . what's his name?'

'The freckled one?' said Olive.

'Puds. His name is Puds,' Grace said quietly. Over the last months, she had met Puds half a dozen times, and she liked him. He was kind – and an extremely talented artist – and she had recognised elements of him in herself; a nervousness created by a parent for whom he'd never be enough. 'And Daniel didn't . . . ask for me?'

Rose frowned. 'No. Why would he?'

'Well—'

'You know what boys are like.'

No, I don't, Grace wanted to say, but the words wouldn't come. Daniel had left! Just left. Without a backward glance. Is that what boys were like? Is that what *friends* were like? 'I was here all day . . . writing in my room—'

Chapter 38

Towerhurst, Tasmania
November 1974

The key to the tower was hidden in a blindingly obvious spot: under a vase that Ben had only picked up to use for a bunch of native waratah he'd found that morning on his walk, a story-board saunter during which he'd stuck resolutely to the road. The flowers were a surprise for Willow, a splash of volcanic red to match the sofa in the front room.

He turned the key slowly over in his hands. It had three large prongs and an ornate handle. There was no question as to where it would fit.

❧

'Wow,' said Willow.

'Wow,' Ben repeated.

'This would make the perfect studio . . .'

'. . . writing bolthole.'

They both paused, glancing at one another. Then Willow laughed. 'After you . . .'

The room at the top of the tower was indeed – as Colette had said – an office, and yet it was so much more than that: hexagonal – six portholes framing the wilderness – with a potbelly stove at its centre, the room full to the brim of dusty, clothbound books.

While Willow peered out the eastern porthole – across the endless rainforest – Ben went to the opposite side of the room, and knelt on a grey chaise longue. It was worn with a dainty indent, as if a child, or a slight woman, had spent endless hours there, gazing at the view beyond, drinking in the spectacular vista of greens and steely blues that stretched as far as the eye could see.

'This is . . .'

'Amazing.'

'It's your perfect office,' Willow conceded, running her hands along the books' spines before she went to the stove, opening it to examine the charred contents with interest. 'A treasure trove. It feels like a long-sealed tomb.'

'Doesn't it?'

She turned to him. 'Great light, though.'

Willow was always on the hunt for *light*. She preferred to paint in the early mornings and late afternoons, maintaining that those golden hours infused her colourful work with a magic she could never capture any other time.

'Shall we share?' He ran his uninjured hand down a pile of classic Australian ballad writers – Henry Lawson, Thomas Kendall, Mary Foott.

'Deal,' she said, which he considered to be very gracious considering the house was much more hers than his.

He went to the closest desk, on which he found a partially written ballad: words scrawled out and replaced with alternatives, an arrow indicating that two lines should be swapped, three stanzas covered in a huge X. Without any difficulty, he understood the inner workings of the writer who had sat here many years before and struggled over this. It was the creative process writ large, a first draft that would never see the light of day. But when he discerned the words beneath, he drew a shallow breath, turning his back to Willow.

She came to here from distant shores,
A place I once did know,
She brought with her a silver fox,
A pendant all a-glow.

The pendant. Ben blinked, trying to push his memories from the mine aside.

This office, he knew, had belonged to Marcus Foxton, who had left Towerhurst after Grace and Rose's departure at the end of the war. It seemed that, one day, he'd put down his pencil – right here – discarding this ballad where it lay. Had it been on the day he left? Who was it about? Rose? Grace? Both? Ben frowned, recalling his interrupted conversation with Ned.

Willow sat on the chaise longue, flicking through a box of notes. 'Seems Grace Grey fancied herself a writer too.' She held out a page. It was another half ballad, and *by Grace Grey* was scrawled across the bottom several times, as if she'd practised taking ownership of the words, which were beautifully written, with a flourish on each G and a long loop that trailed the Y. Ben smiled. The practising of a signature was something he himself had done repeatedly, long before he'd had his first offer of publication.

'And it looks like she was published.' Willow passed him a sheaf of clippings from *The Bulletin* dated from 1941 to 1945. 'The Lads Who Trained in Brighton', 'Knitting for Victory', 'When Copper Won the War' . . . they were all war poems – not of battle, but of life on the Australian home front.

'And that's not all.' From the wall, Willow removed a beautiful painting of a valley, with a patchwork of farmland that rolled to the sea. In its top right-hand corner, it had a dedication – *For Grace*. Something about the style of the artwork looked vaguely familiar to Ben. In its bottom right-hand corner, the name of the artist written in teeny-tiny text.

'Puds?' he said.

Willow glanced up. 'The boy in the Christmas photos? Both of which, by the way, I can't find. They must have fallen out of my bag at Sergeant Griffin's house.'

Even without the photo, Ben recalled the boy's face clearly; that forlorn look he gave Grace. The painting's detail was exquisite: fields of grass rippled with texture, coins of light danced on the bay and the low sun had thrown a golden shawl over the landscape's cool shoulders to keep out the night. It was a moment in time that *meant* something. Feeling flowed through every careful stroke.

And that feeling was *love*. Ben appraised the painting, instinctively knowing, deep in his overactive mind, that it was somehow important, but before he could say anything to Willow, she was gone, down the steps and away, saying it was their last night in the house, and the pasta wouldn't cook itself. He went to the bedroom and slipped the painting into the bottom of his bag. Just another piece of the puzzle that he was sure would one day fit.

❧

As Willow put the finishing touches on her canvas by candle-light that evening in the tower office-studio, Ben watched her work, marvelling at how, only a few years before, they hadn't even met. It was love at first sight, a chance encounter at a gallery event Ben was dragged along to by a colleague from his part-time job tutoring at the university. It wasn't his scene at all, and he'd been loitering by the drinks when Willow had sidled up to him and said with a sympathetic grin: 'At least it's not your birthday.' That was midwinter – June – three years ago, and by spring, he knew they'd be together until the end of their days.

'We'll come back soon, love, I promise,' she said, taking his quietness for upset as she continued work. They'd packed the car and were ready to catch the low tide.

He moved his candle a little closer to where he sat on the chaise longue, overlooking the first clear night they'd had. A silver sprinkling of stars fell on the treetops, and the stroke of Willow's brush and the scratch of his pencil wove together in the room's warm air.

Luckily he was left-handed (but then, he'd always thought left-handers were lucky) and, with his bandaged hand resting in his lap, he was writing a letter to an author friend from London, Roger Masters. They'd met some years before at a writers' retreat in Hobart and become immediate allies. Over a glass or two of whiskey they'd talked late into every night. They'd got on famously, and Roger seemed a down-to-earth kind of guy. It later transpired that his father owned half of Devon, and his tell-all aristocratic biographies were penned under a *nom de plume*.

'What are you writing?' Willow asked.

'I'm getting a start on my selkie short story. It's set at the McGillycuddys'.' The idea had potential, and he planned to run it past his editor when they returned to Launceston.

'Based *loosely* on the McGillycuddys, you mean?'

Ben smiled cheekily. 'Of course.'

Roger had come to Australia on a modern-day grand tour of sorts, and his open invite to London was something that Ben meant to take up when he and Willow were settled. A visit to Europe would be 'just the ticket', as Roger had said, a grand (or not so grand) tour of Ben's own: a stroll around Hyde Park, a visit to Roger's club, a ride on the tube. As always, Ben signed off in shorthand, a little joke between them. 'Your hand couldn't keep up with your brain so you had to learn?' Roger had hooted when he'd first seen his friend's notes.

Ben glanced at the space on the wall where Puds's painting

had been. There was something about Grace . . . the ballads, her love of Daniel, Puds's love for her . . . he wanted to know what had become of her. He wanted to know that it *wasn't* her down that mine. And if anyone could find an aristocrat, it was his friend, Roger Masters.

⁊⁊

The following morning, Ben parked outside Holmes' Grocers, telling Willow he needed some biscuits for the journey.

'I won't be long.'

When he stepped inside the shop, Ben's heart dropped: Mira Holmes, and her penchant for gossip, were absent. In her place, stood a late middle-aged man who merely issued a distracted tilt of his head before turning back to his newspaper.

'Do you have envelopes?'

Without looking up, the man slid one across the counter, and Ben folded the letter inside, writing Roger Masters' address from memory. The two corresponded most months; Roger filling him in on his latest aristocratic exposés (which were truly stranger than fiction), Ben using the titbits to mould into stories of his own.

'This one's for England.'

The man folded his paper away with a sigh as though he might be expected to walk it there himself. 'Collection's not till Monday.'

Damn. Ben had wanted to post the letter in Westford to get ahead of the weekend; if he held onto it much longer, he might well change his mind, and let Grace's memory be lost to the wind. Besides, he didn't want Willow to know he was making enquiries, worried as she was about the current state of his mind.

'Mrs Holmes not in today?'

The man stuck a series of stamps on the envelope's exterior with excruciating slowness. 'Mother? No.'

That hooked nose, those dark eyes ... how had Ben not recognised the likeness?

'It's her day off?'

'Yep.'

Exhaling slowly, Ben attempted to control his frustration, but fatigue stole his calm, and he grappled to retrieve it. He'd slept terribly the night before, tossing and turning, plagued with nightmares that lingered into the morning, as he and Willow had packed their final belongings and driven away. He was filled with a sense that he shouldn't go. That he'd left something behind.

It was no good. He couldn't walk away from Westford without something more to go on. He reached across the counter. 'I'm Ben. We're the new owners of Towerhurst.'

The man raised an eyebrow, taking the proffered hand in a limp grip. 'Richard,' he said. 'So ... you're the one who found the body? Bad business, that.' And there! Yes, there it was ... a flash of Mira Holmes. He eyed Ben with a new-found curiosity. 'There was a suitcase, wasn't there?'

Ben hesitated. 'You have a theory?'

'Grace Grey, isn't it? She left for Hobart, and was never seen again. It was Rose who pushed her, I reckon.'

'What?'

'Oh yes. She hated Grace.'

Ben's mind whirled. 'You knew them? Rose and Grace?'

'Was the first to meet them, wasn't I? Straight off the boat. Rose was sweet on me from day one. We were ... *acquainted* ... for a while.' He said this in a manner so leerish Ben had to look away. 'But she was keener on the uncle, wasn't she?'

'I had heard—'

Richard carried on. 'Bet you hadn't heard, though, that Rose *went away* for a time.' He smeared his lips into a sneer. 'For *work*.'

Ben frowned, completely lost. 'No, I didn't know—'

'Disappeared to Hobart. I saw her, see? I used to drive the army boys from the west coast to the training camp in Brighton.' He said this with the certain sense of superiority of a man who believes that his job is the axis about which all others spin. 'I'd stay in Hobart, before driving back again. Saw Rose, didn't I? Walking down Collins Street, bold as brass, months after she slipped out of Towerhurst without a word to anyone.'

Ben paused, grappling for a comment. 'Walking, was she?'

'Yep.' Richard leaned forward, whispering, though there was no one else in the shop. 'Walking down the road with a pram, a newborn baby swaddled in a pink blanket. She became flustered when she saw me, told me it belonged to a *friend*. She wouldn't say who though. Still, I remember she asked me out for tea, but we'd gone sour by then. What did I want with spoiled goods?'

'What are you implying?'

A shrug. 'Rose Munro had a baby while she lived in Hobart, and when she returned to Towerhurst, there wasn't a sight of that little girl to be seen. I reckon Grace knew about it. Rose carried on cool as a cucumber, like nothing had happened. That was Rose to a T. I've told the sergeant all this, you can be sure of that, but the man's as useless as a . . .'

As Richard talked on, a cool prickle crept up Ben's neck. A *daughter*? He tossed away the thought with a shake of his head, but it seeped back like smoke under a closed door. 'What year was this?'

'1942,' Richard said without hesitation.

Icy fingers closed around Ben's throat. 'You're sure?'

Richard looked at him intently. 'Yep. Winter it was. Right after the Battle of Midway. There was a feeling in Hobart at that time . . . that the war in the Pacific was turning. So I remember it. Wondered how it would go for my job, and all.'

'The Battle of Midway?' The fingers loosened their grip, and Ben could breathe again. 'Wasn't that May?' The date was too early.

'No, not May,' Richard said. 'It was definitely June. June 1942.'

Ben turned from the counter to gather himself. For a moment, he forgot about Grace, about Puds, about the draughts of secrecy that seeped from Towerhurst's darkest corners. Because Rose had had a baby girl in June 1942, and Ned said that she and Marcus Foxton – who had surely set up the Foxton Trust? – had been close. Very close.

June 1942. Willow's birth date.

With a sudden, sickening realisation, Ben knew he'd discovered something important, but not in the way he'd intended.

Chapter 39

Grosvenor Square, London

December 2004

On Saturday evening the aunts announced their departure the following morning.

'Until Christmas Eve,' said Ash. 'We have business in . . .'

'Was supposed to be Geneva, but now it's Oslo,' Ivy said with a huff. This time it was a building they had an interest in, something about Microsoft expanding its footprint. *Microsoft*. Libby knew that was where they'd made their first big win.

'And it will give you a bit of' – Ash wiggled her eyebrows – 'privacy.'

Libby turned away, pretending not to hear. Her aunt was insufferable, though in the most lovable of ways. And anyway, she'd not heard from Sam since the previous morning. But why would she? His overwhelming memory of her would surely be a lingering sense of disappointment, that her excuse for the abrupt end to their conversation was flimsy at best. As Sam had walked away, she'd looked again at the document she'd snatched so hastily from her bag. It was the interview with Olive Foxton, and she'd felt another wave of frustration. Who could she ask to translate it? Placing it more carefully back, she'd turned and headed home.

'By the way,' said Ivy, pushing a glass of wine across the counter, 'we've asked Willow to come for Christmas.'

Two minutes through the door and already Libby couldn't keep up. 'You've done what?'

'And,' said Ash, triumphantly, 'she's said yes!'

Libby dropped her bag at her feet, hoping that the loud thud wasn't her laptop. She'd spent the entire day in the British Library's reading rooms immersed in Stern Publishing's back catalogue: battle ballads, lyrics of love, digests of delightful ditties. Forgotten works hidden amongst a million books where they might never have been read; yet the pages were well-thumbed and Libby had tried to imagine the many readers who'd taken solace from the words. Sam had told her that Lawrence and his mother, Alice, had formed the publishers when they were both under thirty, before they were married in a shotgun wedding several years later. They'd had no money for an office, so *The Albatross* became both their home, and the base for the business. It was, Libby felt, the most beautiful love story she could imagine, and the tale had led her to the library to discover what they'd brought into the world.

'I love imagining them so young, so hopeful,' Sam had added half an hour before Libby would ruin the moment, racing from the café, her past only a single step behind her.

'Is there anything left,' she'd asked, 'of the business?'

'Everything's out of print and the company's dormant. Stern Publishing. Sounds so *serious*, doesn't it?' He'd laughed then. 'The reality is that my parents metaphorically split the boat in half – the bow for living, the stern for working.'

'Sam, that's lovely. When did your dad buy *The Albatross*?'

'Dad? It was Mum's boat long before she met him.'

She'd smiled. Always a pleasure to be surprised.

'And,' continued Ash, bringing her back to the present, 'we bought you a surprise.'

Oh no. Libby stripped off her red coat; a new purchase from a charity shop in Brixton. 'Should I be concerned?'

Ash pushed across a nautical themed paper bag, and Libby peered inside.

'A captain's hat?' It was emblazoned with *The Albatross.*

'A boat-warming present . . .' And even Ivy couldn't help but laugh as Ash saluted their niece and hollered *permission to come aboard.*

≈

Later, Libby sat alone in the front room nursing a Baileys, the sounds of her aunts' packing – opening drawers, zipping suitcases – eliciting a surprise pang of envy. Could it be that she was suddenly of a mind to travel? To see new places? Do new things? She listened to Ash hum – from *Jingle Bells*, she launched straight into *The Twelve Days of Christmas* – realising she would be bereft when her aunts' brief visit was over. But Christmas was only weeks away, and with it, her mum.

Libby could already see Willow. There she was standing at the opposite wall, putting the finishing touches on Ash and Ivy's new – efficiently hung – painting. Those careful strokes, that intense gaze, as though looking straight through the canvas to whatever lay beyond. She'd always loved to watch Willow's work take shape; as a child she'd delighted in shadowing the process with her own tiny easel and palette. Even back then, she'd not failed to notice that her own dabblings were filled with colour while her mother's work was not, though she now understood that hadn't always been the case.

Some years ago, Libby had discovered dozens of paintings in the attic, piled at the back, discarded and covered in dust: seascapes, landscapes, Federation houses, all in her mother's distinctive cubic style, but full to the brim with colour. By the yellow light of a torch, she'd spent an hour flicking through them, realisation dawning – as she turned each canvas over – that all were dated pre-1975. And at the back of the pile, she'd come across something quite different: a small painting of a valley, a beautiful scene from England, or Ireland, eye-catching in a very different way to her mother's work. The golden glow that infused it captured not just a place, but a time: afternoon on an autumn day, Libby could tell, though she couldn't have said why. The artist's name was written in the bottom right-hand corner, and she recalled it now, because it was so unusual.

Puds.

Libby sighed, detaching herself from the past, and glancing away from her mother's work, only to come face to face with Ivy.

'I didn't hear you come in! You scared the life out of me.'

They both paused, listening to Ash, who was – thankfully – on her last round of yelling *fiiiiiveee golden rings.*

'You were a million miles away.'

'Only ten thousand, actually . . .'

'Back in Tassie?'

'Thinking about Mum.'

'Her visit?'

Libby nodded vaguely, as Ivy went to the drinks tray to consider the alarming variety of liquor. 'Sorry about not asking you. We should have. It just . . . came out of Ash's mouth, you know how it goes?

'*And a parrrrr-tridge in a pear tree,*' sang Ash, the rendition finally over.

Libby smiled. 'I do know.'

'You'll be here?'

'Of course.'

'And what about the rest of December? Any plans?'

Libby hesitated. Did Ivy mean: *are you moving out?* 'I haven't . . . I haven't decided about the boat yet.'

A smile. 'Really? And I thought Sam's story was *so* convincing.' Nothing much made it past Ivy. 'But I have to hand it to him, the best way to deal with Ash is to give her a false trail to follow. Otherwise she won't give up until she discovers what was kept from her.'

Libby laughed. 'True.'

'So . . . what *was* kept from her?' said Ivy, with a meaningful look.

'It's not what you think . . .'

'Oh yes? Do tell.'

'Sam is the son of Daniel McGillycuddy's publisher.'

Ivy blew out a held breath. 'Right-o. Well, that wasn't what I was expecting.' She paused, then added: 'Or hoping for.'

A hesitation. 'I've been . . . researching. Dad's satchel.'

'And yet you promised you wouldn't.'

'I did.'

Ivy poured herself a measure of whiskey. 'Just a small one,' she said, 'early flight.'

'I'm sorry.'

'What for?'

'I'm sorry I broke my promise.'

'You're not sorry, love.'

Libby felt a well of affection for her aunt. 'No, I suppose I'm not.'

'It's good to see you like this.'

'Like what?'

'With a fire in your belly.'

Libby *was* aware of a warmth in her stomach, but she'd blamed it on the Baileys. Or perhaps the question she now wanted to ask.

'Ivy?'

'That tone of voice . . .' her aunt said. 'Why do I feel another interrogation is imminent?'

'Why did Mum wait until 1985 to sell Towerhurst?'

A resigned sigh. 'As far as I know — and I don't know much,' she warned, 'the house was left in trust. It couldn't be transferred to your parents until after Willow had married. As I understand it, they had to wait seven years before she was able to sell. Part of the T&Cs.'

'Okay. So why not sell in eighty-two, when the time was up?'

Ivy hesitated. 'You haven't worked it out?'

'Worked what out?'

'You were the brightest little girl. She wanted the best for you. Just as Ben would have.'

And then it dawned on Libby. In 1985 she'd been ten years old. The next year, Year 5, she'd been sent to private school. And private school cost money. 'I thought . . . I guess, looking back, I thought you'd paid for it.'

'Willow Andrews accept a penny from her sisters?' Ivy shook her head. '*Towerhurst* paid for your education, Libby. And your mum couldn't get a reliable estate agent to show the place, remote as it was. So . . . she advertised it herself. Though it cost her dearly to even think about Towerhurst again, let alone go there.'

Libby felt her heart tug. 'But *why*?'

'Your dad's disappearance.'

'Ivy, I don't believe that story.'

'Well, it's true.'

Her aunt was clearly lying, and Libby thought she knew why. That afternoon she'd received a reply from Jess, opening the email with an anticipation that had been matched and further extended.

Dear Libby,

Of course we remember you, you were a part of our journey to Towerhurst . . . without you, we might never have found the cave behind the waterfall! As you can see from the website, we've made a few changes since you were here, but I hope you'll agree we've kept her charm intact.

We have three couples checking in today, so this'll be brief, but . . . regarding the body, I have a document I want to send you, so let me get back to you tomorrow with the full story – trust me, you'll find it's worth waiting for.

Re: Edeline Grey, yes I know a bit about her. Fairly nasty, by the look of things. I'm not sure she visited Towerhurst, but we did discover an example of her handwriting here in the house. It's a very brief letter – Edeline probably wrote it during her incarceration at Holloway – to Rose Munro, who we've since learned lived here in the forties as the chaperone of Edeline's daughter, Grace. It's a bit light on detail, but certainly suggests that life was every bit as complicated in the forties as it is today!

Must run, back to you shortly,

Jess

'I mean,' said Libby, 'that I don't believe Dad's accident was the reason she didn't want to return to Towerhurst.' Silence. Then: 'I've arranged to meet Roger Masters.'

Ivy frowned.

'Dad stayed with him when he was here in London, a writer friend apparently.' Libby paused. 'I imagine he was one of the last people to see Dad alive. I imagine they talked a lot . . .'

'I see.' A shadow flickered over Ivy's face.

'Can I ask a question?'

'Another one?'

'Did Mum ever mention a . . . Rose Munro?' Ivy turned away, and Libby resisted the urge to take the printout of Edeline's letter from her pocket. 'Or did she talk about Marcus Foxton? The owner of Towerhurst?'

Ivy gripped the bridge of her nose between her fingers. 'I

think it's best you ask Willow about these things.' She pushed her glass of whiskey away, as though she blamed it for what she had said, then she stood and went to the window. Tentatively, Libby followed.

'Ivy?'

'Yes?'

'Mum was adopted, wasn't she?'

From her bedroom, Ash had gone quiet, so when Ivy murmured, 'It's not my place to say,' it reverberated around the apartment as if reinforcing the sentiment.

Libby nodded. She'd always wanted siblings, always envied the way that they rallied for one another, stood by each other, the way they showed a singular love tied by blood. Only, in this case, it wasn't. She was overtaken with a flood of affection for her aunts, for her mum, for the way they'd been all these years, despite the reality she now knew. Spontaneously, she leaned in and kissed Ivy's cheek. 'You're the best sister she could ever ask for.' From her pocket, she took Edeline's letter, passing it across.

April 1942

My dearest Rose,

Can't write much, only to say the guards limiting my mail. You mustn't blame yourself about the pregnancy. I can't believe Marcus would have let this happen. I am not there to help, and it breaks my heart that you should have to manage alone. Please keep me informed as you always do.

Yours,

Edeline

'The legacy . . . the dates . . . this Rose Munro was pregnant, wasn't she?' Libby said. 'And Marcus Foxton was Mum's father?

Hence the Foxton Trust, hence the secrecy. It must have been a great scandal. Mum was born in June 1942, so—'

Ivy held up a hand. 'It's conjecture only.'

'You know something . . .'

'Willow . . . suspected. She told me about it some time after Ben's death. I suppose it was the reason he was digging into Edeline Grey. Perhaps he wanted to know more about Willow's heritage. About the Foxton family.'

'And what about Daniel McGillycuddy? Where does he fit into this?'

A sigh. 'I don't know. And I should also tell you that Ash doesn't know either—'

'*Ash doesn't know either* what?' said Ash, who had appeared silently behind them, a pair of festive flashing reindeer antlers on her head.

'Nothi—' Libby began just as Ivy said:

'Your niece has something to tell you.'

Libby gave Ivy a shocked look.

'Well,' said Ash, waggling her antlers, 'I'm all ears.'

'The thing is, Ash . . . well, this is a bit awkward, but Libby discovered today . . .'

'What?!'

'She's in love.'

Libby groaned once . . . then a second time as she was rapidly gathered into a bearhug that took the breath from her. *The best way to deal with Ash is to give her a false trail to follow.* In her own way, Ivy had saved her – by throwing her into the deep end – and it was only when she was finally released from the embrace, muttering quietly that she wasn't sure it was *love* per se, that she realised she still gripped Edeline's letter in her hand.

'What's that?' said Ash, following her gaze.

'A letter,' she said truthfully. 'From Sam.'

It had been the perfect answer because her aunt smiled – and respected her privacy – as Libby bid them both good night. Moments later, she reread the letter once more, before slipping it back in her father's satchel, a vital piece of the puzzle clicking into place: Willow had been adopted, and Marcus Foxton – her father – had anonymously left her a house.

Chapter 40

Launceston, Tasmania

December 1974

For the first time in her life, Willow struggled to get out of bed — not in the way of those mornings at Towerhurst, when she'd lingered luxuriously while Ben had made coffee — but a deep-seated dread that the core of her life and everything she had ever known about herself was about to be ripped away.

'It's not as bad as all that,' Ben had murmured when he'd first sat her down to confess what Richard Holmes had said. 'Your family *are* your family, no matter what. They'll be there for you in the future, just as they have been in the past . . .' He'd trailed off. Naturally, he'd be making private comparisons between their own situations, and in that regard, Willow had most certainly been the lucky one.

'Oh, Ben . . . could it be true?'

'It seems likely. Yes.'

And now Willow turned that name over in her mind as she turned over in bed.

Rose. Rose Munro.

The dates certainly matched, that of her own birth, and the baby that, according to Richard Holmes, had only just been born. June 1942. But what did he know, this Richard? His mother thrived on gossip. The son was probably the same.

had finished with a whoop and, a moment after he'd put down the phone, he'd scooped her off her feet. 'The literary supplement in the *Telegraph*! In the UK! They want a piece of fiction.'

'You can't be *serious*?' And despite her own turmoil, she too had jumped for joy. 'What will you send them?'

He'd rushed to the kitchen, where his tenth draft of 'The Selkie of Ocean Beach' lay on the table. Picking it up, he'd waved it in the air.

'Yes, of course, we'll go to the post office first,' she said now. 'And . . .'

'And?'

'Perhaps I should . . .'

'Yes?'

'I *could* try to talk to Mum. But I'll wait until after Christmas . . .'

Ben squeezed her hand.

'I'll just ask her about my birth. If she hesitates, then . . .' Dina was famous for her inability to tell a lie. Secrets though, she was notoriously good at holding on to.

'It's better to know. Then we can find out—'

'One step at a time.'

'Of course.'

Her own laughter surprised her.

'You haven't laughed in weeks,' Ben said, confirming her thoughts. In that instant, he looked at her with such love, such deep devotion, that she felt everything else fall away.

She had let her suspicions about the legacy become all consuming, blackening her insides. She'd forgotten that outside everything was brighter. What difference did it make if she was adopted? She needn't contact Rose, needn't change a thing, if she didn't want to. Her shoulders dropped. She took a breath, then flicked her gaze to the bed.

'Do you know what else I haven't done in weeks?'

Ben grinned, taking her in his arms; his bandage now removed, his wrist had recovered in remarkably short order. She breathed him in. He seemed to smell of Huon pine, but that was surely just an illusion. Something she was hanging onto. A piece of Towerhurst. She opened her mind, trying to let it go, because whatever occurred there happened thirty years ago.

But this? This was here and now.

Chapter 41

Towerhurst, Tasmania

November 1940

Grace watched Rose open yet another envelope with an air of coy pleasure, the particular smile on her face confirming just one thing: the letter was from Daniel. Two months he'd been gone, and he'd written to her every week. Rose was an object of obsession for every boy in Westford and why, as Aunt Olive had asked with a raised eyebrow, would Daniel be any different? She sighed. Her own letters from Daniel arrived regularly enough, but felt somehow diminished by Rose's reactions.

Marcus breezed into the sitting room. 'I have news.'

Grace sat on the window seat, watching water pour from the gutters. She hadn't been to the waterfall all week, but the waterfall had come to her.

'Grace?'

She turned to him. 'News . . . for me?'

He held out an open copy of a magazine.

'Is this a joke?'

It was *The Bulletin*, and in it was her poem, 'When Copper Won the War'.

'No joke. In fact, they're calling you Tasmania's Pom Poetess.'

Across the room, Rose put aside her letter. 'I'm not sure Edeline would approve.'

Finally, Grace had found something she could do, but more than that, it was something she *enjoyed*. Pleasure, it seemed, was no longer alien to her. She found satisfaction in the *learnin' of it*, as Daniel would have said. And by making her ballads topical, she'd kept up with the news. The war may have ebbed and flowed over the year, but with each tide, its edges lapped ever closer.

In September, Japan had signed an alliance with Germany and Italy. This new enemy felt far closer than Europe, and Tasmanians now kept a weather eye on the horizon. Marches by the second AIF in Launceston woke a dormant patriotic passion, the fever only increasing when mines were found in Bass Strait. Who'd placed them and how they had gone undetected, no one knew. The shallow sea had been closed to shipping, making the island state more isolated than ever. Grace rarely visited Westford, but when she did, she noticed a shift in the mood: the sense of excitement that the outbreak of war had brought with it more than a year ago had become edged with fear as Tasmanians began to contemplate their place in this changing world.

'Don't worry,' Rose had said at the time. 'The state's rather self-sufficient.' She had become an authority on Tasmanian industry since being promoted to personal secretary to Mount Lyell's GM – the appropriately named Mr Claud Greensmith, copper metallurgist and known womaniser – the previous incumbent apparently having been fired.

'Doesn't surprise me,' Aunt Olive had remarked. 'Mabel Martin was in my year at school. Not the sharpest tool in the shed.'

Truthfully, Grace had already overheard such whispers about Mabel, as well as rumours of an affair between her and Mr Greensmith, but whether they were fabricated in Holmes' Grocers, or steeped in reality, Grace had no idea.

Whatever the reason for Mabel's sacking, Rose had taken to the secretarial role like a duck to water, and she had no compunction in sharing her newly acquired knowledge at every available opportunity. 'Tasmania's contributions to the war effort are second-to-none,' she'd said at dinner one night. 'All these businesses reinventing themselves . . . there's a tennis racquet factory in Launceston now makes shell carriers, did you know? And Waverley Woollen Mills are turning out field blankets in the hundreds.' But, according to Rose – which meant: according to Mr Greensmith – Mount Lyell was the crowning jewel, providing much-needed copper for the Allies as the year rolled on . . . and roll on it had.

Uncle Marcus broke Grace's reverie. '*The Bulletin* want more of your work.'

'Really?'

'How about I send off "Spitfire Bingo"?'

She nodded. A flying school had been established in Tasmania's central midlands to take recruits for the Empire Air Training Scheme. This had caused great excitement in Launceston, where daily reports of the war raging over England's skies were front and centre in the newspapers. Funds were being raised – through bingo, Grace had conjectured – to sponsor a Spitfire right here in Tasmania.

When Marcus had left the room, she turned back to the window, sensing Rose's gaze on her as she opened her letter and ran a finger down the page.

She gasped. 'Daniel's coming back for Christmas.'

Rose frowned, then her features smoothed. 'Yes,' she said. 'I know.'

❧

Christmas Eve took an eternity to arrive, but when it finally did, Grace felt a stab of apprehension. She hadn't seen Daniel in over three months, and wasn't sure what to think of him any longer. There were two major complicating factors, and one of them stood next to her, hand raised to knock on the McGillycuddys' front door, and dressed in a skirt of midnight blue that made Grace's own choice of colour – grey – look extremely drab.

'Will we eat inside, do you think?'

'How would I know?' Rose talked through the smile she'd plastered on her face as she waited for the door to open, which it did now to reveal Daniel, dressed in his army uniform.

He paused, his gaze swinging between the two women. When he stepped forward, hand outstretched, Rose walked into his embrace.

Grace was immobilised with feelings she couldn't understand, and those very feelings were the second complicating factor; she wasn't sure how to behave because now, when she thought of Daniel, or read his words, or ran her hand across the smooth stones by the waterfall where he used to sit, her stomach inexplicably flipped, making her feel weak at the knees. The feeling was both good and bad and it gripped her now so that she could only stare, a hot flush rising up her neck.

'Grace?' A gentle hand touched her shoulder. She turned to see a tall man in uniform stood behind her.

'Hello?'

He removed his slouch hat. 'Good to see you again.'

She gasped, then collected her scattered thoughts. 'Puds. I didn't . . .' She paused. 'I didn't recognise you.'

It seemed she wasn't the only one capable of transformation. The assault courses and long marches had done Daniel's friend good. He must have traded in his uniform several times, because he had grown both taller and slimmer in equal measure. He emitted, too, the new confidence that Daniel had alluded to in his letters, suggesting that in his father's absence, Puds had flourished.

As though reading her mind, he said, 'Perhaps I *will* be as tall as my father, after all.'

From within the sawmill, she heard a laugh and turned to see Colette and Ned wrestling a huge garland across the doorway. It must have taken an age to plait the dozen shades of eucalyptus foliage into a rope. Rich red orbs of native waratah flower heads nestled perfectly against the green, the illusion of giant jolly holly berries in a place where there were none.

She looked back over her shoulder to where Rose had blocked the cottage doorway, obscuring Daniel from her own view. She slipped her hand through the crook of Puds's arm and walked away from the scene.

ટঌ

The McGillycuddys had set up a small trestle table in the sawmill, the double doors on each side open so that the building formed a marquee bound by the rainforest. The packed dirt floor was swept smooth, half a dozen storm lanterns hung from the rafters, and the scent of Huon pine infused the sticky air.

Colette placed a marble cake on the already-crowded table, and spread her arms wide – 'Welcome, welcome!' – just as Daniel and Rose arrived, deep in conversation. When he saw Grace, Daniel made his excuses and came to stand beside her.

'You left before I could say hello.'

Ned wound a gramophone and something jolly played in the background – a Celtic jig – and Grace was glad of the noise.

'Well?' she said coolly, taking her seat.

'Well, what?'

'Say hello.'

He almost smiled. 'Hello, Grace.'

'Hello, Daniel.'

'Thank you for your letters.'

Rose took a place at the table, and Grace observed her with a critical eye. 'You're welcome,' she said. All their easy banter from days gone by had evaporated as though their friendship had been a glass of water left on a countertop in summer's midst. Had it been half full or half empty? she wondered, as Daniel frowned at her, taking his place at the table next to Rose, as Grace turned back to Puds.

Ned watched the interaction between Grace and Puds with interest. If those two had sat at the McGillycuddy table on Christmas Eve last year, they would have been unrecognisable from the pair that chatted quietly now. Grace had been replaced with something like a kinder version of Rose, though Colette maintained it was their manner that was similar; their Englishness made them stand out from those around them. Ned didn't work at Towerhurst, so he hadn't observed Grace changing gradually, as his wife had done. Two months ago, he'd dropped by the house to chat with Marcus about some issue with the road and, as they'd chewed the fat, Rose had appeared from a gap in the rainforest shrouded under a hooded coat. He'd waved, calling out, 'A fine, soft day for a walk, Rose.' When she'd pulled back her hood, he'd realised he'd got it wrong: it wasn't Rose at all, and Grace had thrown him a dazzling smile that took his breath away.

Marcus had laughed. 'For goodness' sake, don't ever tell Rose you mistook her like that.'

Now, Ned raised his glass.

'To Patrick and Derek.'

The assembled group clinked their glasses. 'To Patrick and Derek.'

Ned had tried – how he'd *tried* – to dissuade his two boys

from joining up, but his letter about his own experiences (written and posted without Colette's knowledge) had gone unheeded, no matter the pain it caused to write. It had been the same with Daniel, and less than two weeks ago the call-up had been extended to age thirty-three for single men, and Australia's lads were being shipped away in their droves. He'd come to the conclusion that the young just wouldn't listen. His sons were in Libya and, though they hadn't returned to Tasmania for Christmas festivities for years, their absence shone a light through a hole in Ned's heart that had long been there.

His nephew slapped a palm against the table. 'I almost forgot,' he said. From beside his chair, he lifted a large leather satchel. 'I borrowed this from one of the lads at Brighton.' It was a camera. 'His father's a hack. Said I could take it for Christmas.'

He handed it to Ned, who weighed the cool metal in his hands. Truth be told, he'd never held a camera before.

'What do I do with it?'

Daniel laughed. 'C'mon.'

The four kids, and Ned, gathered at the edge of the forest, the mulberry sky heavy with the threat of rain. Trees loomed over them, watching in fascinated silence.

'Right, you lot' – Daniel's voice took on an Australian twang; he'd had quite a lot of Colette's mead and the boy, as far as Ned was aware, wasn't used to the drink – 'no mucking around now.' As the four of them lined up, Daniel played the fool; he'd donned a Christmas hat and was *ho-ho-hoing*, Rose laughing at his drunken antics. Grace was more reserved, standing next to Puds, who'd also had a skinful, but – unlike Daniel – the effect had been melancholic. He looked pale, and the freckles leapt from his skin.

'Should you not be a bit more serious for photos?' Ned said to Daniel, after he'd had his lesson on the shutter. He wondered who would pay for the processing – each image, presumably, wasn't going to be cheap – but more than anything he wanted to get back to his mead and the warm light of the sawmill. Dusk wouldn't be long falling, and tomorrow was Christmas Day. A day off from the mill, a day with Colette and Daniel. A day to think of his boys. 'Ready . . .' He set his finger on the button. 'On three. One . . .'

Rose leaned towards Daniel, using him for shelter, then she tilted her face upwards, lifting onto her toes, and brushing her lips against his.

'Two . . .'

They hovered like that, suspended almost, and Ned couldn't help holding his breath. Rose and Daniel pulled apart.

'Three.' *Click*.

Something indefinable rippled across the scene, and Ned felt uncannily like he was peering through a window of frosted glass. Then Grace turned on her heel, stalking away, Puds just two steps behind. Rose giggled, tipping her face to the heavens as the rain fell like tears of joy on her face.

As Ned retreated to the sanity of his glass of beer, an unexpected shiver crept up his spine. A game was being played by the young'uns, and he wasn't at all sure what it meant. Or where on earth it would lead.

Chapter 42

Northport, Tasmania
Boxing Day 1974

Ash handed Willow a coffee – 'You all right, sis?' – her worried frown framed by a new haircut, a smart dark bob that she spent an inordinate amount of time trying to tame. 'Suits your personality,' Ivy had quipped yesterday, only moments after she'd recounted yet another of Ash's hare-brained business ideas. The twins were on fine form.

'Micro-soft? What kind of name's that?'

'It's derived from microcomputer and software,' Ash had said, sipping her Harvey Wallbanger. She'd made a cocktail for everyone, but while the other glasses were still full, hers was nearly empty. 'I heard about it from Jane Seyors, who went to Harvard. Knows the fella who's starting it. You remember Jane?' she said to the room. Evidently, the room didn't, and the conversation had moved on.

That was Christmas Day, and today Ash's enthusiasm for life had clearly waned. She held a cool cloth to her forehead, and Willow felt for her. At 9 a.m., it was already pushing seventy Fahrenheit. A perfect morning for the beach.

'You'll come, won't you, Mum?' Willow turned to Dina, who was chopping parsley, and humming with a faraway look in her eye.

'Later, darl,' she said absently.

Willow returned her cautious smile, searching her mother's face for her own features. Did anything about them match? Her eyes were an elusive shade; sometimes blue like Willow's until she'd turn towards the light when they'd shift to green. Her hair, though, was without doubt dark, while her smile was wider, too. She was petite like the twins, whereas Willow's tall frame was at odds with the family status quo.

'We're back to Launceston today,' Ash said, 'Ivy and me. The Turners are having a party.'

'Actually,' Dina said, adding the parsley to yesterday's turkey, along with ungodly amounts of mayonnaise, 'I'd like us all to have a Boxing Day lunch.'

Ash patted her flat stomach. 'I'll never fit into my cocktail dress . . .'

'Please?' Dina put a hand on her arm just as Ivy entered the kitchen, dripping and pink from a dip in the sea. 'I have something I want to tell you girls. Something I'd like to say.'

Willow's stomach flipped inside her, like it was trying to get away.

&

After lunch, Dina took Rob's hand in her own, and dropped a bombshell. It was nothing like Willow had expected. She gasped, glancing across the table at her sisters.

'Cancer? What do you mean? When did you find out?'

'A month ago.'

'A *month*?' Willow couldn't believe it, but then she could: her mother had always been good with secrets.

'I didn't want to spoil this one last Christmas, and it was perfect.' She gave that same calm smile she'd thrown Willow that morning in the kitchen before everything had changed.

'One *last* Christmas?' This time it was Ivy who parroted their mum.

'Possibly. Who knows?' Dina said with that same calmness, which was as shocking as it was serene. Willow felt as transparent as both of her sisters looked. For once, they were all a mirror of each other. She began to stand, a flush reaching up her neck.

Rob waved her down. 'I know this is a shock . . .' His words faded as Willow put a hand to her mouth. She wanted to cover her ears, wanted to turn back the clock. Wanted to forget this day. When she considered what she would've put her mum through, what she had planned to ask her that very afternoon, she felt sick inside. She would have unravelled something from Dina's past while her future was so very fragile.

This changed everything. She reached under the table and took Ben's warm hand, and he squeezed it in reply, the gesture confirming what she knew.

Her mum was her mum, that was all that mattered now.

Chapter 43

Tasmania

1941

March 1941

Dear Grace,

Things are changing in the war, aren't they? The lads
say that Tasmania will be a staging post for invasion,
but like Rose always banged on about, we're pretty
self-sufficient with the mine and all the factories. In
Hobart, they've started putting in bunkers, with men
already on patrol.

What do you think? You keep up with these things. I
always said to Puds that I didn't need to read the news –
your ballads kept me knowing what was happening. I
miss them, and your letters. I'm sorry you weren't well
when I came to say goodbye before New Year, because
I would have liked to have seen you. I don't know if he
said, but I wrote to Marcus and he replied saying you
were fine. He also sent a copy of 'Spitfire Bingo'. The
lads here loved it. You must be busy with the learning of
it all. You should get them all published in a book quick
smart – that'd be something, wouldn't it?

What do you think about the WAAAF finally being

formed? Bout time women got a chance to join the air force, I say.

If you get the time, will you write?

Your affectionate friend,

Daniel

PS Someone told me Banjo Paterson died last month. I'm sorry. I'll always be grateful to old 'Benjo', we had a great time with his ballads, didn't we?

April 1941

Dear Grace,

Did you hear about that woman, the Swiss radio presenter, Annette Wagner? They thought she was a Nazi spy, and, lo and behold, it's finally come out that she absconded from Australia more than a year ago. Who'd have thought it? Spies in Sydney. It's like something you'd read in a novel. Gets you pretty downhearted, but our mood here in Brighton is good. I'm learning about the Anzac spirit, and I can tell you it's as real as you or me.

Do you think they'll bring in daylight savings? Ned says he remembers when it happened in Ireland in 1916: he was at the front and his mother — my grandmother — wrote him a whole page about it. She was worried her curtains would fade, and that it might affect her rheumatism. They're saying that an extra hour of daylight would help 'the economy of the war effort'. Couldn't everyone just get up an hour earlier? You could write a ballad about that too.

I read in *The Examiner* they're preparing for air raids in Launceston, getting long hoses and sand and all kinds of things. They've even done a demo of an incendiary bomb at the fire station. Funny, isn't it? When we're ten thousand miles from action.

I know you're busy, but maybe you could write?
Your affectionate friend,
Daniel

June 1941

Dear Grace,

Did you know you can get a free booklet with air raid instructions from the police station? Puds's father sent us two, as if we don't already have enough to be doing. Anyway, what's the catch? As Uncle Ned always said: nothing in life is for free. I wrote to Marcus again, and he says you're doing well. He sent me a copy of 'Blackout Blues' and all the lads here loved it. I especially liked the bit about the faded curtains during daylight savings. Should I take any credit? Would it be rude to ask for a kiss in exchange? I hope you're laughing, like I am as I write this.

I wonder if, on my birthday, you could write me? You'll find some paper and stamps in this envelope so you don't need to get your own – I bought them with my ill-gotten gains from the bet, which we both so want to forget (see what I did there? <u>Bet</u>, <u>forget</u>. You'll make a ballad writer of me . . . <u>yet</u>. Ha!).

Your affectionate friend,
Daniel

Chapter 44

Tasmania

1941

To Daniel,

Thank you for your letters. The paper was nice and thick, and it would have been rude not to reply, seeing as you sent stamps. Aren't you supposed to be saving for home? You must be busy writing so very many letters, and to so many people. Does your captain tell you off? However do you find the time?

I'm glad you liked the ballads. I had already written 'Blackout Blues' when I received your letter, so I'm afraid you can't swap a kiss for it. So, no, there's no credit <u>due</u> and no debt from me to <u>you</u> (see what I did there?). What was it your father used to say? 'Forgetting a debt doesn't mean it's paid'? In this case, there's nothing to forget.

Everything is fine here. Rose is very busy in Queenstown, she's there a lot, although I'm sure you already know that. Since the Minister for Agriculture put out that speech about women being called on to play a larger role in Tasmanian industry, she's been very proud indeed. You'd think she was working the bellows herself. The government's certainly changed their tune since war broke out.

I applied for the WAAAF, but they discovered I lied about my age. But I'll be eighteen in couple of months, and eligible. Funny how boys can get away with it, but girls cannot, isn't it?

Uncle Marcus gave me a copy of Henry Lawson's works, but I'm afraid I can't quite take to them as I did with Banjo's. I was sorry he died, I would have liked to write to him to tell him how much his words mean to me. It seems silly, doesn't it, that we spend all this time in life not saying things to people that we should, and then it's too late?

We think there will always be time.

Sincerely,

Grace

Chapter 45

Tasmania

1941

August 1941

Dear Grace,

Thank you for your letter. It meant a lot to me. I have it in the top left pocket of my uniform. I would like to see you again before we go to Victoria, but I don't think that's possible. Our leave days are as rare as hens' teeth.

I can't write more now because we're packing, but I will when I can.

I just wanted to say thank you.

Love,

Daniel

PS There will be time.

November 1941

Dear Grace,

I wondered if you'd not written again because you were worried that your letters wouldn't reach me. They will – our mail follows us around the world, but I'm not off on some far-flung distant <u>shore</u>, so you shouldn't worry on that <u>score</u>.

Did you read about the blackout rehearsal they did in West Launceston? I don't know if it is necessary or what. Then someone in *The Examiner* was going on about air-raid shelters – why there aren't enough in Australia. He seemed pretty het up about it, saying that bigger cities have subways and the like, but there is no escape in Launceston at all. I reckon they should all move to Westford, seems safe enough to me. Who'd want to invade? Unless they were after the copper, I guess!

I don't suppose I'll be getting much local news now. Can you write me and keep me up to date? I've heard that mainlanders like to pretend Taswegians don't exist, so I'll be relying on you.

Our trip to Victoria went smoothly. On the way over in 1937, I never got to stop in Melbourne like you. You're right about Flinders Street Station – it is pretty impressive. Funny how going somewhere else makes you appreciate a place. Melbourne was busy – you wouldn't believe the number of Americans! Outnumber the Aussies, so they do – and the camp in Victoria is so hot and dry that I missed the west coast a bit. How different my days are from when we used to swim at the waterfall.

Can you believe the HMAS *Sydney* has gone down? What do the Germans want with western Australia, anyway? A good bit of space, I suppose. Have you written a ballad about that? You could finally use the phrase 'wide and distant plains' like 'The Man from Snowy River'. I've learned that ballad by heart, by the way; the lads laughed hearing a Paddy recite Australia's darling poem. I've learned 'The Ma'am from Joey River' by heart too, so you better be careful I don't steal it one day and publish it as my own! Ha!

We're moving to Katherine next, all the way up north. Write soon.

Love,

Daniel

November 1941

Dear Grace,

I have news: I'm just after having won a leave pass in a bet. I know, I know. Anyway, this was more a competition. Long story short, I competed using one of your poems ('Bunkers at Barnacle Rock') and it 'laid them in the aisle' as my mates like to say (I'm trying to say 'mates' instead of 'lads' because I'm getting grief over it). So the pass is mine. I'll be back in early December, so it'll be almost a year since we saw each other (Christmas Eve, if you remember?).

I would like to see you. I know you've been too busy to write again, but . . . I've been thinking about what you said in your letter − 'It seems silly, doesn't it, that we spend all this time in life not saying things to people that we should, and then it's too late?'

I have something to say.

Would you give me the time to say it?

Love,

Daniel

PS I heard that the Tasmanian Government rejected the daylight savings bill. Grandmother − God rest her − would have been pleased for the sake of curtains all across the state.

Chapter 46

Towerhurst, Tasmania

December 1941

The world shifted – for both Grace and the war – the day that Daniel came home on leave. She'd only written to him a handful of times during the past twelve months, though he was constantly on her mind; she was sure she wasn't so much on his. Letters for Rose kept coming, and each time a new one appeared on the hallway table, Grace tried her best to swallow the jealousy, to be happy for Daniel, for Rose, for their love that wasn't unrequited, unlike hers, and instead she focused on nursing her broken heart.

The moment he appeared – walking up Towerhurst's driveway, holding a sprig of white heather – a cool breeze washed right through her. Bravely, she smiled: after all, he had no idea of her pain, and he raised his hand in greeting as she shakily put aside her notebook. She hadn't known what day he'd return, but for the last week she'd dressed carefully in ways she'd neglected the months before. Her resolve to be indifferent began to crumble immediately as she stood and went to the edge of the verandah, where he'd stopped at the bottom of the steps. It was hot, and the overnight rain rose from the forest in gentle wisps.

'Hello, Grace.'

He'd grown more handsome still, and she glanced away, gathering the remains of her indifference. 'Hello, Daniel.'

He removed his slouch hat. 'It's good to be back.'

'I'm afraid Rose isn't here.'

'Rose?' He took a quick step forward. 'Grace . . . I came to see you.'

She laughed a little. 'I hardly think so.'

'I did.'

'I'd have thought after all your letters to—'

He took the steps two at a time. 'Grace, please.' He put the sprig of heather on the seat beside the door, then reached for her hands, the touch sending a shock through her body. 'I came as soon as I arrived.'

'You must be keen to see her.' She pulled one hand free. 'She's in Queenstown and won't be returning until—'

'I came to see *you*.'

She hesitated. Images of that moment on the beach flashed through her mind. *More* than images. She felt the prickle of stinging sand against her legs, smelled the salt tang of the sea, tasted the sweetness of her first kiss, heard the purr of the far-off waves. Then, without warning, the scene morphed, as trees marched over the sand. They brought with them the scent of fresh cut eucalyptus foliage, a mulberry sky, and the first warm plucks of rain. A camera flashed in her memory, then in a swirl of flesh, she became Rose, her laughing lips – their cherry colour made more vibrant by the throes of love – leaning in for a kiss.

She pushed Daniel aside, so that she could race down the steps and away.

&

Behind the waterfall, Grace held her head in her hands. For nearly twelve months, thoughts of Daniel had been her constant companion, filling spaces inside her that she hadn't realised were empty. Her coolness was the perfect protection, but by turning down the temperature, she had frozen stiff. She thought about her mother, and the way her nonchalance had made her feel. She thought about Rose, who may not have been the kindest, but surely deserved a happiness of her own? And, as she had done so many times over the last year, she thought about that girl, Elizabeth Winman, back in Grosvenor Square, who'd held her nerve until the moment her lover had disappeared out of sight, at which point she'd collapsed in a heap and cried.

'Grace?'

She looked up to see Daniel silhouetted by the waterfall. 'Last Christmas Eve—'

'Don't.' She couldn't bear it. The brush of their lips, the shattered glass of her heart.

'I barely even *know* Rose.'

Again, he stepped closer.

'Then why did you kiss her?'

He stopped, spread his arms wide in exasperation. '*She* kissed *me*! She's always flirted with me. I've tried not to encourage her . . . perhaps I gave her the wrong impression?'

His face was still a shadow in the dim cave, and he knelt before her, a half-light spilling across his features. Just as he had done at Towerhurst, he took her hands in his own. They were warmer now; a fire around her fingers.

'The letters—'

He reached out to touch her face, and Grace let out a whimper of misgiving.

'Grace,' he said, 'I'm in love with you.'

A heat travelled through her body until it was extinguished by the chill in her heart. 'You're lying.'

'God knows you don't make it easy,' he said, smiling. Her

mother's voice came unbidden to her mind. *You are very, very difficult to love.* 'But I . . . I love you.'

'Daniel, I . . .' Was it true? Could it be possible? 'Surely not?'

He laughed. 'I do! God, it feels good to say it!'

She was *more* than suspicious; she had been tricked before. 'You *love* me?'

Again, that laugh, exuberant. 'Yes!'

'You always loved me?'

'No. Not always.' He gripped her hands tighter as she tried to pull away. 'But once I got to know you. You're so brave, so full of life . . . and I love that you never knew it.' It was his turn to blush. 'I love you, Grace.'

She felt her heart might burst.

He stepped closer. 'Can I?'

She knew that she was crying, but she felt no embarrassment; the moment took up too much space to let any other emotions in. Letting out a half laugh, her gaze fell over his shoulder to the depths of the cave. 'No observers this time?'

He, too, gave a small laugh, covering his face with his hands, so that she had to reach forward and remove them: his expression was full of regret, full of remorse, and full of something else too.

Love.

She pushed aside her last trace of misgiving, leaned in, and touched her lips to his.

❧

Uncle Marcus was waiting on the verandah when they emerged from the rainforest, his forearms resting on the fence, his gaze a million miles away. Grace felt a flash of guilt, but it did nothing to dispel the butterflies circling in her stomach. Would her flushed skin tell him that today had been the best day of her life?

He straightened when he saw them, his gaze taking in their intertwined hands, but if Grace expected him to be . . . to be what? Protective? . . . she was to be surprised.

He took the steps two at a time.

'Something's happened.' His eyes were wrinkled with worry. In his hand he held his upturned pipe, hot ash fluttering to the ground.

Grace frowned, loosening her grip on Daniel's hand, feeling suddenly self-conscious that they'd been wrapped up in their own world. How long had it been? It felt like minutes, though it might have been hours. She always said that time passed differently once one stepped through the moon gate and beyond.

'Daniel, I'm sorry,' Uncle Marcus said. 'I don't know what this'll mean for you.'

'What is it?' Alarm made Grace's voice hard. 'What's happened?'

A deep, shaky breath. 'The US base, Pearl Harbor, was bombed this morning.'

Daniel frowned. He opened his mouth. Nothing came out.

'It was Japan. Australia has declared war, shoulder to shoulder with America.'

'But . . .' Grace faltered. She'd read that maintaining peace in the Pacific was all that separated Australia from conflict on its shores. 'How do you know?'

'Curtin made an announcement on the wireless.' John Curtin. Australia's new prime minister. According to Uncle Marcus, their new leader had given Australians a certain sense of renewed optimism. This turn of events was unthinkable.

'What do you mean: you don't know what this'll mean for Daniel?'

'Just that.' Uncle Marcus turned back to the house. 'I don't know what it will mean for our troops. For any of us. The war is on our doorstep.'

❧

It meant, of course, that Daniel would be deployed overseas and, a week later, he had word.

'Daniel, you *can't* go. It's not a game any more.'

'I never thought it was.'

Since the waterfall, they'd kissed countless times, and a little more. Grace couldn't get enough of him. Alone at night, she imagined his eyes on her, his fingers moving down her body, his hand touching the bare skin of her legs so gently she would gasp. It was wrong, wasn't it? To want to be touched like that? But, if anything, it felt the opposite of wrong. It felt right, like her past and her future had finally collided. She was no longer alone, no longer afraid. If only Daniel would stay . . . she would do anything to make that happen.

'Where are you going?'

He showed her the telegram. 'Darwin, then . . . I don't know.'

In the days after Pearl Harbor, news came thick and fast of the simultaneous wave of attacks that had hit the Philippines, Guam and Wake Island. Japan advanced into northern Malaya and Thailand, and bombed Singapore, a fortress that – they were assured – would never fall.

'But I think I have an inkling.'

She frowned. 'What do you mean?'

He pulled a letter from his pocket, unfolding the airmail paper carefully. The hand on it was neat and sloping, a million miles from his own. A second sheet fell out. It was a sketch: six men playing cards, a billy boiling over a campfire in the background. 'Puds sent this before leaving camp.'

Dear Daniel,
When you get this we'll be gone. I'm off to catch some more sun, and more tea.

'Will you see Puds again?'

'I don't know.' He took her hand. 'Soon, I hope. He isn't really made for battle.'

'What do you mean?' When she saw him last Christmas he looked stronger and fitter, his former self only a shadow of his present.

'Puds . . . well, he's a gentle giant. He's just different from the others. Without me there, I worry about him.'

'Did you help him through training?'

Daniel smiled. 'A few leg-ups here and there. I owed him. It was *he* who encouraged me to keep writing to you.'

Also to Rose, she thought, but she didn't want to ruin the moment, and her chaperone wouldn't be back from Queenstown for another week.

'So, what's this inkling you have?'

He leaned in to kiss her. His lips were warm, just like the surrounding day. After a moment, she gently pushed him away.

'Really, though?'

He gave her the sketch. Behind the boiling billy, spread out by the campfire was a map, its concertinaed form blending into the grass. She looked closer. It was the nibbled shape of northern Australia, Darwin marked with a star. Off its north-western edge, a long narrow island had been drawn, and faintly circled.

She almost laughed. 'How could a censor miss it?'

'Getting one over the censors is a source of pride in the battalion. We've got a tally on it. Puds is pretty cunning.' He grinned.

'What is it, this island?'

'Timor. That's why he wrote *I'm off to catch some more sun, and more tea*. More tea. Get it?'

'I've never heard of Timor.'

'It's divided between the Portuguese and the Dutch.'

'Aren't the Portuguese neutral?'

He shrugged.

'What's it like there?'

'I don't know. Tropical? Difficult?'

'When are you going?'

'Tomorrow.'

She jumped up, spilling Puds's letter to the floor. '*Tomorrow?*' The wind picked it up, and it scuttled along the verandah.

He rescued the sketch, then turned back to her. 'There's nothing I can—'

'Stay.'

'You know I can't.'

'Stay.'

'Grace, I can't just—'

'Stay.'

He turned her chin towards him. 'Look, the Japanese won't be interested in a tiny island in the middle of nowhere.'

People had been saying that about Tasmania too, though rumours of submarine sightings abounded. Grace stood. She couldn't bear it. In less than a week, she'd found herself, and without him she was scared she'd be lost again.

❧

Later, lying in bed, Grace retraced their day: their walk through the forest, the pause on the sun-warmed rocks to gather breath, the pleasure as they dived into the water and swam under the falls. Then more pleasure later, the kind that made her flesh flush as she recalled it. His hard body against her, the heat of it contrasting against the icy water. How goosebumps sprinkled her arms where he kissed them, and later still, more urgent this time, hidden behind that shimmering screen. He'd pressed his lips against hers, parted them and she'd felt the heat from his mouth fill her whole. They'd entwined, and when he moved inside her, she gasped, her world shifting and twisting on some invisible string until it spun in free fall and she cried out as he held her.

They'd made love, and by tomorrow morning, he would be gone.

Chapter 47

Towerhurst, Tasmania
February 1942

Grace had been at the base of the spiral staircase two days ago when she'd heard it, the announcer's voice fluttering down from the wireless: Timor had surrendered. She recalled it now; how she'd learned the news then walked unsteadily out onto the verandah, falling to her knees.

Of one thing she was certain. Daniel was there, in Timor. Three weeks after his arrival in Darwin he'd sent her a letter, and inside the envelope he'd slipped Puds's campfire sketch: *more tea*. He was two thousand miles away, dead or alive, and she felt herself crumple under the weight of a future without him.

'He'll be captured, that's all,' Uncle Marcus had said, when he found her out there listening to the rain. He couldn't fool her though; she could see he was worried. 'And POWs are well treated. The Geneva Convention sees to that.'

She'd glanced at him through her tears. 'Have the Japanese signed it?'

He'd handed her a mug. 'I forgot the milk,' he said quickly, before disappearing inside. Neither of them usually took it, but still Grace put some in her tea when he returned, the unmixed powder gritty on her teeth.

'What's it like being a prisoner of war?' she asked.

'How did you know?'

Rose had told her on the ship out and Grace had been too caught up in herself to care. Now, next to this gentle man, she felt a stab of guilt that she hadn't realised what it meant.

'Rose said you'd been interned for a time.'

Grace wasn't really sure how Uncle Marcus felt about Rose. There were occasions when they debated heatedly about the war, and times when they'd laugh at a shared joke. In other moments, quiet moments, Uncle Marcus looked at Rose with a strange expression: his brow wrinkled, his eyes searching her face as though trying to recall some far-off memory. For a fleeting moment, Grace had wondered whether there had been a moment of intimacy between them.

'It's true; I was interned for a short time. We escaped, myself and several men from the Fortieth Battalion. I imagine the camps will be less . . . cruel . . . this time round,' Uncle Marcus said, tamping his unlit pipe.

'What makes you think that?'

'We have the previous war to learn from. In my opinion, prisoners will be treated better now.' He looked at the treeline as if it were an advancing army. 'I really believe that.'

≥◆

After Daniel left, Grace had applied for the recently established Australian Women's Army Service, which had been set up to *release men from certain military duties for employment in fighting units*, but as she had none of the skills – driving, cooking, typing – required, she had not been accepted.

'And a good thing too,' Uncle Marcus had said when she received their letter. 'You'd be off to the mainland for one thing, and for another: how would you write your ballads?'

She'd shaken her head, thinking of that day at the waterfall when she'd admitted to Daniel how little she thought about the rest of the world. Now that world teetered: in Europe, the Americans had already arrived in Northern Ireland, bringing much-needed hope with them, but in the Pacific the Imperial Japanese Army advanced further and faster than anyone could ever have anticipated. The Allies and the Axis were on a seesaw, each battle, each victory and loss, changing the balance.

But it was the fall of Singapore, just before Timor was taken, that had shocked every nation; only a month before, the British had begun to retreat to the 'impregnable' fortress, but it had fallen and, with it, the sense of security on the home front in Australia. Days later, Darwin was bombed, and the war inched closer still. The fear was palpable. Pipe shelters had been built in Launceston's Princess Square and trenches in Royal Park. Even in Westford, posters had been strung along its single street: a Japanese soldier running across the globe (*He's Coming South: Fight, Work, or Perish*), a housewife throwing a tin of beans at the enemy (*Food is a Munition of War*), a woman in a blue uniform before a billowing Australian flag (*There's a job for YOU in the WAAAF*). The first American soldiers had arrived in Brisbane in December, and since then their numbers had grown. The most significant changes, though, weren't visible at all; they were buried deep in the Australian psyche. Deep in the *Tasmanian* psyche. They were no longer an island at the end of the world. The world was coming to them.

Only last night Grace had overheard Aunt Olive telling Marcus the latest news from the town.

'What do you mean: a submarine sighting?'

'Just what I said. In Macquarie Harbour,' Aunt Olive had said. Macquarie Harbour was six miles south of Westford and six times the size of Sydney Harbour. In the 1800s convicts had been sent there to fell Huon pine and build ships that would never rot.

'When?'

'Last week. Three fishermen saw it – thought it was a whale at first until it fully surfaced. They're saying it's the Germans, surveying the area.'

'Who's they?'

A hesitation. 'Mira Holmes.'

'Right.'

'Still though, it makes sense: the copper mine . . .'

When Uncle Marcus had only shaken his head, Olive had left the room in a huff.

Now, beneath Grace's bedroom window, a figure crossed the scraggly lawn with quick, determined strides, disappearing through the moon gate and out of sight. It must have been Uncle Marcus, wearing his oversized waxed coat, presumably off to visit the falls.

The falls.

After they'd made love, Grace had lain in the crook of Daniel's arm. They'd brought blankets, and a picnic basket, the contents of the latter spilling across the smooth stone floor.

'I've hidden a tin of my own. Just like your mess tin,' she'd said. 'Can you guess where?'

He'd run a hand lightly through her hair, which had been sun bleached to a golden blonde. 'In your bedroom?'

'No.'

'In the tower?'

She laughed. 'No.'

'Down a mine shaft?'

She shuddered. 'No.'

'Well . . . *where?*' He'd turned to her, following her gaze. Gently, he'd disentangled himself, pulling a second blanket to cover her naked form. Then he reached up into the stone shelf hidden above.

'What's in it?' He gave the Arnott's biscuit tin a noiseless shake, before opening it to reveal two copies of 'The Ma'am from Joey River'.

'One for you, and one for me,' she said.

'Grace, I already told you: I've learned this one by heart.'

Still, he put his copy of the ballad in the pocket of his discarded shorts, then sat, pulling the blanket across himself. Although he'd told her something of his training, his body was a narrative; he was far more muscular than the year before. From the pocket of those same shorts, he removed 'The Man from Snowy River', the copy torn from her birthday book, and given to him as an apology for her rude behaviour after that swimming lesson.

'I want you to look after this for me.'

She raised herself on an elbow. 'Why? What do you mean?' The unspoken lay between them.

'These sheets of paper changed my life, Grace. It was then I saw who you were. They're precious to me. *You're* precious to me. When I get back, you can return them.'

Tears threatened to ruin the moment, so she looked away, slipping the poem into the tin, wondering when they'd be there together again. 'What if I'm sent home?'

'Home?'

She realised he thought her home was now here. She'd barely talked of London as though her past had never been. 'To England.'

Less than three years ago, in another life, she'd had three days' warning before she was put on a boat and sent to an island hanging from the end of the world. She took her pen and notebook from the basket. She never went anywhere without them. 'You'd come for me, wouldn't you?' She scrawled the Grosvenor Square address, and gave it to him.

He frowned, appearing to commit it to memory, before

putting it in his pocket with his copy of 'The Ma'am from Joey River'. 'Your mother won't approve.'

He was right, of course.

'And I'd have to see you without meeting Rose.' He grinned. 'She's in love with me, you know?'

Grace knew that it was said in jest, but now the comment gave her pause. How would Rose feel if she discovered what they'd done?

Before they'd left the falls, Grace had shaken the tin, listening to the papers rustle inside. 'If I return to England I'll leave some money in it, so you can pay your ticket home.' She stood, almost embarrassed at how comfortable she felt around him, wearing her nakedness easily, loving what her body had become; curved and full of life.

He shrugged. 'It won't come to that.'

Now she wasn't sure what it would come to. In the last two weeks she'd suffered a fever, mild at first, but as the days had worn on she felt hot all the time, and when she'd heard the news of Timor, something had shifted deep inside her. It was shock, perhaps, a sickness of the mind.

'Not the mind,' Uncle Marcus had said when he'd come to sit on the end of her bed that morning, 'but the heart.' She was so fatigued – not to mention the nausea that washed over her in waves – that she'd merely nodded in reply.

Chapter 48

Notting Hill, London

December 2004

At 2 p.m., with a certain sense of trepidation, Libby found herself standing outside the apartment of Roger Masters. Nowadays, he lived in Notting Hill.

Taking a deep breath, she knocked on the door hidden within the pillar-porch of a white stucco-fronted house, and stepped back to wait, running a nervous hand over the satchel that hung heavy on her shoulder. Inside, she'd stashed the tin and several newly printed pages, the contents of which had told her something rather incredible.

That morning – an hour after she'd hugged her aunts goodbye – she'd received the promised reply from Jess. The email was still running through her mind.

> Dear Libby,
>
> Me again! Breakfast cleared away, rooms changed . . . our guests off on a boat tour of Macquarie Harbour. So *finally* I have a few minutes to myself. For nearly twenty years Denny and I wondered – like you – about the identity of the body your father found down the mine behind Towerhurst, but it wasn't until a few years ago, when Westford's previous sergeant, Charles Griffin, passed away that we were able to get more information. It was a very cold case by then, and Griffin's replacement arranged for release of the

files on our request (even though we'd asked several times prior!) and we discovered something simply spectacular in there. I've attached details here, but in short . . .

'My *dear*!' Without preamble, Libby was pulled back to the present as the door swung open and she was wrapped in a warm hug by a jovial man who looked as though he'd just returned from a party set thirty years ago. He wore a fetching tweed jacket/waistcoat combination, and his trousers were bright red and flared happily at the ankles. 'I feel as though I already know you!'

'And I you,' said Libby, both trying to catch her breath and surprising herself that the sentiment was true. It wasn't *just* that she'd googled – or oogled, as Miss Winman would have said – Roger Masters before leaving the apartment that morning, it was more than that. She'd *thought* about him, envisioned this meeting and tried to link it with the moment her own father had stood on Roger's doorstep, travel bag in hand, another Tasmanian in London three decades before.

'The very spit of Ben, you know? The spit of him,' he said, bustling her out of the December cold and into a warm, cinnamon-scented hallway.

を

Roger, it seemed, was quite the man about town. Libby's quick internet search had brought up countless photos of him – always wearing exactly what he wore now – and in the company of A- and B-list celebrities: politicians, actors, socialites, most of whom it appeared he had written lengthy biographies about. There they were, lining the hallway, three dozen books at least, and Libby marvelled that any writer could be quite so prolific.

'I've laid out afternoon tea for us. I do hope you're hungry.' He led her into a beautiful Georgian front room where a coffee table groaned with food: sandwiches, a cheese platter, glistening glazed ham, mince pies. Beyond it, an elegant bay window framed a tastefully decorated Christmas tree, and an enormous pile of presents.

'Trinkets from acquaintances, my dear,' he said, following her gaze. 'I seem to collect acquaintances.'

She smiled uncertainly at the hesitation that followed.

'But real friends,' Roger continued, 'like your father, like Ben . . . well, that's the secret to life, isn't it?'

And, with that, Libby's trepidation evaporated and she took the proffered place on the sofa while Roger poured mulled wine, raising a glass of his own to her father.

'I've never toasted Dad before,' she admitted. A sad indictment really, on her and – yes – on Willow, and yet Roger clearly thought nothing of the sort as he lifted his drink a little higher.

'Well, then. For the first time: to your wonderful father,' he nodded with encouragement, 'and also: to doing new things.'

'To Dad,' she said gratefully, tapping his glass with hers, 'and to doing new things.'

☙

Later, all that remained on the table were a few cubes of cheese and the sense that there were unspoken words between them. They'd discussed her (lack of) life in London, and a little about his work, then, finally, she plucked up the courage to ask if Ben had discussed the identity of Willow's mother while he was in London.

'Dina?' Roger said cautiously.

'The other one,' she replied with similar caution.

'I see. You mean . . . Rose?'

She brushed her hand over the satchel. 'I believe Dad was investigating two things before he died. Firstly, Rose Munro.

I guess he wanted to find her? To get to the bottom of the Towerhurst legacy?' At this Roger nodded. 'Secondly, I think he was curious about the identity of the body down the mine.'

'Yes, I recall it well. Quite a mystery. Ben had his theories of course.'

Libby had hers too, formed via the promised email from Jess, the contents of which – and the attachments – had been even more remarkable than she could have expected.

'And how did you acquire Ben's satchel?'

'It's one of the reasons – maybe the real reason – I came to London. The department apparently tried to send it back to Tasmania, but Mum didn't . . .' She trailed off, the unsaid hanging between them.

Roger canted his head, clearly grasping for a filler. 'I was there once, you know? In *Tassie*.'

'Really?'

'Oh, yes. Back in 1972. That's when I met your father. At a writers' retreat in Hobart. We were the only two there who took ourselves less than seriously. The others kept talking about Marx and Trotsky, both of which I had to pretend I'd read. Luckily I knew a lot of Marxist sounding words like . . .'

'Like?'

'Oh, I don't know.' He waved a hand. '*Bourgeois* and *capitalist*, that kind of thing. I think I fooled the others, but not your father.'

'Was it the accent?' Libby laughed. 'And the clothes?'

Roger raised an eyebrow. 'And Lawrence said you were shy!'

She flushed. This conversation – and Roger's warm welcome – *had* inspired a certain confidence in her.

'Yes, well . . . I don't suppose I particularly fit into the proletariat,' he added.

'There's another word for you.'

Roger raised his glass. 'Ha!'

'Roger?' she said, after a moment when they'd both sipped their drinks.

'Yes?'

'What was Dad *like*?'

Roger smiled; a wide expression that told her everything. 'Libby, he was wonderful! Absolutely wonderful! Kind. Intelligent, of course.'

Her heart leapt.

'He was passionate about storytelling, though I got the sense he could be a bit obsessive when a plot line or character caught his fancy.' He gave the satchel a meaningful look. 'And he'd just met your mother a few weeks before the retreat. I've never seen a man so swept off his feet.'

'Really?'

'Oh yes. It was at a gallery opening, you know? Ben was *so* in love.'

What a feeling this was, for Libby to come face to face with someone who had *known* her father – really known him – and who thought nothing of opening up.

'I blamed myself for a long time for his death.'

'What do you mean?'

'It was me who invited him to London for one thing.' He glanced down at his hands. 'But more than that, Libby, I . . . I wasn't at home on the morning he . . . well, you know?'

She nodded.

'I'd left the day before; gone to Edinburgh, and was due back on the Saturday. I recall' – Roger cleared his throat – 'I recall leaving him a little note with a smiley face on it to find. Can you imagine?'

'It's okay.'

'No,' he said. 'It's not.'

'It is.'

'The note was the address of *The Albatross*. If I hadn't left

that, Ben would never have . . .' He hesitated. 'You see . . .
Lawrence was away – taking his son to visit the in-laws, if
I remember rightly – and he'd left one of the McGillycuddy
ballads in the boat's stern. *Tell Ben he can pick it up anytime*, was
what he said. Your father must have walked down to Drayton
Park Station, boarded the train and . . .'

Libby thought of the way she'd blamed herself for Krish's
death, for the moment when she should have called out to stop
him storming away.

'"The Ma'am from Joey River". That was the ballad's name.'
She took the tin from her father's satchel, explaining to Roger
where she'd found it and what the items she'd discovered inside
had meant to her at the time. 'This ballad, in more ways than
I'd ever realised, altered my life for ever.' She resisted the urge
to tear it in two, to scrunch it up and throw it away.

Old Street was the closest station to *The Albatross*, but
Moorgate wasn't much further. Why had her father continued
his journey that morning? Did he fancy the walk? Miss his
stop? Or had he intended to go somewhere else – not to *The
Albatross* at all? She had, of course, studied London's tube map,
and Moorgate was an interchange for three other lines that
spread in a network across the city; the options for where Ben
had intended to go were too numerous to consider.

From the satchel, she removed the map of Ireland, and the
airline tickets, placing them on the table.

'Am I right in assuming Dad was planning to visit Daniel
McGillycuddy?'

Roger squinted at the travel receipt. 'Purchased on the 27th
of February . . .'

'In the afternoon.'

'I'd already left for Edinburgh.'

'It was a last-minute decision, then? He hadn't told you?'

'No.'

'Do you think he wanted to ask Daniel about Rose?'

'I certainly imagine so, my dear.'

Libby frowned. 'Really?'

'Well, Daniel *would* be the one to tell him all about Rose, wouldn't he?' He glanced at her, then frowned. 'Oh, but . . . but, don't you know?'

'Know what?'

'My dear Libby, if your dad booked tickets to Dublin, and planned to travel south to Kerry, well, he . . .'

'He what?'

'Ben must have finally decided to meet Daniel McGillycuddy's wife.'

Chapter 49

McGillycuddy's Fine Timbers, Tasmania

January 1975

Ben hesitated, listening as the tinny jingle of ABC news drifted through the McGillycuddys' Huon pine door by way of greeting. It was 10 a.m. and he should've been halfway back to Launceston by now, but there was something he had to do. He had come to Towerhurst two nights before, alone; Willow was with her mother. In ways he couldn't understand, she had made a connection between the questions she had about her heritage – about Rose – and Dina's illness. She felt guilty that she'd ever wanted to know the truth, had ever thought to challenge her mum. Ben couldn't fathom her thinking, and yet guilt could be like that, couldn't it? Inexplicable. Indefinable. Once it arrived, it simmered, always hiding just beneath the surface. But not knowing where you came from . . . well, Ben could attest that *not knowing* simmered too, all the boys at the home he'd grown up with had battled with it. Even now, he still felt that way every time he saw a child with their mother, every time he saw a child with their father.

Every time he looked into a mirror.

'These things matter,' he'd said to Willow two weeks after Christmas, and she'd sighed in reply.

'Everything matters, Ben,' she'd said after a moment, 'but nothing matters that much.' He'd lost her for a time, he knew that, and the closer he tried to draw her, the further she'd stepped away.

Now, he knocked on the McGillycuddys' door. It was Colette who answered, and it wasn't until she told him that Ned was out – 'Delivering timber' – that he noticed their truck was missing. 'The tea's wet,' she said. 'Come on inside.'

&

On the large, rustic Tasmanian oak dining table – the only item in the kitchen that didn't appear to be made of Huon pine – Ben spread out the letters he'd found the night before. They had been tucked under a subtly tilting floorboard in the bedroom, just a trick of the light he'd thought, until he'd got to his knees and investigated. Five cheap envelopes – five letters from Daniel to Grace.

He reached down to pat Rua, who curled beside the chair, leaning against him. The rhythmic wash of the sea rolled in through an open window as Colette strained fragrant tea into two cups, then placed them, and a plate, on the table.

'Marble cake?' Ben said gleefully. 'My favourite.'

'Is that so?' Colette turned off the radio and sat opposite him. 'I haven't made it in years . . . must have been seeing the light on at Towerhurst last night.'

Ben frowned. He didn't recall telling Colette about his cake preferences.

'This was Grace's favourite.'

'She had good taste, then?' He grinned.

Every time he learned something new about Grace, he tried to piece together the girl that she might have been, though the fragments were too sparse. Which was why finding the letters was such a coup, though really they only told half a story. Because it seemed that although the boy had written to Grace many times, she'd obviously rarely replied.

'Surely these aren't . . .' Colette picked up each letter one by one. 'But look how terrible Daniel's writing is!'

'Your nephew was in love with Grace, wasn't he?'

'He was, o' course.'

'Ned told me a different story; that it was a one-way thing, on Grace's part.'

'Ned!' Colette laughed. 'Even if he'd seen Daniel go down on one knee, he would have thought he was just doing up his shoelace. But Daniel did love her. He told me that he'd admitted it to her the last time he was here.'

'When was that?'

'Oh' – she frowned – 'well, it had to be just before he left for Timor.'

Timor, Ben knew, had surrendered in February 1942. Every Tasmanian knew the story of heroism; the famous 2/40th Battalion that had held the island for three days against unwinnable odds.

'Our nephew ended up on the Death Railway.'

'I'm so sorry.' Sadness opened up in Ben's heart like a flower. He felt cruel, bringing the past up like this, but in discovering those hidden letters, he'd been gripped with such a desire to know more about Daniel, about Grace, that he couldn't help but ask. It was true he'd returned to Towerhurst under the auspices of writing, though his real intention – which he'd hidden from Willow – was to find traces of Rose in the house. He'd found a few photos, but nothing else of interest. Certainly nothing about Rose's time in Hobart or any inkling that she and Marcus had been having an affair. But then, what had he expected to find?

'Whatever happened to Grace?'

'I'm afraid we lost touch.'

'Is it possible that . . . well . . . that Grace never left Westford?'

'I'm not sure what you're asking' – she gave him a knowing look – 'but I know for a fact that Grace and Rose got on that boat in 1945.'

'How?'

'Sergeant Griffin took them. Drove them into Hobart on VJ Day, and dropped them off at the port himself.'

Ben might have been concussed and confused that day in Sergeant Griffin's front room, but Willow had definitely told him later – when his head was clearer – that she'd asked the sergeant about Grace and Rose, and the man had replied that he'd barely known them.

Colette waved a hand. 'He's always played his cards close to his chest. Doesn't like to speak of the past. Daniel saved his life, you know? He'd taken a bullet to the leg, and my nephew pulled him right out of the Timorese jungle, putting him on a boat to Australia. No, there's no doubt about it. Puds is a good man, and he would have done anything for Dan—'

'Puds?'

'Yes, Puds. Charlie Griffin.' Colette laughed. 'Some nickname, isn't it? He doesn't go by it now, but when he and Daniel were young, he was as round as a pudding, bless him. Poor old Puds.' She sighed. 'I think he rather fancied Grace too.'

Ben blinked. Sergeant Griffin was Puds? That was *him* in the Christmas photo from 1940? Why on *earth* didn't he say? Because he was in love with Grace? *He'd* painted her a picture of a beautiful valley that stretched to the sea . . . a painting full of love?

Colette was watching him with a worried expression, and Ben gathered himself. There was no way he could say what he was thinking, he would look even more of a lunatic than he clearly already appeared to be. He cleared his throat and picked up a letter from the top of the pile.

'And Daniel . . . he . . . he . . .'

'Yes?'

'Did he die in Burma, on the railway?'

Colette had a piece of cake halfway to her mouth. She'd chosen the slimmest slice, and it broke, dropping on the table in what might have been a comical moment if it weren't for the look on her face. 'Whatever do you mean?'

'I'm sorry to bring it up . . . it's just that I saw the cenotaph on Westford's green. *D. McGillycuddy 1944.*'

She smiled in that way that only aged grief could conjure. Regret, sadness, acceptance slid across her face in a wave. 'The inscription on the monument is for our son, Derek. He died in Changi. Along with more than eight hundred others.'

'I'm so sorry, Colette. I didn't know.'

'And how would you?' He could tell from her expression that, although it was painful, she was pleased for the chance to say her Derek's name out loud. 'But our eldest son, Patrick . . . he's moving down from Sydney in a year or so, bringing the whole clan with him.'

'I—' A tingle rippled through Ben's body. 'Daniel . . . he's not still *alive*?'

'Last time I checked.' Colette patted his hand affectionately as though she thought him a little mad. 'He never returned to Tasmania after the war, but we do get Christmas cards, that kind of thing. I'd love to visit Kerry – home never quite leaves that spot in your heart, does it? – but Ned . . . he's no fondness for the old country.'

How could Ben not have asked any of this? He shook his head, dislodging a dozen questions.

As if reading his mind, Colette said, 'I thought you and

Ned had discussed him the day you visited? I'd asked him to lend you Daniel's book.'

'His book?'

'It's a collection of ballads. Our nephew started writing during the war.' She smiled, tracing the word 'Spitfire Bingo' on a letter. 'He was inspired, you know, by Grace? She was a fine writer. Tasmania's Pom Poetess they called her. Anyway, before all that, she and Daniel used to read poetry by the waterfall behind Towerhurst. They thought none of us knew.' She grinned. 'It was all very romantic. Ned didn't mention it?'

'No . . .'

She sighed affectionately. 'Let me get our copy for you.'

While she was gone, Ben took a slice of cake and, with a wink, gave Rua a small piece of the sponge, withdrawing his hand guiltily when Colette returned.

'I have no idea where it's got to. I'll find it for your next visit.' She sat at the table, and gave him a quizzical look. 'What *was* it you and Ned talked about that day you visited? He told me you grilled him.'

Ben raised his hands. 'That's a bit of an exaggeration.' He hesitated. Should he mention what Richard had said about meeting Rose in Hobart that day? And Ned *had* implied that Marcus had a child . . .

'I wondered: did . . . did Marcus Foxton and Rose . . .?'

Colette frowned. 'I liked Marcus, so I did. But there were rumours. Olive, though, never gave them credence. She loved that girl like she was her own.'

'Really?'

'Truth was, Ben, I think she saw Rose as an asset. Olive Foxton always liked people to envy her. I think that's why she married Marcus.' A sigh. 'And Rose was a lovely-looking girl. Outshone Grace in every sense of the word when they arrived. And then of course Grace was ill, rheumatic fever,

just when she seemed to be set to shine. She turned out very
well though, in the end.'

In the end. Before she died? Ben pushed the thought aside.

'Presumably the rumours you've heard about Rose came
straight from the large and very active mouth of herself at the
shop?'

'Her son, actually.'

A sigh. 'Richard Holmes was unceremoniously rejected by
Rose. He's held a grudge ever since.'

'A grudge?'

'Him, and half the young men in Westford. They were all
keen on her.'

Ben touched the letters. 'Apart from Daniel.'

'Daniel? Well, not *then*, at any rate.' Colette's face rippled
with distaste, but the moment quickly flickered by, leaving that
familiar warm expression.

'Sorry? What do you mean?'

'Well, he wasn't keen on her *then*. He's certainly keen on
her *now*, of course.'

Ben frowned, slowly leaning forward. Outside, plick-plicks
of rain danced on the tin roof, and yet the sound faded away,
shrinking to nothing so that all other noises became larger,
louder. The drip of the tap. The faraway call of a currawong.
The roaring comprehension that rolled across Ben's mind like
a tide.

'Now? He's sweet on Rose *now*?'

Colette drained her tea. 'I should hope so, Ben. Several
years after the war, we received news that Daniel and Rose
were married and living in Kerry, and they've been that way
ever since.'

Chapter 50

Notting Hill, London
December 2004

'Is this *true*?'

'My dear Libby, it's quite true. Your father heard it from the mouth of Daniel McGillycuddy's aunt not long before he left for London. The admission surprised Ben,' Roger continued, 'because he'd already been told that Rose and Grace's relationship was anything but . . . well, rosy. And the thought that Daniel had gone and married Rose, it didn't sit well with him at all.'

'But according to Lawrence,' Libby said, 'Daniel's wife is still alive. *Rose* is still alive.'

'Good lord.'

And if Rose lived, questions could be answered. 'Do you think Mum knows any of this?'

Roger leaned back on the sofa. 'No. I don't believe she did. I recall that Ben was very concerned about Willow . . . about the way she reacted to news of her adoption. All compounded, of course, because your grandmother was ill. This was all such a long time ago . . .'

'You never asked Mum later? If she knew?'

'Never in as many words. I often sent cards, though I never expected a reply . . .' He sighed. 'I'd have loved to meet her.'

She's coming for Christmas, Libby wanted to say, but instead she said, 'What about at Dad's funeral?'

'It was a very private affair in Tasmania. *Family only,* I was told.' Roger hesitated. 'I know what you're thinking. But I don't judge her for not replying to me or wanting me to come. Perhaps she blamed me? I don't know. It was an unimaginably hard time for her and I've never walked a mile in her shoes.'

Libby marvelled at his attitude. She felt like turning to the *To Do* list in her diary and writing: *Walk in others' shoes.*

'Grief affects each of us in different ways,' he went on. 'Some go inward. Some go outward. Some fill their lives, hoping to keep *so* busy that they might well forget. For me . . . well, when your father died I resolved to *change* my life.'

'What do you mean?'

'Before I met Ben, I had spent years writing about the rich and famous under various pseudonyms. Exposés, really. Mischievous things. Most undesirous for the book's subject, though much desired by everyone else. But in seventy-five my real name slipped through the cracks . . . specifically, the cracks in the doors of the *Sun's* head offices. For a time I was *persona non grata* within London's high society.'

'But you managed to reinstate yourself.'

A nod. 'My notoriety soon preceded me; within no time at all I was flooded with offers to write official biographies. People liked my style, if not my methods. Using my own name unlocked something within me. I became quite . . . prolific.' He paused. 'Your father, he had been right about that.'

'In what way?'

'He encouraged me to stop hiding, to use my own name. *Be proud of what you do,* he'd said, *be brave.*'

Be brave. That sentiment again. Libby pushed the memory of Sam aside.

'Roger,' she admitted, 'I did look you up before I came.' His look of faux horror brought a guilty smile to her lips. She said, 'Apart from my father's influence, this is all in the public domain.'

'Not quite all . . . it was Ben's death that finally encouraged me to heed his words. But I didn't want to simply . . . *fess up*.'

Realisation dawned. 'You leaked your *own* name to the *Sun*?'

He shrugged. 'Sometimes a little white lie can do us the world of good. And sometimes it's the only way we can find our courage.'

'And my father's interest in Edeline Grey? What was that all about? Was it because . . .'

Roger nodded. 'I'm afraid he suspected it was Grace down that mine. The poor girl.'

Poor girl. Jess's email shed a new light on that. Grace was more than she appeared to be. Far more. She reached into the satchel and handed Roger Milton Twiggs' article *A Snippet of Yet Another British Fascist*, but instead of reading it, he laughed.

'What a blast from the past! Your father asked me to look into the Foxton family. Very little had been written about Edeline so I came up with this . . .'

'*You're* Milton Twiggs?'

'Not my most salubrious pseudonym, granted,' Roger smiled sheepishly. 'Edeline – and Grace's – fascist past was news to Ben. He was disappointed, I think, because he thought Grace to be a wonderful ballad writer, a girl with a big heart. Misunderstood.'

Libby came to a decision; she would share what she'd discovered that morning with Roger. His article shed a new light on things: he would *definitely* be fascinated with what she'd learned, and he might also have more to add.

'You might be interested,' she said, 'in this email from Towerhurst's current owners.' Reaching into the satchel, she withdrew the four documents she'd printed that morning. She handed the first to Roger, and with raised eyebrows, he began to read.

Dear Libby,

Me again! Breakfast cleared away, rooms changed . . . our guests off on a
boat tour of Macquarie Harbour. So *finally* I have a few minutes to myself.

For twenty years Denny and I wondered – like you – about the identity of the
body your father found down the mine behind Towerhurst, but it wasn't until
a few years ago, when Westford's previous sergeant, Charles Griffin, passed
away that we were able to get more information. It was a very cold case
by then and Griffin's replacement arranged for release of the files on our
request (even though we'd asked for several times prior!) and we discovered
something simply spectacular in there. I've attached details here.

But first I should highlight something that initially appears unrelated: did you
know that there were half a dozen Nazi submarine sightings in Macquarie
Harbour during WW2? According to an elderly man in the village – who still
owns the grocery shop and considers himself the last word on all matters
historical (and a terrible gossip, if I'm honest) – the Germans were probably
assessing the area for access to the copper. Mount Lyell, you see, was
Australia's largest producer back then, and the Axis were well known to be
short of the stuff.

Anyway, when Denny and I got our hands on the file detailing the contents
of the suitcase found with the body we discovered something fascinating.
It led us to believe, considering the Greys' fascist tendencies, that it was
Grace down the mine. After all, I managed to track down Edeline's death
records from a Parisian record office, but couldn't find any trace of her
daughter. Which means, she's still in hiding, or she's dead and nobody knew
about it.

If my theory is correct, it's a terrible shame, because we found copies of
Grace's published ballads in the tower – Tasmania's Pom Poetess they
called her – as well as piles of work in progress. I've attached some here.
Isn't her writing beautiful? She gave every indication of being as patriotic
as any Australian. No one would have guessed her to be a spy, but then I
suppose that's a job well done.

I would be interested to know what else you learn.

With kind wishes,

Jess

PS Amazing isn't it? How sometimes truth is stranger than fiction . . .

Roger picked up the first attachment. 'A police report? The suitcase . . .' He read on. 'My God! It was full of . . .'

Libby nodded. 'Details of the mine. Blueprints, aerial photos, maps.'

'This is incredible.'

'It's astounding. An agent? Edeline must have been very persuasive considering the girl was only fifteen when she left England. And the Pom Poetess . . .'

Roger's wiry eyebrows leapt up. 'Yes, I remember Ben telling me that, actually. May I see some of her work?'

Of the attached drafts and published ballads, Libby had printed a single one. 'It turns out,' she said, handing it to Roger, 'that it wasn't Daniel McGillycuddy who originally wrote the missing ballad, the one that Lawrence left on the boat for Dad to collect. It was Grace Grey.'

There was her name, written in black ink, that unmistakable writing with the flourish on the G and the long loop that trailed the Y, signed at the bottom of a draft of 'The Ma'am from Joey River'.

'My goodness. Daniel McGillycuddy plagiarised the poem? That's why he didn't want it published?'

'That would be my guess. Maybe he was worried she might read it.'

'But if Grace was dead . . . '

'I guess it means he didn't know? I'm not sure. There are too many moving parts. I mean, for example, did Dad meet Molly Munro, Rose's mother?'

Roger nodded. 'Well, yes! He was due to visit her the morning . . . before the crash. How did you know?'

Libby showed him the business card with Molly's number.

'My, my,' said Roger, 'what a blast from the past.'

'*Did* they meet?'

'I honestly don't know.' Roger appraised her shrewdly. 'Though there is someone who might.'

A frown. 'Who?'

'Rose.'

'You think I should follow my father's footsteps?'

'Yes,' Roger said without hesitation. 'Go to Ireland! Complete his journey!'

Libby felt a surge of adrenaline. 'I can't—'

'Nonsense! Of course you can.'

'I can't arrive in Ballinn *unannounced*.'

Roger raised an eyebrow. 'Well, announce yourself! Write to her.'

'If Rose is still alive – and I'm not *certain* she is – wouldn't it be a little confronting for me to ask about her past like this?'

'Then don't.'

'What do you mean?'

'Don't ask' – he put Daniel's book between them – 'about *her*. You're a literature graduate, aren't you, my dear?'

She nodded.

'Ask about Daniel. Write her a letter and ask about the ballads. His Tasmanian influence. See if she'd be happy to talk.'

'That's a bit . . . sneaky.'

Roger laughed. 'Sometimes a little white lie can do us the world of good; it can help us to be *brave*. You've come this far, my dear' – he patted her hand – 'surely, you have nothing to lose?'

Chapter 51

Launceston, Tasmania

January 1975

When Ben arrived home from Towerhurst, he was greeted at the hall table by an envelope from Roger Masters and he scooped it up eagerly, wondering what on earth it would say. After all, Ben's last letter was the one he'd sent from Westford in November asking for details on the Foxton family and – distracted as he was by the events since – he hadn't written again to Roger. His friend's letter by reply promised to look into it, but that was last month. And since then, everything had changed.

Ben suspected that that poor girl, Grace Grey – the one who'd shed her skin, the one who'd found her voice, the one who'd discovered love – was dead. He'd *seen* that necklace, he was more certain of that than ever. Sergeant Griffin, *Puds*, had lied. Not just about the necklace, but about how well he'd known Rose, and Grace, for whom he'd painted a watercolour full of love. The style of painting, Ben now realised, had been familiar that day they discovered it in the tower because he'd seen it before; lining the walls of Sergeant Griffin's house.

'Locally done, are they?' Ben had asked when he'd returned from visiting the facilities. The sergeant had merely nodded.

And the photo from Christmas 1940? Both copies had

disappeared, and now Ben was convinced that Puds – just as with the necklace? – had taken them.

All this led to one vital question: what did Charles Griffin have to hide?

He'd made (another) detour on his way home, stopping at Westford's empty police station, and waiting for more than half an hour before writing a short message. He'd resisted the urge to address it to 'Puds', instead merely asking the Sergeant to get in touch, then he'd driven back to Launceston, his mind whirling with all that he'd discovered.

'Earth to Ben . . .' Willow stood in the kitchen doorway, watching him with a worried expression. In her hand she held a paintbrush, and her smock was covered in shades of grey.

'I've missed you.'

'Me too. So much.' She conjured a smile, though it was traced with the sadness that had plagued her lately. Dina was never far from her mind. She stepped forward, and embraced him.

'Darling,' he started, 'there's something I need to tell you, something I discovered in Towerhu—'

She pulled back. 'If this is about Rose . . .'

'It is. But not just Rose.'

'Then, right now, I don't want to know.'

'But—'

'Please.' There were tears in her eyes. 'Not right now. I promise . . . listen to me' – she took his face in her hands – 'I promise after Mum's recovered from surgery, and I can think straight again, we *will* revisit this.'

'Willow—'

'How was the house?' she said.

Ben hesitated. He had so much he wanted to stay. 'Fine, fine.'

'Well, that's something then, isn't it?'

He nodded, his gaze alighting on a packed bag blocking the doorway.

'Sorry we have to turn around so quickly' – Willow squeezed his hand – 'I'm keen to get back.'

They were going to Dina and Rob's for the week; Willow had converted the old potting shed into a studio, determined to spend as much time as she could with her mother. When they were there, each dusk mother and daughter sat side by side on the porch, drinking weak gin and tonics flavoured with lemon tree leaves as the condensation pooled on their fingers. *Poor woman's G&T*, Dina had always called it. Many times, Willow had told Ben, the perfect silence had appeared into which her questions could step, but she'd always balked, struggling to find the words.

'You should just come out with it.'

'I will, I will. One day,' she promised with a sincerity he didn't believe.

Her reluctance, however, had been a wakeup call. Were he in Willow's position, Ben would have leapt at the chance to discover the truth. Consequently, he'd upped his attempts to uncover his own heritage, though his search had so far been in vain: the home's staff had vanished, adoption agencies were reticent, and the large facility he'd grown up in had been converted to apartments. In a last-ditch effort, he'd called to make an appointment with Launceston's only private investigator, who wasn't able to see him until early March. Dejectedly, he'd hung up the phone and written down the details of the meeting in his diary, then added a list of documents he needed to gather in preparation.

'And have you,' Willow said now, squeezing his hand so to break his reverie, 'heard anything more from the solicitor?'

Ben had met with him last week – in those plush Doyle & Son offices – in a rendezvous that had been perfunctory at best. 'Sell it *now*?' the lawyer had said. 'You must wait seven years. Before that . . . Well, the time and expense needed to separate the house from the trust would be sizeable.'

'If you'd just give us some more information,' Ben had replied, 'it would give my wife some peace of mind.'

'I don't understand what you mean?'

'The reason for the legacy.'

'You know I'm not at liberty to divulge anything further.'

'Take pity on her.'

Mr Doyle's brow had furrowed at this. It might have been a faint ripple of amusement, if the man had a sense of humour. Ben had left the office with threats to change lawyers, though he'd not yet got round to doing so.

'Mr Doyle's looking into it,' he told Willow.

'Good. Thank you, love.' She kissed him on the lips, then disappeared, off to take a shower before they left.

As Ben heard the shudder of the pipes, he took Roger's letter from his pocket, slicing it open with a bread knife, expecting to read a few words about the Foxton family and some juicy gossip from his friend's latest exposé. But when he read the contents, he flushed.

My dear Ben,

How about that trip to London you've always dreamed of?

　　Apologies for the last-minute invite, but (full disclosure) Geoffrey Dutton's pulled out of the Iliad Club's annual festival of literature and we still want an antipodean voice – so, I suggested someone up-and-coming. You, not to put too fine a point on it. The flights are already booked, we just need to change the name. Bring Willow too – Geoffrey wasn't shy about asking for a ticket for his partner. Why don't you read 'Selkie', that piece you had in the *Telegraph* last week? Perhaps you think I didn't see it! You dark horse! We're all champing at the bit to learn about your inspiration. February 26th is the day, and I suggest you come for a week or two – what do you say? All expenses paid, as long as we can sort things from here.

By this, Ben assumed Roger's club needed some legitimate expenses for a tax write-off. He couldn't believe his luck. His friend had threatened to get him to the UK, one way or another, for years. Now, it seemed, his time had finally come.

On a separate sheet of paper, there was a postscript.

PS I've collected some bits and pieces on the Foxtons. Let's talk about it in person. A fair exchange, yes? Do write/give me a call about your 'Selkie' inspiration, so I can put a few words in the programme.

Ben loved that Roger knew he was already certain to attend. He folded the second page into his pocket and took the invite to show to Willow.

'This is brilliant! You *must* go!' It was one of the many things he loved about her: her unbridled joy anytime anything went his way. She was still warm from the shower and smelled of lavender. 'You can call him from Mum and Dad's house.'

'I will.' He might ask Roger, he thought, to look into Rose Munro . . . on the quiet . . . and perhaps locate a copy of these ballads, the ones by Daniel McGillycuddy.

'Ash and Ivy *will* be jealous!' Willow went on. 'They love London. They've been talking about finding an apartment in the city for years. They have dreams of Mayfair and I have no doubt they'll end up getting what they want.'

Ben hesitated. 'You'll come with me?'

A tilt of the head. 'No.'

'Oh, come on! You've always wanted to travel overseas. We've talked about it a hundred times. London. Rome. Paris. We could tack on a trip, couldn't we?'

She went to the bed to rifle through a mountain of clothes. 'Not this time. There'll be other opportunities. I want to be with Mum.'

Shame needled at him. How could he be so selfish? 'Of course you do.'

'You *must* go, though,' she said, as she buttoned up her shirt. 'And Ben?'

'Yes?'

'Let's forget this legacy nonsense, will we? Let's say no more?'

'I could at least tell you what I discovered about the man who did the painting, about Puds.'

'Please.' She squeezed his hand. 'For now.'

He hesitated. 'If that's really what you want?'

'It is.' She kissed him on the cheek. 'It really is.'

When she stepped back, he resisted the urge to take her in his arms. He loved her more than he'd ever believed possible; he would do anything for her, give her the world, which was exactly why he wanted her to know the truth, but also why he respected her wishes to deny it.

She smiled, and a little of the old Willow – the one who'd never heard of Towerhurst – returned. Lightness lifted her shoulders. 'Let's go?'

He nodded, and smiled too, but as they'd driven the dusty road to Northport, his mind had been full of Grace, Daniel and Rose, and the secretive Sergeant Griffin.

What manner of things did that man – did Puds – have to hide?

Chapter 52

Towerhurst, Tasmania

October 1942

It was the smell that told Puds he was home in Tasmania: the tang of seaweed; eucalyptus; and the sweet nectar of spring wattle on a fresh day. Those things individually might mean nothing to some, but when they mixed with the salt breeze of Southern Ocean . . . well, here it was. *Home.* A place he'd once longed to leave.

What a mistake that had been.

Eight months he'd spent in the hospital in Melbourne. They'd tried to repair him. Rehabilitate him. Recycle him. Fling him back into the Pacific to another place he'd never heard of, to fight the same enemy he didn't understand, but his leg wouldn't heal, and nothing they did would set it right. So he'd limped home to where his father greeted him with a cool disposition. Almost before he'd folded away his uniform, he'd been presented with a new one.

'We'll fast track you to sergeant,' his father had announced without preamble.

That was two days ago; no rest for the wicked. Today, though, was his own. He stood at the edge of the fern-speckled lawn, Towerhurst looming over him, and glanced up at the house's windows, winking in the sunshine. Fighting the urge to run, he steadied himself; he owed today to Daniel, and so much more. As he stepped onto the verandah he wondered, not for the first time, what he would say, and how he would say it. He hadn't been here since Christmas Eve 1940, when he'd walked Grace – and her broken heart – home.

ह

Rose stood in the sitting room, watching a man pace the verandah. He was vaguely familiar. Tall and pale, he walked with a pronounced limp, but his pain, it seemed, was mostly emotional; she could tell by the way he turned his cap as if inspecting its edges for courage. It was only when he ran a hand through his russet hair that Rose realised who he was. Charlie 'Puds' Griffin, it seemed, was no longer worthy of his nickname.

He rapped on the door and she let him wait, wondering at the reason for his discomfort. She hadn't seen him since the Christmas she'd kissed Daniel and watched the inevitable realisation dawn on Grace's face that Rose could always take whatever she wanted, whenever she wanted.

Puds, she supposed, was here for her. She twirled the sherry glass in her hand, pleased at the way the light caught the crystal. It *was* over the yardarm somewhere.

She went to the door.

'Hello Rose.' Puds half bowed, and she almost laughed. Even after what he must have been through, he clearly still wanted her.

'You're back.' She'd only visited Westford once since her return from Hobart, and Mira Holmes had fired gossip with such rapidity that Rose was sure Australia could have set her up on the gun towers in Singapore and the fortress would never have fallen. *Puds was coming home. Four local boys had died in Timor and the rest had surrendered, which meant Daniel might be* dead. *Grace had stopped writing those poems of hers, they say she's deathly ill. A 'turn' of some kind.*

'Rheumatic fever,' Rose had corrected her.

'Yes, yes . . . the sign of a weak immune system, so I heard.'

'I really couldn't say.' Rose had surprised herself in her partial defence of Grace. 'I think it's rather the luck of the draw.' She soon regretted her deflection, because the woman took it as the perfect opportunity to ask about her time in Hobart.

'*Working,* were you?'

Her implication made Rose uneasy. 'Yes. For the war effort, of course.' By then, a small group of local women had gathered at the counter, and she quickly began to throw inconsequential gossip from Hobart at them like stale bread to a flock of ducks.

Gun batteries line the Derwent River.

A Japanese sea plane was spotted over the city.

It's terribly dark at night, on account of the blackout rules.

Her audience had listened with rapt attention. All but Mira Holmes, who had busied herself with the cleaning of the till, clearly irritated. As Rose had turned to leave, she'd scurried from behind the counter, taking her arm, pulling her close to whisper as if they were firm friends and the gaggle of women a nuisance.

'Is it true about your boss? About Claud Greensmith?'

'What about him?'

'That he's finally leaving his wife for Mabel Martin?'

At that very moment, Marcus had crossed the green, and Rose had quickly opened the door and waved. 'My ride . . .' she had said, stepping over the threshold. 'Goodbye, Mrs Holmes.' As she'd turned to go, she'd seen the cogs of the shopkeeper's mind working, her keen eye observing the familiar way Marcus waved his own greeting.

A noise brought her back to the present. 'Rose?' Puds stared at her with concern.

She straightened. Indeed, perhaps she'd had a glass too many for lunchtime, though she didn't feel that she was to blame. Things had been . . . difficult . . . of late.

'How are you?' she asked, as though her mind hadn't drifted and left Puds standing alone on the verandah.

He told her he was returning from the McGillycuddys', that he'd been back in Westford for two days and how little everything had changed. 'I won't,' he said, indicating his leg, 'be returning to the front. I'm joining the police force.'

'Like your father?'

'Yes,' he said with resignation, 'just like my father.'

She'd laughed. There, at least, was something they had in common. An aversion to turning out like a parent.

'Would you like to come in?' He looked like he could do with a drink, and he was better company than no one at all.

'Actually, I was hoping to see Grace.'

Rose frowned.

'Just for a moment.'

She scrutinised him. 'You know she's *ill*?'

'All the more reason to visit.'

'The doctor says . . . it's mostly in her mind now.'

A raised eyebrow. 'I heard she had rheumatic fever.'

'She isn't well, Puds. But if you really want to . . .' She stepped back. 'Be my guest. Go on up.'

❧

Although Uncle Marcus insisted she was improving, Grace felt as though she'd been unwell for an eternity. It was true that, physically, she was able to move about; she washed herself occasionally, and picked a little at her food, but fractured moments of delirium still danced in her mind.

One time – at the height of her fever – she was certain she was back in Grosvenor Square, listening to her father, though she knew him to be dead. He stood before the unlit fire in his immaculate office and lectured her on the state of the tower, the books scattered on the floor.

'No daughter of mine would live like this,' he'd said, before he'd vanished as quickly as he'd arrived.

Another time, her mother had ascended the spiral staircase and sat on the end of her bed just as she had done that day she'd given Grace the oversized dressing gown.

'Yes, *just* like your thirteenth birthday,' her imagined mother had confirmed, 'only now you're nineteen. Nineteen! I hardly recognise you. Your skin's very coarse. I *did* warn you about the sun.'

'I'm sorry, Mother.'

'Now' – Edeline had patted her leg, *there, there* – 'where's Rose?'

One glorious evening, Daniel himself had arrived. He'd worn tattered remnants of a uniform, his slouch hat flattened and tucked under his arm. 'I'm alive, Grace, I'm alive.'

She'd pushed herself up onto her elbow and reached a hand out to him. 'But you haven't written.'

'I'm a prisoner, like your uncle Marcus told you.'

'How do you know he said that?'

'I'm always with you.' Then he'd turned away, and although Grace had shouted, *No*, he'd begun to descend the stairs so that she pulled herself from the chaise longue that had become her bed, and crawled across the floor. 'No. No. No!' she'd repeated *ad nauseam*, until Uncle Marcus had arrived in a flurry of footsteps, wrapping her in his arms, and holding her tight.

                                    ❧

Now Grace sat with notes sprawled all around her. As she'd improved, the words had, once again, begun to flow. But there were problems; she kept searching for traces of Daniel in her work; phrases he might have used, words that reminded her of him. The result was that she'd lost her *voice*; it was as though with Daniel's disappearance a piece of her had died. Nothing she wrote made any sense, just like the face that appeared at the top of the staircase across the room. She shook her head. Had the hallucinations returned? Not for the first time, Grace worried that she'd inherited her great-uncle Cornelius's eccentricity.

The Puds-shaped illusion moved carefully into the room, limping over books scattered on the floor.

'Grace?'

She put her pen aside, confused. 'It speaks.'

A ripple of consternation crossed his features and he lowered himself carefully to sit in the opposite chair, one leg stretched straight in front of him.

'It's me. Puds.'

'Of course,' she said, feeling rather happy. If this was madness, she'd be pleased enough to descend into it.

Puds reached tentatively across and put his hand on hers. *Strange.* To feel such warmth from an apparition. 'You've been very unwell, I hear? Rheumatic fever? They say it's running riot in the US too.' He leaned closer, concern etched on his features. His face had become rather handsome. 'I wanted to see you as soon as I returned.'

She blinked. Where had he returned from? Heaven? She extracted her hand and felt for the top of her yellow blouse, the same one she'd worn out to sea on that fateful day three years before when Daniel had carried her from the waves. A coolness swept over her and she pulled the collar closed.

'I was evacuated from Timor two days before the battalion surrendered. They took me to a hospital in Melbourne. I've been there for the last eight months. I' – he hesitated – 'I asked my father to let Marcus know, but it seems' – again, a hesitation – 'that he didn't?'

She sat up a little straighter, pulling the blanket across her bare legs, although the room was warm. Puds averted his eyes. Ghosts didn't blush.

She slowly observed the chaos of the room, seeing it anew. Each time Uncle Marcus came up, he did a little tidying, but it was like fighting the rising tide. It was hot in here, stuffy. She began to breathe a little faster.

'Perhaps,' she said quietly, pointing to the far porthole, 'if you could open the window?'

From a pile on a chair she took a clean blouse – left some time ago by Uncle Marcus – and, while Puds's back remained turned, replaced the one she wore. Then she pulled on a skirt.

'It's stuck,' Puds said, his back to her.

She stood unsteadily and went to the eastern porthole where her faint reflection stared back. In that instant, she was glad of its transparency, because what she saw frightened her; hollow eyes peering from an even more hollow face. She pulled her hair into a ponytail, then tried, unsuccessfully, to push the porthole open.

She longed, suddenly, for fresh and salty air. Something she hadn't tasted for so long.

'Will we . . . take tea?' She hadn't said such a thing for many months.

He turned from the window slowly as if afraid of what he might see. 'I'd like that very much.'

'Let's go downstairs.'

'You can manage?'

She gave a small laugh; the movement tugging at her insides. 'Probably not.'

He limped over to her, and held out an arm. 'We'll make a fine pair.'

She glanced at his leg. 'What happened to you?'

'War happened to me.'

They hobbled to the top of the spiral staircase. 'What will we talk about?' she said.

'Daniel.'

'He's dead, isn't he?'

He paused, giving her a small smile. It wasn't a happy expression, nor was it the soul-sucking sadness of someone consumed by grief. 'I don't know for sure, but he was almost certainly taken prisoner. I think he survived . . .'

Grace's legs buckled beneath her and Puds reached out a steadying hand.

'I'm fine,' she said, straightening. And for the first time in eight long months, she felt the faintest flicker of hope.

Chapter 53

Hampshire, south-west of London
December 2004

Two days after visiting Roger Masters, Libby found herself in unexpected company and – equally unexpectedly – in a field in the middle of Hampshire.

'I *had* hoped,' she said tentatively, 'we'd just nip down to Borough Market . . .'

Sam, who was striding down the lines of neatly netted pine trees, visibly shuddered. 'And miss out on this?' He turned, spreading his hands wide to encompass the regimented lines of conifers arranged in order of size. 'Where's your festive spirit?'

It was somewhat ironic to hear him say such a thing after the events of that morning, but Libby had to admit that the day *did* feel Christmassy. There was a chill in the pine-scented air that frosted her breath, and several trees had been decorated in full festive regalia, complete with large stars twinkling on top.

'How am I supposed to choose one? They all look the same to me.'

He grinned. 'Allow me to guide you to the choicest specimen.'

She followed him around the corner to the next row, where the trees were bigger. 'Look at these little beauties,' he said, pinching some needles through the netting. 'Nice and firm.'

'It seems quite . . . big?'

But Sam had already turned on his heels, off to find the attendant and Libby smiled, despite her apprehension. She had done *two* things that day that scared her, and at least one of them was already working out.

Moments after posting a letter to Rose McGillycuddy (that was the First Thing that had scared her), she'd been overtaken with a sense of achievement, a sense that she was getting somewhere. A sense that she was discovering a new Libby Andrews – or perhaps rediscovering the old one – someone who no longer put off tasks that needed to be done. 'You've come this far, my dear,' Roger had said to her two days before, 'surely, you have nothing to lose?' The sentiment had been so compelling that – after she'd stepped away from the counter, where she'd paid an ungodly amount of money for express post to Ireland – she'd taken his card out of her diary and written down his words. As she did so, Sam's number had caught her eye. *You have nothing to lose.* Before she could question herself, she'd taken a deep breath and dialled it – thus braving the Second Thing.

When Sam had finally answered, he sounded like he was talking from the climax of a Christmas movie.

'Hello?' he'd yelled.

'Sam . . .'

'Libby! Is that you? I thought you didn't have a mobile?'

She'd pulled the phone a little away from her ear. 'Erm . . .'

'I'm sorry, it's mayhem in here . . .'

'I'll call back lat—'

'I'm in some awful shop in Oxford Street,' he'd said quickly, and a little less loudly, as though he'd realised he might be sounding a little deranged. They hadn't talked since that morning at the café, but did he, despite the chaos, sound pleased to hear from her? It was difficult to tell through the tinny music and screaming children in the background. 'I'm picking up gifts for my friends' kids. They're multiplying, you know.'

'The gifts or the kids?'

'Both.' He'd yelped then, as if someone might have trodden on his foot. 'I *hate* shopping.'

Libby had bitten her lip, trying not to laugh. 'It's no problem, I only wanted to—'

'Are you at the apartment?'

She'd paused. 'What? Now?'

'I could really do with a safe house,' he'd said with a measure of desperation. Sam might have been a soldier, but clearly shopping for My Little Ponies and Dora the Explorer backpacks took more courage than he'd expected.

You have nothing to lose.

'I am at home,' she'd lied so loudly that several people in the post office had turned to look, and she'd flushed, not with embarrassment, but with the anticipation of seeing Sam again.

She'd got back just in time; soon he'd arrived laden with parcels. Had he sported a long white beard, and a few dozen extra pounds, he might have made a convincing Santa but, as it was, his frazzled expression suggested he was more likely to be the labour in Kris Kringle's toyshop than management.

'Traumatised?' she'd asked, trying to keep a straight face.

'I never want to see another reindeer or elf or Christmas tree again.'

'That's a shame,' she'd replied, thinking of the plan she'd come up with on the short walk from the post office, 'because I was hoping you might be able to help me buy one.'

Sam had readily agreed to her request, so long as it meant getting out of the city. He'd returned to Putney only to pick her up an hour later, driving an ancient Volvo which had looked entirely out of place on Grosvenor Square.

As Libby had met Sam at the front door, Miss Winman

bustled down the hallway. 'Good morning,' she'd said distract-
edly as she fished in her handbag. 'I suspect it'll be busy out
there, all those Christmas shoppers, they've got me hot and
bother—' She halted. 'Who's your friend, then?'

'This's Sam.' Libby blushed. 'He's a new friend. We just
met, really . . .'

Sam had come to her rescue with a little white lie. 'I offered
to take Libby Christmas tree shopping, that's all.'

'I see.' Miss Winman smiled. 'Well, that *is* a good shortcut
to friendship, isn't it?'

Shortcut. Something scratched at Libby's mind, and she'd
reached into her bag. 'Am I remembering right, Miss Winman,
that you mentioned you were a secretary during the war?'

'Did I? Well, yes, I was, as a matter of fact. But not for
long. Why do you ask?'

'Do you . . . know shorthand? I have this interview, from
my dad, but I have no idea what it says.'

'I'm a little rusty but perhaps I can . . .' Miss Winman had
taken the slightly crumpled pages from Libby, and glanced at
the first few marks. 'Yes. May I take this? I'd need a proper
look, you know. It's no good guessing.'

'Of course. Thank you. Just . . . call me when you can?'

Sam had watched, looking slightly baffled as Libby thanked
her neighbour again, then turned back to him. 'So, where are
we going for this tree?'

❧

In the end they agreed on a medium-sized fir – smaller than
he'd tried to convince her to buy, and far bigger than she'd
wanted. Lashed to the Volvo's roof rack, it spilled ever so
slightly over the rear window, and Libby wondered how her
aunts would feel about a tree that half-filled the apartment's
front room.

'They'll love it,' said Sam, with the certainty of a man who wouldn't have to deal with the consequences. He seemed so at home out of the city, in his wind fleece and hiking boots, his calm and collected demeanour having returned.

'Well,' she said, one hand on the door. She glanced towards the makeshift café set up in the farm's barn, where rectangle hay bales outside were arranged around several small fire pits that flickered with festive joviality.

'Do you—' she started.

'Do you—' he started.

'Fancy a mulled wine?' he said, just as she said, 'Fancy a hot chocolate?'

She laughed, glancing away. This was silly, wasn't it? Two adults, just friends.

๛

Sam handed her a mulled wine and she gratefully wrapped her fingers around it, relishing the sweet cinnamon scent that wafted up and away in the slowly twirling steam.

'They're predicting Christmas snow, you know.' He sat on the hay bale next to her.

'Really?'

'They do that every year, though. Bloody inconsiderate, getting our hopes up . . .'

Libby laughed. Sam continued to surprise her. He was so much . . . *softer* . . . than the man she'd met in the boat only a couple of weeks before. So changed. But then, was it just *him* who was different?

'It would be wonderful, wouldn't it? A white Christmas.'

'A bit of a change from Tasmania, I suppose?'

She nodded, thinking of the baking Christmases of her childhood. BBQ for lunch, cold drinks on the verandah, the sounds of neighbours playing cricket in the afternoon. So different to this cold crisp day in the countryside where bare hedgerows rimmed the fields, and the smell of mulled wine warmed the belly just as much as the heat from the crackling fire. Unfamiliar, but familiar all the same. After all, she'd grown up reading *A Christmas Carol* each December, watching *The Snowman*, decorating the tree with icicles that would have melted within moments had they been real. She smiled at the memories, and felt a zing of excitement about her first wintery Christmas. But the feeling was quickly followed by apprehension.

Mum's coming over, she thought, then she realised – by the look on Sam's face – that she'd said it out loud.

'That's great. Have you told her about . . .'

She shifted. 'We aren't particularly close.'

'It's okay not to be best friends with your parents,' he said, with an almost forced lightness.

'How's your relationship with Lawrence?'

'It's good,' he admitted, looking down, as though his happy circumstance might somehow take away from her own.

'It's not a bad situation,' Libby clarified. 'It's not like Mum and I don't get along . . . it's more that I don't *know* her. I mean, what was she like before I was born, for example? My aunts told me recently she'd always wanted to travel. You could've knocked me over with a feather! And Roger said that Dad was head over heels in love with Mum, and yet she'd never mentioned how she felt about him.'

'Have you ever said: *Mum, tell me about yourself*?'

She laughed. 'No!'

'I suggest you do.'

'What? Just ask her?'

'Just ask her.'

'I *have* asked about Dad.'

'She won't talk about him?'

'No. Does Lawrence talk about Alice?'

'Yes,' he admitted, 'he does.'

They sat in silence for a moment. 'Sam?'

'Yes?'

'Why did you leave the army?' She didn't know where the question came from, but suddenly she'd been taken with an overwhelming desire to ask. Perhaps it was that they were sat here so comfortably, talking about memories, and Sam himself had encouraged her to be more inquisitive, to voice what was on her mind.

'I . . .'

'I'm sorry.'

'No, it's okay.' He paused. 'I should never have joined up in the first place, to be honest. It was pressure really, from my school. I ended up going to Sandhurst, like so many of the guys I studied with. But, really, I wasn't that interested. I'm outdoorsy, but . . . the army? War?' He sighed, shaking his head.

'What did Lawrence think?'

Sam considered her question, then looked a little sheepish. 'I can't remember really discussing it. He seemed pleased that I appeared to know what I was doing, even though I didn't.'

Libby knew how that felt. 'And you realised it recently? You've left the army, haven't you?'

'I'm on my way out, that's for sure. You don't just hand in your notice one day, then you're free the next.'

'That was . . . *brave*,' she said, using the word he'd applied to her the week before, the one that had made her stomach flutter.

'No, Libby,' he said, 'it wasn't bravery that made me leave.'

'Oh?'

He hesitated. 'It was Simon.'

'Your friend? The one who wrote poetry?'

Sam looked away. 'We'd been on tour for three months . . .'

Libby didn't know what to say. Last year, when the war

started, she'd gone into Launceston city centre to protest, along with millions around the world.

'I was at the field camp when they brought him back to hospital. There was no hope. A stray bullet, friendly fire, though that was never recorded.'

'Sam.'

'No investigation, no accountability. Just swept under the carpet. I struggled on for six months until I finally finished my tour, but I can't go on with that life.' A hesitation. 'This is the most I've ever told anyone about . . . then.'

She took his hand, which was cold, despite the fire, despite the mulled wine. 'I won't share it.'

'No' – he squeezed – 'I know. I'm just surprised. To be able to talk like this.' He smiled sadly. 'I haven't even told Dad the truth about what happened to Simon.'

'I can understand that.'

'I *have* tried.' He ran a hand through his hair.

'Does anything help?' She was asking for him, but she was interested, too, for her. She'd never talked of grief before, not like this. Though, of course, their stories were very different. But grief didn't discriminate, Libby had come to learn. No matter how little, or how well, you knew someone, when they're gone they're gone, and the sorrow that lingers for years also stems from the future that might have been.

Sam took a deep breath. 'It's kind of nerdy, but I've tried . . . writing poetry. A little. Not much.'

'You have?' Libby felt a flush of warmth. For years after she'd graduated, she had thought constantly about the extraordinary power of war poetry. She believed in it wholeheartedly. Not just for generations to follow, but for those who wrote words from the memories they were trying to suppress.

'It's terrible, though.'

Terrible. War was terrible. Writing was not. Libby had

studied hundreds of published war poems, but she had always understood that her own research merely scratched the surface, and in her mind she'd often imagined the countless unseen works that would have told their own story. Notebooks lost to the battlefield. Ballads squeezed onto scraps of paper seized by the enemy. Sketches tucked into letters that never made it home. All of these unpublished works represented outpourings of grief, loss, frustration and love that would never see the light of day, and yet their value had been all in the making of them, rather than that gleaned by those who might read them after.

'It doesn't matter. It's only for you. You don't need to share it.'

More people were spilling into the field now, carrying Christmas trees to their cars as Sam and Libby had done, returning to the barn to warm up with mulled wine and mince pies served on festive paper plates. A family of four came to join them at their fire, and the boy began to throw pieces of hay into the flames.

'I think this is our cue,' Sam whispered.

Libby sensed that it was an excuse, that his time for talking was over. She felt immensely proud of him. She felt his pain. And although they'd barely scratched the surface of what he'd experienced, she sensed that, as he stood and led her away, he walked a little lighter.

He paused when he reached the car. 'Do you fancy a drive?'

She fancied nothing more. 'I do.'

'Good,' he said, opening the passenger door for her like the gentlemen she was beginning to realise he was, 'because I have somewhere I would dearly like to take you.'

Chapter 54

Towerhurst, Tasmania

June 1944

In the year and a half since she'd made her recovery, Grace had developed a celebratory ritual whenever one of her poems was published. Firstly, she took a restorative glass of port. Just one. Liquor – *good* liquor – was in short supply and anyway, if she allowed herself much more, she'd be permanently sloshed, so in demand was her work. Secondly, she allowed herself a little housekeeping. She got to her knees and began to stack sheets of paper, tying them together in logical parcels – one pile: first drafts of 'Across the Water', another pile: notes on the Burma railway – and putting them away in boxes labelled with a month, and a year.

June 1944 she wrote, with a sigh.

When God made time, he made plenty of it, Daniel had said the first time they'd met, under the sassafras so long ago. She counted the years in her head, knowing that more time had passed since Daniel had left than she'd ever spent with him, and yet he was always with her. That itself was a trick of time, which some people thought to be linear. A ridiculous notion. Time looped and turned out and back on itself, a shifting, slippery thing.

The day of Puds's visit to the tower in 1942, she had been

shaken from her stupor, moving back into her bedroom the morning after, though Uncle Marcus insisted she keep the office as her own.

She sighed, gathering more of her papers into a pile. Writing was a messy business. Especially writing about war. Her research was strewn across the tower floor, and newspaper clippings covered every inch of space. She traced her fingers over the familiar tales, written about places she'd never been. The mud, the blood, the horror; she couldn't experience these things, only imagine them and, though she had asked Puds dozens of times for his input, it was nigh impossible to extract a word about what he'd seen in Timor. The only story he'd told her was that of Daniel's bravery. How he'd carried Puds from behind enemy lines, then without hesitation, turned back for those who'd been left behind.

No, aside from articles laced with propaganda, her insight into the war came from Uncle Marcus in unrelenting streams – over breakfast, before dinner – and she eagerly tucked the information away. Aunt Olive scoffed at his insight but Rose always had something to say on the latest battle, though her opinions were never that: *her* opinions; they were invariably formed by someone else and delivered as her own. Just as she'd done in London. Just as she'd done on that first night at Towerhurst when war had been declared.

As the years passed, Grace had begun to understand more and more about the politics of a world she'd once ignored, and memories had surfaced. Slowly at first, then faster as though gaining momentum, spilling over one another into her mind. She recalled events she hadn't understood at the time: of secret rendezvous at Grosvenor Square; of *Mein Kampf* on the coffee table; of Edeline's predilection for black shirts, which she had ceased wearing in 1936 when – Grace had discovered in an old copy of *The Bulletin* – the Public Order Act was enacted, banning the wearing of political uniform. Grace had been blinded by her sheltered life, but now she knew: her mother was a member of the British Union of Fascists.

'Did you know?' she'd asked Uncle Marcus last year.

'Yes.'

They'd talked of it rarely, but Grace had come to understand that her uncle hadn't realised how far to the right Edeline had gone.

'As far as I can tell, she joined the Blackshirts because they gave responsibility to women.'

'I don't understand.'

'It's only my observation but . . . if I were to start a political party, I too would rely on women to politicise the home. They're a weapon that can convert both man and child.'

Grace turned back to the task at hand, filing a newspaper clipping from eighteen months before: late 1942. In it, rumours had been written; stories that Australian POWs had been moved up the Malaya Peninsula and beyond. Some were in Japan, others transported to Singapore. She vaguely recalled Uncle Marcus showing it to her at the time of publication, though she'd been extremely unwell and could barely understand its relevance.

'Keep hoping,' he'd said. 'Hope isn't rationed, you know.'

By September 1943, reliable reports had finally filtered through from Japanese-occupied territory in Asia: the tens of thousands of prisoners of war had been put to work building a railway to link Thailand to Burma and, according to Red Cross representatives – who had been allowed a cursory glance – Daniel was among them. Ned McGillycuddy had told Puds, and Puds came straight to Towerhurst.

Later, when he'd left, she'd curled in a ball, weeping until dawn, sleeping when the sun rose and waking to the realisation that, from then on, she'd have to be stronger. For Daniel, and for herself.

She had taken to asking Puds, every day, to recall his memories of Daniel, thereby bringing them closer. And through their discussions, which often lasted hours, she and Puds became firm friends. A hundred times she nearly spilled the secret she'd kept since Daniel's departure, but she'd never quite found the words, which felt somewhat misleading, considering how candid Puds had been with her.

'I'd do anything for the love of Daniel's life,' he'd said to her once. They'd been skimming rocks at the waterfall, and she'd paused, turning to him.

'Because he saved you?'

'Mostly, yes,' he'd smiled. The sun had peered through a window in the clouds just as she caught his gaze and she gasped. She saw something there that she recognised. Yearning. She'd known, somehow, that it wasn't meant for her. She'd seen it too in the photo taken on that Christmas Eve years before. To others, it might appear that Puds gazed at *her* with longing, but she knew now he'd been looking right past her, to the man on the other side.

'Because you love him, too?'

'Yes,' was all he said, and the clouds had closed as though the sun had reached out to shut the curtains, now that light had shone on Puds's secret. It had rained for days afterwards, and they'd never spoken of it again. It explained so much about Puds, and the way they could be together in such comfort, such companionship.

Both loving the same man.

Chapter 55

Hampshire's country lanes, England
December 2004

'Have I made a terrible mistake?'

'No,' said Sam, 'not at all.' They'd left the tree farm behind, and were weaving their way through the bare hedge-rows of Hampshire's country lanes. 'Sending a letter to Rose McGillycuddy was exactly the right thing to do. You need answers.'

Libby flushed in the face of the praise. 'It was Roger's idea.'

'He's trouble, that one,' Sam said with a grin.

Outside, late afternoon had well and truly taken hold, and in an hour, dusk would fall.

'Where exactly are we going?'

'I tracked down M—'

Libby's phone rang. 'Sorry.' Frantically – if only to stop the embarrassing rendition of 'Jingle Bells' – she dug into the depths of her bag, finding her phone between the pages of the diary that had brought Sam to her aunts' door. When she saw who was calling she leapt to answer.

'Miss Winman!'

Without introduction or confirmation, a familiar voice came down the line. 'Well, this is very interesting.'

Libby couldn't help smiling. Straight to the point. 'You've

been able to read it? The interview?' she asked, her mind already tingling in anticipation.

'First of all, do you have your Christmas tree?'

Libby told her about the farm, and the pleasure of hot mulled wine on a cold day.

'I see,' Miss Winman said. 'You know, dear, your voice changed there.'

A hesitation. 'Sorry?'

'Your voice . . . when you talked about your *new* friend, it changed.'

Libby cleared her throat, glancing surreptitiously at Sam. 'Sorry, I think you're breaking up . . .'

'Really? Well . . . if that's the case, I shan't be able to read out the translated shorthand. I'll call back lat—'

'Wait!' Libby's heart gave a thump. Theatrically, she looked at the phone's screen, then pressed it back to her ear. 'I think we're coming into better reception now.'

'Good. Well, here you are then.' In her clear-cut voice, Miss Winman read out the transcript of Olive Foxton's interview. Then she waited in silence.

'Libby, dear?'

'I'm here.'

'This was . . . not what you were expecting?'

'No,' Libby said, her mouth dry. 'No, Miss Winman, that was not what I was expecting at all.'

Chapter 56

Launceston, Tasmania

February 1975

Before he left for London, there was something Ben was determined to do. He pulled up outside Our Lady of Mercy, a convent that had been converted to a nursing home, the directions to which he'd been given by Colette on the understanding that he wanted to know more of Towerhurst's history.

'She has dementia,' the orderly warned, as he showed Ben to Olive Foxton's room. 'But she's in no way frail and still quite young – just over seventy. Lived alone in some damp place on the west coast for far too long.' Ben had to skip to keep up with the man's whip-quick steps as he strode down the narrow hallway. He was clearly someone with other places to be.

'Yes, I know. That's why I'm—'

'We're short staffed, under-funded, but we do our best.' The place was clean, and jolly prints covered the walls. It wasn't unpleasant, if a little warm in the summer's dry grip. 'Here we are.' The orderly stopped at a closed door, knocking smartly. 'She can be rather . . . acerbic. Good luck.' Without waiting for a reply, he went on his way.

❦

'Marcus?'

Ben hesitated, peering into the gloom. 'No. I'm Ben. Ben Andrews.'

'Ben Andrews . . .' A lamp was switched on, bathing the owner of the voice in yellow light. There she was – Olive Foxton – just a shadow of the woman captured in the photograph he'd seen of her wedding day more than fifty-five years before. Her gaze looked right though him and out the other side.

'Might I come in?'

She gave a regal wave of her hand, and he stepped inside, closing the door behind him. 'Thank you for seeing me,' he said, although he didn't know if anyone had warned her he was coming.

'Hmph.' Clearly his presence didn't alarm her. Quite the reverse: he might not have been there at all.

Ben looked around him. Everything – he supposed – that Olive owned was in this room. Several ornaments, a photograph of a young woman that might have been herself, a remote to a television that he couldn't see. She sat on the only soft chair, and on the small table beside her was a ball of pink wool being knitted into a scarf. There wasn't a book to be seen, though an *Australian Women's Weekly* lay open on the floor beside her.

He indicated a small wooden stool. 'May I?'

Again, she waved her hand, which he took for acquiescence, and he sat quickly, his confidence ebbing away. What *on earth* had he been thinking? Willow would be annoyed with him. But if his suspicions were correct – that it had been Grace Grey down that mine – then Olive might well know the truth. He would need to tread carefully, because if what Richard Holmes had said – and what Ned had implied – was true, that Marcus was the father of Rose's child, he would need to tread carefully, tiptoeing towards answers.

He began. 'I wanted to ask you about a girl who came to stay with you at Towerhurst during the war.'

Olive hesitated, and when she finally spoke, her voice cracked. 'Why?'

Ben repeated what he'd told the orderly. 'I'm writing an article on child evacuees. An old friend of yours, Mira Holmes, told me you might be able to help.'

'Pfft!' Evidently this was the wrong thing to say. Olive snatched her knitting from the bedside table and began jabbing at the stitches. 'What magazine's this for, then?' she said with exaggerated boredom.

Ben's gaze alighted on the bed. '*Australian Women's Weekly*.'

'I don't mind that one,' she said, softening a little.

'I was hoping to ask about R—'

'If you're writing an article why aren't you taking notes?'

Ben smiled amiably and dug into his satchel, then placed a notepad on his knee. This didn't entirely satisfy her, so at the top he wrote *Interview with Olive Foxton, Our Lady of Mercy, February 1975*. That did the trick.

'So then . . .' she said.

'I was hoping to ask you a few questions about your experiences with child evacuees. What life was like. How they coped . . .'

Olive affected an unimpressed expression. 'Useless, wasn't she? Always with her head in a book. Hardly helpful for the war effort, was it? That Grey girl was the ultimate . . .' On the topic of Grace, it seemed Olive was only too happy to comply, launching into a lecture that ranged from Marcus's blindness to her wanton, lazy ways to the fact that she'd spent half a year holed up in the tower, ill and useless.

'I heard she had rheumatic fever. Pretty serious back then, wasn't it?'

Olive ignored him, carrying on as though he hadn't spoken.

'The rest of us, we contributed to the war effort, you know? But not Grace.'

'Surely her patriotic poetry was well received?'

'Poetry! What a load of rubbish. Most women really stepped up. Knitting' – she held hers up – 'making parcels for Changi, working the men's jobs. Take darling Rose, for example.'

Ben leaned forward. 'Rose Munro?'

'How do you know about her?'

'Well, I'm looking into evacuees.'

'Ha! She wasn't an evacuee! Sent away, she was, to look after Grace. I didn't envy her.'

'Rose and Grace . . . they didn't get along?'

'Who on earth would have got along with Grace? Apart from my husband.'

Ben felt for Grace; dismissed as nothing, and yet the work he'd read in the tower had moved him. She'd had a heart, but perhaps Olive hadn't known it? He sighed. With everything going on – Dina's illness, wondering whether he should cancel his imminent trip to London, the endless questions brought up by Towerhurst – he'd noticed he was becoming more sentimental than usual. He made several notes.

'What's wrong with your writing?'

He held it up, glad she evidently couldn't read it. 'It's shorthand.'

'I thought only secretaries used that?'

Ben smiled tightly, pulling on his collar with a glance at the shut curtains. It was stiflingly hot in the room, both in temperature and mood.

'Don't even think about it, young man. You'll let the rain in.' Outside, he knew, the sky was endless blue, but Olive's gaze ran up and down curtains as if observing some imaginary stream. 'It was like this the day they left. Heavy rain, thunder too. I was staying with my mother. I remember it well.'

'They?'

'Rose and Grace. They left without a backward glance.' She pulled at the woollen threads, the scarf unravelling quickly at her feet. 'But Rose was a good girl. She loved me like an older sister.'

'I'm sure she did.'

She pursed her lips, then said, 'What d'you know about it?'

Ben hesitated. The truth was, he didn't know anything about a sibling's love, although in the past three years Ash and Ivy had taught him something of it.

Olive stuck out her bottom lip in a gesture that might have been mildly apologetic. 'Rose was always very independent. Very charismatic. Very *determined*. Everyone loved her, you know. She *adored* me.'

Trying a different tack, he said, 'My article is specifically about child evacuees whose lives changed dramatically during the six years they were here. Some fell in love, some got married, some had children . . . legitimate or otherwise.' He hesitated. 'Rose left Towerhurst for a while, and went to Hobart. Do you remember that?'

As he spoke, Olive frowned, searching her mind for something she didn't seem to know. 'Rose was a good girl,' she repeated like a mantra.

Ben felt guilty about the memories he was about to excavate – if they existed at all – and yet without answers, Willow would never know the truth. 'She had a child, didn't she?'

Olive's laugh was throaty. 'Who . . . who told you that?'

'Richard Holmes.'

Olive snorted. 'It's easier to dam a river than stop that one gossiping, and the mother's even worse.'

'So, it's not true?'

'Rose went to Hobart during the war for work. That's all. I visited several times, don't you think I'd have noticed if she was pregnant?'

Though he wasn't sure he could believe her answer, still he asked: 'You're telling me that Rose Munro *didn't* have a child while in Tasmania?'

Olive scoffed, then looked at him with an unwavering gaze. 'Certainly not!' She snapped her fingers at a jug on the sideboard.

Ben poured a glass of water, noticing how his hands shook. 'Here you go.'

She waved it away. 'Rose up and left the day the bombs dropped on Nagasaki. Never said goodbye. But I understood. I guess she knew the war in the Pacific was finally over. That's what I was told.'

'Told by whom?'

'By Marcus.' She began to pull at her fingers, twisting them this way and that. 'We knew everything, me and Marcus.'

'Knew what?'

'About that vixen, Grace. A fox through and through.'

'What about her?'

'You're asking about Rose, when you should be asking about Grace. What kind of journalist are you?' She waved her hand dismissively at his page of notes. 'She wasn't even married, you know? Who would've wed the little beast?'

'What do you mean?'

Olive tapped her foot in agitation. 'Well, the baby, of course.'

Ben drew a quick breath. '*Grace* had a child?'

'Pfft,' Olive said. She picked up the remote, and pressed a large red button. He thought a hidden TV might come to life. When it didn't, he realised she was calling for assistance.

'I'm tired now, Marcus.' She looked through him once more. 'But *death* put an end to it, didn't it?'

Ben swallowed. 'Death? Grace's death?'

Silence.

'Did Grace die? In childbirth?'

Olive's gaze snapped back to him. 'It was our little secret. Me and you, wasn't it, Marcus? We've never told anyone? Have we? That was the deal.'

He *knew* it. Ben knew it! 'We . . .' he hesitated. 'We made Grace disappear, didn't we, Olive?'

'No, not *Grace*! Her baby! Gone. *Poof.*' She clicked her fingers. 'Even the father never knew.'

'The father?'

Olive began to mutter to herself. 'Why *Rose* married him in the end, I really couldn't say . . .'

'Daniel? Daniel McGillycuddy?'

'Of course!' She laughed. 'But the baby didn't die, Marcus. You know that; it was our little secret. *You* were one who took it away, off to its new home.'

The way she said *it*, made Ben shudder. 'What year did Grace have the baby?'

A huff. 'Don't *speak* to me like that, Marcus,' she said. 'A husband should treat his wife better.'

He was losing her. 'I'm sorry . . . darling,' he said, turning to hide his grimace. 'Would you' – he looked around him for a prop – 'like another glass of water?'

She nodded, pacified.

'Olive, dear' – another grimace – 'I can't recall . . . what year did Grace give birth to her child?'

'You know, Marcus! You took the baby away yourself.'

'Yes . . . but what year did I take her away?'

Olive frowned, hesitating.

'What year?' he repeated.

'Don't you recall? It was 1942.'

The orderly arrived, looking flustered. 'Yes?' he said, summoning a smile.

Olive closed her eyes. 'Tell my husband to leave.' She flapped a hand. 'I don't want to see him today.'

Chapter 57

Towerhurst, Tasmania

July 1944

Grace stepped off the verandah, checking behind her to see whether anyone was watching from the house. She didn't take the path to the waterfall often these days, but a pause in the winter rain, and a shaft of sunlight glinting off water droplets on the moon gate, had drawn her down from her tower room and into the fresh, salty air.

She walked slowly towards the forest, feeling, as always, that tug in her heart. At the small Atlantisite stone now placed next to the moon gate, she stopped, kneeling to brush away the rain, to trace the words carved into its smooth surface. As the cold stone warmed under her hands, she let her mind return to the confusion and pain of 1942, trying, as Uncle Marcus had once told her, to leave the bitterness behind.

It was only because of a conversation she'd once overhead years before that Grace had understood the consequences of what she and Daniel had done. When she'd first had . . . suspicions . . . she found herself recalling the discussion as though it were yesterday, as if the six years since had vanished without a trace. It was 1936 and she'd been twelve years old, hiding, lying on her back reading an encyclopaedia in the front room of Grosvenor Square, on a cold dry day.

Rose and Mother entered, unaware that she lay on the floor behind the sofa.

'Rose,' Mother had purred, sitting and patting the space next to her.

'I'm sorry. I didn't know who else to go to.'

'You've done the right thing. Come here' – *pat, pat* – 'this is not something you can deal with alone. You will always have me to help.'

'Please . . . Edeline . . . don't tell anyone.' Still Rose had stood by the door.

'I won't betray you to Molly. You have my word. I've told you a thousand times, and I'll tell you again: you can come to me with anything. Anything at all.'

'Even this?'

Grace heard the brush of clothing; the light touch of a hand, perhaps? A gesture from her mother that she herself was unfamiliar with.

'Even this.'

'Why? I'm not your responsibility.'

'You live under my roof.'

A sob. 'I shouldn't have let . . . passion . . . get the better of me.'

'If you want to shine like the sun first you have to burn like it.'

'I don't know if this is the time for *Mein Kampf* quotes.'

'Very good.' They both sat. 'What you've done isn't so very bad. Who's the father?'

'You wouldn't know him.'

'Good. I'd have his guts for garters.' Edeline paused. 'You wanted to? It was consensual?'

'Yes.'

'Do you love him?'

'No.'

'Well, that's probably for the best.' The clock on the mantel chimed twice and Grace's stomach gave a low rumble, hidden by the growl of traffic rolling along Grosvenor Square. 'There are many in the party, Rose, who see leadership potential in you, you know?'

'Me?'

'Yes. You were noticed at Selsey.'

This must have pleased Rose, because she gave an embarrassed laugh. 'I don't suppose a baby will help matters?'

'It would be difficult to shake the scandal. Can you marry the boy?'

'I won't!'

'I didn't think so.'

Rose sobbed. 'I'm ruined.'

The sofa sighed again as one of the women leaned towards the other.

'Pregnancy needn't be the end of you.'

Pregnancy? Is that what this was all about? Rose wasn't married and, according to Grace's third from last tutor, only married women could get pregnant.

'When did you last bleed?'

'I've missed one cycle.'

Edeline said carefully: 'At this stage, there are still ways of dealing with . . . your situation. Some things in life need to be destroyed before they destroy you.'

Rose gasped. She said with uncertainty: 'It's illegal, isn't it?'

'In this country.'

'What do you mean?'

'I had hoped to visit Berlin next month. Meet a few . . . political allies. Abortion is legal in Germany. In certain circumstances. I'm sure we could make sure those circumstances apply to you.'

Rose hesitated. 'Surely that's . . . wrong?'

'It's 1936. We are living in a modern age where having a child

with someone you don't love is *wrong*. It only ends in disappointment.' The way she said this made Grace's blood run cold.

'But—'

'There is nothing so very problematic with intercourse outside marriage. You *just* need to be more careful.' As Edeline
described what that meant, Grace put a hand to her mouth. It
took all her willpower not to cry out. A man and a woman
couldn't – *wouldn't* – do those things. The very thought had
repulsed her.

Now, knelt by the Atlantisite stone, Grace realised she'd
been holding her breath. As she took a deep gulp of cool air,
heavy with the tang of leaf mulch, the scene played forward
to 1942. Had that really been two whole years ago? In some
ways it felt like yesterday, in other ways it seemed like an age
had passed since she'd gathered her courage around her and
knocked on Rose's door.

❧

On the night in question, Rose had returned from the mine to
deliver the news that she would be leaving for Hobart immi-
nently, and would not be back for months.

'The ammunitions factory needs to take material direct from
the mine, and Claud' – she had taken to using her boss's first
name of late – 'will be working with them on a new process.
We'll be back and forth throughout the rest of the year. How
exciting 1942 is turning out to be! I'll take a room in Hobart,
get to know the city.'

They'd settled down to dinner, and at this news Aunt Olive
put down her fork. 'Alone?'

'You can always visit. It'll be a blast.'

Uncle Marcus winced. 'These munitions factories can be
dangerous . . .'

'It's a minuscule factory. Anyway, my destiny is *not* to be a canary girl. It's this trip, or back to England, because I can't stay here on the west coast for the rest of my life. I simply can't. I need to be doing more.'

❧

It wasn't until after dinner that Grace had the opportunity to talk to Rose alone. She'd knocked on the door, then nudged it open, acutely aware that what she was about to say was every bit as explosive as a stray hairgrip in a munitions factory.

'Rose?'

From inside, there was a flurry of activity: the sound of papers being knocked to the floor, an intake of breath, the quick steps of socked feet.

'What do you want? I'm busy.'

'Please?' Grace recalled how she'd twisted her fox pendant so that the light from the bedroom caught it. It had thrown a pale glow across Rose's face, and the reflection caught her eye. There was nothing as effective as reminding Rose of her duty to Edeline.

'Give me a minute.' She closed the door and disappeared inside, from where muffled shuffling preceded the scraping of a box across the floor. When she appeared again, the room was clean.

As Grace stepped over the threshold, she'd felt she was walking into the lion's den, but who else could she tell?

❧

Rose had gaped at her.

'I see,' she'd said. 'And the father?'

'Daniel.'

'How could you be so stupid?'

'I love him.' From the look she was given, Grace realised Rose didn't believe the feeling was mutual.

'You don't know anything about love. How many months since you've bled?'

'Three.'

'It's too late to . . . fix . . . the situation.'

A gasp. 'I don't want to *fix* anything.'

'Then what do you suggest?'

'I could go to Hobart with you. Stay in the rooms you're planning on renting.'

'*Room*. A single room in a guesthouse. You can't come with me.'

'Why not?'

Rose had hesitated. 'You just can't.'

'How can I stay here?'

'Marcus will look after you, no doubt.' Grace could hear the malice in her words.

'I can't confess to Uncle Marcus. He'll have to tell Mother.'

Rose had laughed cruelly. 'And you think *I* won't?'

'No,' Grace had said, hoping her bluff would work. 'Because if you do, I'll tell everyone about Berlin.'

'Berlin?'

'Yes. About what you *got up to* in Berlin.' She'd given Rose a meaningful look, but when she only received a blank stare in reply, she'd clarified. 'The abortion.'

Rose had gone to the door and opened it. 'Get out!'

'But—'

'Go!'

And when Grace left, tears wet on her face, she'd known, without a shadow of a doubt, that knocking on Rose's door, that trying to play Rose's games, had been a terrible, terrible mistake.

❧

Just like Rapunzel, Grace had been hidden away in a tower. She hadn't so much agreed as let it happen, because really, what choice did she have? Another girl, another woman, with more life experience, might have found a way to help herself, but Grace could think of nothing. Go to a city? She didn't know anyone. Confide in Colette and Ned? She couldn't bear for them to think poorly of Daniel. Walk around unashamedly while her condition advanced in full view of Westford? Aunt Olive would sooner tie her up than let that happen.

'We'll work it out,' Uncle Marcus had said when he admitted that Olive had told him, and Rose had told her. He'd shown her kindness in spite of his wife's disapproval.

'We'll tell everyone you've caught rheumatic fever. You've been unwell for a month or two anyway,' Aunt Olive had said.

It made sense, but it wasn't the short term that worried Grace most. 'What will we say when the baby finally comes?'

'I'm working on it,' Aunt Olive had said over her shoulder as she stormed out, leaving Grace to wonder what on earth that could mean.

❧

Months later, on the night that Grace had given birth, the sky cried all its tears, and she recalled wanting nothing more than to fling open the tower's portholes and welcome them in, feel the rain on her skin, let it quench the fire that burned inside her. A cruel wind raged down the flue, fanning the potbelly's blaze, and Aunt Olive, surprisingly, had barely left her side. They'd spent more time together in the three days leading up to the birth than they had in the previous three years.

After she'd been in labour for six hours, Uncle Marcus had tentatively approached. 'The tide's on its way down,' he'd said, turning from the room. 'I'm going to fetch the doctor.'

'There's no need.'

Aunt Olive had gone to Grace's side, and put a cold hand on her forehead. 'I'm going to give you something for the pain.

You're just fine, aren't you?' She'd taken a brown glass bottle from her pocket and poured a thimble of amber liquid into its lid, then turned to Uncle Marcus. 'As I said before, this is women's business.'

'I've been thinking about what we—'

'Later,' she'd snapped.

Grace had drunk the bitter liquid, and from there things had become a little hazy. She recalled, though, wondering about loveless marriages. Why didn't people embark on life's biggest journey with both eyes open? Or did they change too slowly to notice they'd already begun to drown? She had imagined Aunt Olive splashing through the sea, clambering over Uncle Marcus to save herself. It had caused her to laugh a little, as the onset of delirium wound its hot tentacles around her mind. And she'd been glad, as she'd watched Uncle Marcus disappear from view, that her good humour was still intact.

୬

Two hours later, every part of her had burned. She'd tried to raise herself onto her elbows, barely moving before Aunt Olive pushed her down. The contractions had been close, but the baby was stubborn. She'd hoped that was a good thing. It was a girl, she'd felt then. She would teach her daughter to be good and kind and generous; she would chase away self-doubt and sorrow with something she herself had never had in her first sixteen years, the greatest weapon: love.

She'd reached out to take a sip of water, and gasped.

It was happening, but something felt very wrong.

୬

When she woke the next morning, the ocean had sighed with a quiet tiredness that seeped into Grace's bones and she'd lain still, examining the sloping ceiling and searching for knots in the golden timber.

She'd been confused as to why she was in the tower. She'd looked around the room to find that it was neater than it had ever been: books stacked away, Uncle Marcus's desks devoid of papers, the potbelly stove polished clean so that the glass showed the last embers from the night before . . .

The night before?

She'd gasped, uselessly trying to lift herself on her elbows. A dozen images, a dozen feelings, a dozen memories had shuffled across her groggy consciousness – the contractions, the burning heat, the understanding that something was wrong – each thought getting heavier and heavier, faster and faster, taking her back there as she'd pulled in thick breaths. She'd put her hands on her tender breasts, then felt down to her belly which had risen in a swell under her palms, but she'd known even then that it was empty, that her baby was gone. She'd held that tiny, swaddled bundle in her arms for only a few seconds before Aunt Olive had swept in, and taken it away.

Summoning the energy from somewhere deep within, she'd called down the staircase.

'Help! Hello? Can anyone hear me?'

Moments later, Uncle Marcus had appeared, his face stricken with a pain that she refused to understand. 'My darling girl.' He'd gathered her into his arms and she was shocked to feel his shoulders rock.

'Why are you crying?' she'd asked, though perhaps she'd already known.

'I'm so sorry,' he'd replied. 'I'm so sorry that this is happening to you.'

'What is happening?'

From across the room, another voice had spoken. 'Your child didn't make it, Grace. In a month or so, we'll tell everyone how well you've recovered from your rheumatic fever. Do you understand?'

Grace hadn't. She hadn't understood.

'It's for the best,' Olive had added, as Uncle Marcus held her tighter.

'I'm sorry,' he'd repeated. 'I'm so, so sorry.'

'But Daniel . . . the baby was all I had of Daniel . . .'

'I know, I know. And when he returns, we'll tell him everything. We'll put things right.'

Grace had sobbed then, just as she did now, two years later. The painful memories made her feel faint and she leaned forward, her forehead resting on the cool stone before her. Her eyes stung as she recalled that moment: the disbelief; the anguish; and how Uncle Marcus had held her as her heart had broken in two.

Chapter 58

Somewhere over Europe

February 1975

So, Olive and Marcus arranged for Grace's baby to be taken away? And they'd told the poor girl her daughter had died? The very thought broke Ben's heart in two.

'More coffee, sir?' The air stewardess reached across, topping up his cup.

'Thank you.'

Beneath him, Europe had appeared, and he glanced out of the window as clouds swallowed up what might have been France. Flying to the other side of the globe had certainly given Ben enough time to think, though he'd arrived at no concrete conclusions. The mystery – *mysteries* in fact; that of the body down the mine, and the identity of Willow's mother – seemed to have the same answer: *Grace*.

Or did they? For a split second, when Olive had said, 'But *death* put an end to it, didn't it?' Ben had been sure that it *was* Grace Grey down that mine, but it was the baby Olive was talking of, and the lie they'd fed her niece. She was good at lying, it seemed. Perhaps she had *lied* to Ben? He hadn't had the opportunity to ask about Grace's current whereabouts – dead or alive – before the orderly had led him out of Our Lady of Mercy without so much as a backward glance.

Perhaps he *had* imagined the necklace after all? And even if he hadn't, either Grace or Rose could still feasibly be Willow's mother. Though if Marcus wasn't the father, who had left Willow the house? It could still have been him; wracked with guilt, perhaps, by his part in the deception. Or Olive – she was the last to live there, and she was a Foxton after all, if only by way of a loveless marriage. Surely Towerhurst was left to her after her husband's death? But if the two didn't get along, Marcus could easily have ensured that his sister, Edeline, inherited.

It was a mess all right, but – Ben considered as his ears popped, the plane commencing its descent – there were plenty of leads. He'd asked Roger to look into details of Rose and Daniel's whereabouts in Kerry; something he might have asked Colette, but couldn't think of a way of doing so without rousing suspicion. He could write to them, sound out what they knew? Visit them? Quickly, he pushed the notion aside. He'd have to learn something more concrete – or something so *shocking* it couldn't be ignored – for him to take the drastic measure of booking a flight to Ireland.

There was no doubt about it, Ben thought, as he fastened his seatbelt, there was a web of lies to be untangled, and he would need to be careful to whom he talked. For now, he'd keep what he knew to himself, though he was troubled by the thought that while a problem shared is a problem halved, secrets multiply in the dark.

❧

Roger Masters waited for him in the Arrivals Hall, a folded newspaper under his arm, chatting to a chauffeur as though they were old friends. Three years had passed since they'd met in Tasmania, and Roger was just the same. In fact, he appeared not to have altered *at all*. Ben would swear in a court of law he'd not even changed his clothes: a tweed jacket unbuttoned over a matching waistcoat. A great juxtaposition to his flared red trousers. His top half appeared to have just returned from a grouse shoot in the highlands, while his bottom half was off to a party.

'My old friend!' He wrapped Ben in a most unmanly hug, sending the chauffeur an embarrassed step back. 'How was it? The journey?'

'Long. I feel like I've been squeezed from a tube.'

Roger laughed heartily. 'Plenty of time for a nap before tonight.'

On the drive to Roger's apartment in Highbury his friend told him that the chauffeur had imparted some juicy gossip about a countess and her gardener lover. 'Quite the Lady Chatterley, by the sound of it.'

'You know that chauffeur?'

'Not at all. Did it seem like it?'

'Yes.'

'Brilliant. That's how you get the info, you know?' He tapped his temple, calmly weaving in and out of cars so rapidly that Ben gripped the dashboard. 'Worth remembering.'

'In what way?'

'For your little investigation.'

'On that—'

Roger waved a hand that Ben wished was attached to the steering wheel. 'Later. Now, tell me: how is Willow? I know it was a last-minute invite, but I had been hoping she'd join you. I would have loved to meet her.'

Willow had remained delighted about Ben's trip until a few days before his departure. 'You're not going to ask about . . . Rose, are you? While you're there in London?' She knew nothing of the things he'd learned – Rose and Daniel's marriage, the revelation about Grace, that either girl could potentially be her mother. Keeping his word was important, though he was bursting with wanting to tell her, and he'd feigned innocence so poorly that she had rolled her eyes.

'Ben!'

'I swear. Look' – they'd been at her parents' house and he leaned in the doorway of her studio – 'I don't have to go.'

It was Dina who had insisted in the end. She was still recovering from surgery, and yet she seemed more whole than ever. 'You'd be mad to miss it. What an adventure,' she'd said. Rob was down at the beach fishing off the rocks, and Willow was with him. 'I always wanted to go to Europe.' At that, the conversation had faltered – the implication heavy – but she'd smoothed over the hesitation by putting an envelope in his hands.

'What's this?' He'd opened it: twenty pounds in crisp notes. She'd ordered them from the bank. 'I can't.' It was too much money, but her thoughtfulness warmed his heart.

She'd pushed the envelope back towards him.

The next day, good news arrived. Dina's surgery looked to have been successful, though it would be months, or years, before they'd know for sure. 'Doesn't mean I'm not going to cark it, so let's see what happens.' She'd taken to talking like that as if *carking it* were nothing at all. It seemed like a perfectly natural coping mechanism to Ben, but Willow said her mother had 'shoved her head in the sand', which – he neglected to point out – was quite the same accusation he could level at her.

'How does she feel about being adopted? About being the child of this Rose Munro?'

Ben resisted the urge to hush his friend, though they were alone in the car. He hesitated, the revelations from his conversation with Olive Foxton on the tip of his tongue. 'How could you?' Willow had said the day she'd overhead him call Roger to confirm his trip while letting slip what he'd learned about

Rose Munro. 'How could you share my *private* information like that?' She hadn't been mad as such, but she'd given off an air of disappointment, and that was somehow worse.

'It's difficult,' he said now to Roger, as they drove through London's thick fog, 'she hadn't yet confronted her parents . . .'

'I understand,' Roger replied. If he noticed Ben was holding back, he didn't show it. Instead, he changed tack. 'I have a surprise for you, tonight at the Iliad Club. *Two* surprises actually.'

'Any hints?'

'None at all, my dear fellow. None at all. You have your secrets, and I have mine.'

❧

Five hours later, they sat together on the tube as it pulled into Moorgate Station. 'Change here for the Circle Line' came the announcement, and they did so, chatting as they went.

'What will the crowd be like? Ben asked, as commuters poured into the carriage.

'Old,' said Roger, 'but not stuffy. You'll like them.'

'To be perfectly frank, I'm a bit nervous.'

'I wouldn't be. They'll already be well lubricated by now.'

Across the aisle, Margaret Thatcher stared out from the front page of a broadsheet, giving Ben a steely look. 'If I can become the first female leader of the Tories,' she seemed to say, 'you can surely read a story to a few half-drunk old men.' She had a good chance of becoming Britain's prime minister in the next election, and she didn't look the sort to take kindly to disagreement.

'Ready?' said Roger.

'Ready,' said Ben. And they spilled out of High Street Kensington.

❧

The Iliad Club oozed the kind of well-worn luxury that could only be purchased with the currency of time: oak panelling stained black with the years, oxblood chesterfields creased with the weight of ten thousand evenings, clothbound books lining floor-to-ceiling shelves. The room was filled with grey-haired men – smoking, talking, drinking – and a large fire burned at one end.

'We get tax breaks for this kind of thing,' said Roger, waving to several men he knew, 'festivals and the like. Inviting visiting speakers.'

So Ben's suspicions had been confirmed?

'But we make sure we donate a nice chunk to the local comprehensive schools, for the upkeep of their libraries and such. Nothing more important than feeding the minds of future generations, is there?'

Ben flushed, ashamed at being so quick to judge. 'No women?' he asked, as a waiter thrust a martini into his hand.

'None yet.'

Ben wondered what Mrs Thatcher would say to that. 'And how many members?'

'Oh, several hundred, I should say. Though only a few dozen, really, are active. In fact' – Roger sipped his drink, giving Ben a keen look – 'I've invited someone you might like to meet.'

'Oh yes?'

'Yes.'

A hesitation. 'Well?'

'Look,' Roger said, as a hush gripped the room, 'they're ready for you.'

ૐ

Ben wasn't alone in taking to the lectern; he'd shared the limelight with an Algerian and a fellow who'd come all the way from Peru. Their stories were cleverly political and he felt rather inadequate in comparison, but when he read 'The Selkie of Ocean Beach' – careful not to stumble over the tricky paragraphs he'd underlined – the audience paid silent attention to every word. When he was asked where the idea came from, he told them about the McGillycuddy's eclectic collection of huts, how they were surrounded by white heather brought by accident many years before.

'Jolly good show,' Roger whispered as he took his seat, and the room filled with applause. 'Most entertaining.'

Ben downed his martini. It *had* gone well, and he couldn't wait to call Willow to let her know.

The MC stood once more. 'Speaking of the McGillycuddys. . .' He nodded to Roger, who stepped up to the lectern, a book in hand.

'Ben,' he said, as the audience watched on, 'I have a treat for you tonight.'

'Me?'

Roger nodded, then he began to read. It was the title poem, he said, from *The Ballads of Daniel McGillycuddy*.

'The Far-Flung Distant Shore.'

Chapter 59

Grosvenor Square, London

February 1975

The morning after the Iliad Club, Ben hopped on the tube –
alone this time – into the city centre, marvelling at everything
he saw: the bobbies, the buses, the bull-nosed black taxis.
Everything was so . . . so *London,* and he had the uncanny
feeling that he'd been shrunk and placed on a Monopoly board
to pick his way around.

In Hyde Park, a light morning mist rose from the damp
grass as he paused at Speakers' Corner, where a small crowd
had gathered before a bearded man gesticulating wildly with a
sheaf of papers. He threw the pages in the air and a cheer rose
over the non-stop traffic of Park Lane. Someone held a placard,
The End is Nigh, while another waved the Hammer and Sickle.
Behind them, on a red double-decker bus rumbling past Marble
Arch, a huge advert for Harrods read *Enter a Different World.*

The collision of these ideologies mimicked precisely how
Ben felt at that very moment. It might have been 1975, but
part of him had been dragged into the past. And it wasn't just
that; it was a sense that he was getting closer to something
important. Last night had told him so.

Later, he stopped, glancing again at the address in his hand, then back up at the towering Georgian terrace house before him. Number 45. It was a stockbroker's office now, and the sharp-suited man leaving the building was testament to that. Glancing down at his own shabby jacket, Ben realised it was the same one he'd worn to Mr Doyle's office all those months ago, before any of this had started.

'I *know* that story,' Ben had said after Roger finished reciting 'The Far-Flung Distant Shore', and the audience began to mingle.

'Really?' Roger handed over the book. It was about eighty pages, just a slip of a thing. 'This copy's for you. It's published by one of our members, you know?'

'I can't believe it.'

'Well, as I said, we have a huge membership list. Truth be told, I've only talked to him a couple of times. Lawrence Littleton's his name. Not particularly active in the club, turns up once a year for Christmas drinks, but I managed to convince him to come tonight . . .' Roger looked around the room. Over by the fire, two men were arguing loudly about *The Odyssey*. One, it seemed, believed it to be a tragedy, while the other was certain it was a comedy. Ben thought it was neither. It was a romance. Everyone knew that.

'Ah, there he is.'

Emerging from the gents was a short fellow with a mop of dark hair, and flares so wide they seemed to hide the little boy trailing behind him, who must have been only four or five.

Roger whispered, 'Normally we don't allow kids at the club; for little Sam we've made an exception. Poor boy lost his mother last year.'

Ben's heart tugged. He knew what it was like to grow up without a mother, to know that, as the years passed, something vital was missing, never a day going by when you didn't wonder what might have been.

'Ah,' Lawrence said, 'our Tasmanian guest. And a fellow fan of Daniel McGillycuddy!'

'Well, I've only just discovered his work' – Ben waved his hand at the book – 'but I *do* know the "The Far-Flung Distant Shore".' He shook the proffered hand, then knelt down. 'Hello, Sam.'

'Hello.'

The boy had large, sad eyes, and Ben reached into his satchel for one of the small koala toys he'd brought along as gifts. 'Something from down under,' he said, in his strongest Aussie accent.

'There you go, Sam. What do you say to that?' Lawrence nodded at his son.

'Thank you.'

'Good boy. Now, take that seat by the fire there, then we'll be off in a minute. It's already past your bedtime.'

Sam smiled at Ben – the expression lit up his face, so that some of the sadness disappeared – then went to sit beside the two men arguing about *The Odyssey*, proceeding to watch them with interest.

'Now,' said Lawrence, waving away the offer of a final drink for the night, 'tell me. "The Far-Flung Distant Shore". You've heard it before? It has a lovely cadence, doesn't it?'

Ben shook his head. 'I'm sorry, what I meant was: I don't know the ballad, but I've heard the *story*.'

'Whatever do you mean?'

'Daniel's uncle told it to me a couple of months ago, about the bet, about the girl up the tree. About the dead snake.' Ben went on to describe the details, opening *The Ballads of Daniel McGillycuddy* to the correct page and, in his excitement (and perhaps buoyed by his second martini), took a pencil from his pocket and underlined *Towerhurst,* and the part about Grace's necklace in an effort to get across his point. 'Getting an insight into Daniel's life like this . . . well, it's . . . fascinating.' But it was *more* than fascinating. Daniel had written a poem about the first time he'd met Grace Grey. She still meant so very much to him, after all those years.

'And what was he *like*?' Here was a man who'd met Daniel McGillycuddy a decade before.

'I never met him, actually.' Lawrence explained that the publication had been done from start to finish by written correspondence.

'Really?' Ben reluctantly recalled his editor, and the face-to-face lecture she'd given him after his last draft. 'Isn't that unusual?'

'Not really. Writers are often shy creatures, after all. Anyway,' continued Lawrence, 'Daniel approached *us*. He merely wanted to bind his poems into a book, a keepsake for the family. Later, when we offered to publish them he agreed, with one condition.'

'Which was?'

'I remove a single poem titled . . . now what was it . . .' Lawrence scratched his chin.

'Perhaps I could see it?'

A frown. 'Oh, I don't think that would be appropriate, to give out something like that.'

'Come now!' said Roger, clapping Lawrence on the back. 'Don't tell me you wouldn't fancy a position on the committee?'

Later, in Roger's sitting room, Ben gave a laugh. 'You sly dog!' Lawrence had not only promised to locate Daniel's ballad – 'for academic reasons only, is it?' – but had also provided an Irish address by which the writer himself could be contacted. Ben had felt a little bad about it, though Roger said that Stern Publishing was languishing as poetry slipped out of favour – 'particularly anything that rhymes' – and Lawrence could do with all the help he could get. A committee position at the Iliad Club would certainly be a boon. 'His wife, Alice, had really been the driving force,' Roger had added sadly.

Ben promised himself he'd make it up to Lawrence Littleton one day, but for now he wasn't sure how.

'Still,' he said, 'in the ballad . . .'

'Yes?' Roger had yawned. It was 3 a.m. for him, but midday for his guest.

'Daniel's watching a boat steam down Kenmare Bay, so he was already back in Ireland when he wrote it. He's older: *It's her memory that haunts me / Of a girl that time forgot decades long before*. This poem is about Grace and, despite marrying Rose, he went on to publish the lament publicly. And Rose didn't mind?'

'Rose and Grace never got along, you say? Perhaps they were reconciled after the war?'

'I don't know . . .'

'Or she married Daniel to . . . assuage a guilt?'

Ben hesitated.

'My dear Ben, I know you're holding back. I'm not quite as indiscreet as I appear.'

'It's not that . . . it's more that I have some things I need to find out, and discuss with Willow. Then I can tell you what I know.'

Roger nodded. 'You'll get no pressure from me.'

The fire crackled. It felt good to talk to someone, at least in part, about the mystery. Grappling for a safe angle, he said, 'Surely Daniel wouldn't have married someone else if he suspected Grace was still alive?' Of course, he had no idea if that was true. The letters he'd read from the lovelorn Daniel were written in 1941, and Grace had lived at Towerhurst until 1945, when she seemed to have vanished off the face of the planet. He turned to Roger. 'In your letter,' he said, 'you wrote that you'd collected some bits and pieces on the Foxtons . . .'

'Oh! Yes. Yes.' Roger went to the sideboard and removed a copy of *The Times* from the top drawer, then handed it over to Ben. It was dated 20th February.

'*A Snippet of Yet Another British Fascist?*' said Ben, before glancing at the by-line. 'Edeline Grey was a Nazi?'

'A fascist. Yes.'

He skim-read the article, pausing on the final line. '*As with so many of Britain's fascists, her current whereabouts remain unknown.* So if Grace did return to England then . . .'

'She may have disappeared with her mother,' said Roger.

Ben's heart sank. That Grace might have any fascist tendencies didn't tally at all with the image he'd painted of her in his mind. 'I'll get in contact with this Milton Twiggs?' he said. 'I'm sure he'll have leads.'

Roger flushed. 'On that . . . there's something I should tell you . . .'

'What?'

A hesitation.

'Oh no!' said Ben, realisation dawning. '*This* is your worst pseudonym yet!'

'Thought I'd squeeze an article out of looking into the Foxtons. Living like this doesn't come cheap, you know,' Roger said, with no little mirth.

Ben glanced around the shabby apartment. 'I thought your father owned half of Devon?'

'Slight exaggeration. But yes. The thing is . . . I've decided to make my own way.'

Ben appraised Roger anew. 'Now to throw off the pseudonyms.'

'Ha!'

'I think you should. And on that topic' – he disappeared into his room, returning with a small cardboard box – 'I brought you something.'

'Oh yes?' Roger removed the lid, then laughed. 'What's this?'

'Business cards.' Ben held one up.

Roger Masters
22 Battledean Road
North London
For all your biography needs

'With your very own name. No more pseudonyms. You can be proud of what you do. Be *brave*.'

A hooting laugh ensued. 'You're not the most subtle chap.'

'But I'm right.'

'Yes, you probably are.' Roger nodded, and Ben fancied he turned a little away, overcome by emotion. 'Thank you.'

'Can I keep the article?'

'Of course, I wrote it for you, after all. I have something else too . . .' He opened his diary, then flipped over one of his new business cards and wrote on the back. 'A friend called to give me this number today . . . it was unlisted, you see? And he's down in Hampshire so he chased it up.'

'Who's it for?'

'Someone,' said Roger, 'you – and probably Willow – might one day like to meet . . .'

ᏋᎧ

And now Ben held Molly Munro's number in his hand as he stared up at 45 Grosvenor Square.

'Seen a ghost?' said a woman of about fifty who had appeared like an apparition at his side. Oddly, she wore a fashionable ski-suit.

'Erm . . . no?'

A hesitation. 'Well, if you don't mind me prying, you've

been standing here an age. I saw you from my sitting-room window.' She gestured over her shoulder to the opposite side of the square.

'Just thinking about the past,' he said.

'Ah yes. The past,' said the woman, 'I know it well.'

Her easy manner made him smile, and he tried to think of an excuse. 'I'm interested in . . . real estate.' Where that came from, he didn't know. Ridiculous. And in London! He wondered vaguely if the value of Towerhurst would purchase even the doorway of a bedsit in Mayfair. Ash and Ivy, however, he mused . . .

'Are you?' she said, clearly surprised. 'Well, the fellow below me has been muttering about selling for the last year. Nice man. I'd say you'd get it for a steal. It's a bit shabby, truth be told. But aren't we all?' She laughed.

'Well, I . . .'

'Have you a pen?'

'I suppose . . .'

She reached for Roger's card. 'This'll do.' Quickly, she scrawled a number on the front. 'I'm always calling, checking if he's okay. Give him a buzz, find the lie of the land.'

'Well . . . thank you.'

'Very well, then.' She glanced at her watch. 'Golly. I'm late for tai chi.'

Five minutes later, Ben stepped into a phone box. First, he called his sisters-in-law in Sydney and left them the number for a shabby apartment they might get for a steal in Grosvenor Square. Then, inspired by the energy of the ski-suit-clad woman he'd met, he dialled the number Roger had scrawled on one of his new business cards in the early hours of the morning.

Chapter 60

Towerhurst, Tasmania
August 1945

The day after America dropped the bomb on Hiroshima, a letter from Edeline arrived. Grace saw her mother's handwriting and, despite herself, looked closer in anticipation. But it was, as ever, for Rose. She shuffled it to the top of the stack anyway; Edeline had always been visible, always above everyone else.

Grace was more preoccupied with the news from Japan. It was sparse, the headlines all of a similar vein – *Atomic Bomb Opens New Epoch in Warfare*; *Big Jap Town May Have Perished*; *Atomic Bomb May End War* – and the world waited to know if the city, and its population, still existed. What was almost certain, though, was that the war would finally be over in a matter of days. And then . . . well, Grace had seen the communication sent to Ned and Colette more than a year ago, and had grasped onto it as proof of Daniel's continued survival. That simple postcard, headed IMPERIAL JAPANESE ARMY, written in August 1944, had brought hope.

I am in *THAILAND*.
My health is excellent.
~~I am ill in hospital.~~

I am working for pay.

~~I am not working.~~

My love to you *DANIEL*

Later, Rose brought Edeline's letter to the sitting room and stood by the crackling fire.

'*I've had word that the first of the evacuated children are already returning to our shores, and I'd like you to join them,*' she read, then looked up to gauge Grace's reaction. When none was forthcoming, she tipped up the envelope, and out spilled a ticket.

Rose was leaving. A wave of relief washed over Grace, and although she was far too old for a chaperone, she realised just how much she still tiptoed around the woman whom Edeline had sent to watch her.

'Looks like we're going back to England,' Rose said, shaking the envelope to dislodge what remained inside. A second ticket tumbled out.

ð

The day after Edeline's letter arrived, Rose gave notice to Claud Greensmith; she would leave her job at the mine immediately. Things had become lemon-sour between them in the last few months, and the timing worked in her favour. The mine was undergoing an audit, and accusations had been made about missing documents, many of the latter only accessible by Claud and, by extension, Rose. Claud hadn't been pleased. He would be left to face the questions alone, and the pathetic man had been so useless at his job – distracted, as he was, by other, more *feminine* interests – that she knew he had none of the answers required. When she asked for her final pay, he withheld it, until she reminded him that she was privy to his darkest secret.

Yesterday, Grace had knocked on her bedroom door. 'When are you leaving?'

The girl – though she was twenty-one already – had refused to contemplate using her own ticket. She was determined to wait for Daniel; it was the ultimate blind hope, and it frustrated Rose more than ever.

'In two days.'

'Two days?' She'd glanced at Rose's suitcase, packed and stored under her bed. 'I thought it was next week?'

'I'm planning to surprise some old friends in Hobart.' In reality, Rose had arranged a room where she would count down the last of her days in Tasmania. She wanted nothing more than to get away from Towerhurst, from Grace's hope and Olive's suffocating adulation. She needed to think. About what she'd do from here. About her own past. About her feelings for Edeline, and how they'd changed in the last years, and a growing concern that she'd been on the wrong side all along.

She recalled sailing away from England, looking back as her shores disappeared, wondering how it would be on her return. Oswald Mosley had argued that appeasement was best, that Hitler's policies would secure England's future. But in the years to follow each new event in the war had planted a little seed of doubt in Rose's mind. Had it begun all the way back when bombs rained on London? She could barely imagine it, those streets she'd once trodden razed to the ground. Or was it when – only months ago – the concentration camps had been discovered? At first she'd dismissed the heinous reports as propaganda, but as images emerged, she could no longer deny what Hitler had done.

She'd written to her mentor seeking clarity, but Edeline's replies had become vague during the last months. In this letter, however, the one Rose held in her hand, she was clear. *It is time for you to be released from both tasks set for you. As I once said: some things in life need to be destroyed before they destroy you.* At the memory – that day Edeline had promised to take her to

Germany – Rose felt such a quickening of her heart, she put a shaking hand to her chest. Edeline had vowed that she would always be there to help, but now she wasn't.

The guesthouse she'd booked was the same one she'd stayed in during her six months in Hobart in 1942. Was that really only three years ago? It felt like a lifetime. Back then, she'd endeared herself to her boss, walking a narrow, and dangerous, line between secretary and confidante. Claud had trusted her with everything. He was a man who rarely acted without an ulterior motive, and the trip had been the perfect excuse to leave Queenstown for a few months, with not only his private secretary in tow, but also the woman who had formerly held the role. Mabel Martin was his lover, and she was already beginning to show when Rose had been persuaded to assist. She cursed the day she'd agreed to take the newborn for a stroll, compelled to do so by her boss, who wanted time alone with his exhausted mistress after the birth of their baby. It was then she'd run into Richard Holmes, whose hungry eyes had taken in the pram. It was impossible to miss his raised eyebrows, and the gleam in his eyes as she'd hastily explained that the baby belonged to a friend, someone he wouldn't know, and he'd quickly hurried off as though eager to spread his own story without delay.

'What about you, Grace?' Olive had asked the previous evening. 'Are you sure you won't go too?' Now that she'd got over the shock of Rose's announcement, it was clear Olive would try to turn the loss to her advantage.

'I'll wait for Daniel. We'll return together.'

Olive had given a nasty smile. 'It'll please Edeline no end when you arrive home with an Irishman.'

'I'm delighted, at least,' Grace had said, 'to know you agree that he's going to return.'

Now, Rose stopped at the tower door and listened. Grace

would be up there, writing, thinking, dreaming, with no concept of how hard life really was. She felt the old envy rise in her chest, then pushed it away. She was no longer obligated to Grace in any way; no longer needed to chase Edeline's affection. It was time to take care of her own future, which would surely be brighter than now.

Slipping on Marcus's waxed coat, she stepped out into the rain.

Chapter 61

Molly's cottage, Hampshire, in the shadow of Foxton Hall

27th February 1975

The Molly Munro who opened the door was not the woman Ben had imagined when he'd heard her voice on the phone. In his mind, he'd painted her image from a photo Roger had dug up from his notes on Edeline Grey. In it, she had been every inch the housekeeper: portly and rosy-cheeked, perfectly overshadowed by the two women who'd flanked her: Edeline and Rose. Kingston Grey – who would die on the first day of the Blitz three years later – had been absent from the informal portrait, but his daughter was there; Grace had been a sickly-looking girl before she'd left for Tasmania, before she'd evidently shed her skin.

'Cuppa?'

Ben followed Molly's slim frame down the hallway, and took a seat at a kitchen table covered in a pile of parsnips.

'Had our first hard frosts this week, so it was time to pull them. Sweeter that way, you know?' Something bubbled on the range, and Ben removed the tweed he'd borrowed from Roger, hanging it over the back of the chair. Molly had clearly expected him to be on time, because the tea was ready to pour.

'So, Mr Andrews—'

'Ben, please.'

She indicated the pile of vegetables and picked up a small sharp knife. 'I hope you don't mind. I hate for my hands to be without work.'

'No, not at all.'

'A hangover from my years in service. Being a kitchen hand feels like a lifetime ago.' She stripped the peel from a parsnip with alarming dexterity, then topped and tailed it with two quick chops.

'A kitchen hand?' he said. 'I thought you were the Greys' housekeeper?'

'I was. After.'

'After what?'

'After Edeline and I left the big house.' She indicated over her shoulder at the towering shell of Foxton Hall visible through the window. It had been destroyed in a fire twenty years before, a sorry end to the Foxtons, of whom, it seemed, none remained. 'When Edeline married Kingston Grey, I left with her for Grosvenor Square as housekeeper. I was only eighteen, can you imagine? Bit of a step up in the world, so my mother said. And my mother was always right . . . according to her.' Molly smiled. 'But you didn't come here to talk about me. Tell me again what you said on the phone? You're looking into the Foxton history, and that of Towerhurst – which you now own?'

He nodded.

'You've uncovered some secrets, no doubt?'

Ben shifted in his seat. 'I don't suppose the fascism was much of a *secret,* was it?'

'The fascism?' Molly paused. 'No, not at all. Edeline wasn't as notorious as Mosley and Mitford, but then, who was?'

'I have some questions about the Foxtons, about Edeline,

about Marcus . . . and also others.' He hesitated. 'I thought you might be able to help, and Rose too. I'd like to talk to her if possible . . .'

A frown. 'You want to talk *to* Rose? I thought you said on the phone you wanted to talk *about* her?'

'Well . . . if you don't mind? And Grace too.'

'Oh. Didn't you say you were interested in information about *Edeline's former disgrace*?'

A clock chimed. Ben had nowhere to be, and yet it made him feel like time was running out. 'No, I wanted to ask about *Edeline's daughter, Grace* . . .'

'Oh. I thought you *knew*.'

'Knew what?'

'Well, the identity of Rose's mother, not to put too fine a point on it.'

A dawning realisation crept up Ben's spine. 'You're telling me Rose Munro *wasn't* your daughter?' But somehow, he had already begun to know it.

Chapter 62

Towerhurst, Tasmania

August 1945

Grace looked down from the tower as rain fell on her baby's grave – the small Atlantisite stone that Uncle Marcus had arranged – and brushed away a tear. How had three years passed since that night when the part of Daniel she'd come to believe would always be with her had died? It felt like yesterday, and yet it was not, though her grief had barely waned. It had been a year since there'd been word of Daniel, but the war in Europe was over, and the Japanese were sure to surrender any day. So Uncle Marcus said, and he was so often right.

There he was now – Grace saw as she leaned a little forward – pausing beneath the moon gate. He glanced over his shoulder so that the hood of his waxed jacket slipped back to reveal a head of platinum hair.

It wasn't Uncle Marcus after all, it was Rose, carrying nothing but a furtive expression and an aura of not wanting to be seen, as she slipped into the forest and disappeared.

Grace knew that Rose disliked the wilderness; she missed, always, the comforts of life in London. She was up to something. She was *always* up to something. It used to drive Molly mad. Poor Molly. Grace thought of her now, how the housekeeper had always been so kind, and yet Rose had treated her mother with ill-disguised contempt. Why hadn't Grace done something? Said something? She should have taken it upon herself to be better. To stick up for Molly when Rose had trodden her down. As Rose disappeared she decided, in that moment, she could no longer stand in the tower, simply looking on.

ε❧

At the edge of the clearing, Grace stopped short as though she'd hit a wall. She froze, unsure of what to do. There was Rose, only twenty yards ahead, kneeling before a towering eucalyptus, its roots a splayed hand, and from between those fingers she withdrew a large suitcase, quickly carrying it to the centre of the clearing. Before her, Grace realised, was the yawning mouth of an old mine shaft; such holes pockmarked the hills behind Towerhurst, a man-made hazard to add to those nature provided.

Rose opened the case, and the surrounding forest held its breath. Even the currawong who flapped on a nearby branch stopped his movement, distracted perhaps by the shiny silver clasps. Quickly, she rifled through the contents, her arms pulled by an invisible string. Why *hide* the travelling case? There was no need for her to sneak away. Unless she had done something terrible? Something she didn't want others to know.

She struck a match, sending sulphur into the breeze.

This was not, Grace realised with sudden clarity, a suitcase packed for travelling. A compulsion to know more propelled her forward, but before she could speak, a twig snapped beneath her weight, and Rose looked up, her fearful expression vanishing as she took in the identity of the intruder.

'Oh, it's you.' She stood, knocking the suitcase so that a sheaf of papers spilled onto the ground. Tables, graphs, reports, a blueprint, headed *Pyritic Copper Smelter*. Urgently, she kneeled, gathering the documents together.

Grace reached down. 'What is all this . . .'

'It is,' Rose said, snatching a document back, 'absolutely *none* of your business.' She leaned forward, her knee pressing a thick piece of card into soft ground.

'These papers are from the mine . . .'

'I worked there, remember? Although I'm sure *real work* is a foreign concept to you.' Rose appeared to try and gather herself then, and when she spoke again, her tone was full of a forced cordiality. 'I was looking after these for Claud, that's all.'

Mr Greensmith? They hadn't parted on good terms, Grace had heard. She frowned, the weight of realisation heavy. Mother's secret letters. Rose's insistence on seeing the mine. The way she'd worked her way up into the top secretarial job. Her diminishing pluck as the war had rolled to its end.

Cautiously, she said: 'Who put you up to this?' She meant: *The Party? Or Edeline?* 'Rose, I know that my mother didn't spend the war at Foxton Hall.'

At the end of 1943, Oswald Mosley had been released from Holloway, and a trickle of fascists had followed. In a small note at the back of *The Examiner* Grace had read that her mother had been one of them, though no one had ever confronted her on the matter. She supposed, in Tasmania, she was known as a Foxton, not a Grey.

Rose paused, taking deep breaths through her nose, her jaw clenched. Carefully, Grace reached forward and picked up an aerial photograph of the mine.

'Did you think the Germans would want . . . *Mount Lyell*?' She almost laughed. It was preposterous.

Still, Rose didn't speak.

'*Why?*'

Above them, the currawong took off in a clatter of wings, the sudden noise seeming to shake Rose from her stupor. 'It's Australia's largest copper producer, but you wouldn't know that,' she said with bitterness, 'lost in your pathetic world of nursery rhymes, and dead Irishmen.'

Grace only shuddered, but Rose carried on. 'Tasmania has munitions factories, food production. We even make blankets.' She said *we* as though she'd worked on the looms herself. 'Edeline told me . . . she said it was everything the Axis needed. She said that *I* could make a difference. That the Nazis were only trying to bring order—'

'Order?' Grace shivered. 'Have you even *read* the news?'

A deep breath, then the case clicked shut with the sound of a misfired gun. 'It wasn't supposed to be like this. England is fading, democracy has outlived its usefulness . . . the individual *isn't* the most important cog in the system.'

They were Mother's words, and Grace had heard them before: endless guests at Grosvenor Square debating Britain's imagined future, shiny and bright under Oswald Mosley's Blackshirts. Edeline had mixed Rose with water, and moulded her like clay.

A new feeling swept over Grace. It was pity. Pity for Rose. Her mother had tried to destroy them both, if in different ways.

'Edeline put you up to this.' As though approaching a wild creature, she tentatively reached out a hand, trying to make peace. 'If no one else knows about this . . .?'

Rose flinched at the touch. 'You're such a disappointment to her.'

This was familiar territory that Grace no longer needed to navigate.

Rose lifted a chain from around her neck, letting it pool in her hand. Then she traced her fingers slowly over the fox pendant. The first drops of rain dripped from its platinum surface like tears. 'You never deserved one of these.'

Grace put a hand to her own chest, feeling the fox near her heart. She still wore it because, although it reminded her somewhat of her mother, it had brought her luck. Through these last years, it had been ever present around her neck. There had been terrible, terrible grief, but there had, too, been love.

There was still love.

Daniel was out there somewhere.

Rose stood, leaving a single piece of card pressed into the ground where she'd knelt.

'What's this?'

A gasp. 'Don't!'

Grace's heart skipped a beat.

> I am in *NAGASAKI CAMP FUKUOKA 14*.
> My health is excellent.
> ~~I am ill in hospital.~~
> I am working for pay.
> ~~I am not working.~~
> My love to you *DANIEL*

'But this is from . . .' Cool fingers of understanding crept up her neck. 'This was sent . . . in *July*? A month ago! *Where* did you get this? Why didn't you—'

Rose snatched the paper, ripping the card in two. 'It's not for you!'

Grace turned over her sliver of sodden paper. Her name had been torn apart.

.. ace Grey.

Rose's knuckles were white, so firmly did she grip the suit-case. Inside it, Grace imagined a hundred letters from Daniel. Proof that he was alive. *Proof* of what she'd known in her heart. Proof that he still loved her, still *thought* of her, and that one day they could be together. The suitcase held the one thing that could win a war when all other weapons failed.

Hope.

'Let him go, Grace. Let him return to Ireland where he belongs. He's not in love with you. He regrets everything. He told me that before he left for Timor.' The words tumbled over themselves, untruths on the move. 'I'm protecting both of you, really.'

Grace's heart thumped. She searched Rose's face, but it was empty of everything save the shiny glow of triumph. But in a way she felt sadness for her. Such bitterness, such anger. 'I'm sorry if you love him, Rose.'

Rose readjusted the suitcase. 'I don't care about that. Or him.' She started towards the ravenous mouth of the mine, and Grace seized her wrist.

'Then *why* would you do this?'

They stood, faces only inches apart.

A hundred emotions traced their way across Rose's expression, and for a moment Grace recognised something like remorse, but almost as soon as it arrived, it vanished, replaced by a look of envy so profound that it took her breath away. 'Because, Grace, you are . . . *very, very* difficult to love.'

Finally, there it was: Rose had become her mother. She'd even stolen the words straight from her mouth, but whereas Edeline had spoken them, on that morning of Grace's thirteenth birthday, without coldness, Rose spat them with bile. It could only mean one thing: she knew they were no longer true.

But before Grace could respond, she was pushed backwards so that she stumbled, falling to her knees only inches from the rock-teeth that edged the waiting mouth of the mine. She reached forward, grabbing for the suitcase.

Quick as lightning, Rose was on her. They wrestled, and Daniel's face flashed before Grace's eyes. If there were more letters, she would have them.

Rose climbed on top of her, pinning her to the ground. 'I tried my best, but you . . . you had to *ruin* everything! Always there, always in the way, always getting what you want. You're so *privileged*, you appreciate *nothing*. Nothing at all. How hard I had to work, always being the housekeeper's daughter, always less . . .' She went on, but Grace couldn't hear; she grappled for breath, for reason, as one of Rose's arms pushed down on her throat, the other reaching for the suitcase.

Grace's eyes bulged as though she'd once again waded out to sea and plunged beneath the waves, unable to surface. She tried to cry out, tried to scream, but the life was being choked from her, and the woman astride her seemed oblivious to it.

Grace felt the sky's cool tears on her face as a tunnel clouded her vision, the circle of light at its centre narrowing to a pinprick. At the end of it, she imagined Daniel was watching, waiting. He smiled, reaching out. Resignation washed over her. She would see Daniel soon, and everything would be as it should be.

But it wouldn't be that way. Because Daniel was *alive*.

Alive!

With a surge of anger, she lifted her hips and shrugged Rose off her as if she were a feather pillow. They rolled one over another, the suitcase a wall between them, and then they fell, scrambling, grappling, crying, into the void.

Chapter 63

Hampshire, England

December 2004

'How did you know she was here?' asked Libby sadly, kneeling down to run her hand over the gravestone.

'Roger rang me,' Sam admitted, his breath fogging in the cold. 'He told me about Molly Munro, and your father's visit, and it got me wondering if she might still be alive. I thought you might be able to meet her. An hour ago, we were pretty certain she was your grandmother.'

She glanced at Sam, then past him to where the jagged edifice of Foxton Hall stood, a solemn sentry casting a watchful eye over the graveyard. Dusk approached, and the clear sky had already begun to burn, bright orange lighting up the shell of the manor as though the fire from all those years ago still raged. Sam told her it had burned to the ground in the fifties after it had been left to the state.

'I'm so sorry . . .' He trailed off, passing Libby a small flower-pot he'd brought from the car. She'd noticed it on her drive, when Ben had stopped on the motorway to fill the car, and at the time had felt a jolt of something – worry? Apprehension? Excitement? – that the flowering heather was for her.

She took the plant carefully and ran a finger over the little purple bells, releasing a delicate, earthy scent.

'Something hardy. To last the winter.'

'It's lovely,' she said, her mind turning to the pressed heather in the rusty Arnott's tin, wondering how many winters the little white flowers had been there before she'd found it.

She looked down at the grave.

Molly Munro
1900–1996

Given what Miss Winman had told her about the contents of Olive's interview, Molly might not be her grandmother after all, but she was one of the last people her father had ever talked to, and she had evidently told him something so profound that he'd booked a flight to Ireland that very afternoon.

'At the time of her death, Molly lived in Foxton Cottage,' Sam said, pointing to a quaint stone house bordering the graveyard and surrounded on three sides by new builds. 'She inherited it from her mother, Joan.' She was impressed at the details of his research. 'Molly's mother, it seemed, had lived in the cottage her whole life – there was an addendum on the deeds to facilitate this, then the Foxtons gifted her the place.'

'They *gave* it to her?'

'Apparently no money changed hands. But you can never be sure of course.'

Molly's tale was just another story simply lost to time. Libby looked down at the overgrown grave. Weeds had sprung from between the cracks and a light sprinkling of moss crept its way up the headstone, and her heart ached that Rose was too far away to tend it.

She pulled the moss away, only to discover something etched beneath.

'What is it?' Sam was beside her.

Libby pulled her collar a little tighter, running her other hand over the epitaph.

A shining star. For ever in our hearts.

'It's . . . it's nothing,' she said, blood thumping in her chest. Though it wasn't nothing, of course. It was everything. Those words were etched on her mind and if she closed her eyes she saw them now. In another place, on another grave. A grave she hadn't visited in nearly five years, because to do so meant that she was lost for weeks and months afterwards. Lost to her mourning, and mourning a lost future.

'These words . . .' she said, wiping her nose with her sleeve. It was running in the cold.

The graveyard in Hobart overlooked the Derwent River, the same river she and Krish had watched a boat sail along as they sat on campus discussing his family and her relationship with her mother. His own family's sprawling house sat on the shores of that river. He was born on its shores, and now he was there for eternity.

Something rested on Libby's hand, but at that moment, wracked with guilt and grief . . . Libby didn't want to be touched. She flinched, moving her hand away, but when she looked down she saw that Sam had merely pressed a tissue into her palm with that same gentleness he'd placed Roger's details there two weeks before. Without making eye contact, she nodded gratefully.

'This epitaph,' she began, 'it's written on so many graves.'

He paused, and in that pause she sensed an understanding, the feeling that he wasn't just observing her, but seeing right into her heart.

'I wanted,' she continued, not knowing where the words came from, 'his grave to be covered with *stories* instead. I wanted it to . . . to explain that this wasn't just another tragic young death: it was *his* tragic young death. I wanted everyone to understand how full of life he had been.' She really had wanted all that, but of course she'd never said as much. Not to his grieving parents, to his siblings, who had lost a little brother they'd known their whole lives.

She looked up to see Sam's expression full of an understanding he surely couldn't have had. Libby hadn't told him the first thing about Krish, not even his name.

'His name,' she said, 'was Krish. He was my first and only love.'

'I'm sorry, Libby.'

She reached down, pulling a weed from the grave. Then another. Then another. It was therapeutic, in a way, and with each pull, each loosening of something that shouldn't have been there, each removal, she felt her mind clear a little as though her emotions, too, were finding their own space.

'I lost him,' she said. It always felt silly putting it that way. *Lost him.* As if she'd merely misplaced him, which couldn't be further from the truth. He had been with her, nestled in her memory where no one could take him away. 'It was nearly six years ago.'

Slowly, carefully, Sam came to kneel beside her. He, too, began to pull the weeds from Molly's grave. When he didn't ask what happened, and perhaps *because* he didn't, Libby continued to speak, unsure from where the words came, but overwhelmed by a feeling of a relief that they did.

'An accidental death; that's what the coroner called it,' she began. 'He was at a party at the house of someone on our course. They had a pool, and everyone was swimming and' – her voice caught – 'and drinking. They started to challenge each other. How far could they swim underwater. One lap, two laps, three . . .'

She trailed off, then glanced up.

'Krish wasn't at heart a competitive person. But, you see . . . we'd had a fight.'

Sam continued to weed as though knowing that to push her into talking was to push her away.

'It was' — she half laughed, a painful sound that came out as an exhalation — 'about study. Stupid, really. He said I put too much into it. Too much time. Too much stress. The truth was I didn't *want* to go to the party because I'm not much of a party person. I was sat at my desk, studying, and he said that life was about more than that. He said I was too driven. And I told him . . . I told him *he* wasn't driven enough. That a little bit of competition might do him good.'

I need to work harder..

You hate med anyway, Libby. Study literature, like you always wanted. Do what you love.

Then he was gone.

'I guess no one was paying attention. At the party. They were drunk, having a great time. The night wore on. And at some point someone went back out to the pool, and Krish was there.'

'Oh, Libby.'

'I have always wondered . . . if I hadn't said that . . .'

'No.'

'Or if we hadn't fought . . .'

'Libby—'

'Would he still be alive?'

The sun had set now, and as the orange fire behind Foxton Hall went out, the first stars began to twinkle. Around them, Christmas lights appeared, one by one: icicles dripping from roofs, bright flashes on trees, gentle warm candles flickering in windows.

Finally, Sam stopped weeding. He spoke.

'I had an interesting conversation with Roger, you know.' Libby looked up at him in surprise. She'd been lost in the past and she'd expected him to be there with her, expected him — if he was to say anything to her – to soothe her. To say *no, no, it's not your fault.*

He continued. 'The evening after you visited him, he called ostensibly to ask after Lawrence: *has the old boy found his land legs?* – that kind of thing.' Sam smiled, eliciting a small upturning of Libby's own lips. Not much, but enough to show she was listening, that she could picture Roger, in his red trousers, the phone pressed between ear and tweed. 'But I believe what he really wanted was to talk about you.'

'Me?' Still, Libby grappled to come back to the present.

'He was worried he'd told you too much. That you would blame him for your father's death.'

She frowned. 'Why would I blame Roger for Dad's death?'

'*He* invited Ben to London.'

'But that's crazy!'

Had she given him the impression she blamed him? She scrambled to recall the details of the conversation, but all she could think of was his generous smile, and the way he'd talked of her father's love for her mother. The way she'd left their afternoon tea both heavier with food and good company, and lighter in her heart. Libby felt unable to bear it. That poor man. It was one of life's horrors to carry guilt of such a magnitude.

She got to her feet and wiped her hands on her trousers. 'I should call him. Or call *on* him? Can you drop me in Notting Hill when we get back? This is nonsense. Roger wasn't to blame.' The words came quickly, and she realised that the thought of such a lovely man being burdened by the heavy, heartbreaking feelings she herself carried was something she couldn't allow. Not when a few simple words might allay his guilt.

Sam pulled the last weed from Molly's grave and stood too. 'I agree. Roger was not to blame. And nor are you.' He said this last with such finality that Libby realised what he was trying to say.

She shivered.

'You're cold,' he said, removing his fleece to wrap it around her shoulders, despite her muffled protests. She *was* cold, inside and out, and exhaustion rolled over her. Today had drained her; she felt squeezed, like a sponge. She'd written to Rose, she'd called Sam, she'd heard of his grief, and she'd told him of hers. And all the while, he'd listened, seeming to understand, and she felt a sense that something inside her was rebuilding, a structure that would not cover the old, but would add to it, so that her history would be incorporated into the walls of something new. Though she wasn't sure what, she had some idea, finally, of what it was she wanted and, as the realisation hit her, she let out a muffled breath, her shoulders dropping as she slowed her breathing. *In and out. In and out.*

'Thank you,' she whispered.

'I'm sorry you'll never know what they discussed. Molly and your father.'

Libby nodded, then leaned her head on Sam's shoulder and stood there for a long time as the lights of Molly's old cottage came on, one by one, and the silhouette of Foxton Hall faded into darkness as the night stole it away.

Chapter 64

In the shadow of Foxton House, Hampshire

27th February 1975

'So, you're telling me that, in exchange for you adopting Rose as your daughter, the Foxton family gifted your mother this cottage?'

A sigh. 'I had very little choice in the matter, Ben.'

'But—'

'Things were different then. My mother had worked at Foxton Hall, in one form or another, her entire adult life. Very loyal to that family, she was — far more so than to her own — and in 1914, despite my protests that I wanted to stay on at school, I was marched up to the house and given the role of kitchen hand.'

'How old were you?'

'Fourteen. The same age as Edeline. We never became what you might call friends, but she grew to trust me after I later became her maid. War had just broken out and most of the estate's staff left during the following months, as did Edeline's brothers, the youngest of which—'

'Marcus?'

'Yes, Marcus . . . well, she was very close to him. He joined his uncle Cornelius's regiment, a Tasmanian battalion, lied about his age and all, as so many did. He was a chatty, charismatic seventeen-year-old when he went to war in 1915, and he returned a quiet old man just three years later. I don't believe Edeline ever got over that; she couldn't understand it. For her the war had meant freedom; without any staff or siblings to keep her in check, she ran a little wild.'

Understanding the implication, Ben said, 'Edeline had the freedom to take a lover? Who was he? Who was Rose's father?'

'I don't know,' said Molly.

Yet another unknown to add to a long list.

'And the truth is, Edeline herself didn't know. She had dalliances with several men at the nearby garrison. I know it all sounds very . . . loose . . . but I think she was lonely. Her parents had left for London and it was just her in the house. In 1917 she received word that her eldest brother had died. And when Marcus came home on leave, she hated how he'd changed. She was deeply unhappy, and at the time I felt sorry for her. I covered for her, made excuses. Lied. She was able to slip away, to do things perhaps she wouldn't have done had circumstances been different, had war never come. And in 1919, she discovered she was pregnant.'

'What happened?'

'She told her mother, who said the baby must be given away. Edeline rallied against this.' Molly paused. 'I've thought about that in the decades since. *Why* was she so intent on keeping the baby? The father, whoever he was, clearly meant nothing to her, and she was only nineteen. Over the years, all I've come up with is that she believed it would fill the hole in her heart left by Marcus's leaving for Tasmania. His uncle Cornelius had told him stories of that remote house in the forest, the one that you now own. I think it appealed to Marcus, the chance to start again, after everything he'd seen, and he followed him there.'

'Surely,' said Ben, thinking of how complicated it would be to explain away Molly turning up with a baby, 'Edeline's parents would have *forced* her to give up the child?'

Molly nodded. 'She was headstrong, I'll give her that. She came up with the plan, and my part in it. What choice did I have but to go along with it? *I* became Rose's mother, and Edeline's disgrace became my own. I agreed to do it because my mother said I must. The cottage was quite an incentive. I was weaker then' – Molly topped and tailed the final parsnip – 'but lies like that wear you down. You have to push back eventually, or you'll disappear altogether.'

Ben thought of Grace, and tried not to make a connection, but he couldn't help himself. Had Grace discovered something – uncovered a lie? – for her to end up down that mine?

'Take Grace, for example,' Molly continued. 'Edeline never loved that poor girl, not *just* because she didn't love her husband, Kingston, but because she resented, I think, that her second-born daughter was entitled to everything she had to deny Rose. A strange kind of thinking, but loss and war and grief does that to people. It can make them bitter in ways we can't understand. Edeline made Rose her political protégé. It was the perfect cover really, though I was sorry I wasn't strong enough then to stop it. I continued the deception until Edeline disappeared. After that, I admit that I thought very little about it. The truth was Rose never loved me; it was as though she somehow knew that she and Edeline were tied by an invisible string.'

'And Rose didn't discover that Edeline was her mother?'

'No, never,' Molly said. 'What I can say, though, was that Edeline enjoyed having Rose to mould. She certainly encouraged the girl's dislike of Grace, a feeling that matched her own. That poor girl. Just a child; the product of a marriage grudgingly undertaken because Kingston was the only suitable candidate in London society who didn't seem to suspect — or perhaps care — that Edeline was spoiled goods. Because there had been plenty of rumours at the time. He was new money, and sometimes new money had to take the aristocratic scraps.'

Ben raised an eyebrow.

'I know that sounds harsh, but there you have it. How the other half live. It was a long time ago.'

Not *that* long, Ben thought. Yesterday evening, in Roger's flat, Ben had browsed stories — penned by his friend — that he now knew mirrored Edeline Foxton's history. Scandalous lovers, rejected children, sibling rivalry. Disputes, debauchery, death.

'But why did Edeline's political view turn so . . . right wing? What happened?'

'Oh, the Blackshirts were stuffed full of aristocrats who'd lamented the changing face of society in the years after the Great War. More than that — something which attracted Edeline was that the BUF encouraged women to take an active role. I think she liked to feel important. It riled Kingston too, another bonus. What started as a kind of rebellion turned into an obsession.' She hesitated. 'I found her, you know?'

Ben looked up in anticipation. 'Who?'

'Edeline. A few years before she died.'

'She's dead? How did you find her?'

Molly waved a hand. 'The truth is, she kept in touch, the odd letter here and there. I guess I was the oldest link to her past by then, aside from Marcus, who she said she never wrote to again after the war. It's true that people were looking for her. Journalists and such . . . it was the reason I went to see her myself. I wondered whether I should give up her location.'

'Which was?'

'Paris.' A nod. 'I wanted to know what had become of her. If she'd changed. Softened?' She paused. 'Repented, even. If she felt guilty about her past. About the fascism. About the way she'd treated Grace.'

'Did she?'

'Edeline lived well enough. But bitterness had aged her in a way that was unnatural.' She picked up a parsnip and turned it over. 'It was as though her cool facade had been peeled back and emotions had got to parts of her that had previously been hidden.' She glanced at Ben. 'It wasn't just the war, though, it was something else.'

'What?'

'Rose had broken her heart.'

Ben didn't think Edeline sounded like the kind of woman who had much of a heart to break. 'How so?'

'Well, Edeline never saw her again.'

So Edeline had left England in disgrace, and Rose had disowned her?

'That's very sad,' Ben said. 'No matter how she felt about Grace, it must have been devastating for her, never seeing either of her daughters again.'

Molly wiped her hands on her apron. 'What do you mean *either* of her daughters?' She wrapped the remains of the marble cake in paper for Ben to take.

Her kindness only made him feel worse about the news he had to share. It had been three decades, but a jumble of nerves danced in Ben's stomach. 'I'm sorry to tell you, Molly, that, a few months ago, I believe I found Grace's body down a mine in western Tasmania. She must have fallen to her death just before the end of the war in the Pacific, because no one has seen her since.'

Molly sat at the table with a patient air. 'You're a writer, aren't you?'

She looked at him with an eyebrow raised in that way people did when they heard about his profession, drawing their own conclusions as to how he lived in his head. Mostly, he had to concede, they were right.

Ben frowned. 'Yes.' He searched her face for grief, even a flicker of it. He'd just told her Grace was most likely dead.

'Yes, well . . . this isn't one of your novels . . .'

A languid air of unease swirled around Ben, wicking away the things he thought he'd known. He felt a strange sensation, like a hook had been cast across the years and sunk into his flesh. Someone tugged the line, and the fine hairs on his arms lifted in goosebumps.

'Make no mistake, Ben, Grace Grey returned to England after the war,' Molly said, with a certain sense of satisfaction. 'I know this because I saw her myself. I *saw* her with my very own eyes.'

Chapter 65

Grosvenor Square, London
December 2004

A week before Christmas, Libby collected the mail to find a letter postmarked Ballinn.

'Seen a ghost, my dear?' said a woman who appeared like an apparition at Libby's side, just as she had a few weeks before, when they'd both been standing in the Friday night bustle of Grosvenor Square. Now, they stood inside, by the four mail boxes in their joined entrance hall, out of the weather that had been blowing cold all day. And Miss Winman was certainly dressed for it.

'No ghosts today, I'm pleased to say.' She had retrieved the shorthand interview, along with a beautifully penned transcript, earlier in the week, and filled her neighbour in on the visit to Molly's grave. Though keen to open this letter from a woman who just might know the truth, Libby hesitated over whether she should invite Miss Winman in.

'I—'

But her neighbour made the decision for her. 'I'm late for tai chi!' she exclaimed, and with a quick squeeze of Libby's arm she rushed out the door and away.

❧

Inside, Libby made herself a cup of tea, then reached into her bag to withdraw the star for which she'd braved John Lewis that very afternoon. It reminded her of Sam, not least because she had to balance precariously on a chair so she could fix the new decoration to the top of the oversized tree.

They'd messaged a few times since their trip to Hampshire, but not seen each other as Sam was busy with his 'cooking sessions', which Libby had come to understand was code for therapy, of the kind the army had insisted he undertake before they accepted his resignation. They needed to be sure, apparently, that he was fully prepared for life outside the services, that he had a plan for what he would do. *What even goes to plan anyway?* she'd wanted to message back, but she hadn't. Their friendship was good for her, and each time they were in touch she realised it had really become that: friendship. Nothing more. And that was great. Just great.

She took a deep breath, sipping her tea as she observed the bustle of Mayfair. A man in a suit descended the stone steps of Number 45, and she tried to imagine Rose returning from Australia, climbing those very same steps to a door she'd walked out of six years before. In that time, London had changed, the world had changed; how would it have felt to step back into the past only to find it altered? And had Grace, too, returned? If what Jess had sent was anything to go by, though, the body down the mine was almost certainly her. Libby tried to push the thoughts aside, but they just kept coming.

Had Rose known about Grace's child? Did she know that *Daniel* was the father? And if she did . . . had she told him? From reading 'The Far-Flung Distant Shore', it was clear that Daniel had still loved Grace, perhaps in his own quiet way, years later . . .

There was no point second-guessing. Life was big and complicated. Daniel had been through a war; according to his ballads, he'd lived through Timor, survived the death railway, been there when the bomb dropped in Nagasaki, and finally returned to Ireland.

Then something happened: Rose had arrived, and they'd married.

On the window seat, the letter called. Libby picked it up, carefully peeling away the seal, and pulling out several pieces of paper. Taking a breath, she scanned the first paragraph, pleased to see that the sentiment was warm, and Libby thought there was something familiar about it. The turn of phrase, perhaps? Did it remind her of her grandmother, Dina, and the letters they'd sent one another in the years before her death? Dina had always said that letters let us express feelings, hope and dreams that we mightn't have the courage to say face to face. Hers had been a perfect example of that: she always signed off with *I love you*, though she'd never said such a thing in person. She and Rob were from a different generation, but Libby knew they'd loved her, as they'd loved Willow, all their lives.

She read on.

Dear Libby,

I'm so pleased to hear from a young woman – for I believe from your tone that you are young? – about ballads. Daniel and I both lamented that the writing, and reading, of them so fell out of fashion when such poetry can be healing. I know; I learned the hard way that life and love and regret can be expressed through the writing and reading of poems. And Daniel, of course, knew that too.

I wanted to write back immediately – express post, as you so kindly sent your letter – because your praise moved me, bringing back memories both good and bad. Daniel was a wonderful man, who stood by me through thick and thin; he had a heart full of forgiveness and bravery. He was of the opinion that ballads can put into words pain we barely understand; heal a wounded soldier; teach even the quietest mouse to find a voice.

You asked if I could share with you 'The Far-Flung Distant Shore' because your book was damaged and you can't locate another? I'm afraid I don't have a printed copy, so I've written it on the attached pages. You also mentioned you had more questions, and I would be glad to correspond, though I can't promise to know all the answers.

Kind regards,
Rose

No matter the importance or otherwise of Daniel's part in Willow's story, Libby realised – with a tug in her heart – how much she would have loved to have met him. With him she felt an affinity, both through his love of ballads, but also because of the things she'd learned about him. Daniel had *also* lost the love of his life, and he had clearly still felt sharp sorrow long after Grace was gone.

She picked up the several pages sent with the letter – a handwritten copy of 'The Far-Flung Distant Shore' – and smiled. The words were *so* familiar to her. After all, she'd read the ballad many times over the last weeks. Yet . . . yet . . . she looked closer, biting her bottom lip. What was it? She recognised *something* . . . not just about the ballad, but the letter too. She held two of the pages at arm's length, then let them fall to the ground, as dawning realisation took her breath away.

Chapter 66

Behind Towerhurst, Tasmania

August 1945

Grace reached out, grappling for something to hold on to, but all she found were the years flashing through her mind. They rolled in reverse, peeling back time like a skin.

She's pacing the tower, waiting for letters from Daniel that never arrive. Her heart aches.

She's smelling the newly turned earth of their baby's grave, which Marcus has marked with Atlantisite stone.

Now she disappears into blackness after giving birth.

She holds her hand over the warm swell of pregnancy.

Her cheeks are flushed as she plans her future.

She sees Daniel for the last time: exquisite ecstasy.

She tastes his lips.

He loves her. He loves her. He loves her.

He is reading 'The Ma'am from Joey River' as he skips around the pool.

Laughter. From her own mouth. For the first time she can recall.

Warm hands save her from the surf.

Her heart shatters on the beach.

Her first — false — kiss.

She meets him under the sassafras tree. Her life spins on a dime, though she doesn't know it yet.

Towerhurst looms over her. She has arrived.

Then . . . Grace's hands found purchase, bringing her back to the present. The stone edge of the mine was slippery, but she hung on. Below her: a dark hole, a lifeless shape at the bottom. Not a single whisper of movement sullied the stillness.

৯

'Marcus . . .' Grace's wracking cries reverberated along the verandah. As best she could, she talked, her hands shaking as her uncle held them tight. Every word burned her throat, and her neck was bruised and swollen.

'She's down there. Not moving. We rolled, wrestled almost . . . there was a suitcase, full of things . . . we fell . . . I'm sorry. I'm sorry. I'm sorry.'

'It's all right,' he said slowly. 'Wait right here.' Then he was gone, off the verandah, disappearing around the side of the house to slip through the moon gate and into the rainforest. Grace pulled the blanket he'd wrapped around her shoulders tighter still.

She wanted to turn back the clock. If she hadn't followed, none of this would have happened. Rose's expression – moments before she'd stood and revealed Daniel's card pressed beneath her knee – had flickered with regret, hadn't it? Then it had vanished, and she'd fixed Grace with a look of such contempt that it had chilled her to the bone.

Had they shared *nothing* growing up? A home? Experiences? A certain proximity to Edeline? Even to think this way, Grace knew that she was only fooling herself. Their two lives had rolled along in distant tandem, far enough apart that their paths never touched, close enough together that when one veered towards the other, they both recoiled to avoid a collision.

Grace spread her muddy fingers on her skirt as she listened to the rain beat on the iron roof, drowned out by a distant thunder. Against the brown and green moss-streaked fabric, the dirt on her hands was dark red. She looked closer. Blood. Dried and congealed, pushed deep under the pad of her nails. Had she scratched Rose? Scratched at her face as she tried to push her off, ripped her fingers along the backs of those perfect, lily-white arms, etched her own desperation on Rose's skin? Feeling nausea rise once more, she leaned over, her head on her knees, feeling a wave of horror drip from the top of her furrowed brow onto the rough wood of the deck.

Grace now understood that, encouraged by Edeline, Rose had been gripped by something worse than madness.

Jealousy. She had been propelled by it.

Leaning her head against Towerhurst's cool wall, Grace recalled the day she'd written her very first ballads, discarded paper spread around her like fallen leaves. After he'd read her work, Uncle Marcus had recognised the pain behind the words and warned that holding on to bitterness, jealousy, anger was like buying poison for another, and drinking it yourself.

'What sort of madman,' he'd asked, 'would ever do that?'

And now as he returned from the mine, he knelt before her, his knees cracking. 'Rose . . . she is most certainly . . .'

Grace muffled a cry.

'It was an accident,' he said without question or doubt. He believed her implicitly, it seemed.

Still, Grace's chest tightened; she was afraid. Everyone in Westford knew there was no love lost between her and Rose. Olive, in particular, blamed Grace for any animosity. For her aunt, Rose could do no wrong.

She found her voice. 'We should go to the station.'

Uncle Marcus hesitated. 'What was in the suitcase?'

The suitcase. She'd forgotten to say. When she'd run, gasping, crying, out of the forest to find Uncle Marcus sat on the verandah, pipe and book in hand, she'd completely *forgotten to say.*

'Espionage?' he said incredulously after she told him. 'You can't be serious?'

A hesitation. 'I think . . . I believe it was my mother who put her up to it.'

Uncle Marcus let out a low breath, and Grace nodded mutely.

'Rose . . . she was very similar to my sister, you know? Not so much like Edeline as a young woman, but a carbon copy of the lady who came to stay some years after Olive and I were married. I discovered a darkness in her then that hadn't existed before.' Uncle Marcus had never talked about Grace's mother in this way. He'd never said a word against her. Pain rippled across his face.

'There were other things in the suitcase,' she said. Things, she thought, that might reflect badly on her, that might make it look as though . . . she'd pushed Rose. A motive.

She told him anyway.

Daniel.

He's alive.

'What do you mean? Daniel's in . . . Nagasaki? Rose hid this from you? From his aunt and uncle?' Something new fizzled in the air. A hesitancy. He stood slowly and went to the murmuring radio in the hallway and turned it off, before coming outside again.

'This won't look good.'

'It wasn't like that!'

He paused for what seemed an age, his brow deeply furrowed. 'Pack your things,' he said finally, glancing at his watch.

She frowned. 'What things?'

'All your things. Pack a suitcase.' She flinched at the word. 'Pack light. You're leaving on the boat.'

'What? I don't understand.'

'You do.'

'No.' She would take responsibility.

Uncle Marcus shook his head. Gone was his pervasive air of vagueness. Gone was the faraway look in his eye. Gone was the sense that he could be somewhere else. He was right here, with her. 'This is your window. We've got an hour left before the tide cuts us off.'

'No, I don't—'

'I need to be here when Olive returns from her mother's tomorrow. To explain that you and Rose have left.'

'I won't—'

He took her hands in his. 'By then, you'll be on the boat. You have to go, Grace. Puds will take you. He'll vouch that Rose got on the boat. Didn't you tell me he would do anything for you?' He searched her face. 'He loves you, you know?'

'Not like that.'

'If you say so.'

The thunderous rain had ebbed to a sob. 'I won't leave. Don't you understand? I've just discovered Daniel's alive! Japan will surrender any day. He'll be home soon. Nothing could compel me to go. I'll face what I've done. I only need to tell the truth.' She stood, and went inside to the hallway mirror to inspect the skin on her neck. It was already turning purple.

He came to stand behind her. 'You should leave, Grace. I don't trust Olive . . . I'm worried about you.' A hesitation. 'You should leave,' he repeated.

'I won't.'

'There's nothing to stay for.' Uncle Marcus flicked a switch, and the wireless buzzed to life, full of the same chatter as before, news that she hadn't heard, but this time, she listened. Finally, when she understood what the announcer was saying, she fell, once more, to her scraped and battered knees.

Nagasaki was gone.

Chapter 67

On the Irish Sea, turning towards Liverpool

October 1945

The eight-week sailing passed in the blink of an eye. Or was it an eternity? Grace hardly knew.

The news out of Nagasaki was devastating. A hundred thousand people had died, and half the city was destroyed, many POW camps with it. On the crossing, she'd tried to find out more. Names of survivors. Where they'd been taken. But she'd been given no indication if Daniel was among them.

She gripped the railing at the bow of the ship. To her right, England's coastline slipped by, its flat, treeless shore seeming strangely foreign to her. To her left, she imagined she might just glimpse Ireland on the hazy horizon. *Ireland.* The place they should have returned to together.

She ached with a longing to be there, though she'd never seen it. To walk on the rolling hills, to smell the purple heather, to see the golden glow on an autumn afternoon. To go to the valley where Daniel's parents lay and explain that their son was perfect. That he was everything she could ever have wanted in life, and more.

That even if he was dead, she loved him still. And she

would move there regardless. To be close to their life as it would have been.

~

When she arrived at Liverpool's dock, a man looked at her papers, then her face. He flicked through a list of names on his clipboard.

He frowned. 'Grace *Grey*?'

She'd almost forgotten that was her name. After being around Uncle Marcus so long, she'd come to think of herself as a Foxton. Speak of the devil: Edeline stood on the dock behind. Her blonde hair was tinged with streaks of silver, but her high cheekbones gave her that look of eternal youth.

'Yes,' she said to the man. 'Grace Grey.'

His frown smeared across his face in a look of disgust. He folded her papers away.

'Come with me.'

Grace's heart skipped a beat.

~

She had assumed that Puds or Uncle Marcus had slipped up; that the authorities in Australia had contacted their counterparts in Britain, and she was a wanted woman, a fugitive. She hung her head in shame as she took a seat in a small, dingy office on the wharf. On the way, she'd lifted a hand to signal her mother and, when Edeline waved enthusiastically, Grace's heart had skipped a beat: for the first time in her life, her mother was pleased to see her. Then Edeline's smile had faltered. Her gaze hovered over Grace's shoulder, looking for someone else.

~

'You're the daughter of Edeline Grey?'

Grace paused. 'I—'

The man looked agitated. 'Are you? Or are you not?'

'Yes.' A flush bloomed on her neck. The bruises had long since faded to a sickly yellow, finally disappearing altogether. At times, she could still feel that pressure on her throat, feel the jealousy that had put it there. Some nights, she'd wondered if she might see Rose's ghost, but she'd seen nothing, and that had been somehow worse.

It was an accident. She wanted to take his hand, and beg her innocence. *She always hated me.* But she knew it was hopeless to argue.

Instead, she said: 'I saw my mother outside.'

This didn't seem to help matters.

'Free as a bird, isn't she? Walking around bold as brass while my son rots in the ground. Her and the rest of those black-shirted bastards . . .'

Grace lowered her eyes.

He took her identity papers and slid them into an envelope. 'I'll be keeping these.'

She wasn't wanted for murder after all, but for being the family member of a fascist.

༄

When Grace was allowed to leave – without her passport – she walked unsteadily back across the wharf to her mother, who wasn't able to hide her disappointment. 'I don't understand . . . where's Rose?'

She looked over Grace's shoulder, as though her protégé might appear at any moment, and Grace had given her the answer she'd been practising.

'She met a man in Hobart when she worked there. I guess they fell in love.'

Edeline was visibly agitated. 'She didn't inform me.'

'She's in love,' Grace repeated, as if it were the answer for everything.

The idea that Rose could love another was too much; Edeline was lost for words, and Grace saw in their absence an emotion that couldn't be expressed. It brought with it a flush of pity for her mother. Edeline had loved Rose, and Rose had loved her, but the truth was, Grace thought calmly, that it no longer hurt.

Her own love had filled the hole in her heart.

She recalled that last hour at Towerhurst, when she and Uncle Marcus stood on the verandah, her uncertain future stretched before her. The easing rain had let a sliver of sunlight through the treeline to the wilderness beyond. 'When Daniel comes back, you'll send him to me, won't you?' she'd said. 'You'll tell him about the baby?' She hated that he'd never known.

Uncle Marcus had paused and taken her hand. 'If Daniel survived Nagasaki' – Grace tried not to hear the doubt in his voice – 'and returns to Tasmania, I'll tell him everything. I'll help, I promise.' He'd turned from her, wiping his eyes. 'Grace . . .'

'Yes?'

'I'll look over your baby.'

Only moments before, she'd knelt at the Atlantisite stone to say her goodbyes. But their child would always be with her, in her heart, no matter what.

Always loved. Never forgotten.

'Thank you,' Grace had said sadly to Uncle Marcus.

'What I mean is—'

'Everything will be fine,' she'd said.

'Grace, I should tell you—'

'Daniel *will* find his way back to me.' She stepped off the verandah. 'I just need ten minutes . . .'

'Grace!' Uncle Marcus had called after her.

But then she was gone, around the back of the house, through the moon gate, down the track through the rainforest. One last time. Her steps were soft on the humus-covered gravel and, just as when she'd first approached the waterfall six years before, she saw water vapour hovering, a low rainbow shimmer colouring the air. This time she didn't round the corner with tentative steps. She picked up her pace as the rainbow lifted up and away, the end of it floating right over the falls.

Right where she was going to hide her treasure.

Inside the cave, she'd taken down the Arnott's biscuit tin, then opened it. Carefully she added the sprig of heather that Daniel had given her the day he'd arrived back from the front – it was pressed now between two small sheets of glass she'd pilfered from empty photo frames, and stuck together with tape. It would tell the love of her life she hadn't forgotten him. She took off her necklace, the fox pendant that had brought her both luck and grief, and laid it on top of 'The Ma'am from Joey River' and the ballad that had inspired her to see the world anew, 'The Man from Snowy River'.

Then she'd fixed the lid on tight.

With any luck, the next person to open the tin would be Daniel, and he could sell the necklace, and pay for his ticket home.

⁂

As the train slid away from the station, Edeline regarded her daughter with a cool eye. 'You've grown up. Marcus said you had.'

'It's been six years.' It was a gap too large to bridge, but perhaps they could start again. She reached out a tentative hand and Edeline flinched, smoothing her skirt, and turning to watch the grey jagged skyline of Liverpool bare its teeth.

'When you disembarked,' she said to Grace's reflection, 'I mistook you for Rose.'

Grace blinked at the sky, its battleship clouds rolling over from Ireland. 'I see,' she said. Cool fingers closed around her heart. When she looked in the mirror, the last thing she wanted was the ghost of Rose Munro staring back.

Chapter 68

Grosvenor Square, London
October 1945

Even though London had changed, the house on Grosvenor Square was broadly the same, aside from the odd missing item, and the dust that lay thick in places it hadn't been before. It had been requisitioned by Churchill during the war, and the Americans had moved in until 1944, when her mother was released from Holloway.

Grace ran her hand along a shelf of empty decanters, marvelling at how they'd once lived. Her father was gone, of course, though as he'd always been absent that gap was filled with only a few sad memories hidden in dark corners: disappointed looks, harsh words, the lingering feeling of a stung cheek where he'd slapped her across the face. Grace wanted to hate him, but how could one hate the dead? It was, she supposed, possible. She wondered vaguely if Rose would have hung on to her own hatred, that ever-present jealousy, if it had been Grace who'd fallen to her end.

Molly was gone too, back to her mother's cottage in the shadows of Foxton Hall.

'She'll be here tomorrow,' Edeline said, a few minutes after they walked through the door.

Grace paused in the hallway, pretending to wrestle with the

buttons on her long coat to hide the shaking of her fingers.
'Molly's . . . coming *here*? To London?'

'Yes.' Though it wasn't a uniform, Edeline was dressed all
in black. Old habits. 'So we can all sit together and *you* can
be the one to explain why Rose stayed in Tasmania with a
man you know nothing about, instead of returning to her
mother.'

ॐ

Later, in her old bedroom, Grace was fascinated by how little
altered it was. The bed – once piled high with pillows at the
doctor's insistence – had been moved, and was now simply
made in a way that suggested a lone occupant had stayed there.
It was as far from the window as it could be, and even the
sun streaming through the remnants of diamond-patterned
blast tape couldn't reach it. This had been her room for fifteen years, and hardly a trace of her remained, and yet . . .
it had always been sparse, hadn't it? No toys, few books, the
fireplace boarded up for fear of draughts. Wasn't that so? She
could hardly recall.

She stepped forward, opening a drawer at random. It was
empty, as was the one beneath. She went to the wardrobe with
the huge mirror that she'd often gazed into, her reflection
somehow unfamiliar, even though she'd looked this way for
years. Most of the clothes she'd left behind were missing –
given away for the war effort, apparently – which was just as
well, because they'd hardly fit now. Only a single, solitary
item remained, draped over a hanger. Tentatively, she reached
out to touch the silk; it was so fine it felt like nothing at all.
She went to the bed, and took off all her clothes, then she put
on the blue dressing gown before turning to face the mirror.

Finally, it fitted. Running a hand over her body, she admired
how she looked. She was curvy now, and she loved the swell

of her stomach: it reminded her of her and Daniel's child, who she would love, in her heart, for ever.

She went to the window, and opened it to look over Grosvenor Square, where there'd once been elegant flower-beds. The trees remained, and she watched as the autumn breeze swirled up a pile of russet leaves, carrying it down the street. She recalled telling Daniel how she'd never noticed the changing seasons in London, but here it was, *the change*, right in front of her. It had happened every year; she'd just never opened her eyes to see.

She unknotted the dressing gown, and slipped it from her shoulders. Then she flung it into the street, where it caught the wind, and flew away.

ॐ

It wasn't until the next morning that Grace was confronted about the pregnancy.

'How could you be so stupid?'

'I love him.'

Edeline gave her a withering look. 'Well, we can put that nonsense to bed. Marcus tells me he was in Nagasaki.'

'There were many survivors.'

'And many more who died.'

'I have faith.'

'Faith? I hope you're not converting to Catholicism.'

Grace sighed. Her mother's barbs were blunt these days. She turned to the newspaper, flicking through the pages. She'd begin, once more, she thought, to collect articles for her ballads. 'I'll be moving to Ireland as soon as he's back. Or even before.'

The vertical lines around Edeline's mouth, which had appeared in the intervening years, creased. 'I don't think so, my dear. I have plans for you.'

'Plans?'

'Marriage. I have four candidates in mind. They've all agreed to meet you.' She hesitated. 'Although you'll have to stay inside from now on. Your skin's become very coarse.'

Grace was amused. 'Who would marry the daughter of a fascist?'

'You think *our* family were the only members of the party?'

'*I* was never a member.'

'I think you'll find you were. I took the liberty.'

Grace paused. 'When will our passports be returned?'

Edeline rolled her eyes. 'Oswald believes taking them away is against the Magna Carta. But he thinks it might realistically be years.'

'How will I travel?'

'You won't.'

There was a knock at the door. Before the war, the house-keeper would have answered, but there was no housekeeper now. A sign of the changing times, and the Greys' altered fortune.

Grace left her mother and walked out into the hallway. She paused, putting a hand to her chest. The enormity of the situation hit her: she was a prisoner and, without her papers, Britain's borders were her bars.

She opened the door, its swollen timber sticking. Her heart leapt to her throat.

'Oh, God.'

It was Molly Munro.

The housekeeper frowned, hesitating on the threshold, a shadow of emotion flitting across her features. *She knows*, Grace thought. Someone has told her.

'Grace?' Molly said in disbelief, looking her up and down.

It was an accident.

An accident.

An accident.

'Molly? It's so . . . lovely . . . to see you again. How wonderful.' She was sincere, and yet her words sounded hollow.

'You're all grown up.' Molly stepped forward and took her hands. 'You look surprised to see me.'

'No, no.' Relief battled with Grace's fear. 'It's not that. I'm just a little thrown from all the travel.' She turned to gather herself, indicating that Molly should come in. 'Please, won't you forgive me?'

Edeline had left the dining room, her half-finished tea still wisping in the cold air. A vicious winter was forecast, and Grace had called for coal that morning. Now a small fire glowed in the grate, making barely a dent in the room's chill. The house smelled damp, but from the look on Molly's face, the neglect didn't surprise her.

Grace fetched a fresh pot of tea.

'You're living back in Hampshire?' she said when she returned to the room.

'My mother passed away . . .'

'I'm sorry to hear it.'

'I've moved into the old cottage. It suits me well.' Her frame had become slim, and she was tanned from what must have been outside work. 'I was on the farms. Thought it a good way to do my bit.'

Grace nodded. One of them would have to mention Rose. She took a breath, but Molly spoke first.

'Rose stayed on in Tasmania?'

The milk was powdered, and Grace stirred the jug energetically. 'Yes. A man in Hobart . . . I don't know who he was. She said she'd write when they're settled.'

'Not to me, I'm sure.'

'I'm sorry, Molly,' she said, for no reason. Or for every reason.

'What on earth for?'

'I . . .' Grace sipped her tea, unsure of how to proceed. At the very moment she thought she might confess, Molly said:

'You've grown up, my dear.' She gave a kind smile, but it slipped as a creak came from the overhead floorboards; Edeline was pacing with vigour.

'I . . . I fell in love.' The tea leaves danced over themselves. They could reuse them tomorrow, Grace thought. Her mother wouldn't like it, but she no longer cared how Edeline felt. 'I fell in love,' she repeated. *And so much more*, she wanted to add. 'He – Daniel – was in Nagasaki, and I've had no word since . . .'

'Does Edeline know?'

'She doesn't approve.'

'Listen,' Molly said, her voice lowered, 'there's something I need to tell you.' The footsteps overhead paused as though they too wanted to listen. 'I always felt bad about the way your mother treated you. I should have done more to stop it. I *wish* I'd done more—'

Grace protested. 'I think we all know Rose was always more of a daughter to my mother than I could ever be.' It no longer hurt to admit it.

'But that's just it' – Molly put her cup aside – 'there's something I've felt guilty about for a very long time.'

'Edeline's a difficult woman.' Grace wouldn't be apologised to by Rose's mother. After what she'd done . . .

'It's more than that,' Molly said. 'There's a reason, you see, that your mother was . . .' A hesitation. 'Rose is—'

The door swung abruptly open, and Edeline entered the room. In her hand she held a pile of mail, which she quickly flicked through.

'I'm *so* sorry to keep you, Molly; I thought you were the coal man.'

Grace hated her mother more than ever at that moment. She'd

watched the coal man arrive herself only hours before, casting a critical eye as Grace directed him around the back of the house. Indifference was one of Edeline's favourite weapons. 'You needn't have come: Rose is returning on a later boat – we should hear from her any day now. It's a wasted trip for you, I'm afraid.'

Molly hadn't stood as she might once have when Edeline entered the room. 'I wanted to see Grace.'

'Goodness. How very charitable of you . . .' Edeline trailed off as she turned a fat envelope over in her hand, frowning as she examined the postmark.

From where she sat, Grace glimpsed familiar spidery hand-writing. Her heart skipped a beat. 'Is that . . .'

'Wrong address.'

'Please . . .'

Edeline sniffed, and went to the fire. 'Your first suitor arrives Friday.' She tossed the envelope into the flames.

'No!' Grace thrust her hand at the paper, though it had already begun to blacken at its edges. She felt the burning kiss of heat before strong arms pulled her back.

'Leave it, love. He'll write again.'

She let herself be pulled into an embrace, her head resting on Molly's warm shoulder. Her gaze lingered on the fire and she watched a small sprig of purple heather roll down the vol-canic red of the coal to rest on the dusty hearth.

Purple heather. Not white.

Daniel was alive! And he was home.

❧

That night, Grace snuck down the stairs in the way she'd once done at Towerhurst, skipping the third step out of habit. She took nothing from the house, only the bag she'd arrived with and never unpacked. She didn't leave Edeline a note: she and her mother were finished.

At Liverpool, she cut and dyed her hair into a short platinum bob. She did it herself, just to be cautious. If Uncle Marcus ever slipped up, or someone found Rose's body, or if Puds betrayed her, though she was sure he never would . . .

When she'd packed her bag in those final rushed hours at Towerhurst, she'd slipped into Rose's room, and gone through her chaperone's papers, searching for more letters from Daniel. There weren't any. Not even from 1940, when he and Rose had apparently written incessantly. Instead, she found envelopes addressed with Rose's name; they were postmarked *Westford*, and the pages inside were scrawled with text copied from newspapers. Stuff and nonsense, random sentences filling the lines. Rose had clearly written them herself, and posted the letters to make Grace jealous, or to play some cruel game. Grace no longer cared which.

In the packed case by her bed, she had found Rose's identification. She added it to her own things so that she could burn it later, then she'd clipped the case shut, and taken it with her. As the ship crossed Bass Strait, making for Melbourne, she'd flung Rose's suitcase over the edge, watching it bob for a moment before it sank to the bottom of that shallow sea.

Now, as another boat took her away from another port, she stood on its deck watching Liverpool fade into the distance. They'd let her through customs with a wink and a cursory glance at her papers. The guard looked very similar to the man who'd questioned her only days before, but she couldn't be sure. That already felt like a lifetime ago and, not for the first time, Grace thanked her lucky stars that she'd kept Rose's papers.

She walked round the stern of the ship to its port side, where the wind whipped at her short hair.

In her hand, she held her new identity. While some might have thought it was remarkable that they looked so very alike, it wasn't strange to Grace. She hadn't got the chance to ask, but she'd guessed what Molly had been going to say.

'Rose is—'

Your sister. She was going to say *sister.*

Despite everything – the hatred, the bitterness, the cruelty – Grace wished that Rose could have discovered the truth. Jealousy was a poison, but to have known that Edeline was her mother would have made Rose happy, and happiness was the antidote to so many of life's ills.

Grace turned towards the horizon. There they were: Ireland's green shores. She'd take a train to Killarney, then rent a hackney. Once, a lifetime ago, Daniel had pointed to the ledge behind the waterfall, and compared it to Ballinn. 'If you know where to look, you'll find it.' She hoped that hadn't changed.

She, on the other hand, would *have* to change, to shed her skin, and be reborn as someone else. The thought conjured an image of the moon gate at Towerhurst, her baby resting beside it and a wave of sadness threatened to engulf her, but she had to do this, and she knew that she could. After all, she'd changed before. She leaned back, her arms straight, hands holding the railing, and said her name one last time. The sound rolled across the water and away, to be forgotten, lost on the shifting tide.

Grace.

Chapter 69

Northport, Tasmania

27th February 1975

That morning, as she'd been standing at the counter of Northport's only bakery, Willow had watched a woman with a tiny baby in a tie-dyed sling waver momentarily over a pile of apple cakes, before ordering the lot and walking out into the dull day. After she'd left the shop, Willow saw them again; they'd been joined by a handsome man, a picnic spread before them on a table by the sighing ocean.

'Excuse me,' the woman had said as Willow passed. 'Could you?' She held out a camera, and Willow had taken two photos of the couple gazing adoringly at their baby. 'Three weeks in and the rolls of film have already cost us a fortune!'

When Willow returned to the house, she'd pulled out the family albums, and spread them around her, turning the pages as the first drops of rain plucked at the tin roof. *1951, 1950, 1949.* She rolled back the years until she reached 1947, when Ash and Ivy were toddlers causing mischief – smeared in messy food, racing in a blur past the camera, tugging at Grandpa's beard – then smaller, sleeping forms in Dina's arms. In the months before that, the swell of Dina's stomach threatened to swamp her. And before that again, there was her father, dressed in his uniform, impossibly handsome under his slouch hat, having returned from war. Several pages before there *she* was, in 1943, held in Dina's arms. She turned back to 1942, and the months preceding it, but they had not been marked in the family pictorial history.

Willow frowned; she'd never noticed that before. She hadn't looked at these albums for a decade, and when she and her sisters had pored over them as children they had always been searching for photos of themselves together, of them *doing* things; not of babies, who all looked the same. Or did they? Willow peered closer, and compared the photos against each other; of her at eight months old, against the girls at the same age, but Ash and Ivy's similarity only distorted the differences between them.

Now Willow set two gin and tonics on the porch table, the lemon tree leaves still swirling listlessly. 'Mum?' She put a mug of cheese straws, fresh from the bakery, next to the drinks. 'I took the liberty.'

Dina closed her book, blinking hard to leave the world she'd been lost in and bring the real one into focus. Behind her, the bay was grey. A solitary gull swooped, kissing the top of the poplars at the bottom of the garden. 'You read my mind.' She reached for her drink, and held it aloft. 'To unpredictable weather.'

Willow proceeded with caution. 'I was looking through the family albums earlier,' she said slowly, not wanting to alarm her mum, just seeing how she might react.

'Oh yes?'

'Ash and Ivy . . . were the cutest babies, weren't they?'

A laugh. 'Deceptively so. They were mischief from the beginning.'

'They look very different from me.'

Dina took a cheese straw and broke it in two. 'Do you think so? I thought you were quite similar, but then everyone said you looked like your grandmother when you first arrived.'

'It's hard to say, because there aren't any photos of me as a newborn.'

'Aren't there—' Dina was interrupted by the slam of the back door. Rob must have returned from the rocks; hopefully with fresh fish for dinner.

'No.'

Her mother's sigh made her heart ache, and Willow felt a prickle of apprehension. 'No, of course there aren't. We didn't buy a camera until your father returned from Japan. There's something about war that finally makes you do these things. That makes you capture the moments that matter.' She leaned forward, patting Willow's hand. 'I'm sorry we don't have photos of you as a newborn. I had a couple taken in the year after, but not enough.'

Rob appeared on the porch, a bucket in hand. His grin told enough of a story; they would be having their fish supper. He looked at their half-empty drinks.

'Another?'

Turning back to the kitchen, he whistled as he went.

≈

After dinner, Willow excused herself and went to the telephone. It was early afternoon in London, and she wasn't sure whether Ben would be at Roger's apartment. But he was, and at the sound of his voice she melted. She'd missed him so much. For months, she'd pushed him away in ways she hadn't meant to, but *of course* he'd wanted to look into her past. He was right to do so. Why shy from the truth? Didn't she deserve to know?

'How far have you got, love?' she asked, after he'd updated her on his reading at the Iliad Club. 'I mean . . . into researching my past . . .'

A hesitation. 'Quite far.'

'I see.'

'I'm so sorry.'

'No, *I'm* sorry,' Willow said. 'I should have behaved better. I should have *been* better. I should have coped better.'

'Shall I tell you what I know?'

Dina poked her head into the hallway. 'Is that Ben?'

A nod.

'Give him our love,' she said. 'There's pudding when you're done.' She smiled, then she was gone.

'I don't think now's the best time.'

'Tomorrow, then?'

Willow paused, nodding, though Ben wouldn't be able to see it. 'Mum and Dad are out in the evening.'

'Darling?'

'Yes.'

'Do you *want* to find your birth parents?'

She thought about her mother and father, how regardless of the truth, she'd love them for ever. Surety coursed through her veins. 'Yes. I do. I want to know the truth.'

'Good,' said Ben, and even from ten thousand miles away she could hear him smiling. 'Because I need to go on a little journey . . . I can buy the tickets this afternoon. I'll reveal all tomorrow.'

'Intriguing.'

'You're brave, opening your heart like this.'

Willow felt her throat catch. 'I'm sorry I wasn't better these last months.'

'It's hard. I know.'

'I'll help you, when you get back to Tasmania . . . we'll find your parents, too.'

'I would love that more than anything in the world.'

She smiled, and wound her fingers around the telephone cord. 'More than *anything*?' She hesitated. 'There's something else I need to tell you. I wasn't sure whether to wait but . . .'

Five minutes later, they said goodbye, and Willow felt her life was finally whole, no matter what the final truth might be.

'I love you, Ben.'

'I love you, Willow.'

'Goodbye.'

'Goodbye.'

Chapter 70

Heathrow Airport
December 2004

You have nothing to lose. Libby had gone over and over Roger's words, eventually deciding that, after everything she'd been through, everything she'd discovered, not just about her father, but about herself, he was right. She would follow Ben's footsteps . . . or at least the ones he'd intended to take.

She stood at security, a boarding pass in her hand, and Sam at her side.

'You're sure about this?' he said.

'No,' she said.

'Well, that's good.' He smiled and she couldn't help but return the grin. Around them, Heathrow swirled; with less than a week till Christmas, the airport hummed with festive anticipation.

'But if "Rose" is Grace, then . . .'

'I don't know,' she said truthfully. 'I don't know what it means.' But her father must have had some idea. The very day he'd met Molly he'd purchased a return ticket to Dublin, and a map of Ireland, and circled the very village where Molly's 'daughter' supposedly lived.

'There is the possibility,' said Sam, 'that the two women simply had . . . remarkably similar handwriting.'

Yesterday, as Libby had held those pages at arm's length, she'd known, almost immediately why they looked so familiar. The tail of the G took up a rude amount of room, and the flourish on the Y was unmistakable.

She'd almost tripped in her race to get to her bedroom, telling herself to *Slow down*, as she'd skidded to a halt and slid the tin from beneath her bed. Carefully, she'd withdrawn the ballad that had so influenced her life – 'The Ma'am from Joey River' – a poem she'd once thought written by Daniel McGillycuddy but that she now knew had been penned by Grace Grey; Jess had sent her the drafts that proved it.

She'd laid the pages side by side, and the writing, she'd been absolutely certain, matched.

Libby sighed. What was she doing? When she'd made the decision the night before to book a flight to Ireland she'd been high on her revelation and she'd not questioned whether it was the right thing to do. But in the cold light of a London morning, it suddenly seemed like madness.

'Well,' said Sam, passing her the hand luggage he'd insisted on carrying from the car, 'I think you're incredibly brave.'

Brave. There it was again, that word. The one he'd used several weeks ago that had made her heart leap. She reached out and took her bag from him, their hands brushing.

Before she'd left for the airport, she'd checked her emails to find a short message from Jess. It had jolted a memory she'd nearly forgotten, about a verse buried in the moss.

Dear Libby

Wonderful, isn't it? Revisiting the past like this. I've sent off enquiries about the Foxton Trust, but I'm hitting walls left, right and centre.

As to your question about the moon gate . . . I'm sorry to tell you that only a few years ago we lost it to a storm which also floored the adjacent sassafras. The silver lining was discovering that the stone next to it was only a memorial, not a grave – the whole patch was stripped to bedrock when the tree fell. Denny was relieved, though I did always say it wasn't a grave! Men and their overactive imaginations :).

I look forward to hearing anything you have to add on Towerhurst's history, though of course only when you've told your mother! Keep me posted, won't you?

Jess x

'Keep me posted, won't you?' Sam said, bringing Libby back to the present. 'You've got my dad and Roger on tenterhooks.'

She hesitated. 'Perhaps I should have . . . I *should* have said something to my mum.'

Sam moved out of the way of a passing family with an over-burdened trolley, then stepped a little closer. 'You can decide to cross that bridge if, and when, it comes to it.'

He smelled of coffee and an aftershave with a piney scent, reminiscent of the tree farm in Hampshire. Even the memory of that afternoon – although it had been one of emotion and sadness – gave Libby joy.

'You're right,' she said. Ballinn might, after all, be a dead end.

He glanced at his watch. 'You better go through.'

'Yes.' Though she felt rooted to the spot.

'And I'll be here when you land.'

'You don't have to be.' She was only going for three days.

'I want to.'

Libby's heart flipped. She hesitated again, looking at him. He was freshly shaven and he wore a neat woollen jumper. Dark chinos. He was more formal than she'd ever seen him and when she'd asked if he had somewhere to go after their early-morning dash to the airport, he'd shaken his head. On their drive here, she'd looked out of the window into a pre-dawn London, and her reflection had thrown back a smile. Sam, she'd realised, had dressed carefully for her.

Now she took in his appearance with an openness that she hadn't before. Those blue eyes rimmed by dark lashes, the long dimples that appeared when he smiled. He was beautiful. There was no doubt about it. And damaged, like her.

'I . . . I'll look forward to it,' she said.

'Me too,' he murmured, stepping just a little closer, so that Libby felt heat rise on her cheeks. She bit her lip, but forced herself to hold his gaze, so that everything around them seemed to fade, or blur, like an old vignette photo in which she and Sam were the focus. And for the first time she could remember, the past moved backwards, away from her, leaving a space just big enough for the present to be where it should be.

Right here.

Right now.

Libby took a deep breath. 'Goodbye,' she said.

'Goodbye,' he murmured.

And, moments before she turned to step from behind her father's footsteps and find her own way, Libby Andrews reached up, took Sam's face between her hands, and kissed him.

Chapter 71

Ballinn, County Kerry, Ireland
October 1945

The scene was just as Daniel had described; a patchwork of green hills that lay like a carpet to the sea. It resembled so closely the painting done by Puds that Grace had taken a moment to gather herself when she stepped out of the hackney. Sunlight bathed the purple heather-clad mountains in gold. County Kerry, it was true, was more beautiful than anything she'd ever seen.

The shopkeeper assessed her quietly. Grace could almost hear the questions crowding behind her lips, but where Mira Holmes would have asked them, the woman merely answered Grace without hesitation, giving her a warm smile. She said that every afternoon in the weeks since he'd returned, Daniel McGillycuddy took a long walk across the valley, following the old butter road that used to lead to Cork. 'Recovering slowly, so he is.' She nodded. 'Gaining his strength. You'll meet him if you follow that boreen.' She pointed out of the window where a track led up and out of the village.

Just as she was leaving, the shopkeeper called after her: 'If you miss him, I'll let him know you came. Who will I say was calling?'

Grace hesitated, then turned towards the woman. 'Rose,' she said with practised tongue. 'Miss Rose Munro.'

❧

From the top of the valley, Daniel watched a golden glow drape the landscape. He sat by his parents' graves. Their resting place had the world's most beautiful view. He sighed and pushed himself up. The light-headedness still came, but that too would pass, so the discharge doctor had told him. He'd spent three weeks on a hospital ship in Nagasaki before they'd planned to send him back to Australia.

'I want to go home,' he'd said.

'Which home?'

He began to walk back down the heather-rimmed boreen.

❧

Grace surveyed the hill, wishing she'd brought Puds's painting with her, but in her haste to leave Towerhurst, she'd forgotten it, along with her beloved copy of *The Collected Verse of A.B. Paterson*. It somehow felt right to have left them there, but she wasn't sure why.

She paused, taking a breath.

When she turned, she saw a figure moving with slow strides down the track. He, too, hesitated, and when he looked up, a thousand emotions crossed his face. He was fifty yards away, and yet she heard him whisper:

'You're . . . here. You're here.'

He wiped his eyes as though he couldn't believe what he saw.

Just as the sun streamed through the clouds, tears began to stream down her face.

'Daniel.'

She called to him as she ran, and when her arms wrapped around his slim, shaking shoulders, she knew that she would never, ever let go.

❧

Later, nestled in the purple heather, they watched a steamer roll down Kenmare Bay. Daniel didn't envy them, those people on that boat. They were going somewhere else, and he only wanted to be here. He recalled his own journey, how a ship had taken him away from his homeland eight years before, and everything that had happened since.

He smiled.

'What is it?'

'I was just thinking of the day we met.' He glanced down at her: her head was on his shoulder. He smelled lavender in her short, platinum hair. 'What would've happened if Uncle Ned hadn't left that dead tiger snake there? On the road to Towerhurst?'

'Dead?' The woman he must now call Rose laughed, pushing him gently. 'I knew it!' Their encounter on the beach came back to him; the first time he'd heard that beautiful sound, her laughter, even after all she'd been through. He blinked, pushing away the tears that threatened once more.

'Daniel, we'd have come together no matter what.' She looked up at him. They kissed gently. The urgency of their first meeting was over: now everything was warm calmness. 'Someday, I'll write you a ballad about how we met. The tree, the snake, the wager.'

'From my point of view?'

'If you like.'

'Yes,' he said. 'I'd like that.'

'We'll publish it under your name.' He began to protest, but she leaned her head back on his shoulder. It felt so right. *She* felt so right. 'I have to leave myself behind, Daniel. I have to leave everything behind.'

'Not me.'

'No,' said Rose Munro, the love of his life. 'Not you.' She plaited her fingers in his as dusk caressed the landscape. 'I'll never leave you behind.'

Chapter 72

Ballinn, County Kerry, Ireland
December 2004

At the top of the descent into Ballinn, Libby hesitated, mesmerised. The view below was spectacular. She pulled her tiny hire car to the side of the road, hopping out and grabbing her jacket from the backseat to wrap it tightly around her.

The scene seemed somehow familiar. Perhaps it was that it was so Irish: that patchwork of fields that led to the sea, those small white farmhouses, the village gathered around a central square. Behind it, the Kenmare Bay sparkled in the clear day, and, above, a wild russet scrubland reached to snow-dusted peaks.

From her car, she took the map of Ireland, unfolding it on the bonnet and looking once more at the circled village of Ballinn. Here she was. Right where her father had intended to be. Emotion tugged at her chest, but she pushed it away. She had come so far; there was no turning back now. Around her, the vegetation chattered, and a breeze stole the map, flipping it over itself to land in the dry grasses at the side of the road.

Libby stepped forward to retrieve it, and as she did, she hesitated. There, at her feet, stretching down the hill, was a sea of another kind; endless dormant heather, the remnants of a few brave purple flowers still clinging on.

Ballinn was gorgeously quaint; two pubs, a charity shop called Threadbare, a corner shop and a glass-fronted terrace that looked perfect for a café but was sadly empty. Festive decorations dressed the street, and a beautiful Christmas tree dominated the green. Even Sam would be impressed at its size. At the thought of him, Libby flushed.

She pulled up to the corner shop – O'Brien's – and hopped out of the car. This was as far as the GPS would take her. Apparently it didn't know the way to Rose's cottage. The address was merely *Heather Cottage, Ballinn, Kerry.* No street name, no number. Nothing. She'd asked about it at the hire car counter at Dublin Airport, but the attendant had only laughed. 'That's Kerry for you. Just ask the locals for directions.'

Libby stepped through the door, pausing to take in the shop. It was small, stocked with packets and cans, an apologetic fresh section tucked away at the back. She made for a small display containing locally baked goods, choosing a Christmas cake and taking it to the counter, where an attractive young woman was flipping through the pages of *The Irish Times* while the proprietor plied her with questions about Dublin. Was it grand being home for Christmas, and did she have a boyfriend yet, and how were the studies coming along? Journalism wasn't it? And how are things at the homeplace, and isn't it sad about the café being empty again this year? *Tut-tut.* A pregnant pause.

Libby, it seemed, had come to the right place for directions.

She cleared her throat, stepping forward, and the young woman gave her a grateful look as she tucked the paper under her arm.

'Bye, Deirdre,' she said to the proprietor.

'Bye, Ellie. God bless,' Deirdre said, though this last was given grudgingly as she watched her leave the shop. 'Now

then,' she said, turning to her next victim. 'You're just visiting
the area, are you? Staying for Christmas? Renting a place? It's
fierce expensive again this year. They say the boom'll never
end. I say it has to. What do you think?'

Not knowing which question to answer first, Libby merely
nodded. 'Yes.'

'You're Australian?'

She had to hand it to the woman, she had an ear for accents.
'Yes.'

'Seamus O'Reilly has a daughter over there. Una's her
name. She's in Sydney.' This was said with an expectation that
Libby might know her and, when she shook her head, Deirdre
continued. 'Ah well. Quite a big place, so.'

'Yes.'

The moment had come. 'I wonder . . .'

'Yes?'

'Can you tell me' – an eager nod – 'Heather Cottage. The
McGillycuddys' house. Can you give me directions?'

The woman looked disappointed. 'Ah yes. *Rose.* Keeps to
herself, so she does.'

That wasn't what Libby had asked. 'It's nearby, I take it?'

'Some of Daniel's people were in Australia somewhere. In
the north, was it?'

Libby didn't correct her.

'You're a relative, are you?' Deirdre was looking at her
intently, examining her features.

'No,' said Libby carefully, 'I'm' – she looked around for an
excuse, and thought of *The Irish Times* tucked under the girl,
Ellie's, arm – 'a journalist. I'm writing an article on Daniel
McGillycuddy's work.'

'Oh.' Clearly Deirdre wasn't a fan of poetry.

'And I'm really very late.' She handed across some euros with
an urgency that matched her expression. Sighing, Deirdre rolled

off a long list of inordinately complicated directions before Libby extracted herself from the shop, and went on her way.

እ

And the way was even more complicated than she'd expected. Several times she'd doubled back, trying to recall the directions, which made less and less sense the further she went. She'd left Ballinn behind half an hour before but – according to the GPS – she was only three miles away.

She noticed a figure, half obscured in a long purple coat, walking briskly along the small track ahead and she slowed the car, rolling down the window so that the cold salty breeze took her breath away. Before she could ask for help, an intersection came into view. There, leaning drunkenly against a fence that was also worse for wear, were two signs: *Ryan* (straight ahead), and *Heather Cottage* (left). Of the two letterboxes in a little shelter beneath the signs, one was stuffed full of letters, suggesting that the owner was away.

Libby wanted to hesitate, but she was now being observed and she resolved to go on so as not to attract attention – particularly after her experience at the shop. The figure, her head hidden by a hood, waved as she passed, and Libby waved in return as she flicked on the indicator and veered left with a sinking feeling in heart: a neglected mailbox, labelled *McGillycuddy,* was a very bad sign indeed.

Chapter 73

Heather Cottage, County Kerry, Ireland
December 2004

As Libby's sinking heart had predicted, Heather Cottage was empty. She knocked several times and listened for the sound of footsteps, but when none were forthcoming she went to the front of the house and perched on a bench that sat facing the sea. Taking deep gulps of air, she heard herself cry out in frustration.

It wasn't something she'd normally do, but then neither was jumping on a plane to Ireland on a whim. Neither was chasing up her father's satchel. Neither was going to an old boys' club and drinking a martini. Neither was . . . neither was kissing a man she'd not long known and yet feeling that she'd known him for ever. She shifted the Christmas cake off her knee and took her phone out of her pocket, longing to call Sam, longing to tell him of the mistake she'd made. But there was, of course, no reception, out here on the edge of the world.

'You don't think you should have at least *written* before?' Sam had asked cautiously on their way to the airport.

'No,' she'd said, bolstered by the confidence of Roger's *what have you got to lose?*

She dug beneath her coat, removing the fox pendant hanging on its chain, turning it this way and that. That fox, she mused, appeared to be running as though it knew where to go. Unlike Libby, who dropped her head in her hands, and felt failure wash over her, and shame that she'd chased her father's footsteps without even talking to her mother, who had tried to erase them altogether, and who had survived her loss for as long as Libby had lived.

❧

'If that's a Christmas cake from O'Brien's, I suppose you'd better come inside.'

The figure in the purple coat Libby had passed on the road minutes before was leaning against the stone wall of the cottage, her face turned to the weak December sun. She'd removed her hood to reveal a short grey bob that curled a little in the fashion of the forties and, though she must have been eighty, there was something youthful about her, a lightness to her nonchalance at finding an unfamiliar woman sitting in despair on her garden bench.

'I'm sorry. I . . .' Libby jumped up, unable to think of a suitable excuse for her rudeness as the woman appraised her, a slight frown on her face.

'Have we met before?'

'No, no, we haven't. I'm afraid I've arrived uninvited. I'm looking for . . . Rose McGillycuddy?'

'And so you've found her,' said the woman without much in the way of curiosity.

'Oh' – Libby put her hand to her heart, felt it thump, felt her old self return, felt the words begin to rush – 'oh! I thought you'd gone away for Christmas. Your post box . . . it was full. And that was you on the road! The woman at the shop didn't mention you weren't here, and she seemed like the type who would, so I just sat, uninvited, on your seat.' Libby looked down at Rose's empty hands. 'And you haven't brought your mail back,' she added, wanting to put a hand over her own mouth to stop the words.

A small smile. 'You sound like my son. With regards to the mail. Though he's rather less . . . talkative than you.'

'I'm sorry.'

Rose raised an eyebrow. 'Well, you can always collect the letters for me, if you like. My son does. Huffing and puffing them into my kitchen as though they are so full of importance he can barely carry them.'

Despite herself, Libby laughed, and Rose gave her another funny look. 'Are you sure we haven't met?'

'No, we haven't.'

'Yes, well, the truth of it is,' Rose continued, unperturbed, and apparently undesirous of an introduction, 'I like, some-times, to pretend that this little place is all that exists. I like to walk on past that post box as if I don't have a care in the world.'

'Blissful,' said Libby.

'Blissful,' said Rose, before adding, 'Ah! Of course! You must be Libby.'

'How did you—'

'Your accent rather gives you away. I haven't met an Australian for many years. It crossed my mind that I might hear from you again . . . though perhaps not quite so soon.' She paused and observed Libby. 'And perhaps not unannounced.'

'I'm sorry, I—'

Rose waved a hand. 'This is Ireland. After six decades you get accustomed to people walking through the front door without warning. Used to drive me up the wall.'

'And now?'

Her lips twitched. 'Are we going to have some of that cake, or not?'

With that, she opened the back door and disappeared inside, leaving Libby hesitating on the doorstep, an uncomfortable feeling seeping into her bones: she was not up to this task.

‒

One step, two steps. Libby made her way slowly along the narrow hall, wondering — for the third time in as many minutes — what on earth she'd been thinking. Her thoughts returned, as they inevitably did, to her mum. She hadn't been honest with Willow and now — here, in Rose McGillycuddy's hallway — the guilt of the deception felt starkly real. She'd been playing with the past, but stood here, it didn't feel like a game any more.

She faltered, alone in the empty hall, while the sound of crockery being laid out spilled from a kitchen. The home was warm, cosy. A dozen pairs of shoes lined the hallway; muddy boots, polished Sunday bests. Once again, she was overtaken with a desire to turn, to run away. It was as though the old Libby and the new Libby were in battle, and a part of her didn't know who she wanted to win.

‒

In the kitchen, Rose indicated the table, and placed two cups at one end. From where she took her seat, Libby had a beautiful view of the sea stretching to an empty horizon, the sun hovering just above.

'When the ballad collection came out we received a few letters from Australian journalists asking about the antipodean turn of phrase . . .' Rose took a copy of *The Ballads of Daniel McGillycuddy* from a shelf that housed an eclectic mix of cookbooks and literature. 'He was influenced by Banjo Paterson and his contemporaries. Funny, isn't it? An Irishman influenced by an Australian who drew on Irish ballads?'

Libby's mouth was dry. 'The full circle . . .'

'Exactly,' said Rose as she sliced the Christmas cake. 'Everything that happens to us, everything we do, weaves into the future as though we're sewing ourselves together with invisible threads.'

A gull landed on the windowsill, and waddled across the vista, pausing to peer in, then took off as suddenly as it had arrived. Libby felt an overwhelming desire to be like that bird, to have the freedom to fly away. Instead, she said, 'I was so very sorry to hear about Daniel's passing.'

A nod. 'He was ill for a long time. His heart had been weakened during the war, so they said. But we were given more than fifty years together. Half a century. I always remind myself that others weren't so lucky.'

Libby leaned forward, grasping her hands on the well-worn kitchen table. Pictures hung above the range: three kids, growing through the years. Then their children, smaller and getting larger. Laughing. A family portrait of at least twenty people.

'Rose . . .'

'Yes?' She poured the tea.

'From what I understand, you were in Tasmania too?'

A hesitation, followed by a small laugh. 'Who on earth told you that?'

Libby cleared her throat. 'It's just that, I've been reading about the history of the Foxton family. I believe you knew the daughter, Grace?'

'I see.' Rose turned away, her tea towel-covered hand hovering over the quietly whistling kettle. 'You're an historian?'

'No . . .'

'Police?'

Libby laughed, partly at the audacity of it, partly to dispel the tension. 'No.'

Finally, Rose took the kettle from the range, leaving silence. She cleared her throat, and poured boiling water into the pot. Wafts of steam curled in the air.

She smiled cautiously. 'What's this all about then?'

'It's all potentially a bit silly really . . .' Libby lost her nerve and trailed off.

'*Silly?*' Rose's eyebrow raised at the word.

'I'm not sure where to begin . . .'

'Do what I always do.'

'What's that?'

'Begin,' said Rose, calmly handing Libby a plate, 'at the very beginning.'

Chapter 74

Heather Cottage, County Kerry, Ireland

December 2004

She might be old, but she doesn't often feel it, only when memories overtake her sense of now and throw her into the past, taking her back there, back to Tasmania, when her name was still Grace, and she was filled with youthful self-doubt and frustration. She can hardly recall those emotions now. It's been such a long time since she cast off the past and learned to live. But Libby's words bring those times flooding back, and she clasps her hands in her lap to stop them from trembling.

Each year brings with it new reasons to be grateful. Her grown children, *their* children, full of hopes and dreams. She's worried, of course, at what this young woman will do with her knowledge, though a part of her feels relief at someone else knowing it. After all, she wanted to confess at the time.

Grace imagines Daniel taking her hand as Libby talks; it was what he would have done. Coming face to face with the past like this would have been more difficult for him than her. He would have worried about the consequences, whereas she feels like she's lived long enough now to face them.

Libby pauses in her narrative, looking concerned, watching

for a response. She has a theory about the body in the mine. It is *Rose*. The person she, Grace, had to become to become the person she wanted to be. Libby knows nothing, of course, of how Rose came to be down there.

Grace only nods. Not a confession, as such, but a confirmation.

'Then you *are* my mother's mother . . .' It's not a question, and Libby's voice cracks as she says it.

Grace shakes her head, then smiles kindly at the young woman, reaching to take her hand. In her green eyes she sees hope. This is a girl who – in taking this journey across the sea to a place she's never been – is shedding a skin that smothered her. Grace knows this, because she's done that before. She recognises that look, the one Libby is giving her. As though her own tenacity surprises her.

She is wrong though, about the facts.

If only their beloved child survived.

If only.

'I'm sorry, Libby,' she says kindly, because she can see that her lack of answers will hurt her. 'I don't know why Towerhurst was left to your mother.'

'I think your uncle Marcus left it to Edeline, who discovered that Willow was *alive*—'

Grace holds up a hand. She likes this Libby, but now she's growing tired. 'As I said, our baby died.' She feels her throat catch. Oh! How raw it still is after all these years.

'I'm sorry . . . but Olive Foxton said that your baby *lived*. And that the truth was hidden from you.'

'Olive was always a bitter woman. Who knows what game she was trying to play?' Sorrow tugs at Grace that her aunt would say such a thing, lie like that. Had she found amusement in her grief? She pushes the thought aside as she watches turmoil scroll across Libby's face. This young woman wants nothing more than to find her mother's history, her own history. It's difficult, though, to completely understand her determination – family isn't just blood, it's love.

'It's just that the timings match,' Libby continues, grasping at any straw she can. 'Nineteen forty-two . . . it couldn't be a coincidence, could it?'

She wants to put this to bed without telling Libby anything more than she already knows. This is her private history, after all, Daniel's and hers – even their children don't know. There's that familiar pull of grief deep in her stomach, and she glances at the photos above the range. She's lucky, so fortunate to have a family. She has to remember this as she forces herself not to recall memories of that stifling room. Of windows that wouldn't open. Of the blurred time that came after. The lies about her 'rheumatic fever', and how she almost believed them herself. Of Puds's visit. How he never once reminded her of how she'd been that day. As she'd boarded the boat, after she'd run from Towerhurst, he had said to her: 'Whatever happens, I'll protect you. No one will ever discover the truth.'

There's silence in the room.

Libby leans forward, insistent. 'Is it true?'

Grace shakes her head sadly, then points to the window, which frames a leafless tree holding bravely to the bare hill outside her home. It is an oak, and it will outlast them all. 'We planted a small memorial here, but our baby's buried behind Towerhurst.'

Libby hesitates, then says quietly, *'Always loved. Never forgotten.'*

Grace gasps.

'I've seen it, the memorial.' She explains that she visited Towerhurst as a child. 'But I don't know how to say this . . . the current owners, they told me a storm uprooted that sassafras last year.'

Grace swallows. The clock ticks in the silence.

'I'm sorry, Grace' – no one has called her that for years

and she draws a rapid breath – 'I don't know how else to say this . . . the grave was empty.'

'That's not . . . that's just not possible.' She tries not to think of that stone being lifted. Of course, it can't have been. She doesn't believe it, and that thought comforts her. Grace knows she must tell Libby what she's been holding back. The private thing she hadn't discovered.

'Please, I think you need to listen to me—'

She holds up a hand. 'Libby, your *mother* cannot be my child.'

A frown. 'But *why*?'

'Because we had a son.'

The colour drains from Libby's face. One moment it is there, the next it's gone. Vanished. Like Grace did all those years before.

'I don't understand.'

'Daniel and I. We had a son.'

'What month?' Libby says, though it's more of a murmur. 'What month did you give birth?'

A sigh. 'September.'

The last of the day's light bathes the old table in a warm glow. Grace knows that golden colour so well; it shrouded Puds's painting, and it lay, too, over the valley on the day she arrived. Later, she recognised it again: those golden flecks in her husband's green eyes.

The kitchen is awash with it. Gold everywhere.

'But,' Libby says, though her voice crackles, 'Ben, my father, never knew his parents . . . is this possible . . .' She trails off, reaching into her bag with a shaking hand, withdrawing an old passport.

Grace can't look.

Libby opens it, turning the photo page towards her.

But she can. She can look.

There he is.

Ben Barton Andrews. Born 3rd September 1942.

Ben? Ben? she thinks immediately of Uncle Marcus. '*Benjo! He'd love that, I'm sure.*'

'It *can't* be true . . .' she whispers.

Libby's biting her lip, looking from the passport to Grace and back again, and her green eyes open wide. For the first time Grace sees their true colour.

They are flecked with gold.

'Oh my . . .'

It's not possible – surely it's not *possible* – and yet, looking at Libby, Grace knows, she *knows*, that it is.

The grave was empty.

Libby's father is her son.

Their son.

Suddenly, she's not rooted to the spot any more. She's on her feet. She moves unsteadily around the table, choking back sobs, and takes Libby's hands in hers. She is crying, and Grace can see it now.

She is Daniel.

She is Grace.

She is their granddaughter.

જી

After what feels like a wonderful eternity, they pull apart. Grace feels her throat catch. 'I can't wait to meet him.' Her tears are hot on her face. 'I can't wait to meet our son.'

But from Libby's expression, she knows immediately that something is very wrong. That she's missed a vital part of the story.

'Oh, Grace.' She gasps, pulling in breath. Then tears run down her cheeks. 'Dad is . . . Dad is . . .'

'Libby,' Grace says, her throat burning with the effort of trying not to understand. 'Libby . . . where is my boy?'

Chapter 75

Drayton Park, London
28th February 1975

Ben stood at Drayton Park Station, excitement swirling in his belly. Everything was going to plan! Willow wanted to find her parents after all, and Ben was damned near certain he knew who they were. *What have I got to lose?* he'd said to himself as he'd stepped into the travel agency yesterday afternoon.

Rose was Grace. He'd known it the moment Molly mentioned the envelope, how — as it curled in the fire — she'd noticed it contained only one thing: a sprig of purple heather. *Purple* heather. He'd understood exactly what it meant. It was from Daniel. And he was in Ireland. Grace had disappeared the next morning, never to be seen again.

But all this, in so many ways, paled in comparison to what he'd learned the afternoon before.

'There's something else I need to tell you,' Willow had said, and he'd imagined her fingers wound in the telephone cord, the way she did when she was nervous. 'I wasn't sure whether to wait but . . .'

'Is it good?' he'd asked nervously.

'Oh, yes,' she'd said, a smile in her voice. 'It's good.'

'How good?'

'*Very* good. Something you've longed for . . .'

'Excuse me,' said a voice, bringing Ben back to the present, back to Drayton Park where the sound of an approaching train hummed in the background. Ben blinked once, twice, then turned to the source of the voice, slipping his map of Ireland – on which he'd circled Killarney and Ballinn, and made a note of the route from Dublin – into the satchel.

'Yes?'

A woman stood next to him, wearing a large jacket and holding the hand of a small girl. 'Are we in the right place for getting to Old Street?' she said in a northern accent, apprehension crossing her features.

'You most certainly are,' said Ben, feeling less the tourist and more the guide. Roger had told him on his first day that this line was famously niche; Old Street was one of only a few stops it made along the way. Ben had caught it several times, but during that first trip – on the way to the Iliad Club – Roger had laughed heartily when he'd opened his notebook, crossing *ride the tube* from his list.

'In fact,' he said now, 'I'm going there myself.'

'To Old Street?'

He nodded.

In her hand, the woman held a tourist map of London, and she glanced at the girl, who stared up with wide blue eyes. 'Only we've never been on the tube before, have we, love?' She turned to Ben. 'She's four years old.'

Four years. Ben tried to flick his mind forward, imagining what it would be like to have a daughter. He grinned at her and she smiled shyly, hugging her teddy tight. It was blue. One of its arms, he noticed, needed stitching, but otherwise it just looked well loved.

When the train arrived, the girl and her mother stayed close, sitting next to Ben and exchanging pleasantries. They were on their way to the zoo: they would walk from Old

Street, and stroll west along Regent's Canal to get there. 'We want to feed the birds, don't we, love?' to which the little girl only nodded.

'A good plan,' said Ben, who told them he was headed to the canal himself. He was excited about getting his hands on the missing ballad, though it was hardly likely to be material now. A small piece of the puzzle, really, but a nice one to have, nonetheless. Besides, according to a note from Roger, Lawrence had left it out for him in the stern of *The Albatross*, and it would be rude to ignore the favour.

'Are you here in London alone?' he asked, feeling almost immediately that the question might be misconstrued, so he added: 'My wife worries about me travelling . . . unaccompanied.' He laughed to show it was a joke, though Willow probably *was* worried, to the extent that he'd get lost on one of his storyboard saunters and end up somewhere in Kent.

The woman looked away. 'My husband died last year, and this is our first trip . . . without him,' she said quietly, with a quick glance at her daughter, who sat on her other side, absorbed in her teddy, who was doing cartwheels on the neighbouring seat. 'I thought it would be good for her.'

Ben's heart dropped. 'I'm so sorry,' he said. The train rocked as they left the bright daylight behind and entered the underground.

She smiled sadly. 'That teddy was his last gift to her. It means the world, you know?'

It seemed to be a question, and he nodded. 'I'm so sorry,' he repeated, unsure of what else to say.

She cleared her throat, then proceeded to ask Ben why he was visiting England, and what was Tasmania like?

'Very different to London.'

'Cities have their place, but we've been here three days, and I'm starved for company.'

He smiled. This place, he imagined, might be lonely without friends already here to greet you. The train began to slow, signs that read *Old Street* flashing past the window.

The two of them stood and waited for the train to stop. It slowed, and slowed.

'Well, good luck,' Ben began as they stepped off, jostling for space between those who wanted to get on.

'Thank you,' the woman smiled back. Then her smile faltered. 'Love? *Love?*'

The little girl had slipped from her mother's grip and was racing towards the door. 'Teddy!' she shouted in a shrill voice. 'Teddy!'

The doors began to close.

'Teddy!'

Ben made a split-second decision. He raced forward, and gently pulled the girl back, hopping onboard himself, squeezing through just as the doors sighed closed. There, on the ground, was Teddy. He picked up the little blue bear, and turned to wave it triumphantly at the window, pointing with his free hand one way, then the other, by which he intended to mean *wait, I'll be right back*. The girl's mother seemed to understand this and nodded, her face flooding with relief as she hugged her crying daughter close, the little girl watching with big, blue eyes through her tears as the train pulled away.

ॐ

Ben sat in the crowded carriage, full of satisfaction at the good deed he'd done and wondering happily how the universe might repay him. He smiled down at Teddy and put him safely on his knee, before opening the satchel to shuffle past Daniel McGillycuddy's ballads, past the article on Edeline Grey by 'Milton Twiggs', past his tickets to Dublin, past the map of Ireland. He was getting close, he knew it, and his growing excitement matched the gathering speed of the train as he withdrew the photo of him and Willow at Towerhurst all those months ago. She looked so happy! Perhaps, once he had confirmed the truth, Willow might want to return there. To Towerhurst. Where it all began. He was sure she could make peace with her past.

After all, they now had a future to think of.

'There's something else I need to tell you,' Willow had said on the phone the night before, that moment after the hesitation. 'I wasn't sure whether to wait, but . . .'

'Is it good?'

'Oh, yes,' she'd said, a smile in her voice. 'It's good.'

'How good?'

'*Very* good. Something you've longed for . . .'

Ben had hesitated. 'You're not saying . . .'

'Yes.'

'You're sure?'

'Yes.'

'How do you know?'

She'd laughed. 'Oh, Ben!'

'You're pregnant?'

'Yes!' Another pause, and concern. 'Are you happy?'

'Happy?' He'd wanted to throw down the phone, and jump on a plane to Australia. 'I'm ecstatic!'

She'd hesitated.

'Are *you* happy?' he'd asked.

'I'm a little afraid,' she'd admitted, 'I mean, will I be a good mother?'

He'd laughed. 'You'll be the best mother anyone could ever hope for.'

'I'm scared.'

'You can do this.'

She'd taken a deep breath, clearly gathering herself. He

could picture her biting her lip. He loved her more in that moment than he'd ever loved her before.

'You *can* do this.'

'With you . . .' she'd finally replied, 'with you I can do anything.'

'Well, that's good,' he'd laughed. 'I'm not going anywhere.'

There'd been silence then, as their future stretched before them.

She'd said, 'We'll call her Libby for a girl, just like you wanted.'

'And what for a boy?'

'We'll cross that bridge when we get to it.'

Now Ben slipped the photo of Towerhurst into his passport, and closed the buckles on his satchel, then sat back in his seat. He was happier than he'd ever been before, and he knew he'd recall this moment for ever. Sitting here on the tube in London, dreaming of the future in Tasmania: he and Willow would have a girl and they'd call her Libby, and Ben would finally, after all these long, long years, have a family to call his own.

They seemed to be arriving very fast at Moorgate Station, and Ben closed his eyes so that he never saw what was happening, and it was over before he even knew it had begun.

Chapter 76

Heathrow Airport, London
December 2004

When Libby stepped through the arrivals gate Sam was there, and her heart did such a flip that her stride faltered. Then she set her shoulders back – as she'd taken to doing – and walked straight into his arms, the several bags slung over her shoulder clinking with the bottles of Irish grog that Ash would presumably consume before the end of the week.

'You're planning a party?' he murmured into her hair.

'Yes,' she said, 'would you like to come?'

'I would.'

'You would?' She glanced up, their bodies still touching. His arms were so strong, he was so tall, and yet when he leaned down to kiss her he was the most gentle man in the world. She breathed him in – coffee, and the smell of wood smoke. He wore his woollen jumper again, but slightly more presentable trousers than the day she'd met him on the boat.

As if reading her mind, he said, 'I've been at *The Albatross*. Getting it ready for its new tenant.'

'Oh,' said Libby, surprised at how this made her feel. She hadn't been seriously thinking about it, had she? It had all just been a joke. 'Ash will be sad about the captain's hat.'

'Yes,' he said, kissing her again. 'But you could always wear it.'

'Erm . . .'

'Oh . . . no.' Suddenly embarrassed, Sam stepped back. 'No, Libby, what I meant was . . .' He laughed.

'What?'

'Well, I wasn't being' – he leaned in and whispered conspiratorially – '*kinky*.' And Libby flushed. 'What I meant was: the houseboat is ready if you should choose to rent it.'

'Me?'

'Of course.'

Alone? she wanted to ask, but didn't know how to do so.

'Just you. But I'll visit' – he paused – 'if you'll have me . . .'

And Libby flushed again.

❧

Before he started the car, Sam turned to her. 'You have a little problem.'

Libby, who had been thinking of her father and everything she wished with all her heart she could have told him, came back to the present. 'What do you mean?'

'Ash and Ivy returned early.'

'Ah.' Libby paused. 'I see.' She *had* planned to get home, put her story in order, then decide what to tell the aunts before she saw Willow.

'Straight to the boat?' she joked.

'They weren't pleased they couldn't contact you . . .'

'I was in Kerry!' she said, as if that was explanation enough.

'They left you several voicemails, apparently.'

'What kind of animal leaves a voicemail?' she grumbled. 'How do you know all this?'

Sam turned the key, and the Volvo rumbled to life. 'Some of us,' he said, 'didn't have the benefit of a comms blackout.'

'They didn't call *you*?' She must have left his number on the coffee table.

'They did,' he said, his expression one of mock horror, then – as though he couldn't stop himself – he leaned forward to tuck a strand of hair behind her ear. The touch sent electricity through her.

'And what did you tell them?'

'I . . . I was put on the spot.'

'Oh dear.'

'All I said was I didn't want to get involved.'

'Involved?' Libby flushed. This time the innuendo was intended.

'I mean . . .' Sam clamoured for words, 'I mean I didn't want to get involved with what you were up to.'

'Sam!'

'I know.'

'Ivy will have read you like a book!'

'I *know*. She did. She says you have some explaining to do.' He hesitated. 'Considering your mum's already at the apartment.'

'She's *what*?! I thought she was leaving today.'

'Honestly, Libby' – Sam shook his head as he drove out of the car park – 'she landed today. She's already here.'

In her rush to unravel the past, Libby had entirely forgotten about the present. 'Do we have to go to Grosvenor Square now?' she said, in more than a little panic. She hadn't had time to gather her thoughts and consider what she'd say to Willow when they came face to face.

She said that to Sam, but he only raised an eyebrow. 'Two days in Kerry where you stayed with – and correct me if I'm wrong – your hitherto unknown grandmother who lives with a false identity . . . then you drove five hours to Dublin, waited at the airport, took the flight . . .'

'Yes, yes.' She squeezed his hand. It was true, she *had* had a lot of time to process what she'd learned, but it was one thing to think about what she'd say to Willow, and quite another thing to say it.

۶۵

On the drive home, Sam hadn't asked what had occurred in Kerry, he'd only nodded as she told him the things she felt she could say. That Daniel McGillycuddy had been her grandfather, and Grace was her grandmother; and in her she'd discovered a wonderful woman who had lived with grief and guilt, who had helped her husband face his part in the war by encouraging him to tell her the stories so she could write ballads that blended the horror with friendship, humour and love. That Kerry was as beautiful as everyone said. That Libby herself had found a confidence she didn't know she had. This last gave her pause to smile, and she glanced at Sam, who nodded in a way that told her she'd been brave.

But there was something else she'd discovered that hadn't surprised her one bit: she had missed Sam. And, when he took her hand and held it in his own, then raised it to his lips and kissed it, she was glad to know that he had missed her too.

Chapter 77

Grosvenor Square, London

The eve of Christmas Eve, 2004

Moments after Libby arrived in the apartment, the aunts – who were clad in glittering party dresses – made themselves scarce, off to buy ingredients, Ivy said, for eggnog. 'A tradition for the eve of Christmas eve,' she explained, pushing a reluctant Ash out the door. In the background, Chris Rea was driving home for Christmas, his soulful tune at odds with Libby and Willow's stilted embrace, which didn't quite hit a festive note.

'How was your journey?' Libby said, just as her mum said, 'How was your journey?'

'Fine, fine. Long.'

'Good. Mine was . . . shorter.' A grimace, to which Willow raised an eyebrow, but to Libby's surprise, she said nothing, only suggested a cup of tea, putting aside the espresso martini which had clearly been forced on her, and which she seemed to find about as unappealing as the conversation Libby knew was to come.

❦

While Libby waited for the kettle to boil, still mulling over what she would say, she investigated the kitchen in which she found two dozen eggs, a kilogram of sugar, enough cream to ensure that everyone in the apartments' cholesterol would go up a point, and a giant bottle of rum. Libby was no mixologist, but she assumed it would be enough to make a couple of litres of eggnog. Perhaps Ivy had forgotten the nutmeg, she thought wryly. She pictured her now, sat with Ash at some plush Mayfair establishment, wondering how long to give mother and daughter before they should return.

☙

When Libby arrived in the sitting room, balancing two teas on a tray, her mother was examining the wall art. 'This is where all my paintings go, then?'

'Your sisters are particular fans of yours.'

'And yours,' said Willow, not missing a beat.

Her mum took a seat on the sofa. 'Come on, sit here beside me,' she said, patting the cushion, 'and tell me' – Libby gulped – 'how you're enjoying London.'

The question was a surprise. A relief. A moment of reprieve before Libby had to explain all the things she'd done. And all the things she'd learned. 'You know, Mum,' she said, 'I like it.'

'It certainly suits you.' A small smile. 'That *colour* certainly suits you.'

Libby ran a hand over her sapphire shirt. 'Thank you,' she said, of the compliment, and of the gentle way their conversation had begun. Still, she took a deep breath, glancing at her aunts' heaving drinks trolley, wishing she'd opted for Dutch courage instead of tea.

'Mum, I did something . . . perhaps I shouldn't have . . .'

Willow nodded, merely biting her lip as though words escaped her. It was, Libby realised, something they both did, a similarity she'd never previously noticed.

'I collected Dad's satchel from—'

'I know. Ivy called me before I left.'

'Ah.'

'She did it for you more than me, I think.' Willow hesitated, then she turned to her daughter, canting her head slowly, considering her next words. 'I wish you had told me.'

'I'm sorry.'

'I might have . . .' A pause. Then a shake of the head. 'No. Who am I kidding? I wouldn't . . .'

'. . . have supported me in following Dad's footsteps?'

At the mention of *Dad* Willow visibly paled. She glanced down at her finger, twirling the ring that she'd once said – in a rare reminiscence – she and Ben had found in an antiques shop in Hobart. Tiny, scattered snippets. That's how Libby had known her father growing up. But everything was different now. Ben might still be gone, but in her mind he had come to life.

'Mum, I'm going to tell you everything. Trust me when I say you'll want to hear it.'

Slowly at first, then gaining pace as the story rolled on, Libby found her voice, cognisant all the while that this tale, this journey she'd been on, belonged just as much, if not more so, to her mother. But in a strange way, in the telling of it, Libby felt an unburdening, a relief, as she peeled back the layers for Willow to discover what was beneath. It was exactly how she'd thought of London when she'd first arrived – layered, the present over the history. She recalled how she considered those London layers to be its people too, how the bustling city had hidden her in plain sight, so that no one looked at her at all. But in the end they had. They'd helped her, supported her. *Seen* her. Miss Winman, Lawrence. Roger. Sam.

'And what of Ireland?' Willow prompted, though she gave no sense of impatience. In fact, she seemed quite in awe of her daughter's newfound confidence.

Libby nodded, describing the valley surrounding Ballinn

and how she'd seen it before. 'The sketch I found in the attic . . .' She briefly jumped forward to the part Puds – who Willow knew as Sergeant Griffin – had played in Grace's rapid departure from Tasmania, and the reason for it.

'That explains his measured reaction to the discovery of the body.'

'Rose,' Libby said. 'The discovery of Rose.'

'And Grace freely told you all this?'

'After some hesitation. She told me everything.'

'And she is . . . she is your grandmother?' Willow asked sadly, but resolutely as though knowing that this moment – the one that had hovered in her future for thirty years – had finally arrived.

'Yes,' Libby whispered, reaching forward to do something she could never recall doing before. She took her mother's hand. It was soft, and cold, and she squeezed it tightly and felt glad when her own hand was squeezed in return. 'Grace and Daniel they were – are – my grandparents, Mum, but not in the way I expected.'

'Not in the way . . .?' Willow frowned, and Libby's heart tugged.

She didn't know how to say this, didn't know how to change everything her mum believed, the things that had driven her these past three decades. But the truth was so powerful, no one else could reveal it. Willow would have to discover it for herself.

'Mum, there's something I want to ask.'

'I can't promise to have the answer.'

'How did the lawyer explain the legacy?'

Slowly, Willow removed her hand from Libby's, and took off her glasses. She set them on the table, and rubbed her eyes. 'I don't understand what you're asking.' Without them, those thick, red frames that were as much a part of Willow as her painting and the armour she wore around Libby, she looked older.

'I mean, what did they tell you at the time?'

'Nothing much. The solicitor said the house had been left in a trust. Wrapped up, I suppose, to ensure anonymity.'

'And it was left *just* to you?'

She laughed a little. 'That was the thing which annoyed me at the time, such old-fashioned nonsense. Not that Ben and I didn't share everything . . .'

Libby drew breath at the free mention of her dad. She leaned forward. 'And?'

'The terms of the trust were that it would only be transferred on the marriage of the . . .' Willow hesitated, her voice breaking. 'On the marriage of the—'

'Mum?'

'On the marriage of the primary beneficiary.'

Libby nodded. 'Grace Grey and Daniel McGillycuddy did have a child in 1942' – Willow's hands began to shake, and Libby gripped them again – 'but it was a *boy*.'

'A boy?'

'Yes. Born in September. And taken away by Olive and Marcus Foxton. To avoid the scandal.'

'But . . . September?' Willow's breath had become quick and shallow.

'It was Dad. It was Dad all along.'

Willow cried out. 'I don't understand.'

'It was—'

'*Ben* . . . *Ben* was the primary beneficiary?'

A nod. 'Yes.'

'I didn't know,' Willow said helplessly, inadequately, her breath shallow. 'I didn't know. After all this time . . . How?'

'He was taken from Grace moments after the birth.' Libby leaned in. 'She thought he had died.'

The room held its breath. 'But he did. He did die,' Willow whispered, putting her hand to her mouth. 'He died in the end. He died because he was looking for *my* past.'

Libby's throat burned with the effort of holding on to her emotions. 'No. Mum. It was an accident.'

'All this time . . . you never had a father because of *me* . . .'

'Mum, stop—'

'Ben was searching for *my* parents.'

'Dad was searching for his *own* parents. Can't you see how powerful that is?'

'I—' Willow's lip began to wobble. 'But he never met them.'

'No,' said Libby, her tears flowing freely now, 'Dad never met them.'

A garbled breath. 'I wish . . . I wish he had.'

Libby whispered, 'I wish he had too.'

A hesitation, a moment wavering between them, a thousand things unsaid. Then Willow dropped her head into her hands, her shoulders shaking as she sobbed and sobbed, the harrowing toll of her loss and each strangled breath drawing Libby closer and closer until she leaned forward and held those slim shoulders in a tight embrace. Their tears flowed together, each lost in their own fading guilt, and grief, and their own acknowledgement that they'd need to accept the past was done and gone, but between them a future remained.

❧

Later, a quarter of a box of tissues down, they sat quietly on the couch. Libby was exhausted, and she could only imagine how her mother felt. Jetlag on top of the revelation that everything she'd thought about Towerhurst, about the reason for the legacy, about the past, had been shattered, not so much in an instant but in a dawning of realisation as they discussed the consequences of what had happened in 1975, and how life might have been.

'Ben . . . he *tried* to get details from them, from the authorities. About his own history. From the orphanage in Launceston, but all the records were either destroyed or closed.' Willow took a long drag of her drink. It was Irish whiskey, one of the bottles Libby had brought back from Kerry. 'After he became interested in my history, he made plans to hire a private investigator to find his own parents. He never told me about it – I suppose he didn't want to upset me after I'd become so opposed to him looking into my past. I discovered the details of the appointment in his diary a year after he died. I never followed up on it. I should have done that, for him.'

'It was important to Dad, wasn't it, to find his parents?'

'The more we discussed having a family, the more vital it became to him. We had trouble . . . conceiving. You were our miracle.' She sighed. 'He never lost faith that you would come along, and he wanted, I think, to be able to tell his children something, anything, about their grandparents.'

Libby gave a sad smile, thinking of Grace, and of Daniel, the love they would have given to Ben if they'd only had the chance.

Willow frowned and the silence stretched. Then she said, 'Do you still have the necklace?'

Libby took it from where it nestled beneath her shirt.

'So Ben really saw it – the other one, Rose's necklace – down the mine?' Willow said.

'Yes. And Puds, Sergeant Griffin, took it to protect Grace and Daniel.'

From outside the door came some muffled laughing. Ash and Ivy were imminent. 'And did Grace . . . your grandmother . . . have a theory?'

'About what?'

'The legacy.'

Libby shook her head. It was something none of them could

answer, and even if they could, what good would it do? The past was over. She went to the drinks trolley, took two fresh glasses, and set them on the table in readiness for her aunts as they spilled through the door. She bent down to kiss her mum on the forehead, and said, in a voice suggesting she was okay with it, 'I guess we'll never know.'

Chapter 78

Grosvenor Square, London
New Year's Eve, 2004

For New Year's Eve, Libby's aunts had gone to town. Not in the literal sense, but the metaphorical. They'd gone out and brought the future right into their Grosvenor Square home. From the comical spectacles that waited by the door, the helium balloons that clung to the ceiling, the bunting that hung from the windows, *2005* was written on everything and Libby knew what her aunts were trying to say.

A new year, a new you. And yet in many ways, Libby had already shed her skin and been surprised that she liked what was hidden underneath; not just a Libby she once knew, but someone even better. She was determined to cherish the parts of the past that deserved to be cherished – the stories of her father, the memories of Krish – but to let go of the feelings that had, for so long, held her back.

'Libby?' Ash's buoyant voice appeared before she did, as her aunt's silver sequinned dress caught the light and flickered across the bedroom wall to signal her arrival. She was like a disco ball and, no doubt, as the events of the evening progressed she would spin in the middle of the room and mimic one, much to everyone's entertainment. 'Oh' – she stopped short – 'you look *spectacular!*'

Libby pushed aside her instinct to brush off the compliment. As the evening's guests had arrived, and champagne began to flow, she'd realised her sapphire shirt wasn't enough. Everyone was – as requested – in cocktail wear, while she herself had run out of time to dress as she'd arranged plates of cheeses and tiny canapés that had arrived in extravagant volume from Fortnum and Mason that morning. Her aunts, it seemed, were quite aware that Libby wasn't a practised host . . . but what did it matter? It was a small party of friends, after all, but as they'd begun to arrive in their suits and smart evening wear, she'd said her greetings, then quietly slipped away. Now, appraising her reflection in the mirror, she considered that she was perhaps wildly overdressed, her emerald-green gown falling to the floor, a split revealing a glimpse of thigh. It was daring, but then, these days, she felt a little bold, a little courageous. A little *brave*.

'Thank you,' she said, 'it's new.'

In the corner of the bedroom, a canvas hid beneath a sheet, and she and Ash exchanged glances, anxious to see what lay beneath. Willow had been working on it during the hazy days between Boxing Day and New Year, appearing from the bedroom occasionally to take tea with her daughter, or accompany her for a 'storyboard saunter' – as she called it – along London's wintery streets.

'Of course, we're not *planning* any stories,' she'd said, each time they wandered.

'Speak for yourself,' Libby had wanted to say, holding her cards close to her chest, thinking of the conversation she'd had with Lawrence several days before, an offer she had promised merely to consider, but was already certain she'd accept. She'd led Willow through Hyde Park and along the Serpentine, pausing to watch the winter swimmers before carrying on to Speakers' Corner, where an elderly bearded man gesticulated wildly with a sheaf of papers before throwing them into the air and proclaiming that the end was nigh. After that, they'd continued northeast, visiting the British Library, then wandering along the frosty edges of Regent's Canal where Libby had showed her mum *The Albatross*, its freshly stencilled name reflecting on the water's glassy surface.

The evening after Boxing Day, Lawrence had called, the raucous din in the background suggesting he was at the Iliad Club.

'My dear,' he'd said, sounding rather jolly, 'I have a proposal.'

'That's a bit forward, I'm already taken,' Libby had quipped, biting her lip immediately, then erupting in laughter just as he did, wondering what manner of trouble this newfound confidence would bring her. Lawrence went on to say that he was considering resurrecting Stern Publishing and he could do with some help.

'It's broadly defunct now, but we have a nice back catalogue.'

'I know, I've read it.' Libby had told him about her day in the library that had taken up time she should have perhaps been using to search for a job.

'Well,' Lawrence had laughed, 'here it is. The job, I mean.'

'What a turn up for the *books*.'

'Very clever!' He'd paused. 'Now, this opportunity: the workload is large and the pay packet very small . . .'

She'd smiled as he'd talked on. Stern Publishing hadn't produced a book for years; it probably needed capital, although Libby already had an inkling of where she might pitch for such a thing.

Shaking off the memories, she followed Ash into the sitting room, where Ivy approached to *ooh* and *ahhh* at her dress.

Of course, the idea of her getting into publishing – something she knew nothing about – was madness. And yet it wasn't. As Lawrence had made his offer, Libby had heard

Krish's voice, as clearly as if he'd spoken yesterday: *do what you love*. And it was true that she had devoured Stern's back catalogue as though she and the books were one. She understood the authors, what they were trying to say, on the page and between the lines. She *believed* in the power of poetry. Not just its ability to capture the past, but to heal it too. The way it brought people together.

'I'll be proposing you for membership here at the Iliad, of course,' Lawrence had added after he finished his pitch.

Listening to the rowdy voices coming down the line, Libby wasn't sure how she felt about this. 'What? A *woman*? At the club?'

'We all must move on, my dear.'

Leaving her aunts to mingle, Libby went searching for Sam, who had apparently been consigned to cocktail duty. Sure enough, she found him in the kitchen, standing at the enormous marble counter, with an open mixology book and an array of ingredients that would inspire jealousy from even Soho's finest bar. He wore a suit that made James Bond look scruffy, and yet his bewildered expression – the same one he'd left with after unexpectedly meeting Ash and Ivy – gave Libby the impression he didn't have a clue how to make a vodka martini, either shaken or stirred.

Grinning, she leaned on the door frame and watched him, unobserved, as he picked up bottles of liquor, one after another, frowning at their labels. He dropped a tray of ice, spilled a measure of Kahlúa, then turned to the coffee machine, muttering about espresso and cocktails and how the two surely wouldn't go together.

'Need help?' she said, coming up behind him, and wrapping her arms around his waist. He was tall, and yet they fitted together perfectly.

'Please,' he said, turning, his eyes – she was delighted to

notice – widening as he held her at arm's length to admire her change of outfit. 'I . . . you . . . hello . . .'

'Normally I'm the one lost for words.'

He cleared his throat. 'It's just that . . . I'm not sure that's . . . entirely appropriate attire for a boat's captain.'

Libby traced a hand down his arm. 'You don't think so?'

He shook his head. 'Very . . . inconvenient. The split up the thigh for one thing. Very cold in *The Albatross* this time of year.'

She had moved her things in that morning, watching the coots glide along the canal through the little (polished) port-holes as she laid her clothing out and made the bed, while Sam set the stove so that she could warm herself with 'just the flick of a match'. Tonight was hardly the evening to traipse across London with a million revellers, but she'd given up her bed to Willow, and had been sleeping on the sofa for a week. And sometimes you just had to take your chances.

'I'll change before we leave.'

'*We* leave?'

'You'll come with me?' she said.

Sam hesitated. 'I'll book you a taxi.'

'Come with me.'

'If you want to take it slow . . .'

'I'm done with slow,' she said, leaning in for an embrace, ready to say what she'd practised saying. 'Let's take the tube.'

'Libby. No.' He hesitated. 'New Year's Eve probably isn't the best night to conquer that particular fear.'

'Who said anything about conquering? I only want to face it.'

He smiled, a slight wrinkle in his forehead. 'You're amazing,' he said.

'It's the perfect time to start again.'

He nodded. 'I won't stay. I'll drop you off and—'

'Sam,' she said, again in a way that made him blush, 'it's the perfect time to start again.'

è♣

Back in the sitting room, Willow stood beside the giant Christmas tree talking to Roger and Miss Winman. The three of them were getting on like a house on fire, and Libby felt her heart swell to see her mum laugh so much. They had talked endlessly during the previous days: on their storyboard saunters, at dinner, in the blissfully quiet times when Ash and Ivy were out. And Libby had marvelled at all Willow had been through, at her resilience in the face of the truth. It had, in fact, opened something wonderful within her, as though the secrets of her past – of Ben's past – had been a closed door which was now unlocked. And behind that door was a revelation that had broken Libby's heart and put it back together again in one fell swoop. Her mother *had* wanted her, so very, very much.

'The last time I spoke to your father,' Willow had confessed, her voice crackling one morning, as dawn began to paint London's skyline and the two of them sat on the window seat overlooking Grosvenor Square, 'I had just discovered I was pregnant. He was ecstatic, Libby. And so was I. *Afraid*, yes, but ecstatic that a piece of Ben and a piece of me would always be together, from that moment forward. But . . .'

'But?'

'But, for all these years I've been *consumed* with guilt, with the fear, the knowledge, that it was because of me that you didn't have a father. It made me . . . cooler than I should have been. Cold even. I was sure, in your heart, you must resent me.'

'No, of course not!'

'Every time I look at you – my beautiful daughter – I see Ben in your eyes, and yet when *you* look in the mirror, he isn't there. He isn't there because you never knew him. Because of me. Because of me . . .' Willow had begun to sob. 'You only had me to raise you.'

'*Only* you?' Libby had said, her throat on fire. '*Only?* Oh Mum . . . you could never be an *only*.'

'I wasn't a good mother. I wasn't enough.'

Libby had felt tears run down her cheeks. 'You were enough,' she'd said, 'you *are* enough.' She had thought of all the people in her life who had lost parents, who had lived without their mothers, or without their fathers, who had struggled and toiled with grief, and blame. She thought about Grace, whose own mother had despised her for no fault of her own. She thought of Sam, who lost his mother at four years old, but smiled at her memory. 'I love you, Mum. Surely that tells you everything?' It had rolled off Libby's tongue without a moment's hesitation, just as the sun peeked over the rooftops south of the square and her mum had taken a deep breath – as though summoning her courage after so many years – and said, 'I love you too, Libby.' She'd reached forward, and spontaneously hugged her, as Ash and Ivy – who had appeared in the sitting room in matching dressing gowns, carrying a tray of coffee – looked on with tears in their eyes.

❧

Time had slipped away and as Ash twirled in the middle of the sitting room, sending reflections of light dancing over the guests, Libby glanced at her watch and gasped. The countdown was only minutes away. She excused herself from Roger – who was explaining the best methods to extract herself from the inevitable *Odyssey* debate at the Iliad Club – 'sit on the fence, my dear' – and went to the kitchen, taking two bottles of Veuve Clicquot from the back of the fridge and pouring them into eight fresh glasses for her friends and family.

She handed them out. Two to Ash and Ivy, who she

loved with all her heart. Three to Lawrence, Roger and Miss Winman, who'd helped her on her journey. One to Sam, who held the key to her future. One glass for her mum, who hesitated before she took it, then pulled her daughter into a hug, kissing her on the forehead and smiling in that way that Libby had always hoped she would – open and happy, honest, with nothing unsaid between them. In her hand, Libby raised the eighth glass, the one for herself, and joined in as the countdown began.

Ten.

Looking around the room, Libby's heart swelled.

Nine.

Lawrence raised his champagne in her direction.

Eight.

Miss Winman patted Libby's arm, and lowered herself onto the sofa, a happy exhausted smile on her face.

Seven.

Roger helped her to sit, his expression all sadness and happiness and everything in between.

Six.

Ivy watched the exchange, and caught her niece's eye. 'I'm so proud of you,' she mouthed.

Five.

Willow nodded and put her arm through Ivy's. She was crying. 'Me too,' she mouthed.

Four.

Ash twirled next to her sisters, throwing Libby a wink.

Three.

Sam moved through the room.

Two.

He was beside her, his arm around her waist.

One.

And they kissed as the room erupted in cheers, and London's

sky was lit by fireworks and Big Ben rang in a new year, and a new you, for the Tasmanian who had traced her past, for the girl who'd been brave, for the woman who had followed in her father's footsteps and eventually found her own. For Libby Andrews.

&

Later – once everyone had kissed and hugged, and drained their champagne, Willow beckoned to her daughter. She led her away from the party to stand before the sheet-covered canvas in Libby's old room.

'I think it's finished, so . . .' Willow removed the sheet and Libby gasped.

'Beautiful. Simply beautiful.' And it was. A patchwork of emerald fields that ran to the sea, a gathering of houses at the shore. It was in her mother's style, but *infused* with colour. So very familiar yet so different to the sketch Libby had found in the attic, the one that Puds had done sixty years ago as a gift from Daniel to the love of his life. Even back then, it had represented a future that he wanted her to have. And now, those green and rolling pastures were part of Libby's future too.

'It's a gift, for Grace,' Willow said, a little nervously. 'Do you think she'll like it?'

'Yes. Yes, Mum. I'm certain she'll like it. She'll *love* it.'

'Good. Because I thought I'd extend my stay. I could go next week. To Kerry. To Ballinn. I can meet Grace. I'm sure she'll want to know all about Ben . . .' She choked back a sob, then sniffed, gathering herself. 'What do you think?'

Libby nodded, lost for words. This would mean the world to Grace. She imagined the picture hung on the wall of Heather Cottage on full display for when her children and grandchildren visited.

'You'll come? You are her granddaughter, after all. I under-stand you have cousins to meet?'

Libby felt the sting of tears in her eyes. 'Of course I'll come.'

'Good, good,' her mum whispered. She stepped forward and traced her hand lightly over the canvas. 'You know, Libby . . . the colour, it makes me hopeful. And that's no bad thing, is it?'

'No, Mum,' said Libby, leaning close, her head on her mother's shoulder, her green dress a match for the emerald hills that kissed the sea. 'That's no bad thing at all.'

Epilogue

Launceston, Tasmania

June 1972

Marcus Foxton ran a hand through the remains of his grey hair. It had thinned since the diagnosis and each strand that fell out felt to him like days dropping away. He tamped his trusty pipe, waiting for Mr Doyle to begin his protestation.

'So, let me get this straight' – Mr Doyle peered over his round glasses – 'you want to amend the will?'

'Yes.' Marcus slid a page across the desk, and Mr Doyle leaned forward. He read without expression until he reached the final line.

'You'd like the legacy to be anonymous?'

Marcus cleared his throat. 'Yes,' he said, 'the boy was—'

Mr Doyle held up a hand. 'Explanations aren't necessary. Towerhurst can be wrapped in the trust,' he said, matter-of-factly. 'It will guarantee your anonymity and might save some inheritance tax. I had hoped Australia would've abolished death duties by now . . .' He began a tirade while Marcus's mind wandered.

Three decades had passed since that September at Towerhurst, when Grace had given birth, and Marcus and Olive had lied to her about the death of her son. Thirty years of deceit. Thirty years of holding onto a burning truth.

Time had disappeared like water down a plughole, and yet it felt like yesterday that he'd promised Grace he'd look out for her baby, moments before she said her final goodbyes and sailed away for ever.

In those first months following her departure, he had been left bereft, paralysed by indecision. Lies tightened around him like a straitjacket, and he alone understood how all the pieces of the puzzle fitted together. Although it was true that Puds was privy to the circumstances of Rose's death, he had no idea about the baby. It was also true that Olive knew the child was alive – something she'd held on to with relish – but she didn't understand why Rose and Grace had up and left without a moment's notice. Colette had no inkling about the baby, though she'd understood that her nephew had loved Grace, and was baffled by his eventual marriage to Rose.

And Ned? It seemed he hadn't even noticed Grace and Daniel's blossoming relationship, he'd only thought it a one-way thing on Grace's part. Marcus envied his neighbour's naïveté; that ability to live life day to day in blissful ignorance of the momentous events. 'And Rose will still write her ballads now that she's gone?' Ned had asked a few weeks after she'd 'left'.

'No. It's *Grace* who writes,' Marcus had clarified. It was ten months before they'd receive word of Daniel's marriage.

'Grace?' Ned had shaken his head. 'I always get them mixed up,' he'd said as he watched the trees croon in the wind, 'those two girls might as well have been sisters.'

At this, Marcus had laughed. Lovable, vague Ned. How it would have been to see the world as he did.

Ben belonged with his parents, but what could Marcus do? Admit his part in the deception? How could he have removed the child from the orphanage without revealing Rose's real identity? The truth was that he couldn't find a way out of the maze he'd built: every turn, every option, led to yet another dead end. So he decided to assuage his guilt with action, and for thirty years, he had.

'You want to leave the trust to both of them? Ben and his new wife?'

'Whoever she may be.' He nodded, hoping it would be this Willow Hawkins to whom Ben had recently got engaged.

In the beginning, his interference had been minor: donations to the orphanage for school clothes, outings and books. Then a university bursary that Ben was sure to apply for. And by the time his great-nephew had become a fine writer – as Marcus always knew he would be – his company, Paterson Publishers, acquired his debut short story collection for a tidy sum. Behind the curtain of his Editorial Director, Marcus had supported Ben's burgeoning career ever since.

Mr Doyle said, 'You do understand, don't you, that as the two are married any inheritance will be, by law, half hers regardless?'

She was a lovely girl, Willow, and with the purchase of her exquisite *The Reckoning* he'd changed her life; it had told the small, clique-ridden Tasmanian art scene that Willow Hawkins had arrived.

'Yes, I understand, however . . . I don't want them to know it's for Ben *specifically*. If they ask the reason perhaps you could' – he hesitated, conjuring an image – 'tell them the benefactor was a particular fan of . . . the arts. Be vague, rather than lie. Lies, I've learned, can be very . . . problematic.' He hesitated. 'I imagine you think this is an odd request?'

'Believe me, I've seen odder.' The corners of Mr Doyle's mouth twitched. In his line of work, presumably, he was privy to all kinds of confessions, and Marcus could see that the man thought Ben was his son.

Lately, he'd got to wondering: would it be more hurtful,

or less, for Ben to discover the truth? That his parents lived on the other side of the world, with a family of their own?

'What about the allocation for your wife?'

Last month, he'd called Social Services. Olive's dementia had nibbled away at her faculties, and she'd stubbornly refused to move out of Towerhurst to a more comfortable arrangement, so he'd had to intervene. He'd experienced no guilt for leaving her all those years before. Bitterness was toxic, and his own remorse was poison enough. 'I've arranged for her to move into a home within the next twelve months. The trust will continue to take care of her expenses until her death,' Marcus said.

Mr Doyle nodded, signing his name at the bottom of a sheet of paper. 'In my experience, Mr Foxton, if you want something buried permanently, then you're better off throwing away the shovel.'

Thirty years ago, Marcus had marked the grave where Ben was supposed to lie with Atlantisite, because his uncle Cornelius believed it had the power to heal memories from past lives. That's why he'd had the moon gate made out of it – stepping through it was like walking into another life. A rebirth. What Marcus had once taken for eccentricity he now saw as wisdom of a sort; after all, lunacy and genius were surely two sides of a coin that might land either way. When he'd read Ben's story about a grieving woman healing herself with the power of Atlantisite, he'd realised just how circular human existence was, and that no matter how hard you tried to shake off the past it was always there, coiling round the years, holding them tight.

'You're probably right, Mr Doyle,' Marcus said, leaning forward to sign his name. 'You're probably right.' He pocketed his pipe and stood. Even if he died tomorrow, he knew that, despite everything – his turmoil about decisions, his worry that he should tell someone the truth – he'd done his best in impossibly difficult circumstances. For Grace. For Ben. And for the next generation who – if life had been different – Marcus would have dearly loved to have met.

Author's Note

It is so often an author's job to weave fact into fiction, to dream of histories that might have been. I adore the process of writing in this way; pivoting my characters' lives around inescapable global events that would have inevitably altered the course of their futures. And as my characters learn about themselves, I tend to learn about the events that shape them, so that gaps in my own knowledge fill, in ways I never expected.

Growing up in Tasmania, I learned very little about life on the World War Two Australian homefront, something I've since discovered wasn't at all unusual. At school, we were taught about the Blitz spirit and the London evacuations, but nothing of rationing in Tasmania or the shelters dug in Launceston's streets. We learned about Dunkirk, the Normandy landings, and the Battle of Britain with the barest nod to the events of the Pacific theatre. It left me with the impression that, viewed from Australia, World War Two had been some distant thing, which of course it wasn't.

Was the Axis planning to invade Australia? Aside from high-level discussions within the Japanese Army, there is no evidence to suggest that it was considered a viable strategy. The country was too vast to control. Instead, the Japanese planned to isolate Australia from the United States by advancing through the South Pacific. The bombing of Darwin (where Daniel and Puds had been stationed before Timor) and the air raids on northern Australia during 1942 and 1943 were designed to prevent the Allies from using these towns as bases. It was true, however, that the Axis was running out of commodities, and copper was at a premium. Edeline Grey foresaw both these things, though whether she'd discussed this with anyone but Rose I'll leave you to ponder. Mount Lyell is no longer Australia's largest copper mine, although it was at the start of World War Two (it was knocked off the top of the podium by Queensland's Mount Isa in 1944). As a geologist, I've studied and explored the rocks of Tasmania's west coast, but it was also something I did long before qualifying. My dad, Adrian, was extremely passionate about that landscape and he knew every detail of the area's history. Many a weekend when I was young was spent gold panning, exploring old mines and wandering Queenstown's wide streets. I'm not sure what he would have thought about the fiction of Mount Lyell being of strategic interest to the Axis; but I believe he'd have thought it just mad enough to be possible.

The perceived threat of a Japanese invasion of Tasmania, however, was very real, as were the Axis's forays into the area. Rumours of flyovers and submarine sightings were later credited as fact. Mines (of the explosive variety) were found in Bass Strait, and Launceston and Hobart – and many smaller towns – built fortifications and undertook drills that would prepare them for battle. By the time Singapore fell on 15th February 1942 (an event that Australians had been assured could never occur) fear within the country reached a fever pitch. With the benefit of hindsight, it can be difficult for us to imagine that feeling, but I did so by reading first-person accounts of wartime life in Tasmania.

As you might have guessed, the 2/40th Battalion was a real Tasmanian unit sent to Timor in December 1941. To learn about these men (many of whom were still boys) to whom we owe a great debt, I highly recommend Peter Henning's

Doomed Battalion and the outstanding interviews recorded by Grant McLachlan with many of the veterans.

Before I leave you, one more point on fact vs fiction: although Hobart, Launceston, Queenstown (and Mount Lyell), Brighton (where the 40th did indeed train) and Ocean Beach (though it's less tidal than depicted) are all real places, Westford is a figment of my imagination, superimposed on the west coast of Tasmania, an incredible and unique landscape every bit as wild and fascinating as it sounds.

Acknowledgements

I would love to thank the following:

To Sherise Hobbs, for donning her shining armour; I'm so grateful for her editorial input and support for *The Moon Gate*: she is everything an editor should be. To Priyal Agrawal and Bea Grabowska for their brilliant insight and thoughts on early drafts of this novel. To Flora Rees, who worked her magic, took my hand and led me through the darkest editing days so I could step out into the light. And to all the team at Headline Review who have championed my work from the very beginning. I really am very grateful.

Becky Ritchie – you're the real deal, aren't you? An incredible agent and a thoroughly lovely person. I've learned so much from you already. Here's to the next literary undertaking!

Those that read the early novel: Mum, of course (my greatest champion!), Jess McCarthy and Sue Lewando.

My immense gratitude to the County Kerry Arts Office who gave me the opportunity to spend time at the Tyrone Guthrie Centre, to the Arts Council of Ireland for the Agility Award, and to the Irish Writers Centre whose Evolution Programme introduced me to so many wonderful writers.

This novel is a work of fiction, but the characters' lives are woven around historical events. Thank you to Marion Sargent, whose research and articles about the Tasmanian home front during World War Two were invaluable. Many snippets of information from them appear in the manuscript, but any errors are completely my own. Without historians like Marion, and the Launceston Historical Society, so much of our precious past would be lost.

To all the friends (including the online writing community) and family (both Geard and Stoffell) who encourage and cheer. To the booksellers who championed *The Midnight House* – especially Una O'Neill, Jill Burton and Jess & Ronan McCarthy – the signings, chats and laughs really spurred me on to do it all over again with *The Moon Gate*!

Penultimately, there is nothing more wonderful than hearing from happy readers. To everyone who gets in touch, or leaves a review, it's just wonderful and makes all the hard work eminently worthwhile.

And finally, to Baz; first reader, soulmate, best friend.